DESIRE

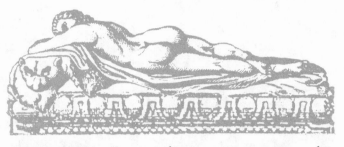

DESIRE

Georgia Hampton

E. P. DUTTON NEW YORK

PUBLISHER'S NOTE: This novel is a work of fiction.
Names, characters, places, and incidents either are
the product of the author's imagination or are used
fictitiously, and any resemblance to actual persons,
living or dead, events, or locales is entirely coincidental.

Published in the United States by E. P. Dutton,
a division of NAL Penguin Inc.,
2 Park Avenue, New York, N.Y. 10016.

Published simultaneously in Canada
by Fitzhenry and Whiteside Limited, Toronto.

Library of Congress Cataloging-in-Publication Data
Hampton, Georgia.
Desire.
I. Title.
PS3558.A4577D4 1989   813'.54   88-20252
ISBN 0-525-24710-6

DESIGNED BY EARL TIDWELL

1 3 5 7 9 10 8 6 4 2

First Edition

To Meg

So many people helped and supported the work that went into the creation of this book. Thanks and appreciation are in order to Barbara Lowenstein, for her energy, diligence, and persistence; Meg Blackstone, for her enthusiasm and guidance; Mercer Warriner, for well-thought-out editorial advice; Ken Robbins, for his unflagging support and great eye; John Ford, for tracking down various bits of esoteric information; and Bill Henderson, for keeping Georgia on her toes. So many others helped in so many ways—Lydia Salant, Priscilla Bowden Potter, Jeffrey Potter, George Caldwell, Jorge Castello, Jason Harootunian, Norman Kurz, and last, but not least, Deborah Morrison.

DESIRE

Prologue

It is autumn 1988. I keep an apartment in the Carlyle Hotel now. Very fancy, very nice. My windows look out on Madison Avenue. The Whitney Museum is next door, and all up and down the Avenue, from 57th Street to 96th Street, are shops displaying the most expensive objects in the world. Jellackman's has a Philadelphia highboy (not the best I've seen) for forty thousand dollars. Mannequins stare out from the windows of Yves St. Laurent and Calvin Klein, draped in one-occasion frocks that run to fifty thousand dollars.

These are just the trifles. The real heart of Madison Avenue—the real light that attracts all those other moths—is the art. Not just some art, but all the art of all the ages. Would you care to see (or better yet, to own) the notorious *Odalisque* sketches of Raphael? Or perhaps these jewel-encrusted treasure boxes that once belonged to Suleiman the Magnificent? How about a sculpture by Henry Moore, a painting by Jackson Pollock? A private viewing can be arranged.

In all those white-walled, gray-carpeted galleries, the dealers dance like hunting cobras, and the collectors, mesmerized, press forward, oh so eager to be the prey. *Ars gratia pecuniae*—art for money's sake. Art to the highest bidder. Art to the highest roller. Art to make your reputation. Art to impress your friends. Art to hedge inflation. Art to ease recession. And, win or lose, the dealer takes it all.

Don't for a minute think that what's on the block down there is just art. It's the heart's blood of the artist, too. Every canvas, every chiseled piece of stone, every pencil scratch on every piece of rag paper shimmers with the inner light of some artist's genius and inspiration— of some poor bastard's soul.

But, as you'll see, this story is mostly not about art. It is about love and the power of love. The kind of love that laughs at civilized restraints, ignores all inhibitions, and grabs you by the soul. At least that's how it was for us—for all of us. We came together by chance and happenstance at a time of such enormous hope and energy that even the oldest and wisest among us felt that virtually anything was possible. We were lovers and we were friends. Between and among us there was a full measure, believe me, of everything sublime, and everything infernal, too. I'll leave it to you to decide which was which. I have invented nothing. I have changed nothing. What I give to you are my memories.

I'm sitting now looking out this window over the tops of the buildings, across Central Park. The sun is falling into the Hudson River, the time the French call *le crépuscule*. In the failing light, the window becomes a mirror in which I am floating like a presence at a séance, superimposed on the darkening city. Proust had his scents. I have my music. It is Charlie Mingus who plays, not here on a record in my fashionable tower in the sky, but on a warm, sweet night in 1955 at the Five Spot in Greenwich Village. It is the perfect music for my odyssey back in time. It was the music that perfectly echoed the moods of our era, swinging easily between cool blue lows and wild hot highs. And Greenwich Village was the only place in the world to be if you were young and brave and hungry for adventure.

PART

I

I was twenty years old when I took
the Trailways bus to New York City. I can still see myself, fresh off the
bus, miraculously standing on the sidewalk by Seventh Avenue, in
Greenwich Village, listening to the music that filtered up the stairs from
the Village Vanguard. I was in love with everything I saw, everything
I smelled, with the sounds of the saxophone, the traffic, and the street
people. It was all somehow just as I had pictured it when I first decided
to leave school.

Only yesterday I had been a junior at Syracuse University, majoring
in education, minoring in art, and dying of boredom. Campus life was
the essence of fifties style, and every coed was decked out in ponytail and
bobby sox, circle skirt and circle pin—all symbols of sweetness and
virginity. Back then there were only two possible destinations for nice
girls leaving home: a carefully chaperoned dorm room at college, or a
husband's house when she married. If you'd opted for college and hadn't

found your man by graduation, you faced the three terrible T's of spinsterhood—Type, Teach, or Travel, the latter only in the company of a proper (read *elderly*) female companion. Such were the choices in 1955.

My hometown was a suburb of Dayton, Ohio, called Singing Hills, though there were no hills at all and precious little to sing about. My parents, Walter and Mary Alice Green, were simple, pleasant folks. We lived in a white shuttered house on Maple Lane—me and my three older sisters and an older brother. Singing Hills was a bedroom community —the men commuted to Dayton and came home to sleep—so weekdays revolved around the comings and goings of the commuter trains that shuttled the husbands and fathers to and from the city. I remember mornings when I was very young—too young for school—my sisters would argue over clothes, Dad and Joey would talk baseball over breakfast; school buses would beep their horns, cars would start up in driveways, and then my brother and sisters would be off to school, and my father would be on the 8:05, and suddenly it was only Mom and me alone in the house. And I remember the quiet. Quiet streets, the neighborhood empty except for us, the women and children of suburban America.

My Mom cooked, cleaned, shopped, went to the beauty parlor once a week, and played canasta with the girls at the Singing Hills Country Club two afternoons a week, but in a way I think her life was in a kind of suspension while the others were all away. Life didn't really seem to begin again until the school buses rumbled home and the 5:45 whistled its arrival.

My father walked through the front door at six o'clock every day of his working life—hung up his hat, kissed my mother, and sat down to his dinner. We ate steak one night and chicken the next. Vegetables were strictly frozen or out of a can. It was years before I realized that peas and carrots did not grow on the same stalk or that string beans didn't grow naturally in a swamp of Campbell's Cream of Mushroom Soup. Desserts were not an occasional treat but an intrinsic and important part of the meal, and every night we looked forward to Mom's cookies, pies, cakes, and fudge.

My brother played basketball and chased girls. My sisters practiced cheerleading, baton twirling, ballet, and cock-teasing, at which they were all three particularly adept. In the evening we all watched television until it was time to say a cheery "good night" and go to bed. My parents valued cheerfulness above all other things. They also loved their country, their God, their President, their hometown, and their family. I suppose you might say they loved one another, too. In any case, if either of them harbored any feelings of ennui or discontent, ambition or passion, I was never aware of it. No one ever questioned the Singing Hills way of life—not out loud, in any case, and certainly never to me.

Nothing bad ever happened in my childhood. In fact, nothing much ever happened at all. I did have an experience, though, a kind of epiphany, really, that I can't quite explain—it was such a simple un-dramatic thing—but I know it changed my life and it set me on the road that has taken me where I am—and that's a long way from Singing Hills. I was fifteen years old and it was a Saturday. Four of my friends and I had caught the train to go into Dayton. We were going to have lunch in the Rose Tearoom at Rike's department store and then go to the movies, and I suppose we were pretty excited, because for us, you see, that was a real adventure—lunch at the Rose Tearoom! And to leave home, unchaperoned! To catch the train into the city! To eat lunch in fashionable surroundings! We all wore our best suits, stockings with seams that needed constant straightening, high-heeled shoes on our feet and white cotton gloves on our hands. And every one of us—skinny little things that we were—wore a breathtakingly tight girdle underneath our clothes. Can you imagine?

We acted carefully blasé as we waited for the hostess to seat us and soon we were studying the menu intently, though of course we knew we were all going to order club sandwiches and Cokes. And then, well, nothing really happened—no flash of light, no voice from the burning bush, but it was just at that very moment, I remember it so well, I seemed to awake for the first time. It really felt like that. I was listening to the clinking glasses and the silverware and the soft sounds of the waitresses' rubber-soled shoes, and I looked up at my friends and I suddenly realized that they looked exactly like the sea of carefully coiffed, starchily dressed middle-aged women all around us. And the thought made me ill. I looked around and saw all these women, with their immaculate linens and their proper values, and their comfortable, ordered lives and they seemed so unreal to me. And I knew, just then I knew—and I have never forgotten it—that I was different. There had to be more to life than the Rose Tearoom, and I was going to find it. Of course, my friends would never have understood. I simply told them I was ill and left.

From that day on I was as restless as a bitch in heat. Not unhappy, exactly, but restless. I was the first female I knew (I'd bet anything on this) to get laid just for the hell of it. I was the first to dream of any kind of career, and the first female in my family to go away to college. Indeed, for two years I lived for the day I would begin my real life in college. But

I must confess that I found very little that looked like real life on campus. By junior year I was wondering whether it was the others who were crazy, or was it me?

It was about that time that I met up with Boyce Benson, a graduate student in art and the proctor of my still life class. He was tall, thin, and very pale, with a beakish nose and unruly hair. All the girls had a crush on him, although, in retrospect, he wasn't much to write home about. Maybe it was his intensity about art—the terribly earnest way he had of telling us that Art and Art alone could profoundly change our lives —that made him so attractive. He had actually lived in New York City, and he spoke endlessly about the circle of artists he knew there. He dropped tantalizing, magical names: Abstract Expressionists, Art Students League, Waldorf Cafeteria, Museum of Modern Art . . . He had been a regular at the Cedar Bar, legendary hangout of Jackson Pollock, Willem de Kooning, Franz Kline, Jasper Johns, and all the other greats of New York's art scene.

I was dazzled. I started coming around after class, asking questions, volunteering to clean brushes or stretch canvases. We had long discussions about Art and the meaning of life (he mostly talked; I mostly listened). We had coffee, went for walks, had dinner, and finally, one afternoon, we had sex. Boyce lived in a tiny room over a laundry, and the whole place smelled of soapsuds, starch, and hot irons. It had a bed, a bathroom, and a lovely weeping willow outside the window, and to me it was heaven.

I remember the willow tree particularly because when we lay on his bed that afternoon the sun streamed through the leaves, making wavy patterns on the bedcovers (I thought myself terribly artistic to have noticed). All the gropings and pawings that constituted my sexual experience up to that time had taken place in backseats or less than totally private conditions, and almost always they had taken place in the dark. Imagine my disappointment, then, when, rather than taking full advantage of our sunlit privacy, Boyce covered his nakedness chastely with a quilt before beckoning me to join him. I had never before taken off all my clothes with anyone, and the initial shock of his skin against mine was gloriously exciting. If Boyce was somewhat shy and inhibited, I discovered, a bit to my surprise, that I was not.

Under the covers with Boyce, things had reached the point of no return. He was on top of me. "Are you ready?" he asked unnecessarily. I was ready. He put himself inside me and I remember thinking how stiff and strong he was all of a sudden. And then I stopped thinking altogether. I could have gone on for hours, but I felt Boyce shuddering against me and suddenly it was all over. I made sure the next time was better. And the time after that was better still.

So. I had found passion of a sort, but freedom was still quite elusive. No matter how many nights he said he'd spent at the Cedar Bar, Boyce was no bohemian. Words like "family," "tenure," "pay scale," and "savings" began to creep into his casual conversation, and our steamy little love nest over the laundry was starting to feel a lot like a low-rent version of Singing Hills. He hadn't actually said it, but I knew Boyce had marriage and the graduate school housing project on his mind.

Once I realized that, it didn't take me long to organize my next move. I packed my bags, bought a bus ticket to New York City, and never looked back. A ship in port is safe, I reminded myself, but that's not what ships are built for.

2

N ew York was everything I'd hoped for and much, much more. I felt as if I had finally come home to the place where I belonged. Within weeks I had a job modeling at the Art Students League, I was waitressing nights at the Figaro, and I had a boyfriend of sorts—Jake Woolf.

Jake was in his early forties, tall, thin, tweedy, and sarcastic. Reluctantly, he taught several of the life-drawing classes at the League, considering himself an artist first and foremost, and a teacher only out of necessity. In reality, I'm afraid he lacked the will and maybe also the talent to make it purely as an artist, and I'm afraid, too, that his students more than occasionally suffered for his failings.

I must say I liked modeling, though. I never found it demeaning or exhausting or even particularly boring. The posing was actually restful and often interesting. I worked up a series of poses based on classical paintings I had studied, and developed a rhythm—pose two minutes, switch; pose two minutes, switch. It was like a very slow, studied sort of dancing. I enjoyed watching the students' intense concentration as they tried to re-create on paper the lines of my limbs or the contours of my breasts and buttocks. I got a stretch break every twenty minutes or so, and I liked to walk around looking at their easels to see the progress they had made. More often I simply forgot about the students altogether and let my mind wander into daydreams and fantasies.

More than once I caught Jake staring at me in a way that made it clear he was having some fantasies of his own, and that was how it started with us. It was a game in a way. Lying naked on the platform, I watched Jake make love to me in his mind, and I must say it excited me so much I could scarcely hold still. When he finally did grab me in reality, quite suddenly thrusting his hand inside my robe, he had no more than to touch me between my legs and I instantly had an orgasm. A few minutes later, on the couch, Jake did, too.

Unfortunately, that kind of instant gratification, exhilarating though it was for a first encounter, set the pattern for all our future sexual encounters as well. It never seemed to occur to the man that sex might be more fun if it lasted longer than a minute and a half. I'm not sure he ever did really like it.

What Jake did like to do was talk. In the end that was really okay with me, especially since he was one of those people who looked better out of bed than in it. Without his pipe and his glasses and his tweed jacket, his charm all but disappeared. He was a good talker, though, and he taught me a lot about what was going on with artists in the Village at that time.

We went to the galleries, museums, and artists' studios. We went to look at art. In those days I hardly knew what to make of most of the art we saw. It was called Abstract Expressionism. I knew that much. But what was it? It had no subject. What was I supposed to see? "Not see," Jake corrected, "feel." Well, all right, then, feel. Mostly, I felt nothing. But sometimes I would feel a little something—a vague impression of energy and motion. And sometimes, just sometimes, I would feel a kind of trembling awe, an emotion so strong I didn't have a word for it. Slowly I came to understand that the ones who made me tremble were geniuses, but that all of them—all but the most blatantly and blindly imitative—were a new breed of artist, possessed and challenged by the utter freedom of a brand-new form that seemed then to lack all boundaries. I'm here to tell you it was pretty damned exciting.

Of course everybody was dirt-poor. We lived and worked and partied in lofts and basements and walk-ups that even the rats had abandoned (well, not quite)—miserable spaces with holes in the floor-boards and plaster falling from the ceiling, toilets in hallways, bathtubs in kitchens—but few of us noticed or cared.

Oh, people pretended to live in terror of the Con Ed collector, especially on Fridays, because even if you came up with the cash you couldn't get turned back on until Monday, but the truth was, everyone kept votive candles, the kind that came in little glass containers, on hand for such emergencies, and people got by all right. If the rent was due and you didn't have it, no sweat. You threw a rent party. Word got out, people came, brought food and liquor, and contributed a couple of bucks toward the rent. By the time the party was over, everybody had had a great time and, *voilà,* there was the rent.

So poets wrote poems about the roaches, and painters painted pedestrian legs and feet (or whatever else they could see from their basement windows), and beatnik wives swapped recipes for chicken-back stew. At Horn & Hardart you could get a bowl of beans and a cup of coffee for twenty-five cents. Ketchup and crackers were free. In China-town, late at night (or early in the morning, depending on your frame of mind), chop suey could be had for fifty cents a bowl. Subways were fifteen cents, a jug of Gallo wine one dollar. Entertainment was found in the streets. Talk was everything, and musicians played jazz all night in Washington Square. The artists were content with anything as long as they could work. But, they were never content about their work.

Jake liked to take me to the Cedar Bar to show me how accepted he was by the other artists. He also enjoyed the admiring glances his friends would throw my way. I looked okay. I had good legs and what was known in those days as a "well-developed bust." I had curly red-brown hair, a wide mouth, a big laugh. Not for me the black turtlenecks and wrap skirts of the beatniks; I still wore tight sweaters, cinch belts, and kick pleats. I hoped I looked like Marilyn Monroe before she bleached her hair, but in reality I think I looked more like Donna Reed with tits. I was still very much the new girl in town and people were curious about me. I was certainly curious about them.

The Cedar Bar. This was the center of our bohemia. It was a dull-looking place. Brown. Yes, I would say brown was the dominant color (or lack of it). It was scruffy and dark and smelly and by the time I got there it already had a store of legends and stories. Everybody knew about the time Franz Kline started beating on Jackson Pollock, and Pollock, much bigger than Kline, started laughing and trying to evade the furious blows, while he kept whispering to Kline, "Not so hard, not so hard." And about the time Pollock himself lost his temper and broke down the door to the men's room in a fit of fury. And about the time de Kooning smashed a bunch of furniture into little bits. The stories went on and on and everything that was happening that mattered was happening there. Artists continued to gather there. Older, established artists. Comers. New, undiscovered talent. Even the hangers-on had a place at the long row of stools against the dark bar. To understand the Cedar, you have to understand that artists are nourished more by each other than by the public. Oh yes, they all want critical acclaim, but they know that ultimately to give one's work to the world at large is an experience of surprising emptiness. Like throwing a bottle with a message into the sea. What matters most is the recognition of your fellow artists. Did they understand? Did they? That was the big, anxious question. No matter how far outside the establishment you stood, at the Cedar you were not alone.

Writers had their own hangout. The White Horse, over on the West Side, was the literary bar. Mailer, Styron, and, of course, Dylan Thomas used to hang out over there when he was still alive. The word was that the writers were even more violent than the artists, maybe because their work was so much less physical, and the fights that broke out at the White Horse could be truly frightening.

I used to go to the Cedar whenever I was free, for lunch, after work, at midnight. I would order a beer or a bowl of clam chowder and sit and watch. I remember one time I had slipped and fallen on the ice outside my apartment. I must have sprained my hand in falling, because by the time I got to the Cedar it was throbbing with pain and swollen up to twice its normal size. Franz Kline and Lawrence Ferlinghetti were sitting together at the bar. Franz Kline was in his mid-forties then and just making it. He had money for the first time in his life and he was buying drinks for everyone. When he saw my hand, he demanded ice from the bartender and wrapped it in a handkerchief of his. "Why didn't you go to a doctor?" he asked with real concern. And I said, "I would have, but I didn't want to miss anything." He smiled and bought me a second drink. He understood. The Cedar was the place to be if you were any part of the Village scene in the fifties. If you missed it, you missed everything.

One particular night, the atmosphere at the Cedar was crackling, as usual, with excitement. The walls of the tavern hummed with intense talking and violently expressed opinions: "In nature there are no lines, only curves." "In the abstract there are lines but no boundaries." "Bullshit! You're much too influenced by Mondrian." "There are always boundaries." "Are you saying the abstract is formal structure? Well, you're pissing against the wind." "Oh, get off it! You either paint good pictures or bad ones." "I say the reason you use so much black is you're too cheap to buy pigment!"

Jake and I took a back booth. I had just lit up a cigarette when a young painter named Piri Morales slid into the booth beside me. "Hey, man, how's it goin'?" he greeted Jake, but his eyes never stopped traveling from my bosom to my face. "Who's the new *muchacha?*"

Jake introduced us. Piri slithered closer until his thigh was heating up next to mine. "You modelin', babe? I could use someone like you at my place."

"Come off it, Piri. What do you need a model for?" Jake laughed, explaining, "Piri paints boxes inside boxes. I don't think he knows how to draw anything with a curve to it."

"Hey, you shut up, man." Piri continued ogling me. "Just 'cause I don't paint 'em, don't mean I can't appreciate good-looking curves when I see them. But seriously, Jake-o, I got something to talk to you about. Buy me a beer? I . . . uh . . . forgot my wallet."

"You never had a wallet, Pir." Jake handed me some money. "Get us some beers, babe?"

When I returned with the drinks, the two men were deep in conversation. It seemed that a number of artists had decided to band together and open a cooperative gallery. It was a good idea. Everybody had a lot of work to show and nowhere to show it. The only galleries in those days were uptown on 57th Street, with a small sprinkling on Tenth Street. The biggest art scene downtown was right here at the Cedar, and it was all talk and nothing to see.

A dozen artists had banded together, rented a space on East Ninth Street, and promptly run out of money. The only recourse was go out and get more artists to join up. Jake was thrilled. He even overlooked the fact that he was in the second string of painters to be asked. At last someone was offering him a chance to show his pictures. While the two men hashed out the details of Jake's participation, my eyes wandered around the room and I happened to notice a man at the bar who had not been there before. Jake, too, caught sight of the newcomer and, raising his hand in a beckoning gesture, said, "Great! Here's Ivan."

Ivan St. Peters walked over and pulled a chair up to our booth, and so I came to meet the man who is at the heart of this story. I've thought about that evening a thousand times, trying to recall every moment, every gesture. What was I feeling as he greeted us, as he raised my hand to his lips and looked into my eyes? Was it love at first sight? Did the rest of the room fade into a blur, leaving only him? Well, not exactly, but I know that I was aware of a growing excitement, of a sense that suddenly the evening had taken a most interesting turn.

Ivan was most remarkable because he was so different from everyone else. He seemed more vibrant, more intense than anyone else in the room. His very blue eyes were brighter, more attentive; his smile warmer, more dazzling; his gestures more animated and dramatic; his voice more resonant and certainly more interesting, with the lilting inflections of his accent. I couldn't place it then. I would have been astounded to know it was Russian. He was wearing an outfit that made him look like some sort of a Gypsy cowboy—a white embroidered Cossack shirt over tight-fitting dungarees. On his feet were a pair of pointy western boots. A lesser man might have looked a trifle theatrical or a little ridiculous, but Ivan simply made everyone else look boring.

"I am collecting friends, blithe spirits, to come to a small party for Dance Duprey. He has arranged to have some of his poems set to music, and he wants friends to listen and to sing them. Do you sing?" he turned to me.

"Only in the shower. I'm a humanitarian."

"Oh yes? But such a beautiful one. Come along anyway. You will be the decorative element."

There are times, so rare you could cry, when everything—large and small—falls into place in the most incredible way. No effort, no thought—you just sit back and things happen, and they are perfect—you couldn't will them better. Then for a space of time anything can happen; for a while everything is possible, even happiness. No matter what comes after, you never forget those times, and that evening, by God, was one of them. Jake and Piri were too involved with making plans for the gallery to go to a party, which is how it came to be that Ivan and I left together and walked through the warm May night.

3

On the way to the party we talked and I began to discover this exotic and handsome man. He was a sculptor and he had come to this country seven years before, from Paris. Somewhat mindlessly I said I had always thought that artists preferred Paris to New York. Ivan said yes, yes, that had been true once, but no more, not since the war. America, he said, was thriving. After all, the war did not take place here. Europe was still staggering in the aftermath of the war's devastation. Everything interesting in art, he said, was happening here, now.

He let me believe that he had simply decided that he would work better in New York and so he came. It wasn't until much later that I learned his family had all died in Russia, and that he had spent his adolescent years during the war in a German work camp. It was only after the war that he had been able to find his way to Paris, walking the entire distance at age seventeen from a relocation center in Austria.

He told me that in Russia his mother had been a ballerina and his father had been a pianist and composer. He said most of the rest of his family had died or disappeared during the Revolution, before he was born. My head was spinning as he talked. What did I know about Russia, revolutions, Paris, or even World War II? All these events that had been so real to Ivan and his family had been nothing but subjects in history class to me. I was thinking about what an ordinary life I had led in comparison, when Ivan asked me if my parents were still alive.

"Oh yes," I said. "Alive and quite well. My father's retired and they spend their time happily interfering in the lives of their children and grandchildren. Luckily I have three sisters and a brother and they're all married, with children."

"Do you see them often?" he wanted to know.

"Not really. Ohio's pretty far away, you know. Lucky for me, I guess." I gave a little laugh but for some reason I felt uncomfortable. I had never talked to anyone like Ivan before.

"So, Maisie, tell me, how is this lucky? Does it not make them sad to have their daughter so far away?"

"I suppose in a way it does, but in another way it is better. You see, they don't really approve of the way I live and what I want out of life."

"No, no, Maisie, that is nonsense. They love you, don't they? Your life is your own. No one can change that. What you do with it is your decision. But to deny your parents the tenderness, the affection that is their due in their old age, this is truly regrettable. You must write to your parents, to your mother who nursed you and loved you through all the years of your childhood, and you must visit them as often as possible to kiss them and lavish them with daughterly love. Will you do this, Maisie?"

We had been walking all this time, through Little Italy and Chinatown, to Wall Street, and now we found ourselves in the very nethermost reaches of lower Manhattan. We had stopped while Ivan awaited my answer to his urgent question. It felt as if we had left all of civilization behind, and there was no one else on the street. Not even the drunks and derelicts seemed to find Water Street hospitable.

"I'll write home tomorrow. A nice, long letter, I promise." We were standing under a streetlight and I looked up at him to show my sincerity, although I was feeling not a little sheepish. I was about to say some other silly thing when Ivan kissed me.

It's a funny thing about kissing. To describe a kiss physically, to analyze it, is to miss the point because, you know, it's really kind of an absurd gesture at times. This was not one of those times. His kiss simply took my breath away. "What the hell, I'll write home every day," I said when we had separated and I managed to speak.

"Ah, Maisie, Maisie. Amazing Maisie," Ivan crooned. "You are a delectable, delicious girl. Come, let us go to see my friend Dance. Let us sing with Dance. Let us dance with Dance. For this is truly an enchanted evening."

With this exuberant statement he led me to the dark, locked double glass doors of a huge deserted office building. He pressed a button. We stood waiting for a long long time. I wondered if he'd lost his mind, but I didn't really care.

At last a dim light came on inside, and a small woman with a mass of gray fizzy hair fumbled with the locked doors and managed to open them at last. Our hostess, Hortense Loudon, was a poet. She and her husband, Jonathan Greenwood, a set designer, were in their early fifties, devoted to the arts and to giving theatrical, literary parties in their remote penthouse apartment.

Hortense led us into a huge elevator, hopped onto the operator's stool, and proceeded to work the manual controls to bring us up twenty-one floors to their penthouse. Dressed in an outfit straight out of an army-navy surplus store, she looked like a slightly demented sea captain.

The party was in full swing when we arrived, and from the looks of things it was an interesting gathering. However, I was mostly aware of Ivan and very little else. His kiss burned my mouth. I could not stop thinking about him, wondering what was going to happen next, wondering how he could suddenly turn into a gregarious, dancing, singing partygoer when such a momentous event as our kiss had taken place. Most of all I kept wondering when he was going to kiss me again.

Ivan was hailed by everyone. He caught my hand and settled us down on a pile of cushions as Dance and a young woman who was about to make her debut at the Metropolitan Opera sang poems he had written and set to music. They made a lovely pair of songbirds and I wondered if they were also romantically linked, romance being very much on my mind. Later on I discovered that Dance was never romantically linked with anyone, and that while hundreds of people all over New York believed him to be their closest and most intimate friend, the only person he was really close to was Ivan St. Peters.

After the recital, Ivan disappeared into the kitchen to hustle up something to drink and I was left to study the crowd. It was not your usual gathering. Sometimes at the Cedar, the word would spread that so-and-so was giving a party for an uptown dealer or collector. Then, like locusts, a body of people would swarm and descend on the startled host, each uninvited guest bearing a jug of Gallo or a six-pack of cheap beer. This gathering had much more panache. The women wore real clothes as opposed to thrift-shop bargains. The talk seemed more sophisticated. There were many theatrical people there, such as Julian and Judith Beck, whose Living Theater would send shock waves through the New York theater world. I recognized some of the Beat poets—Allen Ginsberg in particular, who used to come into the Figaro and read very late at night and who, they said, had just gotten out of Bellevue. All in all, it seemed to me quite a glittering crowd. I was so enthralled I didn't notice Dance Duprey until he was standing right next to me.

I had never met Dance Duprey before, though I had seen him many times. He used to come late to the Cedar, usually very drunk but never loud or obnoxious. He lived in the Village and I had seen him often enough—poking around in the curio shops on Bleecker Street or strolling through Washington Square Park—to know that he was a man of not inconsiderable flair. He favored white linen trousers, tailored shirts, expensive shoes, and Panama hats. Puffing at small thin cigars through a carved ivory holder, he looked every inch the elegant poet and dramatist he was. Of course, he was already a great success by the time I met him. His poetry was widely published and highly praised in literary circles. But he was best known for the startling, provocative, often hilarious plays which he produced himself in a tiny theater on St. Mark's Place. His latest play, *Bananas,* was in verse and it was about madness.

He was famous for his Sunday afternoon parties, to which came the uptown society types who idolized him, the columnists who wrote about him, his Village friends—mostly fellow artists and writers—and often as not, people off the street, workmen or fortune-tellers or shop owners he had just met. He had a particularly quirky, and I must say, charming way of speaking—his voice dripped with Southern honey, his speech was studded with baroque, Southern-style figures, yet one's overall sense of him was pure New York—erratic and charged with nervous energy. Often he would leave his sentences uncompleted, as if convinced that every listener knew precisely what he was saying and would understand the rest.

Everyone seemed to love him. And that night I, too, came to love Dance. How could I not with an opening line like this:

"I want to know all about you." He said leading me away from the heart of the party to a relatively quiet alcove.

"You do?" I said. "Why?"

"Because you sparkle and because I don't think I've ever seen anyone quite so pretty as you. You remind me of the girls in the murals at the Café des Artistes. Been there?"

I shook my head.

"Well, good. Then I'll take you there for lunch and show them to you myself." Dance had the most beautiful green eyes I had ever seen and there was no doubt in my mind his compliment was sincere. I was flushed with pleasure. Dance grinned a sleepy sort of grin until he saw my empty hands. "Why, honey, you don't have a drink. Good Lord. You do drink, don't you?" He pulled a silver flask out of his pocket and offered it to me. "I can't stand people who don't drink."

"Of course I do. Ivan's gone to get us some wine . . ." My voice trailed off, realizing Ivan had been gone for an awfully long time. Dance realized that, too.

"Don't worry. He'll be back. It's just that the wine is in the kitchen and so are a gaggle of Ivan's most devoted fans."

I sniffed. "Devoted *women* fans?"

Dance laughed. "Yes. They say that Ivan goes through women like water. I've wondered about that. It's an appealing notion, isn't it?"

"I guess it depends on whether you're the women or the water." I wasn't making any sense at all but Dance laughed again as if I were the wittiest of conversationalists.

"You know," he whispered, "there's a woman here who just told our hostess that Ivan is the only evidence of God she's found on this planet."

"Well, that is impressive," I said, wondering what the hell all this was leading up to. "I take it this woman wonders what planet I'm from."

"I'm not doing a very good job of being subtle, am I? Subtlety is such a devious affectation, and so very difficult if you're drunk, which I am. But I've been told I'm rather touching when I'm drunk. Yes. And this particular woman is in love with Ivan. I'm afraid most women are. Are you?"

His question caught me quite off guard. "I just met him," I said, and then, thinking I'd better assert myself quickly: "But, come to think of it, yes. I think I am in love with Ivan."

"Good girl. It doesn't do not to love him. Now come with me. We must sing of your love. I have written a charming little musicale, an ode to lovely, lovable love." He led me to the piano and began passing out sheet music with lyrics to the assembled guests.

However, it was not of love we sang that night, it was vegetables. I was a tomato.

At the piano, Dance showed not the slightest sign of his intoxication, and he played with great assurance as we all gathered round and sang. At first people sang with hesitation, but it was a truly charming and hilarious bit of writing, and in the end we were all belting out the parts assigned to us with great gusto and good humor. When the musicale finally came to an end we were all in fine high spirits, and there was much hugging, kissing, and back-slapping. I was sort of hoping that Ivan would feel the need to kiss me again, but I was disappointed.

Suddenly our hosts appeared from the kitchen—Hortense handing out paper plates and spoons, with Jonathan behind her, carrying an enormous pot of mashed potatoes. Up till now there had been plenty to drink but nothing at all in the way of food. In fact we had all worked up quite an appetite. The mashed potatoes were delicious. I often wonder how it was possible that it didn't seem the least bit strange to find myself sitting on the floor of a penthouse apartment in downtown Manhattan, surrounded by a crowd of quite bizarre strangers, drinking like crazy and eating mashed potatoes with a spoon.

The party broke up shortly after three o'clock in the morning. Naturally, Ivan took me home. Despite the late hour, neither one of us was a bit tired. Our feet barely touched the pavement and our words never stopped flowing.

Would I like to be twenty-one again, walking home through the streets of New York on a morning in May just as the sun is about to come up, with Ivan's arm around my shoulders? What do you think?

I had an apartment on Eighth Street, half a block west of Fifth Avenue. It was a third-floor walk-up with a tiny alcove kitchen, a bathroom with a deep, claw-footed tub, and one enormous room with high ceilings and a fireplace. The wall with the fireplace was all exposed brick, and the rest of the walls were painted white. Most of the windows—they were at least six feet tall—looked out on a courtyard made up of small backyard gardens. From my windows I saw trees, grass, birds, and squirrels, and the sounds I heard were country sounds. Every day I lived there, I savored the contrast between the noisy bustle of Eighth Street, which was very much the heart of the Village, and the cozy serenity of my apartment. Three flights of stairs were the magic passageway from one world to another. To this day, when I dream of home, when I dream of the place in which I was most comfortable and happy, it is that apartment I dream of. It is difficult to reconcile the vividness of my vision of that place—so complete with color, sound, and even smell—with the fact that that building was long ago demolished.

Ivan came home with me. We had walked all the way back from Water Street, and all the way I had been intensely aware of his physical presence. When he touched me, whether to hold my hand, steer my elbow, or simply rest his fingers lightly on the back of my neck, I felt a hot pleasure flow from the point of contact and suffuse my entire body. When we entered my apartment the sun was just rising and there was no need for more light. The light came on its own, increasing with our intimacy and passion. The morning chorus of birdsong was our music. We made love more slowly than I had thought possible, and for a long time. When we awoke, it was to the full brightness of noon.

We were ravenous and happy. As I prepared eggs, bacon, and coffee, we chatted with the ease of old friends, and I marveled that there was none of the anxious discomfort that marks the conversation of lovers who are still strangers. Ivan wandered around, examining my books, records, photographs. Nothing was exempt from his curious scrutiny—not my mail, not my wardrobe, not the contents of my medicine chest. Yet, amazingly enough, I was neither offended nor threatened. Rather I was flattered to be the subject of such intense curiosity. He reminded me of a child hard at work on a jigsaw puzzle, who needs to examine each individual piece before connecting it to a larger picture.

Describing Ivan is not an easy task. He was handsome, but not in the way Hollywood had taught us to think of masculine good looks. Everything about him was excessive, exaggerated, larger than life. His hair was jet black and fell in shocks around a high forehead and prominent cheekbones. You could appreciate the features of his face, a fine nose, high-bridged and faintly Romanesque, and the long, almond shape of his eyes. The legacy of foreign lands and ancient blood was everywhere in him. But it was the way he held himself, the arrogance and swagger in his bearing, that commanded your real attention. It was a confidence born of strength. His shoulders were broad and his arms incredibly strong, and yet he moved easily, even delicately in the small spaces of my apartment. All in all, his looks would have been overpowering had he not possessed the most beautiful mouth I had ever seen. The hawklike features, the squared chest, the dramatic coloring all were softened by his mouth. It was a mouth made for laughing and for kissing. It was a full, sensitive mouth, and when he was pleased, when he smiled, it was so indescribably sweet that my stomach took a dozen back flips as I sat stealing glances at him across the table.

□

We ate, and drank many cups of coffee. Ivan smoked and told me more about himself and his life. I asked him about his work and he paused for a long time, the smoke from his cigarette curling in front of his face and his eyes burning so brightly as if to penetrate something that was just there beyond the wall of blue haze. Then he said: "When I was little boy they took me once to see my mother dance. I was very excited because I love my mother and I am feeling very grown up and important, being allowed to stay up late and be with my father. We sat in a red velvet box and I could see everything—the crush of people coming into the theater, the orchestra tuning their instruments in the pit. I could feel the excitement in the air, the anticipation. Then the lights went down and it was suddenly very quiet and the curtain came up. It was magic. The dancers in costume, the bright lights, the sets, the makeup, the make-believe. My heart was pounding and I thought it splendid but I kept looking at my father, wondering when my mother would appear. Suddenly she did, and my whole young life is shattering in million fragments. She was not anymore my mother, she was an enchantress in flight, her passion burn like fire. She hurl herself through the air, her body becomes the music, the music transformed her. When the dance was over she lifted her eyes to my father and what passed between them was so strong I could see it, feel it. They understood what had happened. She and the dance have become one. I know from that moment that I would search for that in my own life, trying to find in myself what I saw her achieve that night. It is what I do. Struggle as she did, as every artist does, to give voice to things that have never been said."

The telephone rang but I ignored it, then promptly took the receiver off the hook and stuffed it in a drawer.

"What a wonderful story," I breathed. "What wonderful parents."

"Yes. They were," Ivan said thoughtfully. "They believed in their work and the joy of it."

I sighed. "I grew up wondering how my parents could stand their lives. It all seemed so obvious and dull and preordained. I wanted to scream at them, to wake them up from that terrible conformity that seemed to hem us in."

"But, Maisie, I don't understand this place you come from."

"Yeah. Neither do I. It sure as hell isn't Greenwich Village. It's the suburbs. There's a hush out there, all across America. The suburbs are so quiet. The streets are empty. People don't call to one another. They don't lean out windows or even look out windows. All the sounds are kept inside. It's a world that likes to remind itself whenever possible that it is lucky to be what it is: well-fed, middle-class, American, adjusted, and empty-headed."

"They like to be empty-headed? No."

"Yes," I said, "they do."

"Your parents feel this way?"

I sighed again. "That's the trouble. I think of my mom and I see her making costumes for the school plays out of crepe paper. And my dad. He has all these funny old jokes that never make anyone laugh but him. They're not bad people. But they never change, every day of their lives is closed, uneventful, monotonous." We were silent for a moment. Then I said, "What happened to your parents, Ivan?"

He shrugged. "They died when I was nine years old. A fire. They were in the provinces, performing in an antiquated theater. I can imagine it. I do imagine it. The dancers, the music. Suddenly the stage is engulfed in black smoke. The audience panicked. Over three hundred people died in a matter of minutes. And that is life, Maisie. One moment you are dancing, the next moment, pouff! *Fini!* The end."

"My God, how awful. For them and for you. What did you do then?"

Ivan laughed. A booming, completely inappropriate laugh, considering the serious bent of our conversation. He took my hand. "What you will give me if I tell you there is a fifty-cent piece in your hand?" he teased.

"Well, there isn't," I said. "So I'll give you whatever you like."

"Oh, Maisie, you have made big promise." He turned my hand up, and there was a fifty-cent piece. Then he passed his open palm over mine and the coin was gone, only to reappear again at the bottom of my coffee cup.

"You asked what I did?" he boomed, sunny with mischief. "I did what any boy would do. I joined the circus!" I got no more out of him after that. He was intent on claiming his prize.

He drew me back to the bed to resume our more intimate activities. I think it was then I realized that the same curiosity that Ivan exhibited in his examination of my apartment was one of the qualities that made him a sensational lover. All his interest, all his attention was focused on me so that not a gesture or a tremor was lost on him. He studied me and explored me and I opened up to him as I had never done to anyone before.

"You are fantastic," Ivan said. "Like a beautiful ripe peach you are bursting, bursting with a pure sweetness." He kissed me and held me close to him and I felt as if I had been swallowed up into some nether-world of flesh and sensation. "I cannot get enough of you. I want every bit of you, every part of you." Then he pulled away from me and his great hands ran over my body, stopping here, caressing there. He massaged my back, my neck, my buttocks, his hands touching my skin as if it were silk. And I was like a melting thing, dissolving blissfully to the magic of his touch.

Then he asked me to raise my arms over my head. "Ah, yes." He smiled. "You see this curve," and his finger traced the line from my elbow, along the soft underside of my arm, into the deep hollows and then to the rounded cups of my breasts. I could feel my nipples stiffen and my breath catch in my throat. His hands rested softly on my breasts, but he could see how aroused I was. He knew exactly what to do and where to go next. "I love how you look. You are woman in fullness of her sex. You have the scent of one who is ready to make love. Your skin glows with pleasure. Your cheeks are hot and your lips are full and red." As he said this, he parted my legs and gently began to caress the soft dark places there. My legs willingly fell apart and I felt an urgency, a wonderful openness, a rush to something I had never known. It was as if we had all the time in the world. He was perfectly expert. The waves of heat started to build. There was something about him, the way he looked at me. I knew he wanted to please me. I knew that by giving everything to him I would please him. I had never trusted anyone the way I trusted Ivan in that moment. I abandoned myself to him. My body was his and he took it.

Afterward he hugged me and petted me and kissed me and I cried, my face buried in his neck. I was so happy.

In the evening we went out to a little French restaurant in the West Village. We ate coq au vin and drank a bottle of Bordeaux. We walked back to my place through the soft night and I don't think I have ever been more content in my whole life. The following morning Ivan left early to return to his studio. As he was leaving he tipped up my chin and gently kissed my lips.

"Au revoir, Maisie," he said, then whispered something in my ear that I shall not reveal. He left me laughing, but when the door closed I felt as though the sun had been eclipsed.

5

I was in love. Butterflies-in-the-stomach kind of love. Schmaltzy lyrics, heart-yearning, blood-pounding kind of love. In the days that followed I thought about Ivan constantly, replaying every moment, every word, every touch. Sometimes I wanted him so badly my legs would shake, and I would have to stop whatever I was doing and sit very still until the waves of desire and passion calmed to a small ripple.

I lost no time in telling Jake that our "relationship" had moved on to a new and platonic plateau. He puffed on his pipe and said, "Ah! Another fair damsel falls for Ivan the Terrible. You disappoint me, Maisie. Frankly, you don't seem like his type."

"Frankly, Jake," I answered, "up yours."

I could see Jake felt little more than a slightly bruised ego, and to his credit, he could see that, too. He puffed thoughtfully some more on the pipe and then we moved quickly on to other topics of interest. Namely the cooperative gallery. They were looking for someone to be its director. "Hard work," Jake warned. "Big responsibility . . . no pay in the beginning, of course . . ." Was I interested? Indeed I was.

It was two weeks before I saw Ivan again. He and Dance came into the Figaro very late one night, and very drunk. Clinging to them was a cute little actressy type, and, oh my, wasn't she just full of herself, like a cat with a big bowl of cream. Never mind that I had probably looked that way the night I met Ivan, I loathed that woman. I watched them out of the corner of my eye. Ivan was obviously turning on the charm, she was batting her lashes a mile a minute, and Dance kept leaning over and peering down the front of her dress as if the fate of the world hung there in the balance. After a while, Miss Pert got up and made her way through the crowded room to the rest room in back. I watched and followed her. The Café Figaro's one tiny cubicle that served us all was past the kitchen, down a few stairs, the last door before you got to the alley. Sometimes the boss locked it if the toilet was broken, or if he smelled marijuana, and then he'd send customers out through the alley into the back door of the bar next door.

I knew where he kept the key. I could hear her peeing as I locked her in. Then I hustled myself, quick as a fox, right over to Ivan's table. "Okay, boys. What's your pleasure? Speak up. Order up. Last call for a last round in the Last Chance Bar." I hiked one leg up on the empty chair and blessed myself for shaving my legs that very afternoon.

Ivan immediately wrapped his large hands around my calf, groping like a blind man. "I know this leg. I know this leg very well. I love this leg. I want this leg. Maybe I put this leg in my pocket and take it home. Okay?" Dance smiled a lazy, droopy kind of smile. Then he nodded a few times. "It's a good leg. Do you think it's got a friend?"

"Sure, it's got a friend. A nice friend. Hey, leg, you got a nice friend for my buddy here?" His hands started traveling up my leg, under my skirt. I didn't move, not a muscle. Ivan hesitated. His hand climbed higher. Still I didn't move. I was daring him, and he took the dare. His finger gently stroked the soft, hollowed-out place on the inner part of my thigh. I held still, then he looked up, directly into my eyes, and as a thousand volts of electricity passed between us, I slowly removed his hand and lowered my foot to the floor.

"As I was saying, what's your pleasure?"

"Maisie? Yes, it's Maisie," said Ivan, looking very much more sober than he had when he came in. He was turned on and so was I. Dance, on the other hand, was fast losing the battle for consciousness.

"I think we should get him out of here, don't you?" I said. "I mean while he's still awake. It'll be easier." Ivan jumped up, agreeing.

I hadn't forgotten the girl locked in the bathroom, but clearly Ivan had, which was fine with me, but the sooner we got out of there the better. I signaled one of the other waitresses to cover for me and then together we got Dance back to his apartment. We placed him gently on the bed. Ivan removed his shoes and I tucked the covers around him and brushed his hair out of his face.

"He's beautiful, isn't he?" I said, staring down on the poet, who looked like a sleeping child, his face flushed, a tiny bit damp, but so peaceful and innocent. "I've never seen him sober," I said. "Is he always drunk?"

Ivan shrugged. "Yes, but not always with alcohol. Sometimes he is drunk on words. Sometimes he is drunk with pleasure. It is all the same." Ivan smiled. "When you know him better, you will see what I see. Without the drink he thinks he will go mad. But let us leave him now to sleep."

We crept out of the bedroom and closed the door. I was thrilled by Ivan's assumption that I would get to know Dance better. Ivan went about the room turning off the lights, and as I watched him I knew I didn't want to wait until we got to my place or his. What we had started back there at the Figaro wanted to be consummated right then and there. The look on Ivan's face told me it was exactly what he had in mind as well.

He put his hands on either side of my head and kissed me hard. I was no shrinking violet. My lips, my breasts felt swollen with a desire so intense I know I must have moaned. I wanted him now! On the floor. On the table. Anywhere. My hands tugged at the buttons of his shirt and the zipper of his pants. He reached under my blouse and with one deft snap my bra was off and I gasped as his fingers teased and twisted my nipples. My skirt was pulled roughly above my hips and he let me go long enough for me to wiggle out of my underwear while he kicked off his jeans. Then his hands cupped my bare bottom and he picked me up and pressed me against the wall as I wrapped my legs around him. He looked at me then and his hair was slightly disheveled, his face intent, his eyes radiating unbounded lust, a smile of pure happiness on his lips. I cried out for him and then I felt him stiff and hard against me. I came once when he thrust himself inside me and again, and then again. I had never known that could happen. I had never known anything *like* that could happen. My body no longer belonged to me. I had no control, nor did I want any. But he had no more control than I did, and he buried his face in my hair and came inside me with tremendous force.

We were immobile for a few seconds and I marveled at his strength. His shoulders were wet with the sweat of our bodies, but he held me as lightly as a child would hold a doll. I traced the line of muscle in his arm, then, on an impulse that was as irresistible as it was strange, I sank my teeth into his shoulder. It must have hurt because I heard him catch his breath, but at the same time I felt him swell and harden inside me and we were off again. This time we made it to the sofa before we burst into another glorious orgasm. Then we were laughing. We clung to each other until we were weak with the laughter, shushing each other so as not to wake up Dance, only to start up all over again.

Later we drank wine, wrapped in each other's arms, on the sofa. My hands rested on his head as he pressed against me, and I twisted his thick hair through my fingers. I felt so happy. Not giddy or silly, but the kind of happiness that fills you up. I never wanted to let him go. I wanted to tell him how I felt. I wanted to tell him I loved him. Lucky for me, I didn't.

The next morning it was pouring rain. I could hear it raking against the windows, and the sound lulled me in and out of the nicest dream until I suddenly woke up. I wasn't in my apartment, in my own bed, and for a second I didn't know where I was. I was wrapped in a warm cashmere blanket on a deep green velvet sofa. Except for the rain it was quiet, and I thought I was alone until I saw Dance sitting at the large round oak table that dominated the room. He was perfectly still, wearing a white silk dressing gown. He could have been a marble statue.

I felt awkward and wished desperately that I had gone home the night before instead of falling asleep in Ivan's arms. Ivan! Where the hell was he? I had to pee terribly.

Suddenly Dance looked at me, all beaming smiles, not a trace of hangover. "You're awake. It's all that way." He waved back toward the bedroom. "Shower if you like, but don't get dressed. Wear a robe to breakfast. It's much cozier. There's one in the bath."

I nodded gratefully, and clutching the blanket, I stumbled out of the room. When I came out I was showered, brushed, and combed and wearing a beautiful blue paisley robe. The table, I saw, was set with jars of jam and marmalade, hot fresh bread, and a large pot of rich black coffee.

"Now I can say it like a real, live human being," I said. "Good morning, Dance. Looks like you got stuck with me. Where's Ivan?"

"Oh, honey, he's working. He left hours ago, but there's a note for you. Have some coffee first and clear the cobwebs."

I read Ivan's message immediately. "I kiss you awake and leave you for now. Dance will take good care. Ivan."

I guess I must have looked fairly forlorn because Dance laughed and said, "Now, now. Don't go all down at the mouth. It will give you wrinkles. Ivan does as he likes. It doesn't do to get all droopy about it. If you want him, make sure your rope is at least five miles long. That one needs a lot of leeway."

"I do want him. But I get the feeling I'm part of a large crowd of hopefuls," I said, wishing Dance would say this wasn't true, but he didn't. He sort of smiled and nodded, but didn't say a word. "Oh well," I sighed, biting into a large chunk of bread, "woman cannot live on hope alone."

"That's the spirit. But then, never give up hope." He pushed a silver tray over to me with three little jars on it, each filled with a different kind of jam or marmalade. I spread some neatly on the crust of bread. It was delicious.

I looked around the apartment. It was clean, spare, and polished. There was an austerity to it that surprised me because Dance Duprey did not strike me as austere. We talked amicably for a while—loose, disjointed, pleasant sort of talk, as if we'd been having morning coffee together for years—and then Dance asked me, "Why are you here? I mean here in New York. Are you ambitious, artistic?"

"God, no. It's nothing nearly so neat. I'm here because I didn't want to be *there*, I guess. I suppose I thought I would find out what I wanted if I could just get to New York. Why are you here?"

"Oh, I wanted to make my presence known in a certain way. There's a kind of energy you find here that you don't find anywhere else in the world. The past is never present, and the present is somewhere in the future. Everything happens according to a different set of rules, and the primary rule is that there are no rules. I like that. I like relinquishing all notions of control. I like relinquishing all notions of everything. It's a purifying experience, don't you think?"

"I suppose so, but then I haven't quite gotten to the pure part yet. No matter how much I try to tell myself I'm free to do anything I want to, I always have this sneaking suspicion that Mrs. Shacter is waiting for me just around the corner."

"A name from the past?"

I nodded. "Mrs. Shacter was the principal of my elementary school back in Ohio. She was also the keeper of the Permanent Record. Everything you did went on Permanent Record, and I believed it was really permanent. You know, like written in stone for life! No redress. I thought Mrs. Shacter had a direct line to the ear of God. It wasn't until much later that I realized the Permanent Record was just some moldy old ledger book in her office. But I still worry about it."

Dance laughed. "Yes. I suppose we all have one of her in our lives. For me it was a governess."

"You had a governess?"

"Oh yes. I was an only child and my father was away most of the time. He was in shipping." He stopped and grinned. "Banana boats. And my mother was . . . well, the expression they used in Savannah was 'not herself.' In fact, she was plumb loco. Hence the governess, and she was, by God, the real thing. Straight from the pages of Frances Hodgson Burnett—the spinster daughter of impoverished English gentlefolk. And she was as sane and sensible and right-thinking as my mother was vague and childish and given to fits of nonstop chatter. Her name was Miss Clarisse Appleton and I adored her because she was so sure of the things that 'mattered.' It was her favorite word. Certain things mattered and other things did not matter. Nothing eluded her quick and unsparing judgment. The South did not suit her at all. She said it was one big madhouse, and she was right. Miss Clarisse never could grasp the simple fact that to a Southerner there's no charm in sanity. Indeed, it's a downright gloomy idea. Our way is all contradiction and colorful behavior. Hers was all consistency and conscience. But she was determined to influence my young life. What mattered most to Miss Appleton was structure. She could talk for hours about the great houses of England, the antiquities of Italy, and the architecture of Paris. Her life had been filled with insufferable humiliations as a poor relation, second-rate hotels and package tours, but be that as it may, by God, she knew that what mattered most was only found in Europe. As soon as I could, I left to study in England and France."

"Not in second-rate hotels, I'll bet."

"Heavens, no. My introductions and accommodations were befitting the scion of Savannah's steamer king. I went first to England and read ancient languages at Cambridge. But I found England dreary and depressed from the war. So as soon as I could, I left for Paris.

"Of course, I loved Paris. Everywhere I looked there was something old and beautiful to behold. Every building, street, monument was steeped in history and meaning. I felt as if Paris were my soul mate. Everything seemed so very grand and solid. My acquaintances were all much older than I. I was engulfed by the intelligentsia. I'm afraid I was turning into rather an academic prig. But then one afternoon I went to a gathering at the studio of the great sculptor Constantin Brancusi, and that's where . . ."

"You met Ivan." I said with satisfaction. At last we had come to the point of Dance's recitation. I leaned eagerly toward him.

Dance grinned. He was enjoying his story as much as I. "Brancusi was a very beautiful old man, like a sage, with a great gray beard and small sparkling blue eyes. He was very colorful and very childlike, grinning and pleased as anything over the smallest triffling thing. I had brought him a box of Havana cigars and, oh my, he carried on over them, sniffing and touching them and playing with the tiny brass lock on the box as if it housed the rarest jewels. His studio was in great disarray—the beginnings of plaster sculptures lay about in no particular order, some things seemed to be discarded, some put aside for the moment. There were giant marble boulders, wood blocks, uneven shelves filled with black tools and rusty forms, and here and there a bouquet of flowers. The whole effect was terribly, terribly chaotic, but the energy of the place—darling, there was some very great energy going round, and it was very infectious. There were so many people there that day, and so much talking and shouting. I swear my senses were positively reeling. But I noticed Ivan right away. I couldn't very well help it. He was buck naked and covered in mud.

"It had rained that morning and Ivan had stripped off his clothes and he was stomping around in the mud and the puddles of the courtyard singing a Russian drinking song. Soon others joined in the refrain and they were just like pigs in the proverbial . . . Well, I was amazed. I confess I had expected something far more elevated from the afternoon. More intellectual, I guess. Brancusi and I watched them together and then he leaned back in his chair, warming his back against a big old stove, and he said, 'The day you are no longer a child, you're already dead. Never forget that!'

"Ivan must have noticed the perplexity I felt, because he came lumbering over like a bear after honey and he just laughed and threw his big old wet, muddy arms around me like he was about to squeeze the daylights out of me. Well, a great hush came over the place, because I think everyone thought that I must take offense. But no! It was such a grand and generous gesture. Really it was. The man was without fear or anxiety—still is. Now, this will sound a bit much, but I tell you I knew in that moment my life had taken a turn. Ivan was not afraid to expose himself naked to the world, physically as well as in his mind, in his spirit. It was the beginning of our friendship. I spent a lot of time with him after that. For the first time I saw that one could live without the weight of possessions. Ivan made do with a chair, a table, and a rolled army-surplus sleeping bag. That was all his comfort, but he acted as though he lived in luxury. It came from inside him. It was the way he saw things, the way he took pleasure in them. What he made me come to realize was that the Old World, the traditions that we were so carefully taught to view as things that 'mattered,' were frozen in the past. 'Look at the past, study the past, appreciate the past . . . and then let it go,' he said. 'The work is never about the past. Look for something else. Look for something you've never seen.' I began to realize that in Paris and London nobody listened or looked at anything unless they were told to. It was like living in a museum. The images were frozen icons. I came to see Europe the way you did your moldy old ledger book."

"God. That's a lot more interesting than Mrs. Shacter," I said. "So then you and Ivan moved to New York?"

"Yes. I came first. It was easy for me, of course. I just had to book passage. But Ivan needed work permits and visas and an American sponsor. It's not easy for a foreigner to get into this country. But finally he got cleared. He came here as a stonecutter. A skilled worker." Dance paused remembering something. "When he came through Immigration I was waiting for him outside on the pier. He was grinning from ear to ear. 'I come to the New World and I am a new man with a new name!' he exclaimed to me. 'This is a wonderful omen.' What he meant was that the customs official couldn't pronounce his long and complicated Russian surname, so when he saw Ivan's birthplace, St. Petersburg, he simply wrote 'Ivan St. Peters.' He was sent to the Catskills to work the bluestone quarries, but an artist in Woodstock discovered him and got him a job in New York, carving monuments and statuary for the city. I got him his loft and paid a few months' rent on it, but Ivan wouldn't let me do more than that."

I was mesmerized with what Dance was saying. I felt as if I were being pulled out of myself and propelled into a world that was much bigger, much more exciting, much more dazzling than anything I had ever experienced.

"I wish I knew more. I wish I knew just what you're talking about. I wish I'd been to Europe," I said passionately. "You and Ivan come out of such a different world than the one I know. Oh, I envy you."

"Don't. Envy wastes a lot of time. And I'm not so sure my world is very different, after all is said and done. Ivan's is, yes, but you must remember that for Ivan, the world he came from is now a graveyard." Dance stopped, and I could sense the sadness he felt. There was real pain in something he knew about Ivan, but I didn't want to press. But then he brightened. "Ivan's a wonderful combination of Old World tradition, charm, and intellect, and yet his energy and his sensibilities are very raw and brash and American. Have you seen his work? No? Oh, Maisie, I envy you the experience of seeing it for the first time. He understands beauty like no one else. You know, when Rilke saw Rodin's sculpture for the first time, he was thunderstruck. He said, 'Your work is the voice I harken amid the silence that surrounds me, the dawn and twilight of all my days and the sky of my nights.' That is just how I feel about Ivan's work, and one day when I'm as good a poet as Rilke was, I will tell him so in my own words. To me, Ivan is a very special kind of genius."

"He's a very special kind of lover."

"Yes. I'm sure he is. But to an artist there is only one love affair." He filled my cup. "You don't strike me as the kind of girl who's looking for a permanent setup. But if you are, don't waste much time on Ivan."

In truth, I didn't know what I was looking for. And I said so. I only knew I didn't want to lose sight of Ivan St. Peters. He had chanced into my life twice now. I wanted to make sure there was a third time. I got the feeling Dance was trying to tell me how. "I take it I'm not the first girl he's left behind on your sofa," I said.

Dance shrugged. "Not the first."

"So what are you saying?"

"I guess I'm trying to tell you to think about what you want before you get more involved. Ivan needs a woman who can take care of him, who understands what he is and who he is—someone who won't make demands on his time or his emotions. You can handle Ivan easily if you can accept things as they are, but I'm afraid most women can't. They want to go about changing things. Sooner or later they try to force him into a corner. That is always fatal. Ivan's life is his work. Nothing—not friendship, love, or anything else—will ever be as important to him."

I felt flattered that Dance was taking me and my brief relationship with Ivan so seriously. He had a way of saying things that made me feel wonderfully right. In time I was to learn that one of Dance's most endearing qualities was his capacity for friendship. Where friends were concerned, he stinted on nothing. When you were with Dance, time was suspended. He never rushed you, never so much as thought about doing anything other than just being with you, grasping every nuance of what you wished to say, without needing to be told all the boring details. I'll never forget that morning I spent with Dance, wrapped in blue paisley, with the rain holding us hostage. We talked on into the morning about many things, not just Ivan. Even the most mundane subject shone in the glow of his interest. The talk fed on itself and we began to make the connections that would bind us in the closest kind of friendship. I don't know what he saw in me that he hadn't seen in the dozens of other women who had fallen for Ivan, but it was understood from that morning on that now there were two of us looking after him.

In the following months I spent every minute I could with Ivan and Dance, and in their own ways, both were to change my life completely.

6

Ivan and I became lovers. I managed to accept the fact that there would be no regular rhythm to our times together. The intensity that I had witnessed in Ivan proved to be but a tip of the iceberg compared to the energy he brought to his work. I quickly discovered that when Ivan worked he did not make love, at least not to me or any other living woman.

I don't think I had ever realized just what went into the making of a sculpture. The first thing that struck me, watching him at work in the studio, was the sheer physical labor and drudgery of it all. Ivan would go at it like a drone, hauling dozens of hundred-pound sacks of clay up the four flights to his studio, mixing it in great tubs like witches' cauldrons, then building the armatures, the frames on which the rough clay shapes would be molded. Then there was the sculpting itself, and Ivan the drone became Ivan the artist possessed, bobbing and weaving around his creation like a boxer looking for an opening in his opponent's defenses, suddenly swooping low with tool in hand to deepen a line here or whirling about with a growl of fury to eradicate an imperfection there. Stymied even for a moment, he would groan as if in pain, holding his head in his huge hands, his body a perfect model of despair; then the solution would come to him and he'd pounce lovingly, caressing, teasing shape and life into the reluctant mass. If the work went well, he would grin as he sculpted, murmuring and muttering as you would to a lover, or to a coma victim to urge him back to consciousness. My God, he was beautiful.

Like an insatiable lover, Ivan was never exactly "finished" with a sculpture unless it was physically taken from his presence (a ruse to which Julian would later frequently resort). If his fertile brain hadn't constantly provided him with new objects for his physical attentions, I believe he could have happily worked the rest of his life revising a single piece.

His sculptures were first of all gouged and scraped and brought to life from the blank, dead gray clay. Then, if he could afford it, the models were sent to a foundry where castings were made from poured bronze. The bronzed roughs, crude and covered with slag, would come back to the studio for finishing, which for Ivan meant an incredibly intricate labor called chase work—the detailing that was virtually his signature —then long, arduous hours of sanding, and finally the patina. At any given time you could see works at every stage of creation, standing with endless patience in their carelessly assigned spots around the huge studio.

In the studio, he sculpted and observed nothing but his inner vision. Outside the studio, he did little else but observe. I've never known anyone with such hungry eyes. He would roam the streets, searching, his eyes moving restlessly over people, objects, patterns of light and shadow, fleeting scenes of drama or comedy. One day he took me to the Museum of Modern Art to see Brancusi's piece called *Bird in Space.*

"You see here," he explained as we walked around the great bronze abstraction. "It is not an abstract image of a bird, but rather he has formed the image of flight itself."

Ivan did not align himself with any school or movement in art. "I am a student of the Old World, a pioneer in the New," he would say. And it was true. You could see in his work the influence of Brancusi, Rodin, even classical Greece, and yet he dwarfed these influences with his own expansive measure and style. He loved America. He loved Americans. He had good reason to.

Ivan never talked about the grim realities of his past. The memories were ugly and harsh. He didn't like to tell me about the war or the Germans or the work camps. About these he talked only to Dance. But Ivan told stories, wonderful stories, peopled by the characters of his boyhood. He could fill a room with his stories. In time I was able to piece as much of Ivan's past together as I think was possible. I don't believe he fabricated his past, but I do think the world he came from was so erased from this planet by the time I knew him that perhaps, in memory, it became a part of another, larger, more colorful dimension than it actually was. Then again, perhaps not.

He was born in the city of Peter the Great, the capital of all the Russias, a cosmopolitan city of beauty, sophistication, and learning. It was the site of the Winter Palace, the Palace of Art, the great university with all its attendant libraries and cultural institutions. Of course, it was the scene of the Revolution itself in 1917, when suddenly it was no longer St. Petersburg.

So Ivan came into the world in a place of great beauty, but at a time of great drama and chaos. When his parents died, years later, in the fire that burned down an entire theater, an uncle—a flamboyant scalawag who managed a traveling tent show, a small single-ring circus—took him in, and Ivan found himself traveling in caravans from one end of Russia to another, along with parrots, leopards, dancing bears, and tigers.

I have never been to Russia, but I've been to the circus many times. How easy it is to imagine the lively and curious boy that Ivan surely was at nine years of age at the center of this sawdust world. Never mind that the circus had fallen on hard times and its resources had dwindled considerably. It was a world where illusion and showmanship were everything, and Ivan was at home there.

It was there he met the magician called Kournos the Magnificent. Not so many years ago, while browsing in the Gotham Book Mart, I came across a book on magicians, and to my delight there he was. And he certainly was magnificent, a suave man in evening clothes, white gloves, a silk hat, and a cape.

Part of his appeal, Ivan told me, was that he was a talking magician. He delighted his audiences with jokes and leisurely philosophical monologues. He could cause a coin to gallop end over end across the backs of his fingers, or he might balance a deck of cards on the toe of his boot, flip it in the air, and catch a perfect fan of fifty-two cards. From his top hat he could produce a hundred yards of sash ribbon, a dozen bottles of champagne and twenty champagne glasses, thousands of playing cards, a skull, a canary in a cage, seven lighted lamps, and a bowl of water with a goldfish in it, all the while amusing himself and his audience with commentary on everything from the events of his day to the mysteries of the universe.

Ivan loved him, he said, like no other. Night after night he would sit in the darkness just outside the glow of the incandescent lamps and wait patiently through the clown act, the jugglers, the animal turn, the acrobats. "And then," Ivan whispered, "the tent go black. No music plays, no fanfare. All the people waiting—waiting in the dark. Silence all around. But now inside the sawdust ring lights start to glow, burning hotter, brighter until suddenly—POUFF!—big explosion and much white smoke. Kournos is there! Kournos the Magnificent, smiling, talking, pulling us into the magic circle where reason dares not go."

"Ah," Ivan would sigh. "You see, Maisie, the whole secret of art is the illusions it creates."

Kournos and Ivan were together for four years. The mentor and the protégé. Ivan was being groomed to inherit the magician's mantle when the time came. But that was not to be.

He grew to be a strapping boy who looked much older than his years. And on his thirteenth birthday Kournos gave Ivan the coin, an ancient icon passed down from one magician to another, and told the boy, "I have taught you everything I know. Tonight you will perform. Tonight you shall enter the magic circle with me."

That day Ivan was picked up by the Germans while walking along the street. In less than four hours he was on a crowded train bound for Germany, for the work camps. It was 1941. He would never see his uncle, the circus, Kournos the Magnificent, or Russia again. Only the coin, tucked in the deepest corner of his coat, was left as a reminder of the world he had left behind.

Like millions of others, Ivan St. Peters was swallowed up in the apocalypse of World War II.

Four years, a lifetime to a boy forced overnight to become a man. A harsh, grim, gray existence surrounded by cruelty, hunger, and death. His work was heavy labor, clearing rubble from the bombs, rebuilding houses, shoveling coal for fuel, and, because the Germans were so very patriotic, reconstructing destroyed monuments. Perhaps this was what saved him. He had talent. He could reconstruct the faces of stone statues. He could even hammer out a new one.

And then, when he was seventeen years old, it was over.

"For weeks there had been rumors," he told me. "The Americans were coming. The war would soon be over. It not seem possible. And then, suddenly, the war *was* over. Germany lay in the rubble of defeat, and everywhere there were the Americans. First came the soldiers and then supplies. There were doctors in first-aid tents and boxes and boxes of blankets and shoes and coats and gloves. But most of all, there was food. Food. Real food. Hot, filling food.

"I tell you a story. I attached myself to a medical unit. I could help with translation, tell the Americans what the people needed, give them information. The magician, he spoke seven languages, one for each day of the week, so I was pretty good. Soon I was living at the hospital. There were American soldiers there, and I used to do sketches of them to send home to their sweethearts.

"It looks like all Europe was on the move. On the roads, thousands people are walking, pulling carts or pushing bicycles all piled high with what was left of their belongings. The roads were full. Everyone is trying to get somewhere so life could begin again. One day in hospital they bring in little old man who has collapsed. His face was like old raisin. He didn't speak English and he is so scared. He is shaking so much his jaw make a rattle. Under his coat he is holding something that he would not let go. I was supposed to undress him for the delousing, but he fight me like a tiger. Finally I find what he is hiding—it is an old, dry piece of black bread. So I try to talk to him. I speak to him in French and Polish and then Russian and I could see he recognized that language. I told him they want to help him, to wash him and make him feel better, but he doesn't believe. I can see he has lost most of his teeth and his gums were raw. The pain must have been great. You know, I said to the doctors, it is better to let him be. Why should he believe me? Why should he believe anyone? So we leave him. All day he is huddled in his bed, watching the nurses, watching the doctors. And then it is dinnertime. In are coming big tables of hot food. Fried chickens and steaks and green vegetables and butter and milk. And there was also a giant pyramid of white, fresh-baked rolls. So soft and good smelling. I watch the little man. He sit up and look and he smell and then he begin to smile. And suddenly from under his coat he is taking his black rock of bread and making perfect aim he throws it out the window. The Americans, you know, they were like gods. They were food. They were nourishment. They were plenty. They were the road back to life."

7

In due course the gallery opened on the top floor of a charmless old building on Ninth Street between Second and Third avenues. Today this is the fashionable East Village, but back then it was a down-at-the-heels neighborhood of dusty old shops and dismal gray stone buildings. The artists loved it, though—not for esthetics but because the rents were cheap.

To get to the gallery, one had to weave one's way past the winos, step over sleeping bums, and sprint up four flights of stairs in a building that was redolent of boiling cabbage and garlic. Not that any of this put a damper on our high spirits and lofty dreams. We were serving art (and ourselves), and there was, we thought, no higher cause than that. We worked for weeks, sometimes clear through the night, stripping plaster from the walls to expose the brick, sanding and hand-polishing the wood floors, even knocking down interior walls to make one open, uncluttered space.

That was the easy part. The hard part was trying to get the twenty or so opinionated, egocentric artist members of this so-called cooperative to agree on anything. Every meeting was marked by hysterical outbursts and violent dissent. For three whole weeks they argued about the particular shade of white that the wall must be painted. In my ignorance I had gone out and bought the cheapest white paint I could find, only to discover that there's no such thing as simple white. There's yellow white and pink white and blue white and gray white. At one point I was ready to send all of them over to Bellevue to have their heads examined. But in truth I was having the time of my life, blissfully in love with Ivan and playing den mother to everyone else.

Money, of course, was the big problem, and there were moments when even the most optimistic among us doubted we would actually make it to the opening, but somehow, something always saved us.

On opening night the wine was the cheapest we could find, and there was no food until the mother of one of the artists showed up with a huge vat of chopped chicken liver. But the excitement, as the artists and their friends jammed into the gallery, more than made up for any lack of éclat. It wasn't until later in the week that we were forced to admit that we had opened to thundering silence as far as the rest of the art world was concerned. Not one critic had come, no dealers, no curators from museums, and certainly no collectors. Of course, no one had seriously expected sales on that first night, and of course there were none; but after a month our obscure little gallery could boast not a single sale to raise our flagging spirits.

It was summer, and the people who mattered had all left town. We had decided to shut down for most of the week, but I dutifully sat behind my desk every Saturday and Sunday through July and the sweltering heat of August, hoping against hope that something interesting would happen. Mostly only the artists dropped in to adjust their paintings and complain about the space that had been allotted to their work or about the quality of light that illuminated their pieces, while I tried to appear competent and maintain an air of sympathy toward each one. As August gave way to September, Mrs. Preobrazhansky from the second floor took to dropping in to bring me a bowl of borscht or a cup of hot, strong, very sweet tea. Once she came up with her husband, who had, touchingly, put on a tie and jacket for the occasion. They walked slowly around, looking carefully at each picture, and whispered to each other in Polish, but I don't think they said anything kind about our exhibition. After that they treated me as if I were a prisoner, clearly considering it their duty to keep me as comfortable as possible for the duration of my captivity.

☐

I was tending the gallery one Saturday afternoon, feeling bored and not a little melancholy. The autumn weather had turned unseasonably wet and cold and I had more or less decided that the day was to be a bust, when a Wall Street type in gray flannel walked in. From the look of him, I guessed, sardonically, that he was either lost or was looking to get out of the rain. I guessed wrong.

I pretended I was busy at my desk and watched him out of the corner of my eye. He was around thirty and good-looking in a pale, Waspy sort of way. Everything about him was just so—neat, tidy, and Ivy League all the way. Not at all my type, I said to myself, but in truth I had always been a bit intrigued by a certain kind of upper-class, Down East arrogance that bespoke good family, all the right schooling, and the right kind of bank account, too, of course. Sure enough, underneath a somewhat bland exterior, this guy was arrogant as hell. He was in no hurry, walking slowly from piece to piece, carefully studying every picture, every sculpture. After a while he zeroed in on the single piece of Ivan's work, and for a solid half hour he looked at nothing else. My landlady at the time had once been a showgirl. Now in her dotage, she was never short on advice. "Always look at the shoes," she had said to me more times than I could count. "Shoes make the man." I looked. Exquisite, handmade, expensive leather boots. It was time for Maisie Green to make her move.

I slid out from behind my desk, smoothed my skirt, straightened my seams, and walked over to stand beside him. "I don't wish to disturb you," I said in my best imitation of a finishing-school accent, "but should you have any questions, I'd be only too happy to answer them."

"Yes. Thank you." He didn't even bother to look at me. "I'm curious about this St. Peters." He gestured toward Ivan's sculpture, which dominated the center of the room. It was a beautiful bronze, very physical and energetic but quite delicately executed. Ivan had titled it simply *Nude 9*, because it had taken him nine renderings to get it right. It was a very sensual and feminine piece, and I often wished I had inspired it, but the piece had been cast before I came on the scene.

"This is from a series the artist calls The Sirens."

"Then there are more?"

"Oh yes. Not all of them have been cast as yet, but the models are available." Ivan had gone for months living on little more than bread and water to scrape the money together to have this piece cast.

"It is a strong piece. Very moving. I should like to see more of this man's work. Does he see people at his studio?"

I could feel my heart beating. His Harvard accent and confident manner were impressive. Maybe he could do something for Ivan. I remember wondering if Mr. Uptown Gray Flannel Suit had any idea what Ivan's studio might be like. Ivan lived in a place over by the Hudson River that was so rundown you could actually peer through the floorboards into the factory below, where dozens of Puerto Rican women worked in twelve-hour shifts making toilet seats. If it was cold out today, it was sure to be even colder in the loft, but what the hell. Nothing ventured, nothing gained. I looked at my watch.

"It's getting to be closing time. If you'd like to meet Ivan St. Peters —I mean, if you'd like to see more of his work—I could take you to his studio."

Apparently I had said the right thing. He nodded and extended his hand. "My name is Julian Slade and I want very much to meet the man who created this."

I beamed. "I'm Maisie Green. I hope that overcoat of yours is warm, because I can't promise you any heat where we're going."

"I'm eager to go wherever you're taking me, Miss Green. That's the nice thing about wanting something, isn't it? It generates its own heat."

During the the cab ride over to Hudson and West 12th streets we chatted amiably about the gallery, how long it had been in operation, my position there, the general reception of the show, some of the other artists; and by the time Julian had paid the driver and taken my arm outside Ivan's building, I felt as if I had broken through some of Julian Slade's reserve. But possibly it was the other way round. As usual, I realized that it was I who had done most of the talking. Apart from his name, I knew nothing about Julian Slade.

8

I'm sure it was difficult for Julian to imagine how anyone could live the way Ivan did, but nothing in his pleasant, carefully composed demeanor betrayed either his excitement at being on the verge of a big discovery or his dismay at seeing Ivan's circumstances. There could be no doubt that Ivan St. Peters's loft housed a working artist. The living area—one curtained-off room— could be taken in at a glance. An industrial sink and a bathtub occupied one wall; the opposite wall was lined with industrial steel shelving that held all the necessities of Ivan's spartan personal life: a hot plate, a teakettle, one large pot, a couple of plates and mugs, a few neatly folded clothes, and a lot of books. Chairs, a table, and lamps had been scavenged from the streets of New York. Dominating the room was a large double bed, raised on a platform, covered with a fur bedspread. It looked like a stage piece, and it was. Ivan had received the bed, complete with an eight-foot-high, ornately carved headboard, from a set designer at the

Metropolitan Opera in exchange for work Ivan had done at the opera house. On that bed and on that very fur, countless Desdemonas had died in Otello's arms.

Ivan had put a kettle of water on to boil, and in a matter of minutes he was handing out steaming mugs of tea laced with dark Jamaican rum. "This will fortify you for the studio, my friend," Ivan said. "When it rains, the damp chills the bones and sometimes the spirits. I would not like for you to see my work in poor spirit."

"You are very kind to let me come unannounced, Mr. St. Peters."

"Ivan," Ivan bellowed. "You like my work. You are friend and must call me Ivan."

"Then you must call me Julian."

Ivan threw his arms around the surprised Julian in a gesture of warmth and friendship, and despite Julian's natural reserve, I could see he felt himself warming to the man and the place. When at last the tea was drunk, Julian was allowed beyond the curtained wall into the studio. It was a vast, open loft with walls of exposed brick and seventeen floor-to-ceiling windows. At this time of day the light was dim and diffuse. But it did not seem to matter. It wasn't hard to see that Julian was astonished at what he saw. Only a half-dozen sculptures had been cast, but even the clay figures were vibrant with feeling and sensuality. Ivan's accomplishments were stunning in their range, originality, and impact.

Julian stood rapt in silent admiration. Slowly, methodically, he examined each piece, and the expression on his face was one of pure joy. Neither Ivan nor Julian spoke for a long time, and yet they seemed to have a perfect understanding.

But later, after Julian had taken us out to dinner and later still over drinks at the Cedar Bar, the conversation flowed. Each man recognized in the other a true passion for art. They talked for hours, long into the night.

"You know," Julian said thoughtfully, "no matter what words I use, what vocabulary I may have developed over the years to describe a particular work of art, in the long run I always judge its worth by a purely irrational feeling. It's something that happens in the gut. I trust it more than any other factor. The very first time I experienced it was at a much-touted exhibit in the Metropolitan Museum when I was sixteen years old.

"What I saw were two figures carved in wood. A man and a woman embracing. I was young. I knew nothing, and I looked at it, and I walked on. But something made me turn back. Something made me study the piece until my eyes ached. And what had seemed at first a simple portrayal of a man and a woman embracing now took on so many layers of feeling, such complexity of meaning. Love, passion, death, and agony were all visible to me in the clutch of those young lovers. And there was beauty. An ethereal, untouchable beauty that defied my senses and filled me with a happiness that I'd never known existed. It fascinated me. I went back to the museum the next day and the next until I was sure that what I felt was not some sort of transient adolescent emotion—not just an excess of hormones." Julian smiled. "From that point on, my life and the pursuit of art were inextricably linked. What I've seen of your work today gives me that same feeling."

Ivan nodded, smiling. He was not inclined to disagree.

"You know you're far too good to be showing in that little gallery." Julian's abrupt change of mood caught us both off guard. "The sculptures I saw today should be seen together for their greatest impact. But surely you know all this. You should be seen uptown. Your work should be seen as a whole, not piecemeal."

Ivan shrugged. "I like of course my work to have wider audience, and it will. This gallery is only to begin. Perhaps when my art begin to sell . . ."

Julian smiled thinly. "You cannot expect sales from that place. You and the gallery are unknown. You have no way to reach the people who must recognize you. You have no money for announcements, advertising, photographs. No money, I might even venture to guess, for postage stamps. Frankly, I'm amazed that you have managed to cast as many pieces as you have. I know something of what that costs."

"But we have much energy and talent," Ivan protested. "It takes time for good art to develop. Longer still to be appreciated. I am willing to wait."

"For whom? For what? Why should you wait? You know as well as I do that your work cries out for an audience. The right audience will appreciate it, and pay for their appreciation. But those people look to the established galleries and dealers for direction. It is important, very important, not just to be bought, but to be bought by the right buyer. I'm afraid you would be hard-pressed to find that person climbing up four flights of stairs on Ninth Street."

"That is very well," said Ivan, "but what do you suggest?"

"Simple." Julian smiled. "I suggest you let me represent you."

"You are dealer?"

"No. Not exactly. Not yet. What I am is a stockbroker on Wall Street. And I'm very good at it. I've been successful at telling other people what to do with their money. But I don't intend to be a stockbroker forever, only long enough to acquire enough capital to go into business on my own. My own gallery, my own collection, my own stable of artists."

Ivan whistled in appreciation. "Let us hope it will be soon," he said. That would be . . . mmmmm . . . welcome."

"If you mean that, then I'll promise you this: the sculptures I saw today will be showing uptown in a matter of a few months. Shall we drink to that? Shall we drink to the beginning of a long, profitable, and happy relationship?"

They did just that, but not before Ivan had leaned across the table and kissed Julian forcefully on each cheek.

That night Ivan and I sat up until dawn. I had never seen him so happy and excited. We discussed what a fine person Julian Slade appeared to be, and wondered who of the many girls floating around the Village should be presented to him as an affectionate companion.

Julian came around almost every day. Sometimes I would make spaghetti, sometimes we'd just sit and drink the wine Julian brought, eating bread with fresh mozzarella from an Italian cheese maker down the street. Mostly, Julian looked at Ivan's work. He wanted to see and know everything. Ivan showed him not only his sculptures, but all his sketches, drawings, and notebooks as well.

I was witnessing the beginning of an intense, complicated, and lifelong love affair between Ivan and Julian. I don't mean to suggest for a minute that they were actually lovers in the physical sense, but they experienced the same joys, jealousies, and feelings of possessiveness and betrayal that any other lovers do. They were bound by admiration, loyalty, and, most of all, need. It was perfectly obvious that Ivan needed Julian. And although the reasons for it were less immediately obvious, Julian needed Ivan. He needed Ivan not just because Ivan was an artist whose works he greatly admired, but because Ivan represented everything that Julian himself could never be but desperately craved.

Of course, Julian put it to Ivan in a much more practical way. "I need you," he said, getting straight to the point, "because you are unknown. I need a discovery. I need someone with your talent on whom I can hang my hat, make my presence felt in the art world. At present there are five top galleries in New York. I have no desire to work for any of them. I want to compete with them. I want my own gallery, my own place to represent my taste. But frankly I haven't the capital or the visibility I would need. So I've approached Millicent Selby, and she's agreed to take me on as silent partner."

"Millicent Selby!" My heart fell. Jake and I had spent many Saturday afternoons doing the uptown galleries and we had been to the Selby Gallery several times. The gallery was okay but Millicent was something of a joke in the art world "I don't know, Julian," I said, "I've heard some pretty weird stories about that woman. I'm not sure that Ivan's virtue will be safe with her, if you know what I mean." Julian laughed while Ivan looked pleased but confused.

"What Maisie means," he explained to Ivan, "is that Mrs. Selby, a rich and respectable widow, takes a very passionate interest in the lives and careers of the artists she represents. Millicent Selby is an eccentric and she is very much on the fringes of the established art world. But it would be a mistake to underestimate her. She has a flair and a very good eye for what is truly good in an artist's work. And she is unswervingly loyal to those whom she represents. What she lacks is even a modicum of business sense, but that's where I come in, you see. I can and will put the gallery on a firm business footing, and in due course it is I who will be selecting the new artists for the gallery and mounting all the important exhibits."

In a month's time we learned that Julian had meant every word he said. He had selected nine sculptures from The Sirens series, and they were being shipped uptown to Millicent Selby's gallery. Even more important, he advanced Ivan enough money to cast half a dozen new sculptures. As far as Ivan was concerned, he had hit the big time. He was rich. Of course, to Ivan, rich simply meant that he could afford to do his work. Whether he ate or not never even entered his mind.

I remember a conversation that took place as the sculptures were being packed for shipment uptown. Ivan had been trying to find the words to thank Julian for everything. He really was feeling somewhat overwhelmed by this amazing turn in his fortunes. Julian impatiently waved him aside. "Don't waste time thanking me, don't waste time on anything. Get on with your work. That is all that matters. Get on with your work and I'll get on with mine. You and I need each other, Ivan. I believe I can do for you what you can't do for yourself. I can make the whole world love your work as I do."

If there are other words that an artist would rather hear, I surely don't know what they might be.

9

I suppose this is as good a time as any to introduce Miss Emma Blackstone of Boston, Massachusetts, who was, at the time I met her, engaged to be married to Mr. Julian Slade III, also of Boston, Massachusetts, and currently residing in New York, New York.

We saw a lot of Julian in the next few months. He was courting Ivan, and Ivan was happily encouraging Julian's advances. We liked Julian. He was different from everyone else in our circle of friends. Certainly we could see that he was a bit of a pompous ass, but he was kind, he was interested in everything Ivan did, he was generous, and he was good company. I think both Ivan and I felt a little proprietary about him. We had found him, adopted him, and even if he was a bit of a funny duck, he was ours and we loved him. We were still trying to find just the right girl for Julian when he announced one evening that his fiancée was coming to New York, and he would like to bring her by to meet us.

Ivan was all enthusiasm. "Dear Julian, how perfectly good. Of course you must bring your fiancée to us. We will receive her with much love, much joy. This is opportunity I am waiting for. Together you will choose the sculpture that will be wedding gift. You sly dog. How long you have known this mademoiselle?"

"All my life." Julian smiled. "Our fathers were friends."

We were sitting around Ivan's kitchen table enjoying the warmth of Ivan's newly installed heaters and eating cabbage soup. Ivan used to make the best cabbage soup in the world. We had gone shopping that morning over on First Avenue and Seventh Street, a little world populated by Russians, Poles, and Ukrainians. Everyone, of course, knew and loved Ivan. The butcher gave him bones for soup, with enough meat on them to make several meals and garlic sausage that he made himself every week. The little bakery a few doors down had real Jewish sour rye, "the kind of bread a man can chew," Ivan said. Another little store for pickles where fat, laughing, toothless Katya always handed us a dill pickle each, to eat dripping, out of hand, as we continued our wanderings in Little Ukraine. At the greengrocer's, Ivan taught me to shop like a French housewife—to choose only the most perfect little potatoes, to inspect the cabbage, to feel each onion for unacceptable soft spots. I helped with the shopping and did much of the cleaning but Ivan always did the cooking. He must have known instinctively that a girl from Singing Hills, Ohio, might know how to work appliances but not how to cook the kind of food to satisfy a hungry Russian bear. Truly, I think my mother would have fainted dead away at the sight and smell of all the garlic, hot peppers, onions, and other "exotic" stuff that went into Ivan's soups. For that was all he made—huge vats of soup swimming with lovely cabbages, potatoes, tomatoes, beets; floating with aromatic sausages and little bits of smoky bacon. On special occasions, such as that particular evening when Julian was dining with us, a bowl of sour cream was passed around to dollop into the soup. With the soup we ate great chunks of heavy bread on which we spread layers of unsalted butter. All these tastes were new to me and I loved them. They were new for Julian, too. He ate with great gusto, and I could tell that he was delighted with our bohemian charms and comforts.

Needless to say, I was intensely curious to know more about Julian's fiancée, and Ivan was, too, because he poured another round of iced vodka, which we drank out of tiny shot glasses, and plied him with questions.

"I can see that I'm going to have to tell you our whole story," Julian said, openly enjoying the attention. "My father and Emma's father were friends from boyhood, and remained so all their lives. I can remember when Emma was born. Everyone was so excited and going on about the good luck of her being a girl. They felt the future, ah . . . *solidarity* of the two families was assured because you see they assumed, rightly, I guess, that when we grew up I would marry Emma. But at the time I looked at this tiny, ugly baby with fat cheeks, and I was not in the least amused. I was seven years old.

"That summer our two families went to Dark Harbor, Maine, as we did every summer, and one day my father went sailing with Jack and Bettina, Emma's parents. Nothing unusual about that. Sailing was one of the great pastimes at Dark Harbor, and they were both very expert at it—sailed all the time—but that time they just . . . never came back." Julian shrugged. "A sudden squall, some said a seventh wave, and pfft! they were gone."

"Oh, Julian, how awful! You were so young to lose your father!" I interrupted. It seemed so faraway and so romantic, I remember secretly wishing that I had had some dramatic tragedy in my childhood. "Luckily your mother was spared," I added stupidly.

"Yes, that's what everyone said," said Julian. "Only sometimes I'm not so sure. Certainly she was never the same again. She only got vaguer and vaguer over the years. But that's neither here nor there. Of course, I was lucky to still have my mother. Emma wasn't yet a year old. She was completely orphaned, raised by her grandparents, Jack's people.

"That fall I went away to Exeter, and for many years I wasn't aware of Emma, really. Oh, naturally I saw her regularly. Our families, what was left of them, remained very close, but I was growing up, you see, and she was just a little girl. I think I first really noticed Emma when I was eighteen and she turned eleven. Emma's grandmother, Louise Blackstone, had arranged a party to celebrate my new status as a college man. I arrived a little early, no other guests were there yet. Louise and I were chatting in the hall and I heard a greeting and turned, and there she was coming down the stairs. Her hair was tied back in a ribbon and she looked like a tall, skinny Alice in Wonderland. Everyone had always said she would grow up to be a beauty. The genes were all there, of course, from both her parents, and she had the most extraordinary coloring—burnished gold hair, a very fair complexion, but dark, dark, brown eyes. That day she reminded me of a newborn colt I had seen once on a friend's horse farm in Kentucky—she was all long limbs, long neck, and big, soft brown eyes. I knew immediately that in a few years Emma Blackstone was going to be an extraordinary young woman."

"Tiens," whispered Ivan, his imagination inflamed. "Your Emma sounds most enchanting."

Tiens, I said to myself, she sounds like trouble. "Do you mean to tell me," I said aloud, "that you became engaged to an eleven-year-old girl?"

"No, no," Julian laughed. "I was caught up in college and life went on. Occasionally we wrote to each other, but they were simple, innocent letters of an older brother to his little sister. No, it wasn't until I was about to go to graduate school that I realized I was in love with fifteen-year-old Emma. And it wasn't until the following year that we became engaged. I remember the day I went to talk to her grandparents as clearly as if it were yesterday. Frankly, I did not think much of my chances. Emma herself was of course much too young to be officially engaged. But the biggest black mark against me was that my grandmother had recently died, and we, that is my mother and I, were shocked to discover that far from leaving us the fortune we had expected, she had left nothing but debts. In short, I had no money of my own in the world. I didn't think the Blackstones would look favorably on my situation, but I was wrong. John and Louise were in my camp. Even my reversal of fortunes did not put them off. John assured me that Emma would have plenty of money of her own. He knew I was a steady young man, and apparently all those years of family jokes about my marrying Emma had not been jokes at all, but dearly cherished hopes. I promised that we would wait until Emma was twenty to marry. Then I drove her out to Walden Pond and proposed to her. We would have been married by now, only John died suddenly a year ago and Emma wanted to wait a little longer. She felt her grandmother needed her, and of course she was right."

What a paragon of beauty and virtue, I thought to myself, hating the creeping envy I felt in my gut. "Well," I said, smiling brightly, "I, for one, can't wait to meet her."

1o

And meet her we did. Hardly a week later. She had come to New York in the midst of all her busy wedding preparations to house-hunt with Julian. When I first laid eyes on Emma Blackstone I thought, Now here's the real thing. She was a rich girl who'd never thought about money for even one day in her life. Everything about her spelled class—the good plain tailored suit, the simple handmade shoes, the gloves, the hat, and the makeup that wasn't there.

Back in Ohio, girls in my high school dreamed out loud about marrying into the world of country clubs and fur coats. To them the rich were different because of what they owned. But I had discovered there were other things that really made the difference. For one thing, rich young people were not searching for a sense of themselves; they had assured futures and family power behind them to guarantee those futures. They were comfortable with their possessions, not thrilled and delighted by them, and they moved through the world with enviable ease. That was Emma Blackstone. Or at least that was the way she appeared to me when I met her.

I had been quite keyed up when Julian and Emma arrived at the loft, gushing and carrying on and embarrassing myself. Somehow, in the presence of this tall, elegant, beautiful girl I couldn't shut up. Julian made introductions all around, and when he came to me, she extended her hand and softly repeated my name as if it meant something to her. Unreasonably, I felt my back go up. Here was the perfect woman. Touchingly perfect, really, but I feared the loss of the spotlight. I could feel it shining on Emma and I felt outclassed. That alone was enough to make me resent her.

I tried to behave myself. I made tea, served cookies, smiled, and chattered away about this and that. Ivan, oozing charm, called for vodka. "Maisie!" he shouted. "Bring glasses."

Emma protested, as if alcohol had never crossed her virgin lips, but in the end she tossed it back like a pro. In the end they always do. Then we all watched as her pale, perfect skin turned a pretty shade of pink. So very becoming. So proper. So demure.

Oh, what a bitch I am! No, that's not true. What a bitch I almost was.

Ivan took Emma around the studio, showing her some of his works in progress. She oohed and aahed softly and was generally very ladylike and very quiet. Once or twice I caught him looking at her in that strangely intense way of his, but then nothing visual was ever lost on Ivan, and there was no quarreling with the fact that Emma Blackstone was a visual banquet. I had another pang or two when I saw Ivan showing her his sketchbooks—something he never did with strangers. Oh, I tried not to be so possessive. I tried to remember everything Dance had lectured me about, but it wasn't easy. I was insanely in love with Ivan, and no amount of lecturing would change that.

"Julian," I said, "sit down and stop staring a hole in your lovely girl. I swear, you look like you're about to burst." He did, too. I had never seen him quite so worked up, fussing over Emma like a stage mother at an audition. He flushed a little and sat down obediently. "More vodka?" I wagged the bottle in the air.

He grinned and pushed his glass toward me. "Why not? It's a day for celebration, and she is lovely, isn't she, Maisie? Don't you think she is quite the loveliest girl in the world?"

"Absolutely," I said. "And she does wonders for you, Julian. You look positively human—losing your well-pressed, hand-tailored edges. It becomes you."

He laughed. "I am a little foolish over her, I admit. I want everything to be perfect, I guess. And it is. Everything is perfect." We both turned to gaze at our respective loved ones. They seemed deep in conversation.

"So tell me, Julian. Are you nervous about getting married? I mean, nervous about marching down the aisle and all that?"

"Not in the least. I don't have to march down the aisle. That's the nice thing about being the groom. You don't have to do very much of anything except show up. Damned nuisance, waiting this extra year, though. I guess I won't feel entirely safe until the actual vows are said."

I nodded. "You mean, 'Many a slip twixt the cup and the lip'?"

Julian smiled thinly. "That's what they say, isn't it? Still, if that's what Louise Blackstone thinks is suitable, then so do I."

"Tell me, what is Grandmother Blackstone like? I have a feeling she might not find me at all a suitable friend for her Emma."

"Well, Emma's grandmother is old-fashioned—as old-fashioned as you are modern, Maisie. In fact, I doubt that she has any idea that people like you actually exist. But she's a lovely old woman in her own way. I can't help admiring her. She's been a good friend to me, and now she's entrusting me with the care of the only person in the world who means anything to her."

Streams of sunlight coming through the windows had caught the dusty air of the studio so that Ivan and Emma looked almost dreamlike in the bright white haze at the far end of the room.

Ivan seemed to be dazzling Emma. He was gesturing grandly, and she was lapping it up. I could hear the inflections of Ivan's voice, but only caught snippets of what he was saying.

"Uh-oh. I think poor Emma is getting the full treatment."

"The what?" Julian said.

"You know, the tormented love-of-art speech. I think she's getting an earful. Oh God." I heaved a great sigh. "Love. Doesn't it have the most insidious way of creeping into every conversation? Is what you feel for Emma torment, Julian?"

"No. Of course not. Why should it be? Emma and I are alike. We think alike. We understand each other. We enjoy the same things and we look forward to the same things. Torment has nothing to do with it. Contentment is more like it."

"How very dull," I said. "Like the Bobbsey twins. Don't you ever just want to grab Emma and take her off to some shack in the woods, lose yourself in passion and all that?"

I expected a laugh, but Julian seemed rattled. He leaned toward me, clearly struggling with several conflicting emotions. "I know we must seem dull to you. But that's exactly how I mean to sound. You and Ivan can torment yourselves. You can indulge in passions because that is your nature. You're free spirits. You can do anything you like, and believe me, I don't think any the less of you for it. Maybe I even envy it. Emma and I can't step out of character—it's just not in us to do that. But don't ever think we don't feel as strongly as you do."

I applauded. "Julian Slade, you are passionate after all. Let's drink to that. And let's drink to perfection and the best of all possible weddings. To you and to Emma and to a long and happy marriage." I held up my glass.

"If you have one more drink you'll be on your face."

"Pity. I'd rather be on my back," I said, rather too loudly, and then clapped my hands over my mouth in a burlesque of regret. "Whoooops. Don't let Granny Blackstone hear that!"

Julian grimaced and started to say something, but then Ivan was calling to us. He came up to Julian and slapped him on the back.

"Too much talking!" Ivan shouted. "We need celebration. Come, come, I am very happy and I would like very much to invite you to have dinner with me tonight." He squeezed my shoulder and then turned to Emma and, taking her hand in his, said, "You will say yes, Emmachka? You would do me great honor."

Emmachka? Oh, brother!

11

In Emma's diaries, which I have now read at length, I was able to meet that innocent creature in the most intimate way. She began keeping a diary when she was nine years old. By the time she was twenty, they had become quite remarkable pieces of writing.

When I was growing up, I must have been given dozens of those cute little quilted diaries with dreamy teenagers printed on the covers and little gold locks with little gold keys that I promptly lost. My attempts to journalize my life were sporadic (and embarrassing in retrospect) at best, but lists were my strong suit. Things like The Ten Cutest Boys in Eighth Grade, or A Wish List for Christmas. On one page I had written Tab Hunter's name one hundred times. There were doodles and notations on the weather (always rain, since clement weather was unlikely to give rise to much introspection), and only a very few vague stabs at digging out my thoughts. My last entry (and my best) was from my fifteenth year, when the love of my life, Luke Walton, threw me over for a cheerleader named Dee Dee McGraw. "My love," I wrote, "is like a cold, cold pizza."

Emma's diaries, by contrast, were bound in fine morocco leather. Between gold-stamped covers, in a neat and fluid hand, not daily, but often and at length, she confided her thoughts, observations, and feelings. Her version of that day in the studio is, as you can well imagine, completely different from mine.

I give you Emma's diary: December 1956.

I think today has been the most exciting day of my life. In many ways I felt as if I were floating through a dream. Looking at those houses was extremely dreamlike—real and unreal at the same time. I liked the one on East 69th Street the best, but I have such a hard time picturing my life there. Mr. and Mrs. Slade of 55 East 69th Street. I still wish I could have persuaded Julian to start our life in New York in a small, anonymous apartment. I've never lived in an apartment, and it seems so very appealing to me. But not to Julian. "Your grandfather wanted us to have a house, a real home, a real foundation for our married life." Of course, he's right.

Darling Julian. He is so grounded where I am not. So reasonable where I am just silly. So clever and sophisticated about New York. Yet he surprises me with hidden aspects of himself. I've always known that he loves art, but I don't think I've ever really begun to understand how deeply he feels and how important sheer beauty is to him. When we went to the Frick Museum today he talked about how his grandmother used to take him there every weekend. "Clayton Frick. That is the man I should have married," she would say to her impressionable grandson. Then the two of them would dream about what their lives would have been like, living in the grand mansion on Fifth Avenue and 70th Street. I think deep in his heart Julian really aspires to grandeur like that, only I don't think it's at all selfish on his part, but a kind of quest for the ultimate in beauty.

After lunch we took a taxi downtown to meet Ivan St. Peters, a new friend of Julian's, a sculptor whose work Julian admires greatly. The taxi deposited us on the doorstep of a building that looked like a huge warehouse. It seemed very forbidding and was quite unlike any place I'd ever been. We walked up endless flights of stairs so that I was out of breath when we finally knocked on his door.

But, oh, what a magical world I stepped into! We were greeted by Ivan and a pretty girl called Maisie Green. We drank a cup of tea and ate some delicious cookies. I couldn't help staring at the living arrangements—everything in one room—one room to cook, eat, bathe, sleep, and read. And love in—for it was immediately obvious that Maisie and Ivan were lovers. Halfway through our tea, Ivan leapt to his feet, shouting, "No, no, no, no, no! But you Americans are intolerable. *C'est incroyable!* This is great moment in our lives and we are drinking tea! This does not do. Maisie, get vodka glasses."

"It is tradition," Ivan said, handing tiny glasses filled with vodka around. "You must drink. The whole glass. All at once. Not to lose a drop. Every drop spills or wasted is bad luck. So, *na zdorovye!* My friends! And he gulped back all the vodka in his glass. Then Maisie and Julian did the same, and then even I threw all caution to the wind and gulped it down. Everyone was laughing as though we'd been the best of friends forever.

"Vodka is good for the studio," Ivan beamed, pouring another round. "Maisie tells me it is very cold in there, but for me it does not matter. I am used to it. You have only to know one Russian winter, then you laugh at what people are calling cold here." And the way he said "Russian" and "winter," I could almost hear the wolves howling in the icy night.

He looked at me then and said, "Now you can see my work." He pulled aside the heavy draperies and we walked back into his studio.

I wonder why Julian hadn't prepared me for what I saw there. Perhaps he hadn't the words to describe the extraordinary beauty of Ivan's sculptures. Perhaps he worried that I might be shocked if he told me that they were, in a word, erotic. There were many female nudes, and men, too, but mostly I saw figures coupled, entwined. I certainly wasn't shocked, but I was staggered by what I saw. As I walked around the studio, I felt the strange sensation that I was walking outside myself. But at the same time I felt wrapped in an almost luxurious warmth. His work filled me with wonder.

"What you think of my art, eh?" Ivan asked me as he took my arm and began walking with me around the studio. I looked for Julian to join us, but he was talking to Maisie. Ivan continually ran his hands over his sculptures and I noticed that his hands are very beautiful, so strong-looking, and so expressive and eloquent. I could well imagine those hands forming and shaping these extraordinary objects.

I've never heard anyone talk as Ivan did. He was quite impassioned and very very blunt. We stood before a sculpture of a man holding a woman in his arms. But it was not an embrace. It seemed they were struggling with one another. The faces were distorted and the muscles bulged with tension. "What you think of this, Emma?" he demanded. "I call it *The Lovers.*"

"Are they lovers?" I said slowly. "I can't say whether they're fighting or embracing." And it was true. There was such ferocity. "I see pain more than love."

"Ah, but are they not the same thing?"

"Are they?" I said, surprised.

"Love is such gentle word for the madness in human heart, is not so?" He grinned and squinted slightly, as if he were searching for just the right words. "These lovers are far beyond the . . . romance." He tossed his head contemptuously. "See, they know for each of them there is no other life—no other life—but that they *must* be together. And yet they struggle."

He laughed a big, booming laugh. "Maybe this is what only the artist knows. Like inspiration. Most people don't know about love. They say they love, but they know nothing. They don't want to know. They wear masks and clothespins on noses, and they don't touch the shit—excuse me—and they think then it doesn't smell. But love is not so nice always; love is fearful. It demands you to lose control. It is a very great madness. It is ultimate surrender. In art, too. Art and love are the same—surrender is everything."

Suddenly, Ivan turned to me, and in a low voice, so low the others could not hear, he said, "Do you understand, Emma, what I say? Do you?"

I couldn't speak. He overwhelmed me. I had no idea what I should say or how I should react. But I did understand him. I nodded and then I felt so very exposed and so very, very alone. Was I going to cry? Ivan said nothing more, but turned and signaled to the others. He was very jovial and went up to Julian and slapped him on the back.

"But we must not talk anymore," he shouted. "I think we need celebration. Come, come, I am very happy, and I would like it very much to invite you to have dinner with me tonight." He turned and took my hand in his. "You will say yes, won't you, Emmachka? You would do me great honor."

12

efore Julian and Emma left the
loft, Ivan rushed to a telephone. I heard him rattling away in French
(which was infinitely smoother than his English), making arrangements
for dinner at Le Pavilion. In those days, Le Pavilion was not only the
best French restaurant in New York, which meant also all of America,
it was the best restaurant, period. How Ivan knew this, living impoverished on the water's edge of Manhattan Island, was one of those mysteries about him that intrigued me. Julian and Emma left, and it was agreed
we would meet again at nine o'clock that evening.

I managed to pull together what I thought was an appropriate outfit
from my thrift-store costume collection—a red taffeta number with a
halter top and a very full skirt. Dance let me borrow his opera cape, and
I was all set. Ivan looked spectacular in his black tie (another hand-me-
down from the Metropolitan Opera), and off we went in some splendor,
I must say. Throwing caution and economy to the wind, we went by taxi

to Park Avenue and 57th Street. Christmas was in the air. The night was cold and crisp, and along Park Avenue a million tiny lights sparkled and glowed. New York had never before seemed so beautiful, and life had never seemed to hold quite so much promise.

A uniformed doorman helped me out of the cab, and in seconds we were through the revolving doors and inside the fabled Le Pavilion. Everything in the large room proclaimed luxury and good taste. Henri Soulé himself greeted us and led us to our table. While Ivan discussed the menu with M. Soulé, I watched the entrance, waiting to see Emma and Julian arrive. A bottle of Dom Perignon arrived at our table, and just as the waiter was placing the fluted glasses, I saw them. I looked at Emma and I'm afraid I lost a little of my Christmas spirit. She was stunning. Everything about her was simple, and simply beautiful. Her unbelievable hair, heavy and exactly the color of burnished gold, was wound into a chignon at the base of her neck. Her soft dark eyes glowed with pleasure and anticipation. She wore no jewelry and didn't need any. The black velvet dress, cut close at the bodice and flared out around the knees, set off her fair complexion so that she herself looked like a jewel from Cartier's. They say that black on the body of a beautiful woman makes all colors seem fatuous. How true it was that night. Next to her, I felt like the tinsel on a Christmas tree. But, having made this silent observation, I decided, what the hell! Live and let live. She couldn't help being who she was, any more than I could help being me. Anyway, I liked her. There was, after all, nothing snooty about her. Emma Blackstone was open, friendly, and extremely appealing. I decided to relax and enjoy the evening.

Ivan, in consultation with M. Soulé, had organized our entire dinner. We started with a pilaf of mussels. When that was removed and we had finished the champagne, our tournedos Rossini arrived, along with a wonderful red wine the like of which I had never tasted before. Ivan was in his best form, very animated and perhaps a little loud for the hushed surroundings, but enormously charming and irresistible. He was filled with stories about Paris and then drifted back in time to Russia and the circus world. He even showed us a few magic tricks. Very corny things, but still amazing. Forks and spoons appeared and disappeared, and no matter how hard we concentrated, we couldn't catch the methods of his tricks.

"It's very simple, my friends. Most things are," Ivan said. "I have seen doves turned into cheetahs, I have seen beautiful ladies disappear in thin air. It is not mirrors. Magic is in the eye. The eye is everything. What the eye will see, the brain believes. But the eye, he is a lazy fellow.

Oh yes. He see but he don't understand and so he is easy to fool. I tell you a story. Only yesterday I was walking, and it was dull, gray day—*sero*, we say in Russian, not raining, you know, but *sero*. I turn corner and there is walking toward me a man with yellow box. It is very yellow, so yellow it make everything else disappear. He is tiny man and the box, which is shoeshine box, is enormous. I stop. I am dead in my tracks. And I say to him, 'You have beautiful shoeshine box.' Little man, he look at me like he don't believe me, but then he see I really like his box, and he is relaxing. He don't speak much good English—not me either, huh? —and so we are talking very happy in Italian. He tells me he is at corner of 34th and Fifth Avenue for years and years, shining shoes, and no one ever admires his box, so he is pleased, very pleased, that I am seeing the beauty of yellow box. Then he says, 'If you like this, you come to my corner on Friday and I show you most beautiful shoeshine box in the world.' "

"But that's tomorrow," Emma said. "I hope you're going."

"Oh yes. I will be there. Tomorrow morning. I must see most beautiful shoeshine box in world. Don't you?" We all agreed that yes, of course we would, and then the conversation drifted on to other things and was forgotten. We ate and talked and laughed as if we were old friends, and I wondered at how easy it was to accustom myself to the sensations of luxury. Dessert was sensational—oeufs à la neige, so sweet and silky, light and rich. The bitter taste of espresso was a welcome stimulant and a perfect ending to a fabulous meal.

"But evening is very young, my friends," Ivan said. "Let us continue celebration with dancing." We were all agreed, and off we went to Roseland.

I had the feeling that this kind of an evening was a novelty for Emma, that she was used to a much more buttoned-up existence. But we were mellow, gay, and carefree, and even Julian was relaxed and loose, telling anecdotes and stories about colleagues at work and the oddities of art collectors. Ivan, of course, loved to dance and was marvelous at it, so that his enthusiasm was completely contagious. We danced a rhumba and a fox trot, and as we returned to our table the first strains of a waltz floated through the air. I was flushed and happy as I sat down, and I didn't mind in the least when Ivan held out his hand and invited Emma to join him on the dance floor. Julian lit my cigarette and we agreed that for the moment we were happy to sit and watch the dancers as they twirled by. My head was buzzing from all the wine and the after-dinner cognac. As I peered through the smoke of my cigarette, I felt as though I were watching one of those spectacular ballroom scenes in an epic movie—*War and Peace, Gone With the Wind*—the pretty, lilting music and all the couples swaying to and fro, whirling and stepping in time to the waltz. Ivan and Emma made a beautiful pair, both tall and so very graceful. When the waltz ended, I felt a moment of regret as Ivan bowed slightly and led Emma back to the table. Then the orchestra took up the throbbing rhythms of a tango. Ivan stopped and turned to Emma, and she looked up at him, seemed to hesitate, then nodded, smiling her sweet, shy smile. He took her in his arms and they began a sinuous and seductive tango. At first their steps seemed correct, although a little hesitant, but as they became caught up in the rhythm of the dance—the insistent and unyielding slow, quick, slow, slow pattern—their bodies seemed to merge and they danced as one. His arms encircled her and yet she held her distance, the color high on her cheeks. The flounce of her skirt whirled to reveal the length of her perfect legs. How to describe the elegant, sensual movements of that dance, the dramatic pauses that made one's heart stop, the slow follow-through and then the circling, twirling forms, so correct and yet so very explicitly indecent? The tango is a dance of passion, of romance, of mystery and desire; Julian and I sat mute and rather stunned, I think, to be witness to such wild emotions.

"Where on earth did you learn to dance like that?" Julian demanded when Ivan and Emma finally returned to the table.

"In dancing school, of course," Emma answered him, and she was so jaunty and unexpectedly saucy in the way she said it that we all burst out laughing.

13

The next day Ivan left my apartment at dawn, filled with an energy I could not fathom. Somewhat the worse for my night on the town, I opened the gallery at noon.

At the corner of 34th and Fifth Avenue, a little old man was sitting on top of a throne. Intricately carved and painted, it could hardly be called a mere shoeshine box, for it was constructed of five separate pieces and it towered over the crowd. The little old man sat on top like a king surveying his realm. Emma was there first, and as she watched, enraptured, I'm sure she must have known without looking that Ivan was there beside her. Just as I'm sure he wept for the joy of it, no doubt congratulating the man and hugging Emma at the same time. Because, truly, it was the most beautiful shoeshine box in the world.

It must have been quite a powerful experience indeed. Though in time I would hear some of the details of that day from both of them, I think I can imagine it completely. It was one of those moments in life that change everything.

So the two of them spent the rest of the morning together, walking the streets of New York, poking into curious little shops, stopping to warm themselves with coffee and freshly made donuts from a kiosk. They hopped a bus and rode downtown all the way to Chinatown, where they bought a string of tiny colored lanterns for Emma's Christmas tree. Then he grabbed her hand and announced he was taking her to lunch where she would have the best spaghetti "with a sauce that smells of the Italian sun."

It was a restaurant called Mama Rosa's in Little Italy, and there they talked for hours. Ivan asked her all sorts of questions and at first she answered hesitantly, unused to such questions and unused to talking at length about herself, but Ivan was driven by a desire to connect things, and out of these connections came the drama that was soon to unfold.

"Who are you, Emma Blackstone? What do you think? What do you feel? What do you see? I want to know. I want to know about you everything I can. There is so little time."

Emma nodded, thinking perhaps he meant the minutes that were flying by on this extraordinary day. But in her heart she felt a certain, surprising apprehension. Indeed, there was so little time. She was going home the next day. To Boston and to Gram and to her wedding. To another reality altogether.

She shook her head and laughed. "Right now—right this very moment—I feel as if I've walked into a kaleidoscope. Everything seems to be bright and swirling and very very beautiful, but it makes me dizzy because nothing stands still. I suppose it's New York. I've never experienced New York the way I have in the past few days."

But of course it wasn't New York. It was the man. Emma blushed, remembering her dream. It had awakened her before dawn and, restless in her suite at the hotel, she had written it down in her diary, not stopping until she had filled page after page with her thoughts.

I am standing at the altar next to Julian. It is our wedding day. Everyone is there. The bishop is reading the vows. Suddenly there is an enormous clamor outside the church and the great doors burst open. I hear someone calling my name and I run down the aisle and out into the sunlight. Outside, there is an enormous field filled with people having a picnic. I run through the grass, and the harder I run the more excited I feel. Sexually excited. It is so strong. Exquisite pain. I am filled to bursting. I stop, panting for breath, and I know, suddenly, there is someone behind me. I feel danger, but it is delicious and enchanting. I start to turn to see who it is, my heart is throbbing in my chest, and I feel such joy . . . I wake up from the pounding of my heart.

I am confused. I feel there is so much to discover, so much mystery, so much adventure in life. I am afraid to think of it.

She got up and got dressed and went down to the Edwardian Room for breakfast. But she was restless and the attendant waiters hovering about her made her even more so. Promptly at ten she marched into Bergdorf-Goodman. It was early and she was almost the only customer in the store. It made her uncomfortable and so she left. And since it was a clear day, she decided to walk. And all the while she knew exactly where she was going.

"Did you know I would be there this morning?" she asked Ivan.

"I didn't know. I hoped. I wanted so much to see you again." He paused and looked at her. "Emma. Emmachka. Forgive me. You see, we Russians cannot make do with just one name for a person. We need a million names. A name for every mood and occasion. So do not be offended if I change your name to suit what I am saying to you. I think you will not understand why I am saying this, but truly, life is stranger than all fiction. When things happen, so sudden, so unexpected, then perhaps they were meant to happen. I wanted you to come today, I willed you to come to me today because I want one last moment with you before you become wife of Julian. I am wanting to tell you how deeply I honor meeting you. When you come into studio yesterday, for me everything was standing still and I am not believing my eyes because you are a vision I have had before. I had to see you again." He reached his hand to her face, to her cheek. "You are so beautiful."

She felt her mouth go dry at his touch.

Neither of them spoke, and then Ivan pushed back his chair.

"Emma, Emma. I cannot tell you what it is that excites me so. I am poor fellow with words. I must show you. You must come with me now. I must show you. Will you come?"

But he hardly waited for her answer. He called for the check and quickly paid it, then got her coat and his, and tied his long woolen scarf around her neck against the cold. It was well into the afternoon now, and the light was beginning to fade to the deep sapphires and golds of an early winter sunset. About ten blocks from the restaurant they came to a heavy, dark office building that housed dozens of novelty wholesalers. The large front windows were thick with grime, and inside Emma could see dim displays of plastic dolls, masks, and masses of ornaments. Ivan rang a bell at the service entrance. Clearly he was well known to the watchman, who waved them in. Ivan greeted him in Russian and they proceeded to speak for a minute or so, talk punctuated with much laughter and back-slapping. Then Ivan led Emma to the service elevator and slowly it rose to the top of the building. On the way Ivan explained:

"When I come to America, I am working cleaning and making new the monuments and statues. Many are on tops of buildings. New York has much beauty in the sky, but it is museum only for pigeons. But there you find beautiful gargoyles, angels, goddesses, even small Roman temples. I have seen reproductions of Islamic mosques and statues of all presidents of United States. I don't do the work anymore, but I enjoy to come up here to this building because . . . well, you will soon see why."

When they got off the elevator, there were two flights of stairs to climb. At last Ivan opened a small steel door and Emma stepped out onto the roof of the building. She gasped with delight. She could see for blocks and blocks out across Greenwich Village and down to Wall Street. Uptown there was a clear view of the Empire State Building, which was all lit up in red and green lights for Christmas. At the edges of the roof around them was a series of twelve stone statues.

"The twelve months of the year." Ivan gestured. "All the ladies you see here are carved fifty years ago. They are in a terrible condition when I come, but I fix to almost perfect. Except for August. She was beyond fixing. Owners of building don't care if one month is missing, but I cannot let August disappear. August is special month, filled with bounty of earth. So I create her again. My August carries basket of fruit and wheat, and to me she brings peace and health and wisdom. I want you to see her, Emma."

Emma stared at the statue for the longest time and then looked at Ivan.

"When did you say you made this?"

"About five years ago."

"I don't understand. It looks like . . ."

"Exactly. She looks like you, she is you. Do you understand why I call you vision? Do you understand why I must see you? When you walk through my door, I see the face I have dreamed of for long, very long time." He stopped and fumbled his hand deep into his greatcoat and pulled out a coin. "I tell you this now because maybe we never have such time again. I cannot stop myself. It is like no other story you will hear. You see this coin? It is very old. Greek. It is very worn from the ages and from use. A magician give it to me. It was coin he use in magic. This coin, he make it dance on his fingers, gallop like a horse, end over end, on back of his hand. It was a coin that could appear and disappear when he say. He told me the coin was magic and I believe him. But there came many, many dark days that I don't believe him. It was wartime, and I don't believe in nothing but fear. On the day the magician gave me the coin I am picked up by Germans and sent to work camps. Somehow I keep the coin with me, and as days turns to months of labor and starving, that coin was only thing to keep me alive. In blackest days I only touch it, touch it and I am remembering time when world is not so foul. You see, Emma, there is a face on it. So worn you can hardly see. It is beautiful face—most beautiful face on earth, you understand? This woman's face is my only reality. She keeps me warm. She gives me nourishment. I know her like no other. I know the long neck and the slope of shoulders, the beautiful gold hair. I feel I know the touch of her skin."

He came close to Emma, his finger tracing the soft curve of her cheek. "It is your face, Emma. I don't believe such thing has come true for me. After the war I know there is only one life for me. Millions have died and I am survived, true, but I am very alone. All people that was my life—they are gone. But I have still the coin with my woman who is in my heart, and I am wanting—no, I am burning—to make such beauty to wipe away the shame of war. I go to Paris to learn . . . and there I begin my searching for you.

"I was wishing for you with all my heart. But when I come to America, I give up wishing. I think you only live in my heart and so I put you in my work. I carve you, I mold you, I create you over and over . . ." He took her hand, which was trembling violently, and held it in his until it was calm again. Then he took the coin and pressed it into her palm.

"This is for you. You must have it now."

"But I couldn't. You must keep it always . . ." she stammered.

"Why? The magic has already worked. It brings me you. I have no more need . . . If you marry Julian it doesn't matter. You will be other man's wife, but always you will be mine. You are reflection of me, part of me, and the image of you is always, will be always in my heart."

Emma tried to speak but she couldn't. Ivan shook his head, smiling. "There is nothing to say."

14

The Emma Blackstone who returned to Boston was outwardly the same one who had left, but inwardly she was a changed woman. She could not forget even for a minute the eyes of Ivan St. Peters and the way they seemed to drink her in. She was experiencing a sense of urgency quite unlike anything she had ever known before. What had she known, this proper Bostonian, this girl who lived locked up in diaries?

I think she was not so much a lonely child as an isolated one. Her grandparents were obviously kind and loving to her, but they were clearly of another generation, and not much inclined or able to change their Victorian ideas about child-raising. They had suffered terribly over the death of their son, the heir to all they had preserved and accomplished, and I suspect that in Emma they saw a chance to redeem their loss. No expense or effort was too great for their granddaughter—the best schools, the best toys, the best holidays. But Emma never had many close friends. There were no slumber parties recorded in her diaries, no all-night confessionals, no raids on the icebox, no escapades of any sort. She didn't scorn those things; like a child in a glass bubble, she was just never exposed to them.

Indeed, what passed for fun seemed to center mainly on subdued outings to "the Club," where Grandfather retired to the billiards room and Gram played bridge on the veranda. As often as not, the adolescent Emma swam all by herself in the pool, or perhaps had a "deplorable" game of tennis with a stray club member.

Summers were spent in Winter Harbor, Maine, where life took a slightly jauntier turn. Gram would lose some of her starch and join Emma on nature walks. They would pick berries (for Mrs. Malone, the cook, to make jam from), or collect seashells, which were then cunningly glued to wooden boxes for Christmas gifts.

Back in Boston, schools were strictly of the country day variety and Emma was whisked to and from them in the family sedan, driven by Mrs. Malone, who, curiously, seems to have doubled as the chauffeur.

Ruthie Beyer appears to have been Emma's best and only friend in all her childhood years. They met in the sixth grade. Ruthie had lived in more than a dozen foster homes before coming to Emma's school on scholarship. "No one wanted me," she told Emma, "because I was too ugly."

At the age of fourteen, Ruthie, who had never been particularly hale, came down with polio. The result was an even uglier girl with a twisted hump on her left shoulder and a crippled leg, but Emma never gave up on her and spent all her free time keeping the girl cheerful and amused. At age fifteen the poor girl died of pneumonia, and Emma was devastated.

At sixteen, as Emma's debutante days approached, she went to a few cotillions and attended her cousin's coming-out party. Other "outings" seemed to consist mainly of paying formal calls on Gram's old friends. Then Julian appeared on the scene and Emma found herself "unofficially" engaged. In Emma's diary she sees Julian as a worldly man who will be her lover and her teacher—in short, the person who will lead her into real life.

That is precisely what he did. The girl on the train back to Boston had been turned inside out by "real life." She felt it fluttering in her belly, burning in her heart, darting like arrows in the hidden corners of her mind. And in her pocket she gripped a gold coin in the palm of her hand.

□

The next day found Emma at the photographer's studio, where, dressed in her white lace gown and veils, she posed in virginal splendor for her wedding portrait. The room was oppressively hot, and done up, it seemed to her, in undertaker's gray. Gray curtains were draped behind her. A raised gray carpeted platform was under her. There were no windows, there was no air. The only sound was the bored voice of the photographer as he asked her, politely but firmly, to hold her head this way or that—eyes up, eyes down. A nervous, fluttery assistant tugged and pulled at the hem of Emma's dress, pinning its folds to the carpet so that she was a prisoner where she stood. All at once her legs began to tremble and she sensed a dangerous hysteria deep inside her that threatened utterly to undo whatever composure she had mustered. She fought to hold back tears, but the tight bodice was suffocating her—squeezing the life out of her. She felt a flash of heat, then a chill. Suddenly the room was spinning, and as the blood fled from her tortured brain, Emma Blackstone fainted dead away.

When she revived, minutes later, she found herself dressed in a silk kimono and lying on a divan in the dressing room with a cold damp cloth on her forehead. Beyond the curtained door she could hear the photographer's voice soothing her grandmother. "They all go through it, Mrs. Blackstone. Prenuptial nerves . . . common as can be . . . seen it a thousand times . . . reschedule the session, Mrs. Blackstone. Don't worry . . ."

Emma sobbed silently into her hands. What was happening to her? She could not compose a single coherent thought without its being overwhelmed, overtaken, by thoughts of Ivan St. Peters. Even as she was waking from a swoon, his face swam maddeningly before her eyes.

And then, in yesterday's mail she had received the one thing for which she had not dared to hope, and with which she could least well contend.

It had been a small square package carefully wrapped and tied with string. There was no return address, but instinctively, in spite of the many packages containing wedding gifts that were arriving each day, Emma had known. She opened it carefully, upstairs in her bedroom. Inside, in a simple frame, was a drawing of herself.

During the short drive back to the house from the photographer's, Emma was pale and still trembling. Neither she nor her grandmother spoke, but once home, her grandmother called for tea and led Emma to the sitting room.

"I'm so sorry, Gram," Emma said weakly, after the maid had left and she had composed herself.

"Darling Emma." Louise Blackstone did not look at her granddaughter. "I feel I must speak to you about what you're going through. You must try to believe me, dear, I do understand. It is very difficult, I know, but you must place your faith and trust in Julian. He is a gentleman and he loves you very much."

Emma had no idea what her grandmother was talking about.

"When I married your grandfather, no one spoke of these things," she continued. "It just wasn't done. Girls were expected to be innocent of all knowledge before the wedding and to . . . to accept whatever happened on the wedding night without a murmur. Quite cruel, really. But somehow I thought that, well, in these days and times, you might have learned of these things from your girlfriends."

Slowly it dawned on Emma. Her grandmother was talking about sex.

"No. No. You don't understand. It's not that. It's not that at all." Emma was sobbing now. "Oh, Gram. I just don't know if I want to get married. Not now, anyway. Not now, before my life has started. It's not Julian. It's . . . I don't know. Why do I feel like my life is ending? I want to do the right thing, but I don't know what that is."

"Emma, listen to me. Drink your tea and calm yourself and then listen very hard to what I am saying. Marriage is not the end of anything. It is a wonderful beginning. I thank God every day that you haven't picked up any modern notions about careers or any of the other unfortunate ideas young women seem to be seized by these days. You're going to make an excellent wife for Julian, a caring hostess, and when the time comes you'll be a loving mother for his children. You will carry on the traditions of the family and the responsibilities of your social position as all the women in our family have done. I know what I'm saying. I know because I, too, had these feelings you're having now. My dear, I was petrified of marriage. I was barely eighteen years old and I had hardly spent ten minutes with your grandfather, outside of strictly formal meetings. I cried, too, though no one knew it. But, darling, it all rights itself in the end. You'll see. Once the wedding is over and you and Julian have had some time together, you . . . Emma? Why, Emma!"

But Emma was not there. She had fled from the room.

She lay miserably on her bed all afternoon and into the evening. There was no one she could turn to, no one she could talk to. Julian had come to see her late in the day—she was sure her grandmother had called him—but Emma had refused to dress or come downstairs. A tray of soup lay tepid by her bed. She could neither eat nor sleep. She studied the drawing Ivan had sent her. It was an extravagantly beautiful woman portrayed there, not only beautiful, but vibrantly alive and proud and determined as well—not exactly the kind of woman Emma had always imagined herself to be, and yet she recognized herself in that drawing —not, perhaps, her everyday self, not the one she shared with Julian, but a secret self she had never shared with anyone. Now she could not doubt that Ivan St. Peters had seen that secret self, had spied on her very soul.

She reached inside the drawer by her bed and took out the coin. As she held it in the hollow of her palm, it grew warmer until it burned and seemed to glow. She looked at the drawing and then at the coin. It was like magic, almost an enchantment, as the two objects blurred and merged in her sight.

She loved him. She felt like a shooting star hurtling through space. Everything around her was wild and bright. Love. She had never known it before. The great mystery of it, the thing that had always eluded her, was now here. And it was so very clear to her what she had to do.

15

W hat on earth is going on, Julian? If this is some sort of joke, I simply won't have it!" Louise Blackstone handed Julian the note she had found only an hour earlier. "She can't possibly mean this."

Julian read the note and then read it again. It was brief. In Emma's neat hand, on her personal writing paper, it said,

Dear Gram,
    Please try to understand and forgive me. I cannot marry Julian. I love another.

His mind went suddenly and totally blank. "When did you find this?" he said finally.

"There's another one, for you." Louise Blackstone watched his face carefully as he read. His expression did not encourage her.

Dear Julian,

I cannot hope for you to understand, but please try to forgive me. The love I feel for you is the love of a sister for a brother. In that way, I will always love you. My heart has given itself to Ivan. Let us be grateful that I've discovered this before it was truly too late.

"My God! She must be ill," Julian stuttered. "Her mind has come unhinged. She's having a nervous breakdown, become unbalanced . . ."

"My granddaughter is not unbalanced. She is the most normal of girls, of that I am sure. But something or someone has made her leave this house. Perhaps you ought to gather your thoughts, Julian. Perhaps you ought to think back over the past few weeks. Have you two quarreled? Have you upset her in any way? You haven't made improper advances, have you? What happened in New York? She's been changed ever since that trip."

Julian drew himself up indignantly. "Emma and I have not had any sort of argument, and as for 'advances,' I can only assure you that we have both been content to wait. I think you are upset, as am I, and I don't think it will do either one of us, or Emma, any good if we continue in this vein."

"You're right, Julian. Please forgive me." The elderly woman sat heavily in a chair. She ran her hand over her eyes. "Will you permit me to read your note?"

He passed it to her, feeling like a man suddenly caught in a whirlpool. He was struggling to maintain his equilibrium, but he felt as if he were being sucked down. He watched as Emma's grandmother read and then reread the note. Then she folded it and passed it back to him.

"I don't understand whom she's talking about or where she's gone. Who is this person she names? This . . . Ivan?"

"He's an artist," said Julian, swallowing a knot of bile that was threatening to make him physically ill. "A sculptor in New York. I introduced them. He has a woman of his own, or perhaps I should say he *did* have. They're dirt-poor. They live in a garret. He is a genius. Oh my God, I don't know what else to tell you. He . . . he is supposedly a friend of mine. But she can't mean this. They can't do this to me. They wouldn't. She's probably regretting this even now; perhaps she's afraid to come back . . ."

"Julian, get hold of yourself. If you know where this person lives, I suggest you go there immediately. I have no idea what's going on here, but what I do know, and you should, too, is that Emma has never said she would do a thing and then not done it."

"Yes, of course, I must go. I'm sure there's an explanation and that it's not as serious as it seems." Julian's voice was soothing now. "I know Emma's been upset in the last few days, but she would never walk out on me. I know her, I'm confident of that."

In reality, Julian was confident of nothing. Again and again, a vision of Emma dancing in Ivan's arms flashed before his eyes. How impossible to accept, and yet deep in his gut he knew it was true. Emma was with Ivan St. Peters. He only hoped it hadn't gone too far. Ivan the artist was a genius. Ivan the man, Julian felt he knew, was a cad. Emma had been so impressed, but Julian, stupid Julian, had presumed to think it was the art, not the artist, that had so taken her. And now she had made her move. And he had been a fool not to have seen it coming.

16

W here was I while Emma sat on that train to New York? I was in Singing Hills, Ohio, home for the holidays. What was I doing as she ran breathlessly up those stairs to the studio? Probably sitting around the kitchen table at my sister's, telling her about my exotic life in New York. And what precisely was I saying as Ivan and Emma became lovers, flesh to flesh, heart to heart? I don't know—nothing important. Nothing at all.

The morning had threatened snow, and by early afternoon, as Emma emerged from Penn Station, the straining sky lay down its load of swirling flakes that softened and silenced the city. When Emma arrived at Ivan's door, she was breathless as much from excitement as from the exertion of taking the four flights of stairs at a dead run. Such an innocent creature she was. What if he hadn't been home? What if I had answered her bold knock at his door? But the planets were all in their proper places for Emma that day, and it was Ivan, alone, who greeted her.

"I had to come," she said simply.

He reached for her hand and drew her into the room, brushing the snowflakes from her hair. "Your hands are freezing. Come here. Let me warm them in mine."

"I've left Julian. I cannot marry him. I've left Boston." Her eyes had a feverish shine, her voice a manic edge. Ivan could see how taut was the thread of her sanity at that moment, how near to breaking, and he soothed her as he took her coat.

"Hush now. We don't talk now," he cooed. "First we get you warm, darling girl. Black tea—that's what you need. Shush, Emmachka."

But Emma could not sit still, and while he made the tea, she wandered about the room, now and then touching something, inspecting it, like a child in a new place. The door to the workroom was open and she went in. She was astonished to see sketches of her everywhere. Hundreds of them, it seemed.

"I told you that I possessed you. Do you see how?" He was by her side. His voice was low.

Her hands were shaking, her whole body trembled, and she tried to say something but she couldn't. Her arms went around his neck like a sigh. Touching him, holding him like this released the tension of which she had been unaware, and she began to cry—small sobs at first, then deep, wracking spasms. Ivan said nothing, but held her in his bearlike embrace and murmured softly to her as if calming a frantic animal.

"All the way down here on the train I thought of what I wanted to say to you. I even rehearsed a speech, but I can't remember a word of it now," she whispered.

"Now, now. We have much to say. So much, and we must go very slowly just now. Don't you agree?"

"I don't know. I don't know anything other than that I had to come here to you."

"I'm glad you come. My God, I thank heaven you come. I never, never expect to see you." He drew her close to him and gazed into her face. For a moment he feared that she could not really know as yet how irrevocable the consequences of her actions would be.

"We shall talk and you will tell me just what has happened. Does Julian know you are here?" he asked.

"Yes. I expect he does by now. I left him a note. I left my grandmother a note. I told them both I couldn't go through with the wedding and that I was coming here."

"Ah." Ivan sighed deeply. "They will be very upset and worried. And Julian will be . . ."

"No. No. Please don't talk about all that. Don't you think I know how upset they'll be? I know. But there was nothing else I could do. Its easier this way for everyone. I love you, Ivan. I want to tell you how much I love you. Oh, I have no words. It seems ridiculous to try and tell you. You must know it. I am crazy with love of you—I have been since that night we danced. And the coin, Ivan. It *is* a magic coin. I can feel it. In my hand it comes alive, and it's brought me back to you." Her face had gone very white again and she looked at him, struck now for the first time with uncertainty. "Please say something, Ivan. Say something or kiss me or hold me."

Suddenly he caught her up and kissed her. His mouth covered hers, and she was soft and moist and so sweet, so indescribably sweet to him. And a kind of madness seized him so that it was he, rather than she, who felt breathless. Emma held him closer still, feeling herself drawn into him, feeling the currents of passion and need pass between them. He kissed her again, a long and tender kiss, feeling her heart beat against his, kissing her until he was filled up with her, exhilarated by her flesh, her nearness, her scent, her soft yielding body. It was too much. He buried his face in her hair and whispered, "You are mine now. Truly and forever."

She nodded, and then they did not speak.

Outside the snow fell silently and steadily, shutting out noise, shutting down traffic, shutting everyone in.

17

Julian did not call Ivan. His only thought was to confront Emma, to look in her eyes, to know that she was still his. It wasn't until the door to the loft on Hudson Street opened that his worst fears were confirmed. The woman who greeted him, her face radiant with defiance and joy, her glorious hair unbound, streaming down her back almost to the floor, her stance proud and determined, was not the Emma Blackstone he had known and loved.

They talked, but there was nothing he could say that would make a difference. "I feel sorry for you, Emma. It is you and not I who will have to live with this. Your grandmother is devastated, and I think you owe it to her, at least, to come home immediately."

Emma looked openly back at him. "Julian, it wasn't my purpose to hurt you or her. There isn't anything I wouldn't give to keep anyone from being hurt. And if I had a million years I couldn't tell you how this happened. All I know is that it did and there's no going back."

Ivan stepped toward Julian and made as if to touch his shoulder, but he shrank from the gesture with disdain. "I have nothing to say to you. You don't really love her. You can't. All you love is yourself. You and your colossal ego—you think you can take whatever suits you. You have the morals of a filthy alley cat. If you had any decency you would leave Emma out of your bordello. Go amuse yourself with some whore and keep your hands off decent women. I've come for Emma and she's leaving with me now."

"No, my friend. I am sorry, but you are wrong. Everything happens so fast, is not seeming real, but I am telling you it is real. Emma and I love each other and we will be together. Some things don't need time. Emma and I both feel this."

"He's lying, Emma," Julian snapped. "What he says isn't true. He hasn't the courage to admit it to you, but you must see it. You can't possibly know what's in your heart and mind in so short a time. You're throwing away everything that means anything on a chance meeting and a few hours in bed. You can't have any notion of how little that means."

"It means everything, Julian." Emma came toward him. She stood directly in front of him. "Julian, do you see me? I mean, do you really see me, because I don't think you ever have before. What you've seen is what you've wanted to see, but this is the real me. I came to him, Julian; Ivan never asked me to come. And now that I'm here, I won't leave. I can't. Please try to understand. I mean what I say. I love him."

"But you don't! You can't." Julian was whining now, and desperate. "You only think you love him. You couldn't possibly think so little of yourself and me. You've confused love, real love, with sex. I am your fiancé. For the love of God pull yourself together and come away from here with me now."

"No, Julian. Please don't make me say it again." Her voice was steady and calm and low. But there was a steeliness in it that Julian had never heard before.

They stood in silence for what seemed a long time. And then Emma said, "Ivan has asked me to marry him. And I have accepted. I will marry him, Julian, no matter what anyone says. I will go to Boston and tell Gram myself, but I want you to tell her first. Tell her how we feel and what has happened and why there can be no turning away from it. You would never have been truly happy with me, Julian. Because you never really knew me. Tomorrow is Christmas. I want to be with Ivan tomorrow, but I will go to see Gram the day after."

She was beautiful as she spoke, her face aglow with an inner light. She was self-assured and somehow serene. Beneath the thin silk kimono she wore, he could see the outline of her breasts. It almost made him ill. He felt as if he had seen a rare work of art vandalized and defiled. He searched her face for the old Emma, but she was not there. Still he knew he would never forget her as she had been, and never forget what he had lost.

"You should at least go home for Christmas, Emma," Julian said. "I promised her that. I promised I'd bring you home for Christmas."

Emma smiled. "I am home, Julian."

18

E/mma's Diary:

December 25, 1956

For as long as I can remember, I have been plagued by the notion that somehow life was leaving me behind. No matter what I was doing, it seemed to me that real life was what was happening somewhere else. It hardly seems possible now that by the simple act of taking a train to New York I left my girlhood behind. But I know in my heart that I will always measure the beginning of my real life from the moment that Ivan took me in his arms and kissed me.

I will never understand where I got the courage to go to him. I think that I was truly possessed by a power outside myself. But when I looked into his eyes, I knew that everything was all right.

When we kissed, it was as though the shadow of an older memory, a memory not of the mind but of the blood, came to the surface and I knew that we had loved before. I came to Ivan with no experience of physical love, with almost no experience of physical pleasure, and yet I responded to him as a woman of the world. Julian has never once kissed me the way Ivan kissed me, and yet I knew exactly how to kiss. My lips opened of their own accord, the taste of him was heaven to my senses, and I felt myself wanting to take him into my body, into my very soul. I look into his eyes, those blue pools of light and love, and I am drowning in sensations, even now. He penetrates my soul and we are born again inside each other's arms.

I've read descriptions of sex, everything from the purely clinical to the overblown romantic; I've imagined it thousands of times. What I was unprepared for was the sheer delight in making love to a body one loves better than one's own. Nor did I know at all about the aching tenderness of love, the simple, childlike yielding to another's whim. And most of all I did not know about the generosity of love. We make love over and over again, and just when it seems that our passion has been spent, a look, a touch, a word, and we are at it once again, teasing, coaxing, urging each other on to new heights of pleasure.

What amazes me, and perhaps Ivan as well, is that I feel no shame, no modesty, no reluctance to expose myself in any way he wishes. We interrupt our lovemaking so that he can make sketches. I lie there, naked and exposed. I watch his face, but mostly I watch his hands. His hands are beautiful, with long, tapered fingers, holding the charcoal exactly as he held my nipple just a while ago. Soon my breathing changes and Ivan can tell by looking in my eyes how I feel, how I want him again.

I looked in the mirror a little while ago, and for the first time in my life I saw that I was beautiful.

19

I knew something was up when I got off the plane and saw Dance waiting for me on the tarmac. He was bundled up against the cold in a vintage raccoon coat that hung almost to the ground. It was like Dance to do things like this, meet friends at airports on cold winter nights, but despite his smile and his bear hug, I knew there was trouble. It was in his eyes. In those eyes, nothing was hidden. I saw sympathy there, and the pain of knowing something that was going to bring pain.

To Dance had fallen the unhappy task of telling me about Ivan and Emma, and I confess I didn't make it easy for him. I was devastated. I felt as if all the breath had been knocked out of me. And yet, even as I cried bitter tears in his arms, I realized that I had known Ivan wouldn't be mine forever. There had been a great deal of lust and a lot of laughter between us. Perhaps I'd hoped something more would come in time, but I had been living mostly for the moment. Of course, these thoughts hardly made the moment less painful. I sobbed loudly in the back of the cab all the way to my apartment.

I was a mess, in spite of Dance's efforts throughout the night to comfort me. I wept and railed and drank. I threw up. I vowed never to have another thing to do with men and announced my intention to sequester myself in a cabin in the woods and mourn my loss alone with nature. I couldn't believe I had been so stupid as to leave Ivan alone for Christmas while I went home to Singing Hills. My ego was shattered, and I swore I would never get over it.

Dance listened patiently to it all, and then sometime late, late in the night, as he stroked my hair, he asked softly, "What do you want to happen now?"

"I want to die," I said miserably.

"I mean after that."

"I want Emma Blackstone to die. Oh Christ. I don't mean that. But why is it one always hates the other woman so much? Why don't I hate Ivan? Why do I think he's the innocent victim and Emma is the wicked one? Oh God, Dance, I really do hate her."

"Honey, you don't hate anybody. You just hate what's happening. You know, none of this means you won't see Ivan again. You'll go on being friends."

"Ha! Who wants to be friends? Friends I've got, but I'll never have another Ivan St. Peters."

"Well, it doesn't do any good to think of it that way. Ivan's a rare bird, but maybe he wasn't the best kind of bird for you. Do you remember that morning at my apartment when we first talked? I was thinking mostly of Ivan, what was best for him. I really wasn't thinking much about you. But now I know how good and caring and generous you are. You're the rare one, Maisie. And you don't deserve a life with a man who's only going to give you a small piece of himself."

"Bullshit, Dance. Don't hand me that 'you deserve better' speech. I'm miserable. And I intend to stay miserable. I've been happy-go-lucky Maisie, the sunshine girl, the party girl, the good-time girl long enough. And what has it gotten me? Nothing, that's what. Does Emma Blackstone care about my feelings? In a pig's eye! No one cares about my feelings. No one thinks I have feelings. They think I'm too busy cracking jokes. But what about me, Dance?" I was feeling good and sorry for myself.

"I care, Maisie. I care very much about you. And you may not believe it right now, but so do Ivan and Emma. Please be kind to yourself. Misery and hate and jealousy are only going to hurt you further. They want to see you, Maisie. Ivan especially. Look. It's happened. Nothing is going to change that."

"Oh shit! I don't fucking believe this! There's got to be another way. How about if Emma gets lost? I'll take that. Or how about if I wake up and find this is only a stupid dream?"

"How about your getting undressed and into bed and me getting in bed with you, and I promise I'll rub your back until you go to sleep."

I was exhausted. I did as I was told. Dance rubbed my neck and shoulders, easing away the stiff knots. He rubbed my back, my legs, my feet, my arms, my hands until I lay limp and relaxed. Then he undressed and got under the sheets with me, holding me close. There was nothing remotely sexual about our being naked together in my bed, and I was surprised at how natural and comfortable it felt.

"Dance?" I whispered.

"Shush. You're supposed to be asleep."

"I am asleep. I just wanted to ask you something. It's very personal."

He didn't say anything but I sensed it was all right.

"Ever since I've known you, you've never been with anyone. I mean, I've never known you to have a lover. Do you . . . well, do you ever have sex?"

His arm was relaxed around my shoulders. "Do you want me to make love to you?"

"I don't know. Yes. If you want to."

"All right." He smiled and brought me closer to him. Then he kissed me softly on the mouth. There was nothing hesitant or shy about him. He was a strange lover. Very sweet, affectionate, and quite virile. But there was none of the passion in him that I had grown used to with Ivan. His instincts were quite natural and pure and honest. It was clear he was not inexperienced, and yet, when it was over, I felt it had not happened at all. He was exactly as he had been before.

I lay in bed next to him, staring blindly at the ceiling in the dark. When I heard his breathing become regular, I started to get up. But his hand, which had been loosely holding mine, tightened.

"I never answered your question, did I?" he said.

"It's all right. You don't have to."

"But it wants an answer. I've never had a lover, not in the way other people do. I've never felt a passionate attachment to one person, but I have been, and am, in love with my friends. It's a very intense feeling and perhaps not unlike what you feel for Ivan. But for some reason, for me it seems to apply to everyone. It's not unusual for me to make love to my friends, too. Sexually, platonically. Everyone has a different need. But for me it's all the same. I either love or I don't. That's always the way it has been with me. I can't make any other distinctions."

"But you're closer than anyone else to Ivan."

"Yes." He paused, and I could sense the intensity of his feelings. "Ivan and I come from the same place. We share the same knowledge. We're brothers. And I love Ivan in a way that has nothing to do with this earth."

We were quiet again. I was trying to take this all in. Trying to understand. But before I could think too much, I was sound asleep.

20

Emma went to Boston, and the meeting with her grandmother was not a peaceful one. Louise Blackstone was unyielding. She found it incredible that Emma would say and feel the things she did. Louise Blackstone belonged to a society whose members married their own kind and honored the rituals of their caste. They were, above all else, the careful stewards of their own good fortune. The young were to succeed them in the quiet privileges that their parents had preserved, and deviations from the norm were unacceptable.

An artist, a foreigner, living in a loft with no means of support, no prospects, no family, was not acceptable. She turned a deaf ear to everything Emma said. She could not and would not condone such behavior.

"I am too old, Emma, to go against everything I have believed in all my life. You have made a public promise to Julian. A sacred oath.

I expect you to honor it, regardless of what you may think or feel. You have made a contract and you are bound by it—if Julian will still have you."

Emma, pale but firm in her resolve, shook her head. "That is no longer possible, Gram. I'm sorry. I was wrong to expect you to understand. I love you, Gram, but I can't do what you ask. I hope that someday you will forgive me."

But the older woman shook her head and moved away. If Emma chose to throw away her life and marry the likes of Ivan St. Peters, so be it; it was no longer any concern of hers. In doing so, however, she not only turned her back on any further contact with her family, but she would be cut off from any family support. None of the family fortune would come to her. Her case rested on this hard fact. The Blackstone fortune was sizable. It was unthinkable that Emma would be allowed to fritter it away in a world that was dubious at best, degenerate at worst. Never, never would Louise Blackstone relent on that front.

She urged her granddaughter to take some time to think this over. She hoped against hope that Ivan would not be so irresponsible as to allow Emma to lose her entire fortune. She even hoped that perhaps, devoid of her fortune, Emma would lose the larger part of her appeal to this unscrupulous foreigner. In all this she was wrong. Perhaps it's just as well she never knew how very wrong she was, for neither Ivan nor Emma ever gave a moment's thought to what that money might have meant to them.

"Gram understands nothing," Emma wrote in her diary. "I don't attach any particular importance to money. I never have. She thinks of money as a way to keep the world at arm's length. Money insulates Gram, but it suffocates me. I am in Paradise. I want Ivan. I choose his life and every bit of its uncertainty. I don't want an assured future. I only want what's now! To wait would only defile what we feel. I am committed to Ivan, to our love, and to our life together."

She returned to New York and Ivan. Less than a week later they were married at City Hall, and despite everything I had said, I was the maid of honor and was fairly stalwart throughout, if I say so myself. Ivan had a way about him that could weaken the firmest resolve. And anyway, one look at the man and I knew I had lost him forever. I may be a fool, and perhaps no judge of character, but even a fool knows the look of a man deeply in love when she sees it.

After the wedding, we all took a subway to Grand Central Station, where we ate and drank, toasting the happy couple at the Oyster Bar until it was time for the train that would take them up the Hudson to Rhinebeck for their honeymoon. Dance and I gaily waved them off from the platform, but when the train was out of sight, I turned and collapsed in tears into Dance's arms.

Dance took me home and I must have slept for two days. But when I woke up I knew it was time for me to take charge of my life. Surprisingly, it was Julian Slade who came to my rescue.

21

I hadn't actually seen Julian since the night the four of us went to Roseland, but I found myself one afternoon about two months later near the Selby Gallery, at 67th and Madison, and decided on impulse to drop in. I was impressed. The place reeked of money. Millicent Selby may have had an eccentric reputation, but her taste was impeccable.

Julian rather blanched when he saw me. "Maisie! What brings you uptown?" he said.

"Just slumming," I joked feebly, but Julian was nice enough to offer me a polite if tight smile. "Actually, I was on an interview for a job near here. I was curious to see you, Julian. How are you?"

"Fine. And you?"

"Oh, I'm fine, too." We stood awkwardly for a minute and then I started looking around. "Whose work is this?" I asked.

"His name is Carlos Sassi. He's a Spaniard. It's dreadful, isn't it?"

"Hey. That's a new sales technique."

"If I thought you were buying, I'd say Mr. Sassi was an artist whose gifts were just now being given serious notice in America. But since I assume you're not buying, I can tell you he's simply a hangover from one of Millicent's past indiscretions, and there was no way out of her contract with him without a messy lawsuit. The critics were not kind, the show has been a dud, and mercifully it will be done and out of here next week. Why are you interviewing for jobs?"

"Oh, you know," I sighed, "change of scene and all that."

He nodded. There was a long pause and then he said, "And how is the happy couple?"

"Back from the honeymoon and busy living happily ever after, I guess, or whatever it is happy couples do." The expression on Julian's face was truly painful to see. I couldn't help myself. There was no one else in the gallery, and I put my arms around him and held him. He stood there stiffly, but he didn't pull away. I think he might even have hugged me back if someone hadn't come in just then. Julian excused himself and asked me to wait while he saw to whatever it was. When he came back he asked me to lunch.

Strangely enough, Emma and Ivan were never mentioned over lunch. Julian talked about the gallery and his plans.

"There's a whole new wave coming, Maisie," he told me. "It's not like the art world we know. There's no school, no center, no central group like the Abstract Expressionists. It's happening in London, in San Francisco, and here in New York, too. I call it Factory art. Abstract is dead. This new breed is something else, and I'm going to make my name on it."

"What about Millicent? Is she going along with you?"

Julian gave a short laugh. "Millicent has very little choice if she wants to stay in business. And she does. The gallery is her whole life, but she's mismanaged it practically to the point of bankruptcy. She needs me, and frankly, she knows it. I can save her hide. But listen, Maisie. How serious are you about wanting a job?"

"Well, according to my bank account I'm very serious."

"Good. Because the gallery needs an associate director. Someone who can run the gallery on a day-to-day basis."

"But I thought that was your job."

"No. I'm a partner. I've got plans for the future of this gallery, and I need someone like you whom I can trust. Someone who can stay on top of all the details of organization. You can do that, Maisie. You're good with people. You can deal with the artists and keep track of them.

See that the openings run smoothly, stay on top of the paperwork. But most of all I need you to keep Millicent out of my way. She's impossible, but you'll like her. You and I could make a great team. What do you say?"

What could I say? I was thrilled.

This sudden turn of events put us both in a buoyant mood, and before I knew it, Julian had insisted on taking me out to celebrate. I agreed to meet him at an opening at the Museum of Modern Art at six. It was here, for the first time, that I rubbed elbows with the fabled uptown art crowd. Naïvely, I still thought art was the point of an opening, but of course it isn't. The people are. Who they are. What they wear. Who they're with. That's the show. And that night it was a good one. Julian was everywhere and clearly making inroads. He was poised, friendly without being overly familiar, and charming with just that touch of aloofness that suggested he might know a thing or two they didn't. I've never seen anyone work a crowd the way he did, quickly, easily, and purposefully. That having been accomplished, he took me by the arm and we were off.

We went to a restaurant called Gino's, which was quite in at the time and packed with a handsome breed of East Sider. It was a sea of pinstriped young men in English haircuts paying court to sleek, blond young women of the Gucci/Pucci persuasion. Julian was very gallant, ordering champagne to celebrate my new appointment. We drank a great deal that night, and as the evening wore on I got the feeling that Julian was somehow clinging to me, that he didn't want to let me go.

When finally he brought me to my door, he seemed so genuinely sorry the evening was over, what could I do? I took him in.

Julian Slade and Maisie Green were not meant to be lovers. That night we tried. It was a disaster. I have an image of Julian standing in the half-light from the bathroom in nothing but his socks and shirt, looking about as miserable as a banker at an orgy.

"It's all right, Julian," I said, patting the empty side of the bed and feeling like a courtesan. He climbed in and we embraced. Nothing stirred. We embraced again and he kissed me. Nothing again. Julian pressed valiantly on. Sex with the wrong person is no joke—maybe that's why we both started to laugh at the same time. We'd reached an impasse. Julian sort of groaned and flopped back on the bed.

"It's all right, Julian," I said again. "It doesn't matter. Let's just talk."

"I must have had too much to drink," Julian began lamely.

"Yes. That and about ten other reasons. Let's face it, Julian. You and me as lovers makes about as much sense as . . . as . . ." I couldn't think of anything. I could feel him in the silence, feel the tension in his body, the emotions breathing in the air.

"Nothing much makes sense, Maisie. Not anymore." His voice was low and miserable. I was glad we were in the dark. I could sense he wanted to talk, and it would have been unthinkable in the light.

Julian Slade was not the confessional sort, but that night he told me about as much as he was capable of telling anyone. His voice was that of a man stunned by a blow. We had both been jilted, but Julian had been stripped naked. We talked all through the night, or what was left of it, and I learned that he had few friends. Emma had been everything to him—friend, sweetheart, family. The rest of the world could have disappeared, for all he had cared.

By dawn we were both exhausted. I could see his face now, and his eyes were hollow. I leaned over and touched him.

"I wish there were something I could do for you," I whispered. "I wish I could make love to you and help you forget. Someday, someone will. You have to believe that, Julian." He didn't even look at me, but stared hard at the opposite wall. And then I was asleep.

At eight o'clock I was torn awake by the jangling alarm clock. Julian was gone, but propped up on the coffeepot was a note.

Dear Associate,
      Our workday begins at ten o'clock.
      The Selby Gallery

I groaned, drank a steaming mug of the thick black coffee, and then struggled into a paisley silk dress, a Christmas gift from my mother.

And so began my bout with a career.

My first day on the job, Millicent Selby swept into my office, accompanied (as she usually was) by a beautiful white cockatoo. Her flaming red hair was done up in a beehive, and she wore an elegant black crepe sheath with masses of heavy gold and paste jewelry. She stopped, tapped a long, perfectly manicured purple fingernail on my desk, and said, "Life is difficult and brief, so you might as well make it lively." With that, she left. The cockatoo lingered only long enough to shit on my carpet, then scurried after her.

Millicent was at least intriguing, but the bird, whom she adored, I loathed and feared from that moment on. She would stalk the gallery with that creature on her shoulder, looking like some kind of freaked-out pirate in drag, and would chuckle indulgently whenever it flew screeching at some unsuspecting prey—more often than not an important collector. When she was out, the bird, whose name was Echo, roamed the gallery freely and on several occasions nipped my ankles.

It did not take long to see Julian's dilemma. He was a businessman, but Millicent clearly was not a businesswoman. He had a genuine feeling for new trends, but he was equally adept at the difficult, often boring job of grooming, publicizing, and generally launching new talent. Millicent, in contrast, found business a bore and spent her time at the gallery primarily on theatrics, intrigue, and romance.

Before Julian had taken the helm of Millicent's gallery, there was no "line" followed there. Mere whim had dictated Millicent's exhibition policy—that and the physical attractiveness (and cooperativeness) of the artist. All this, of course, had done nothing to enhance her reputation in the art world.

She had come to New York as a rich young widow before the war, loving modern art and, of course, the artists who created it. When she first appeared on the scene, she was like a fairy godmother descending on drafty lofts and studios. She liked to buy pictures directly from the artists, and she went, dressed in her extraordinary furs, cash in hand. There were few who could resist. In a short time she had amassed a sizable and impressive collection.

In the early days of her gallery, her artists had been devoted to her; there were so few other dealers who appreciated and supported what they were doing. Among the galleries showing Abstract Expressionist work, the Selby Gallery earned for itself a certain amount of fame. The remodeled town house on 67th Street was considered an exquisite space in which to show, but by the mid-fifties, Millicent's rather unorthodox "eye," coupled with her dramatic and self-centered manner, had begun to put both buyers and artists off. She was deemed unreliable.

By contrast, Julian had a way about him that proclaimed authority and boosted confidence. In the space of a few months he had effectively reduced Millicent's visability in the gallery and brought in a whole new clientele. The art market was rife with a new breed of collector who looked at art in terms of dollars and cents. Whereas Millicent wanted people to buy for beauty, for love, for emotion, Julian persuaded his clients that art was an excellent investment.

As a result, business hummed on 67th Street and Millicent enjoyed the rebirth of her gallery. For the first few months of my job, she made life easier for all of us by falling in love with a tall, blond Dutch artist who spoke little English but who had electrified New York by staging one of its very first "happenings." It was a curious event that took place in an abandoned subway station in Queens. The invited guests entered the station through a manhole in the street. Down below was a perfectly ordinary party complete with champagne, food, even a strolling musician, while the walls of the station reflected flashing lights and film clips of express subways rushing through crowded, rush-hour stations. The effect was physically nauseating. Everyone loved it.

I was beginning to learn a lot about the art world, and much of it confused me. It was a world of cunning and sometimes outright dishonesty. I saw how art was manipulated, promoted, and publicized. New collectors, anxious to get in on the act, were seduced by the dealers, whipped into a frenzy of buying so that they often literally begged to be allowed to purchase pieces that just a week before had been gathering dust in some warehouse. They reminded me of sheep begging to be fleeced.

"The business of art is business," Julian was fond of saying whenever I questioned something.

"Yes. And the same is true of selling used cars," I retorted, "and frankly, Julian, I don't see much difference."

"Ah, but there is a difference," Julian laughed. "There's much more money in art than there is in used cars. You're too sentimental, Maisie. We are here to sell, and there is no room for sentiment when it comes to selling. Least of all in the art world. Don't be so down on the poor dealer. Even the most high-minded collector wants to know that his purchase might be worth more in the future. Profit is always on everyone's mind, Maisie, not just the dealer's. Pay close attention. You'll see I'm right."

But I didn't believe him. I didn't want to.

22

Meanwhile, trouble was brewing in paradise. Down on Hudson Street, Ivan and Emma were finding that after a few months the intensity of togetherness and poverty were beginning to wear on them. Dance was worried. Emma had sold off her good clothes to the resale shops.

"Oh no!" I said. "How awful. Not all those cunning little cashmere numbers. What will she do, now that she has to dress like the rest of us?" Dance ignored me.

Ivan, he said, was making small clay sculptures that Emma was selling at the street art fairs that sprang up in the Village on weekends. Dance was horrified. "Imagine," he said. "Ivan's sculptures selling to tourists from New Jersey for ten dollars!" There were times, Dance said, when they barely had enough to eat.

"So let them live on love," was my reply. But I regretted it the minute I said it, because Dance looked so pained that I felt like the world's worst bitch. That was the thing about Dance—he always made you want to be a better person.

So, when a distraught and tearful Emma St. Peters showed up at my door early the very next day, I tried to get past my initial astonishment and be the better person Dance would have wanted me to be.

She virtually threw herself into my arms. "Oh, Maisie; oh, Maisie," she kept saying. "I don't know what to do. I didn't know where to go."

"My God, what's happened?" I said, suspecting that Ivan was either dead or, more likely, sleeping with another woman. Feeling acutely uncomfortable, I led her over to a chair and sat her down.

"Emma, please, blow your nose and start from the beginning. What has happened?" It took her a while to calm down, then slowly the story emerged.

Well, they had gone to sleep as usual, but she had awakened at three in the morning to find Ivan gone. He had never before left her alone in the middle of the night. "I was terrified, Maisie. I've never been so frightened. I didn't know what was happening to us."

I couldn't help feeling sorry for this sobbing, wretched creature, but frankly, I couldn't see what the fuss was about and I said so.

"It's all so confusing," Emma sniffed. "In the beginning he hardly let me out of his sight. Even when I wasn't posing, he wanted me to stay there in the studio. He said he worked better with me there. But now he is so moody. Sometimes this terrible gloom comes over him, and for no reason. Sometimes he comes in from the studio and hardly looks at me. He makes me feel like I'm in the way or something. I know he needs his solitude and I try so hard to be quiet, to read or do my embroidery, but I always seem to irritate him somehow."

"What you're telling me," I said finally, "is that you two have had a fight."

Emma nodded solemnly. "A terrible fight. He didn't come home until six o'clock. And instead of apologizing or explaining, he was mean and cold and furious. He said horrible things, Maisie. He said I was provincial and naïve."

"That's horrible?"

"Well, it was the *way* he said it," she wailed. "I couldn't stay there. I just threw on the first thing I could find and left. Oh, I'm so sorry, Maisie. I have no right to impose all this on you, of all people. You must hate me, but I didn't know where else to go. What shall I do? You know Ivan. You know about men. Please tell me what to do."

I sat and watched the weeping Emma, and I felt sorry for her, I really did, but I was helpless in situations like this. Other people always seemed to know just what to do, just what to say in the face of tears, heartbreak, and emotional setback. Dance was one of those people. Why hadn't Emma gone to Dance? She sobbed uncontrollably, little gasping noises that were truly pitiful to hear.

The sorrier I felt for her, the angrier I got at Ivan. The bastard. He sweeps this poor innocent creature off her feet, she gives up scads of money and a respectable marriage for him, and now, a mere three months later, he's furious because he can't go catting around at all hours of the night.

I made her go into the bathroom and wash her face with cold water. Then I brewed a large pot of coffee and made her drink it strong and black.

"Look, Emma. You love Ivan and I know he loves you. But you've got to realize that living with him every day is not going to be easy. You can't let him upset you like this. Honey," I told her, "he's an artist. He's crazy. It comes with the territory. They're all crazy. If they weren't, they wouldn't be artists. They don't do things like normal people, and they don't understand things like normal people. Next time he steps out of line like that, why don't you just smack his face for him?"

Emma gasped. "Really? Do you think so?"

The whole idea was so appealing that we both burst out laughing. "Sure," I said, "knock out a few teeth, if you can. You know what Ivan wants from you—what all artists want from their women? All you have to do is inspire him like a muse, support his fifty-ton ego, nurse him like a mother, fuck him like a whore, put up with his insults like a saint, clean his house like a maid, cook his food like Escoffier, and stay the hell out of his way the rest of the time."

Emma laughed heartily, then sighed. "I'm afraid you're right, you know, but it's worth it." Her reply was so ingenuous that I couldn't help feeling that perhaps, after all, they were meant for one another.

We were relaxed in each other's company now, and I was beginning to feel as if I hadn't handled it so badly after all. I was beginning to think that Dance would finally be proud of me.

"Look," I said, "you've had a fight. Personally, I love fights. I figure it keeps things interesting and clears the air at the same time. I'll bet Ivan is chewing his nails right now, worried to death about you."

Her eyes began to fill with tears again. "Should I go back?"

"Let him stew for a while. But of course you're going back. And you'll keep going back because, believe me, this isn't the last fight you'll have. You're married, after all. The only other option is to leave him."

"Oh, I couldn't leave him! I couldn't live without Ivan."

I shrugged. "There you go. Your problem is solved."

"It is?"

"Sure. Because there is no problem. Now comes the good part. Making up."

Emma looked thoughtful for a moment, and then she grinned. "Maisie, you're a very clever person. I'm glad I came here."

We talked for the better part of the morning. Emma was a good storyteller and had a surprising sense of humor. Not ribald, mind you, but she could laugh at herself—and did. She told me a lot about her life and how she felt about Ivan. I discovered that she wasn't quite as prissy and mild as I had imagined, and she discovered I wasn't as self-confident and ballsy as I tried to make people believe.

By the afternoon we were still having a good time, and I got the idea to go up to the Gypsy Tea Room and have our fortunes read by Pandora.

"Do you believe in fortune-telling?" Emma asked me excitedly.

"Well, not really. But I love it all the same. I mean everyone is so cool and skeptical about it, but you get them to a reading and look at their faces. They're like children greedy for the next installment of an adventure story. Aren't you longing to know what's going to happen to you next?"

"I certainly am at the moment," Emma admitted. "Let's go."

The Gypsy Tea Room was then at the corner of 42nd Street and Fifth Avenue, and Pandora was an exceptional fortune-teller. She held Emma's hand in hers for a long moment. "You're going to take on a new responsibility very soon," she said. "Someone near to you has upset you, but your new endeavor will make this person very happy. You are a dreamer, my dear, and reality can seem quite terrifying when one has done nothing but dream. Don't worry, you will land on your feet. You've a strong will, and you'll never be governed by fear."

Emma was thrilled with her prophecy and quite ready to face Ivan again by the time I left her on Hudson Street. She hugged me before she went inside. "I'm so glad we're friends," she said.

Later that night I caught up with Dance at a party.

"You'll be pleased to know that Emma and I are, as of this afternoon, bosom buddies," I said, making a wry face.

"I heard. Ivan was all over the place today, looking for her. He made me sit in the loft while he roamed the streets, so I was there when she came in. We had a nice little chat."

"About me?"

"Some. Emma thinks you're the most wonderfully clever person. I told her she was quite right. But we mostly talked about Ivan."

"So what else is new?"

"She said something very interesting, as a matter of fact. I asked her what she loved most about Ivan, and do you know what she said? She said, 'I know he's handsome and sexual and talented and worldly and all those head-turning things, but what I love most about him is the child I see when I look in his eyes. It's the child in him I love.' She knows, Maisie, if Ivan ever loses that quality, he'll lose his art. She understands that, and she's willing to commit her life to standing between him and the hard world. Emma's got her feet on the ground. She knows what he's about." He smiled and took my arm. "Now come with me. I'm on my way to a cast party for the Polish Theater for the Dead. Guaranteed fun, if you don't speak Polish."

"Or if you're dead," I said. "Which I am. No. You go. I'm going home." We kissed and I turned to go, but Dance caught my arm.

"Hey, what did Pandora say to you?"

"She said I was going to take a long ocean voyage and meet a tall, handsome stranger." I shrugged. "So? She's gotta make a living, right?"

He laughed. "I love you, Maisie."

"And I love you, Dance."

23

"She's going to have a baby. Did you hear me, Julian? I said Emma is going to have a baby. She's pregnant. She just found out." I was standing in the doorway to his office, and now I stepped in and quietly shut the door.

Julian had gone very pale. He got up abruptly from his desk and strode to the window. "And what do I say to that, Maisie? Hurray for Mother Nature?"

"Well, no . . . not unless you want to. I'd rather you did something about it."

"What am I supposed to do about it? Send a silver rattle?"

"For Christ's sake, don't snap at me. I thought you'd like to know. And frankly, I think you ought to do something. They're flat broke. You've got half of Ivan's sculptures sitting in the warehouse. Why don't you start burying the hatchet and do something about selling Ivan's work?"

"I have no agreements with Ivan St. Peters, and don't intend to have any. As for his things in the warehouse, they're still in crates. He can have them any time—at his expense, of course."

"That's very unwise of you, Julian. Other dealers are interested in Ivan now. But he is holding out for you. He says you're the only person he trusts."

"Trust! The man knows nothing about trust."

"Well, he does, but he doesn't know anything about business. You ought to see what he's doing these days, Julian. It's fantastic. It's changed. The scale has all changed. Everything is much more fluid, more delicate. The Marlborough Gallery has been sniffing around down there, and so have some of your other competitors. With the baby coming, he's got to make money, so I don't know how much longer he'll hold out. I've been around here long enough to know you'll be cutting your own throat if you let another gallery have him. What do you say to just going down and having a look?"

Julian said nothing, but I could see him thinking. I had a feeling he wouldn't be able to resist seeing Ivan's latest work, and I was right. Finally he turned to me and with a tight expression he nodded. "I'll go when I can."

I started to leave. "And, Maisie," he said, with the barest smile hovering about his lips, "for your information, the Marlborough Gallery never 'sniffs' around the studios of unknowns. If you're going to meddle, get your facts straight. A lie is only as good as its truth."

I clicked my heels and saluted. "Right, boss."

He visited the loft a week later, and I was amazed at how smoothly it went. Of course, there were a few awkward moments in the beginning, but once Julian was in the studio, once he saw what Ivan was doing, well, it was a piece of cake. Something wonderful had happened to Ivan's work since Emma. It was the beginning of the elegance and tranquility that would mark the famous pieces of his maturity. The overt eroticism had given way to a much deeper, more intense vision. She was everywhere in his work. I wondered how Julian felt about this. Whatever he felt, he certainly didn't react unfavorably. He seemed, if anything, more appreciative than he had ever been of Ivan's talent. Julian even bought a piece outright to establish his good intentions. As he laid the check for five hundred dollars on the table, there wasn't a dry eye in the place.

He left, promising Ivan a show and congratulating Emma on the baby, and the three of us collapsed in one another's arms with relief. The truth of it was that not only were there no other galleries interested in Ivan's work, but the times were changing, just as Julian had predicted.

Pop Art was going to dominate the next decade, and nothing could have been further from the spirit of Ivan's work. And they *were* broke. As poor as they could be. They had found an art-loving doctor who would deliver the baby in exchange for three of Ivan's pieces, but other expenses loomed. They needed an angel, and to my mind it had to be Julian. I knew that Julian had the money to help if he chose to. Hindsight, of course, would tell me that Julian Slade was no angel. What I didn't realize was how deeply he had been humiliated, and in what complicated ways that fact had changed him. It was only in the years to come that these bits and pieces of his nature would surface. But even then I was witness to a shrewd and extremely ambitious man. He had an uncanny, persuasive way about him, so that artists, clients, and even the critics came away totally unaware of how he had manipulated them. Hidden underneath a carefully manicured layer of good breeding and manners was a driving need to control, to pull all the strings.

Not in our wildest dreams would one of us ever have suspected that before Julian had come to the studio, he had also been to see Emma's grandmother. A child on the way has been known to effect miraculous family reconciliations, and the ugly truth was that Julian was not about to encourage or even tolerate such a happy eventuality. His influence on Louise Blackstone was substantial. They were both, he had suggested many times, the victims of a willful, capricious young woman who had turned her back on everything that they stood for and loved. It wasn't terribly difficult, given Julian's powers of persuasion, to convince this proud, bereaved, and aged woman that no reconciliation whatever would be possible. And it probably wasn't much more of a strain to convince her that the trust fund she would no doubt want to establish for her great-grandchild ought to be administered, not by the child's irresponsible mother nor by its bohemian father, but rather by someone who understood business matters.

Louise died in her sleep shortly before the baby was born, and never beheld the beautiful Natalia Louise St. Peters, who came into the world on a crisp November morning in 1957. A million-dollar trust fund was quietly accruing interest for that baby. A trust administered by Julian Slade in any way he saw fit.

But we knew none of this. And wouldn't for more than twenty years.

24

The old year ended. It was now 1958. I had lovers of my own, a substantial number of them, in fact, and each in his turn was welcomed into the fold like family, but they were a transient lot. The constants in my downtown life were Emma and Ivan and Dance. And what a full life we had: ice skating at Rockefeller Center, with the tiny Tally wrapped in fur like a papoose on Ivan's back; drinking champagne at midnight on the boardwalk at Coney Island; hitting Chinatown at five in the morning for egg rolls and chow mein; listening to poetry and jazz; boozing and dancing. Not just we, but the whole art world seemed to be caught up in a frenzy of activity. Our world then was young, and in love with being young. There was a brotherhood, a bond that united every creative spirit in the Village. No danger lurked, no anxiety gnawed. Everything was new and fresh and exhilarating. We believed in our art and our music, our poetry and our theater. We believed the impact of it would ripple out across America from the lofts and garrets and galleries, from the dance halls on St. Mark's Place and the tables at the Cedar and the blue-lit stage of the Five Spot. There was something in the air then, a sense of possibility, a feeling of immortality. Oh, there was struggle aplenty, and more than enough heartbreak to go around, but in spite of it all, we thought that we would live forever.

One night, after attending a black-tie premiere of the ballet, and after several hours of making the rounds of nightclubs and bars, Dance, with some of his uptown friends, wove his way into a subway station to head downtown. The subway car was mostly empty and he dozed off for a few minutes. When he woke up, the train was just pulling out of the Eighth Street station. Somehow it must have seemed profoundly urgent to him that he get off just there. He wanted to have a last nightcap, he said, with his pals at the Cedar Bar. He started to climb out of the window of the now-speeding train and was decapitated.

Dance Duprey died an ugly, senseless death. As the terrible news spread, his friends, and they were legion, all crowded into the Cedar. We were devastated. The mood was shattered and quiet; no one seemed to know what to say, but after a while someone got up and started reading one of Dance's poems. It was a beautiful love poem, filled with sparkling images and words that seemed to float in the air. I had heard Dance recite it many times. He loved to recite and people loved to hear him, loved the sound of his voice, not just for the soft Southern accent but for the way he had of transporting his listeners. He had been a man who possessed the rarest of all gifts, the gift of friendship. He had graced the world with his presence and he had given us all such pleasure.

Emma made all the arrangements for his body to be shipped to his family in Savannah, and Ivan spent weeks carving a headstone for the grave of his best friend. When it was completed, I made the trip south to see that it was placed properly in the cemetery.

No one knew it at the time, but looking back, Dance's sudden, shocking, and ultimately meaningless death was for us the turning point of a decade, of an era. Suddenly we all felt terribly mortal and vulnerable and a little afraid. Somehow, at that point, the fifties, our fifties, the scene in Greenwich Village, the artists and writers as a community, perhaps even the exuberance and excitement we felt, all began to fade. The sense of enchantment and struggle seemed gone. Most of us, if not all, knew that our special place in time was fast on its way to becoming history.

Within a year, Ivan borrowed enough money from Julian to leave the city with his family. They had decided to move out to the tiny hamlet of Springs, on eastern Long Island, where so many other artists had moved.

On moving day, Emma and I sat on unused packing boxes in the now-empty loft. A truck had come for the furnishings and work tools, and Ivan was downstairs, supervising the loading. Tally lay soundlessly asleep in Emma's lap.

"Nothing will ever be the same," I said morosely.

"No. I expect not," she answered softly, adjusting the blanket around Tally. "Things change because life changes. Ivan couldn't stand living here anymore. We'll have a good life in the country. It will be different but perhaps better, who knows? What we knew, what we had here"—she looked around the loft—"is gone. I can feel it. Can't you?"

"I worry about you being so far away."

"And I worry about you here in the city."

"I'll come for weekends . . ."

"And we'll come in . . ."

"Oh shit." I started to cry.

When Ivan came in, we knew it was time. The three of us hugged, and then Ivan and Emma and Tally went down the stairs. I held back for a minute, my eyes darting around the space, looking for something. I didn't know what. A sign? A souvenir? Something tangible to take away with me? But Emma had been right. This was no longer our place.

They drove away in an old green Packard for which Ivan had traded one of his sculptures to a fellow artist. My eyes blurred, but I kept on waving until the car was out of sight. How could I know then that it would be half a decade before I saw them again?

PART

II

25

There is a corny old joke my father loved to tell. It's about a man and his wife who had many children. The woman was a good mother and a wonderful wife. She took care of everything, and dinner was always ready on the table when the man came home. He was a very stern and aloof man, and the children always felt that he took their mother too much for granted and never paid enough attention to her. One day the woman was called away from home in the middle of the day and she couldn't get back until late in the evening. The oldest daughter made dinner, the younger children set the table, and by the time their father came home, everything was ready and perfect as always. All nine children sat at their places, waiting for their father to join them. He walked in, looked around, smashed his fist into the table, and shouted, "Where the hell is everybody?"

After Dance died and Ivan and Emma left for the country, that's exactly how New York felt to me. I was surrounded by people, but everybody was gone. I was bored, lonely, and dissatisfied. New York felt cold and empty. And coldest of all was my job. My days were spent issuing polite but firm rejections to hopeful young artists. The Selby Gallery was fast becoming the center of the avant-garde scene, and artists from every loft and garret in New York made their way uptown with high hopes and a box of slides in hand. I sat at a small desk on the main floor of the gallery and I could see them through the window with their scruffy clothes, dirty fingernails, and unkempt hair. How romantic and bohemian they looked in the hangouts downtown, and how very out of place in the rarefied atmosphere of Madison Avenue. The word was out that Julian was the moving force behind the Selby Gallery, and while many of them could have gotten to Millicent, they demanded instead to see Julian Slade. I felt like posting a sign reading "Abandon Hope, All Ye Who Enter Here," for Julian made a point of never seeing anyone who merely walked in off the street. There was nothing Julian so abhorred as a hungry, importunate artist smelling up his clean, spare space. I was to buzz him with a special code if there were any untouchables hanging out downstairs, and he would then use the back exit to avoid confrontations. God, he was a bastard.

I knew well that I needed to do something about my life, but I thought I hadn't a clue as to what it might be. I was wrong; Dance had told me exactly what I should do years before. And one day as I walked up Fifth Avenue on my way to work, his words came back to me from out of the blue: "When you don't know what else to do, go to Paris." Without a moment's further thought, I walked into a travel agency and put down a deposit on a one-way passage to Europe on the first available ship. There was one sailing in two weeks, which left me just enough time to pare down my possessions to what could fit inside two suitcases and quit my job.

Julian thought I was crazy. And I suppose I did, too. It was just that very element of craziness that made it so appealing. The day I was to sail, I bought a bottle of champagne to toast my courage and invoke the gods of good sailing. It was dismal November weather, but I stood on the deck sipping my champagne feeling as light and buoyant as the bubbles in my glass. As the giant ship slipped from her berth, I smiled and tossed the nosegay of violets I had bought for myself into the murky waters of the Hudson River. While I watched the tiny bouquet bobbing up and down, I laughed aloud with sheer happiness. I knew that I was doing the right thing, and I thought gratefully of Dance, who was once again steering me in the right direction.

"They say people take sea voyages to find love or to run away from it." I turned and came face-to-face with a tall, friendly looking man who had gray hair and the kindest brown eyes I'd ever seen. He was quite a bit older than I, but his eyes were young and his smile was enchanting. His name, he told me, was Henry McCann.

"Well, I guess you could say I'm running away, but not from love or to it, I don't think."

"Ah," he said, "that sounds intriguing. Are you a fugitive from the law?"

I laughed. "No, not from the law." I turned and looked at the skyline of the city, receding into the mist. "From New York. It betrayed me, left me, and now I'm done with it. I thought Paris would be a perfect antidote. The timeless city and all that. Would you like some champagne?"

"I'd love some." He took the glass and drank and then handed it back to me. It was starting to rain by now and we were wrapped in a dense gray fog. The gulls, the water, the sounds of the ship's engines and foghorn were muted and almost dreamy.

"I feel like we're in that movie *Outward Bound*. Do you know it? The one where the passengers on the ship find out they've all died and that their souls are on the way to the judgment gates."

"Well, I'm not so sure about myself, but may I say you look very much alive. That's why I couldn't resist coming over to talk to you. I hope you don't mind." He smiled again.

I smiled back, finding I didn't mind at all. We stood there in the rain, drinking and laughing until we were both shivering. He walked me to my cabin and I agreed to meet him in the main salon for cocktails. Then it was dinner.

The first-class dining room looked very posh indeed. I remember worrying about my dress because it was the first night out and everyone was dressed to kill—the men were in black tie and the women were all done up in furs and jewels. Henry waved away my worries. "You have your own sparkle and it makes their jewels look like dull stones. In fact, I can't remember when I've seen anyone so pretty as you."

Who was this lovely man? I wondered. Why was he traveling alone? Would we have more than dinner together? I certainly hoped so. So far, I liked what I saw. I liked the man and I liked his first-class approach to traveling. We started our dinner with caviar, mounds and mounds of it, ladled out of large, chilled silver bowls, and with it the driest champagne I had ever tasted. After that, what we ate and drank seemed less important. We talked. The more we talked, the less important everything else seemed to be as well.

Naturally we talked about ourselves and I found myself telling him the most minute details of my life. My mysterious escort was a great listener, the kind of person who listens with his eyes, not just his ears. The more I told him about myself, the more he seemed to like me. And it was clearly more than just sex, although I could tell he liked me pretty well that way, too. There was respect and admiration in the way he talked to me and treated me. He was fascinated with my "bohemian" life in the Village, and I climbed to new conversational heights, recounting odd bits of stories about the people and places I had known.

"But I'm doing all of the talking and I don't know a thing about you," I exclaimed. "I've been trying to figure you out, but nothing fits. I think maybe you're a novelist. Somehow you make me think of Somerset Maugham."

He laughed. "I'm delighted you think so, because I'm afraid my real story would bore you to tears. So—let us say that your instincts are quite correct. I am a very successful writer and this is the kind of chance meeting that will work its way inevitably into one of my books. Now let me see. I am about to start a new book and my thoughts have been churning around, searching for just the right moment to begin. My story, so far, is about a man—oh, let's say a man in his early fifties. On the surface he seems a very straightforward fellow. A businessman. From the Midwest, let's say."

I groaned. "Not the Midwest. I'm from the Midwest and I hate businessmen."

"Ah." He nodded sadly, but then he brightened. "But don't give up on my man so easily. Where are you from, by the way?" When I told him, he grinned. "Well, our fellow comes from a town called Madison, Indiana. Really not more than fifty miles from Singing Hills."

I settled back in my chair. Madison, Indiana, was a charming old town with huge Victorian mansions perched atop bluffs overlooking a bend in the Ohio River. I had been there once with my parents, and even then, as a teenager, I had been impressed. It was one of the prettiest places I had ever seen.

"Yes. Madison, Indiana. And there on the busy river, a boy grows up in a life of wealth and all the security of an American middle-class family. He has brothers and sisters and nursemaids and ponies and a summer house on the Michigan shore. His father puts him down for Yale and expects him to come into the family business when he graduates. The family business dominates the town, and half of Madison is employed by it. But ever since our boy was a small child, he has been fascinated not with the stuff of manufacturing and the great American way, but with opera and antiquity and all things French. French languages, French cooking, French literature. The boy, you see, has a very peculiar mother. Well, peculiar for Madison. She is a frail woman of extraordinarily delicate sensibility. She hides in the closet when it thunders, and weeps at almost anything having to do with music and poetry, things her husband has no time for. Her greatest joy is indulging her eldest son's interests. Finally she persuades her husband to send the boy, now an honors graduate from Yale, to Europe for a year. It is 1927. The family business is booming. The father bows to this request and even sends the boy off with his blessings and a sizable allowance, so that he can move easily throughout the continent. The young man is twenty-one years old and it is spring. He falls in love with Paris the way only a boy of twenty-one from a small American town can fall in love. It is complete. It is total. Paris is everything to him.

"His money and manners and introductions serve him well. He is swept up into that extraordinary group of writers and artists who converged on Paris in the twenties. The Fitzgeralds, Hemingway, Picasso, Cole Porter, the Murphys, and so many others. It is a breathless time. Everything seems fresh and newly invented. He has found his spiritual home. He realizes he can never go back to Indiana. His life, for better or for worse, is in France.

"He spends his money freely, even extravagantly. He is confident that before long he, too, will begin a life in the arts. In the meantime, his family indulges him. He has no worries. He finds he is much sought after. He is young and attractive and pleasant. He falls in love with a beautiful girl from a very old French family. The courtship is intense. Soon, very soon, he expects to ask her father for her hand.

"And so now we come to 1929. Black Thursday. Our young man is in the country with his girl when the news of the collapse of the stock market reaches him. Upon his hasty return to Paris, he finds he has become a pauper overnight. When you're rich, when you've had all the worldly goods handed to you without so much as lifting a finger, it is a fearsome shock when all that is suddenly snatched away. It is awful and terrifying. Our hero has no experience in dealing in the harsher realities of the world. Suddenly doors are slammed, landlords are issuing evictions, creditors hound him, and worst of all, his would-be fiancée no longer cares to see him.

"He has just enough money to get back to America, traveling steerage on a horrible old tank out of Rotterdam. When he gets home, everything is a shambles. His father is dead of a heart attack. Everyone in the town is out of work. People are starving. They are looking to him for help. He knows what he must do. He works. He works hard for ten years and is able to save the company and put many people back on the payroll.

"Then the war comes. The small business lands an enormous government contract, making uniforms for the army, and he accumulates a fortune. He marries but it is not a success.

"And then one day he turns fifty. Suddenly he realizes he has spent over twenty-five years working at something that means nothing to him. The person he knew, the person he wanted to be, is still back there in Paris. So he throws over everything and buys a ticket to Paris and sets out to find his life again."

Henry stopped, and looked at me rather sheepishly. I got the feeling that this might have been the longest speech he had ever made.

"Go on," I said. "What happens then?"

"Well, let's see. On the ship he meets a girl, a lovely girl, and he tells her his story."

"Go on," I said.

"I can't." He said helplessly. "Perhaps our fellow is rather at a loss as to what to do next."

"Yes. I can see he is," I said, taking up the story line. "Well, he mustn't let the girl get away. Not now. Not just yet, because there is something about him that she must know. Perhaps if he can only find a way to tell her, she will be his."

"I see. But what does he do?"

"Well, he asks her to dance. He thinks if he can hold her in his arms, perhaps she will realize what it is he wants so badly for her to know."

Henry pushed his chair back and held his hand out to me. The orchestra was playing one of my favorite songs, "Night and Day." We danced, twirling slowly around the floor. Henry held me very close. When the music stopped, we stood in the center of the floor, hardly daring to move away from one another. Finally he spoke very softly.

"And what is it he wants her to know so badly?"

My voice sounded husky. I could hardly keep it steady. "He wants her to know that underneath that well-mannered and orderly façade is a man with a deep strain of poetic feeling, and underneath that feeling is a man who is an ardent lover."

It had taken me about three hours to realize Henry McCann was one of the most interesting human beings I had ever met. And about three minutes to know this was the man I wanted to spend the rest of my life with.

We were married by the ship's captain the night before the ship docked at Le Havre.

26

There never was an easier, happier marriage than the one I had to my darling Henry. I had to laugh when I came to this passage in Emma's diary: "Incredible, wonderful news! Maisie's gone and married herself a millionaire." It was true.

We bought a wonderful house on the Ile St. Louis. Every room had a view, so from our nest we saw the Seine with all its boats and barges, the spires of Notre Dame, and a panorama of Paris that was spectacular. It was not a grand house, but it had a certain grandeur to it because it was old and there was a timeless feeling in the way it rambled up four stories and then reached across a tiny, ancient street onto the roof of another house.

It is beyond my powers to convey what fun it is to find yourself suddenly and effortlessly rich. It's not so much the having of wealth that makes you happy, it's the worlds you discover that you never dreamed were there. I've known plenty of people who were miserable whether they had money or not, but if you were ready to enjoy yourself, there was no question about it, money opened doors and paved the way. Henry and I were in a frenzy of not wanting to miss anything—and we didn't. We combed the showrooms and shops of Paris, buying anything that pleased us. Henry was happy to indulge my love of clothes, and even took a great interest in them himself. I learned that spending money was easy, but that spending money *well* was a refined art. I was an excellent student.

Henry was the warmest and most genial of men and possessed a special charm that naturally made people feel at ease. Hordes of Americans streamed through Paris in the early sixties, and it seemed as if most of them found their way to our door at one time or another. Indeed, it was joked that swarms of small boys met incoming trains and sold our address to homesick-looking Americans. There were writers, painters, senators, newspapermen, racing stable owners, movie producers, tall Texas girls looking for titled European husbands, the newly married, the newly divorced, people looking for loans—a multifarious assortment, all needing to be looked after. Henry was never known to turn anybody away, and it was left to me to ferret out the worst of the freeloaders, a job I quite liked. I soon gained the reputation of having a wicked mouth and a propensity for deflating overblown egos. Henry and I made a superb team.

I was at home in Paris in a way that I would never be in any other city in the world. This has remained true all my life. Paris never changes. It never disappoints. It is always beautiful, charming, easy, and lighthearted. Today, as then, I can walk on the boulevards or sit in the cafés and give myself up to that delicious trance in which nothing but the sensations of the moment seem to matter. The colors, the scents, the sounds of the city all envelop and comfort me like a delicious warm bath.

Letters flew back and forth across the Atlantic. Also cryptic notes scribbled on the backs of shopping lists; clippings from newspapers; snapshots of Tally; a single word dropped in an envelope; funny sketches from Ivan, cartooning life in the country; antique postcards; a pressed flower; joke presents. Within the year there was a notice of Ivan's show at the Selby Gallery and subsequent clips of his reviews, all of which were splendid.

One September evening I was sitting alone at Café Lipp, waiting for Henry, who had gone on his own to the opera, when I recognized a familiar figure weaving across the crowded floor.

"Maisie. Dear, sweet, Maisie," her voice brayed, and her extensive feather boa trailed across the small tables, in and out of drinks and ashtrays. She took no notice. It was Millicent Selby.

"Millicent! Whatever are you doing in Paris?" She swooped down into the chair opposite me and blew a dozen little kisses vaguely in my direction.

"Darling, I've come for good. I had to leave America. Simply pack up and leave. What else could I do? It was awful. I couldn't stay on in New York. Not with that beastly man in the same city." She lit a violet-colored cigarette, inhaled deeply, and blew the smoke out of her nostrils. She was wearing an oriental pajama costume of an ill-considered hue for which the feather boa did nothing at all. With her lips painted a brilliant red and the smoke issuing from her nose, she looked like a Chinese dragon. I had no idea what she was talking about, but I imagined it was about a man and yet another difficult love affair.

"Well," I said sympathetically, "Paris is a great city for getting over a broken heart."

"Oh?" Millicent's voice dipped a few octaves. "Are you heartbroken?"

"No. I thought you were."

"God, no. Far from it." She peered around the room. "My heart throbs with a new passion. He's here somewhere. A darling young man. And so talented."

"Then what were you saying? I mean about leaving New York?"

"Tut, my dear. You mean to say you haven't heard? You haven't heard of the treachery that was done to me. You don't know of my *crise?*" Millicent's voice never failed to stun people. It was rather like a brass band suddenly striking up the national anthem. It roared and punctuated itself with hoots and barks. I felt myself turn crimson as people in the café stared at us. But my curiosity was whetted. I shook my head and acknowledged my ignorance.

"Then I will tell you everything," she declared. "But first I want a drink. Shall we have a bottle of absinthe?"

"Absinthe is illegal. How about Pernod?" She bowed to my suggestion and in due time the waiter placed a bottle and a tall siphon of soda water in front of us. Millicent batted her false eyelashes at him while he prepared her drink.

"Ah, Paris," she said drinking deeply from her glass. "I feel so safe here. So far from the pursuit of tricksters and con men. But sad. So very sad for the evil that was done me. You were smart. You saw him for what he was and left town, left the country. Oh, when I think of how trusting I was, how generous, how—"

"Millicent," I said, "who are we talking about?"

"Julian Slade, that's who. My all-too-recent partner."

"Are you telling me that you and Julian aren't partners anymore? What happened? Have you closed the gallery?"

"Closed! I wish I'd burned it down! No, the gallery is there, but I am . . . here." She extracted a lace handkerchief from the folds of her bosom and blew her nose into it. "You know, Maisie, I was never happy about taking Julian on as a partner. Oh, I know what everyone said, that I needed him, that I didn't have a head for business, that I was too much 'involved' with my artists. Well, perhaps they were right, but so what! I love art and artists! Not business and everything reduced to a lot of little numbers on a ledger sheet! I was having a ball, and I was never in it for the money anyway. You know, I don't think I would have minded all that much if my gallery had gone under or failed or whatever all my well-meaning friends warned me about, but what I don't seem to be able to stand," and here two large tears plowed heroically through the heavy rouge and makeup, "was being booted out!"

Feeling sorry for Millicent was not easy. She was simply not the kind of woman who appealed to one's sympathy, and I confess I was more intrigued with the facts of her story than its sentiment. I waited a moment for her to collect herself.

"God, Millicent. How awful for you! And, what do you mean, booted out? I thought you and Julian were equal partners."

"Equal? I found him quite inferior, if you must know. But that's not what you mean. Yes, we were equal partners as far as making decisions went. On paper I owned more shares than he did, but then there were the silent partners." On the word "silent," Millicent's voice pierced the room. "Pantywaists, all of them. Greedy turncoats. They saw a good thing and they sold out. Julian offered them a bundle for their shares, and we all knew the gallery was not known for its profits. Oh God, money. I hate the word."

"You mean you didn't get any?"

"Oh, I got money, all right. Julian's offer was disgustingly generous. But I had no choice in the matter. It was take it and go. A one-way street for me. He got everything. He owns it all. And the worst of it, Maisie," she yelped, "was that he didn't even have the decency to release some cock-and-bull story about my 'early retirement' up and down the street. Everyone knows I was shut out of my own business."

Well, that was a piece of news. I wondered how Julian had managed to get his hands on what sounded like a fair amount of money, but Millicent didn't know.

"Julian came into some money, I think. I don't know. The man's an enigma as far as I'm concerned. Oh, the gallery is doing well enough. Julian's loaded it down with all these Pop artists. Frankly, Maisie, I don't know what's to become of art. God. The things he hung on my walls. Art is in the gutter as far as I'm concerned. In fact, we *exhibited* a gutter. I mean it. A gutter was constructed in my lovely space, complete with authentic trash and filth from the street. Oh, my dear, you have no idea how I've suffered."

At that moment a slender young man with thick black hair, dark eyes, and olive skin that revealed his Italian origins came up to our table and laid a possessive hand on Millicent's shoulder. Millicent's eyes devoured him and she batted her lashes in a grotesque parody of a young girl. Then she turned back to me. "Here is my new discovery. Such vision, my dear. And sooooo intense! He paints lovely clouds in the bluest skies imaginable. Such skilled hands . . ." I could see in an instant that Millicent was no longer suffering.

I tried to find out from her how Ivan was faring, but she was no longer interested in the artists back in New York.

"He doesn't sell, darling," she told me placidly. "He creates beautiful things. Therefore he doesn't sell. If they were ugly, maybe . . . or if he made giant plastic hamburgers instead of reclining nudes. They want neon, darling, and crushed beer cans. No one wants beauty anymore. No one"—she patted her young man's hand—"except me."

I lost no time in shooting a letter to Springs. "I heard the most extraordinary story from Millicent Selby," I wrote, and I asked what they could add to her garbled version of the death of the Selby-Slade partnership. The return letter left no doubts as to where the St. Peterses stood.

"I can't think that Millicent understood even remotely how generously Julian treated her," Emma wrote. "Ivan says she is a ridiculous woman and that Julian was quite right to 'boot her out,' as she says. Julian is doing very well for himself and has renamed the gallery Slade International. Don't you think it grand? Ivan's show, though a success, has not brought in many sales, but Julian has high hopes and so do we. It's only a matter of time . . ."

Clearly they were very much on Julian's side. I gave the whole incident no further thought.

Indeed, I was preoccupied with Henry, whose health of late had not been good. As a boy he had suffered from tuberculosis. The disease was threatening him again. We went to Switzerland for treatments.

I loved Switzerland as I had loved Paris, though for entirely different reasons. We were high in the Alps. It was beautiful and the people were lovely. We took up hiking and spent hours of every day alone in the clean mountain air. It worked wonders for Henry.

By our fifth year together, he was recovered enough to travel again. We decided to go back to America.

I n the days before the Expressway was extended, it could take as long as four hours to drive from New York City to Springs, on the end of Long Island. Of course, it can take as long or longer today, but for different and less pleasant reasons. That June day when Henry and I drove out to see Emma and Ivan, we passed through endless small towns, stopping to buy ice cream cones in Smithtown, duck livers at the Big Duck in Riverhead, and freshly picked strawberries from a little stand in Sagaponack. We were charmed by the rural landscape, surrounded on every side by sparkling blue waters of ocean, bays, and inlets.

Henry asked me if I had ever been out here before, and I told him about the time . . . oh, how it all came rolling back over me. It was 1956. We had been at the Cedar Bar one hot August night. Not many people were there. Anyone with any sense had gotten himself out of town by hook or by crook—for the month, if at all possible—but Dance, who must have had hundreds of such invitations, was in town with us. He was perverse about things like hot summer nights and had elected to wear a tie, a Panama hat, his white linen suit, and black patent shoes. He was drinking bourbon, though both Ivan and I had been reduced by the heat to iced Cokes. We were at the bar, it was about ten at night, and for once no one had much to say. Just then the door swung open and someone, I can't remember who, walked in. He stood there for the longest time until everyone felt his presence and then he said, "Jackson Pollock is dead. Dead in a car crash in Springs." We were stunned. It didn't seem possible. No one knew what to say or to do. No one except Dance. He walked out onto the street and hailed a cab. Then he got Ivan and me, and damned if he didn't talk that cabbie into driving us all the way out Long Island to Springs. When we got there, we drove the same road Pollock had driven only hours earlier. We saw police barricades. We saw the car overturned in a small clump of trees. On down the road, we saw people gathered in Pollock's house. But we hadn't come to gawk. We had come because Jackson Pollock was an artist and a great one. We had come to be near. We had come because we could do nothing else. Dance instructed the cabbie, who was really kind of a swell fellow, to drive us up and down these dark country roads until finally we came to the end of a small peninsula not far from Pollock's house. I remember we got out of the taxi and walked down on the beach. The sky was freckled with stars. The moon disappeared as an occasional cloud scudded by. It was heavenly. I mean really like heaven. No one said much. We just stood there letting the magnitude of the sky envelop our feelings, and then Dance picked up a rock and threw it into the glassy water. "There is no difference between life and art," he said finally. I don't know how long we stood there, but when we drove back by Pollock's house it was dark and quiet. We got back to New York while the sky was turning a pale gray.

"Dance wrote a poem about that night," I told Henry. "He called it 'Fatal Paradise.'" There were tears in my voice and Henry reached over and patted my hand. "I guess I'm feeling a little emotional about seeing everyone again," I said, rolling down my window to smell the sea air.

"Of course you are. It's been a long time. It's one of the things I love about you most. You have an enormous capacity for people. You care about them so much. That's a rare commodity, darling."

I nodded, but my thoughts were churning. I wondered if we would all like each other as much, now that our lives had taken such separate paths. Letters were one thing, but after all this time, surely they had changed. Surely I had changed. God, I thought, what if we run out of things to talk about?

The highway had narrowed to local roads as we passed through the famous resort towns of Southampton, Bridgehampton, and East Hampton. Between the towns were open fields and farmland where row upon row of potato plants ran to the white dunes and the sea. It was late afternoon and the sun bathed the sky and land in a soft golden light.

At East Hampton we took a left fork by an old windmill and followed the signs pointing to the hamlet of Springs.

"Okay, now. Slow down just here, I think," I said, reading to Henry from a scrap of paper. 'Go past the country store and turn right on the first dirt road with a blue mailbox in front.' I see it!" We drove up a bumpy winding lane for almost a quarter of a mile. The late-afternoon air was heavy with the perfume of honeysuckle and briar roses. Finally we came out into a clearing and pulled up to a weathered gray farmhouse with a big front porch.

"Oh, look, Henry. It's them. Stop. It's Emma and Tally!" If I had had any doubts about how we would take to one another again, they vanished in a split second. I jumped from the car. "Emma, Emma. I can't believe I'm finally here. And Tally. Is that really you? My baby girl, all grown up?" I hugged first one and then the other and then both at the same time. We were laughing and crying and talking all at once.

Emma looked marvelous. Her amber-colored hair hung down her back in one thick, long plait. Her skin had a warm peachy glow and she sparkled with happiness and vitality. I couldn't help staring at Emma's costume. She was wearing a flowered peasant skirt and a man's white T-shirt knotted at the waist. On top of that was an army jacket faded to a pale jungle green and on her feet, those beautiful, long, elegant feet were heavy lumberjack boots. On anyone else it would have looked hideous, but Emma still managed to looked elegant and chic. Dance had once described Emma as an example of American aristocracy. "It's all in the bones," he said. "Long, slender, and very fine, like a purebred Borzoi." I hadn't wanted to hear it then, but looking at her now, I knew exactly what he meant.

"I don't know how you do it, Emma," I told her. "Here I am, turned out in Vogue's best version of the well-dressed woman on a country weekend. My shoes are Gucci, my scarf is Hermès, my trousers are St. Laurent, and my sweater was handknit by a little old lady in Scotland. And I look like a frump next to you. And here you are . . ."

"Dressed like a farm girl." Emma grinned. "And it's all thanks to Elvis and Agway."

I looked at her in bewilderment. "Darling, I've been out of the country for five years. Whatever are you talking about?"

"Elvis is where I shop for haute couture. It's the thrift shop run by the Ladies' Village Improvement Society—LVIS . . ."

"Get it?" little Tally chimed in. "It's just like Elvis Presley. I got my overalls there. We go every Saturday." Tally was six years old. She was tall, skinny, and shockingly pretty. Who could expect otherwise? She had inherited Ivan's blue eyes, but her hair and complexion were all Emma. Perhaps the most startling thing about her was her precocious charm and composure. She was the first to acknowledge that Henry had remained standing unintroduced and ignored by me and Emma.

"You must be Uncle Henry," she said. "I recognize you from the pictures Aunt Maisie sent. Would you like to see my baby goats?" With that, she put her small hand in his and led him off to a ramshackle barnyard. I could tell Henry was enchanted. He adored children and I knew that Tally would have him wound around her little finger in no time at all.

"Evidently," I said, "living in the country agrees with you. Tally is a beauty and you look spectacular, with or without Elvis. I've brought her some clothes from Paris. Do you think she'll be disappointed? Most children hate to get clothes."

"She'll be beside herself. She already is. She thinks you're her fairy godmother and I think you are, too." Emma stopped and hugged me again. "I'm so happy you're here. He's charming, your Henry. So attractive."

"Well, I couldn't let you be the only girl on the block with a handsome husband. How is our Russian bear, anyway? Has the great outdoors changed him?"

"I don't know. In some way he hasn't changed at all. He disappears into his studio and works like a demon, but now he also works outdoors —in the garden, chopping wood. His energy is incredible . . . but it always was. I need my eight hours of sleep every night or I'm a mess. But Ivan . . . if he sleeps three or four hours it's a lot. Sound familiar?"

I nodded. "How is his work going? Is he selling anything?"

"His work is wonderful. You'll see for yourself. That barn over there is his studio. As for sales . . ." She shrugged without finishing her sentence. "In fact, speak of the devil . . ."

At that point Ivan emerged, covered with white plaster dust, looking every bit as gorgeous as I remembered him. Propriety be damned, I thought, and ran into his arms.

"Maisie, Maisie, Maisie." He picked me up and swung me around and around until I begged him to stop. I'd forgotten how big he was and how good it felt to be in his arms. I'd forgotten how it felt to look into his blue, blue eyes and feel myself drowning. I'd forgotten how the world could slip away at times like this and leave me feeling that there was no one in it but Ivan and me. For one tiny moment I was crazy with wanting him, wild with desire. Then I remembered Henry and pulled myself together fast.

"Beautiful, wonderful Maisie. You are here at last." Ivan's voice was happy and untroubled by the turmoil in my eyes. "We have not been happy one day since we don't have you. And where is the man who has stolen you away from us for so long?"

"He's been spirited off by your daughter," I said when I had caught my breath. "But there they are now. Come and meet my catch."

A half hour later we were settled on the porch, drinking the burgundy we had brought from France. The sun was low and the view was splendid. The land dipped away from the high ground of the farm to an unspoiled inlet of clear blue water bordered by luxurious stretches of green sea grass. Everything was still except for a few ducks flying in low to their nests. It was beautiful.

Years later I heard someone at a party talking about the artists in the Hamptons. She was spouting a theory that the realist painters all lived by the ocean because of the views and landscapes, and that the Abstract Expressionists had moved to Springs because of the light. I thought this was a lot of baloney. They moved to Springs because it was cheaper, I said. But I learned later, from a talk I had with a painter, that there is something special about the light in Springs. It turns out that there is something that happens to light when the land is surrounded by water on several sides. And in Springs the water is everywhere.

"That's Accabonac Harbor," Emma said. "The community of Springs is more or less centered around the harbor, and the local people, the fishermen and farmers, call themselves Bonakers. A lot of them are descended from families that settled here three hundred years ago. There are clams and scallops by the bushel in those waters, free for the picking."

"You don't mean you actually wade out there and collect clams!"

"Oh yes. We practically lived on clams the first year we were out here. Now I have a garden and we even keep chickens out behind Ivan's studio." She sipped her drink and let her head fall back with pleasure. "Mmmmmm . . . this truly is fantastic. Vintage wine is not high on our list of staples, as you might imagine."

"But what does that matter," Ivan said, "when we can call this land our own? Everything you see"—he waved his arm in an expansive circle —"is ours. Forty acres."

"Forty!" I exclaimed. It seemed like a awful lot of land.

"I put every penny I had and borrowed more to get it," Ivan said proudly. "I have passion for the land. It flows in my blood. We have been lucky, yes, my darling?" Ivan had his arm around Emma's waist. She had dropped her head onto his shoulder and was looking up at him. Then a very amazing thing happened. They exchanged a look of such intimacy, such intense connectedness, that to this day, when I recall it, I get goose bumps. It only lasted a second, but the impression it made has lasted all my life.

"Look," I said, "we want to take you out to dinner tonight. But before that, I want to look around. I want to see the house, the garden, the baby goats, the works." Tally looked at me approvingly. "Ivan," I said, "Henry is too shy to ask, but he is dying to see your work and the studio. Why don't you two get lost for a while? I want to gossip with Emma and Tally all by myself."

"Maisie is so subtle, isn't she?" Henry said, as he and Ivan went off together to the barn.

"Okay, girls," I said. "Let's dish. Isn't my Henry the cutest thing you've ever seen?"

Tally giggled and off we went to look at the barnyard. And a barnyard it was, complete with goats, chickens, and a crazed rooster who kept attacking my shoes. "What on earth do you do with all these chickens?" I asked, wrinkling my nose at the smell and the din. "Do you eat them?" I feared the worst.

"No," said Emma, "that is, hardly ever. We keep them for the eggs." I watched as Tally poked around inside the coop, dislodging crotchety hens from their nests, carefully sliding her slim brown hand underneath the feathery bulk. She found two eggs and handed them to me, smiling shyly.

"Here, Aunt Maisie, feel them. They're still warm from being inside the chicken."

Indeed they were. The eggs had a strange and magical warmth, and I felt a similar warmth spreading through my chest as I watched Tally skipping lightly along the path that led to the vegetable garden. She was a little girl who was truly as remarkable as her parents.

No one felt like eating what they called a fancy dinner, so we had pizza at Ma Bergman's. While we ate, Ivan and Emma spoke of what their life had been like since they'd moved to the country.

"I guess it took us a little while to adjust to the change. I think that first winter was the hardest. Strangely enough, the thing that took us both by surprise was the absolute quiet of those long winter nights. We didn't know anyone at all, and it seemed as though the few people who lived here in the winter all hibernated in their own houses. There was one day in February when we couldn't stand it one more day. Do you remember, Ivan? It was getting on toward evening, and we looked at each other, bundled up Tally, and drove all the way to New York. We went to Chinatown for dinner and then went over to the Cedar. Tally slept with her head in my lap and we hung around until closing time. Then we got back into the car and drove home."

Ivan chuckled. "You remember that morning? We feel wild and crazy from extravagance. We know sun is rising soon, so my driver here went all the way out to Montauk Point. There we are, at the end of the earth, watching a most magnificent sunrise."

"After that," Emma continued, "we settled down. Soon it was spring. Time to start the garden. Our neighbor, Mary, gave me some chicks. Ivan was working night and day. Now we hardly ever go into the city. Only when Julian insists on a command performance."

"Speaking of Julian," I said, "fill me in on his lordship." I meant it as a joke, but Ivan and Emma fell into raptures about how great Julian was. The details were sketchy, but there was no doubt that Julian had risen in the art world. He was doing well enough to be essentially supporting them. They'd made a deal, it seemed. Julian paid for Ivan's materials, for foundry time, for everything he needed to keep working. In addition, he paid them a monthly living allowance. He visited them periodically and took away with him everything Ivan made. Few of them were shown, however, and fewer still (if any) sold. All things considered, it was, as Ivan and Emma both pointed out, an extremely generous arrangement. "It is artist's dream come true," Ivan intoned solemnly. "Julian Slade is our patron saint."

For some reason I felt irritated to hear Julian praised so extravagantly. "But don't you see," I said, "you're being very naïve! When you are recognized for the great artist you are, Ivan, Julian will stand to make a great big fat packet of money selling the sculptures you have sweated blood to create. So it behooves him to be generous now."

"Dearest Maisie." Ivan looked at me like a fond papa. "You are forever our greatest cynic."

As things turned out, of course, I wasn't nearly cynical enough.

28

We stayed the night in Emma and Ivan's tiny guest room. I couldn't fall asleep for a long time because my mind was abuzz with so many new impressions. I wondered what Dance would have thought about this country life. Not much, I guessed. Dance had been a city boy through and through. He needed people, noise, events, activities. I'd asked him once when he ever had time to write. He was never alone, he was never not doing something. "All the time, honeybunch. I write all the time. I write on menus, theater programs, napkins, newspapers, even my shirtsleeves." His had obviously not been a solitary muse. More like a party girl, I thought, leading him from one merry gathering to another, and maybe even to his death. I shuddered and felt my stomach tie itself into the old familiar knots. I hadn't allowed myself to think about Dance in a long time, but seeing Emma and Ivan brought all the memories back. I didn't want to relive the past, though, and so I played a little game in which I pretended that he was still alive.

I pictured him coming out to Springs, carrying provisions from Zabar's or Balducci's. Caviar, smoked salmon, bagels, Brie, rare fruits and vegetables. Delicacies that were to Dance the necessities of survival. He would complain about the country air, the country noises, the lack of elegance and comfort. But he would come, and his visits would always be the high points of the year. In my game I introduced him to Henry, and was pleased to see how well and easily they got along. Then I thought about a strange thing: I imagined all of us as we would be with the passing of time, ten, twenty, thirty years. I watched Tally grow up, saw myself get older, lazier, more set in my ways. I pictured Emma and Ivan looking rather grand and prosperous in their old age. Both wrinkled, gray, distinguished, and still beautiful. But no matter how I tried, I couldn't picture Dance. I couldn't even get him into his forties, much less his sixties. And then I wondered if we had all always known somehow that he'd die young, that somehow he was meant to die young, that he had not been made to endure the changes and ravages of time.

I don't know why I was lying awake thinking these things. Perhaps for the first time in my life I myself was becoming aware of the passing years and the changes they would bring. Certainly seeing Tally so grown up had made a strong impression on me. I couldn't get her out of my mind. The last time I had seen her, she had been a toddler. But now I was fascinated. Tally had grown into a real person with her own definite personality, poise, and charm. Oh, you could see her resemblance to Emma and to Ivan, but what was most striking about her was a quality that was entirely her own. And even at the age of six I couldn't help noticing that of the three of them, there was a way in which she seemed the most grown up. I had an image of Ivan and Emma floating through their lives with their heads in the clouds and their feet not quite touching the ground, and little Tally, just the opposite, very much with her feet on the ground.

I don't mean to suggest that Emma wasn't in control; she was the active heart of that family, the center that held everything together. It was extraordinary to realize how far this girl from Boston's Back Bay had strayed from the life that once seemed her destiny. Instead of managing a household of servants, she did everything that servants would have done for her, and more. Ivan, like every other artist I've known, was ridiculously helpless when it came to dealing with any aspect of life other than his art. He didn't drive a car if he could help it, had no concept of money, and did nothing around the house. He relied on Emma for everything. And within this hubbub of necessity and dependence, Emma flourished. She nurtured Ivan, mothered Tally, raised her own vegetables, milked goats, kept poultry, baked bread, and indulged in what seemed like a hundred and one craft projects. Mind you, she was not what my mother would call a good housekeeper. Their house was, to put it mildly, a pigsty. Dishes piled up in the sink until there were no more clean ones left. Everywhere you looked, there were the beginnings of new projects fighting for space with works in progress. Bread was rising in a bowl, seeds were sprouting in a jar, seedlings were rooting in peat pots, soup was cooking on the stove, beans were soaking in a pot, and on and on. Books, magazines, and newspapers were everywhere, along with crayons, drawing pencils, and sketchpads. Laundry lay about in heaps, some of it waiting to be folded and put away, the rest waiting its turn to be put through the hand-cranked washing machine and hung outside to dry. Their living room was dominated by a loom and a quilting frame, and Emma was quite capable of dropping whatever she was doing at any given moment to spend an hour or so at her weaving or quilting. But within this seeming chaos they thrived. Friends were always welcome, and refreshments of one kind or another materialized without visible effort on Emma's part.

"I know we live close to the bone," Emma had told me as I admired her garden, "but I like being self-sufficient. All my life I was pampered and coddled. I was taught to do things, but no one ever expected that I would use that knowledge. I remember my grandmother sent me down to the kitchen one time to see how jams were made. And the reason she did this was so that I would be able to judge whether my own cook, when I had one, was doing it properly. Now Tally and I gather our own berries and make our own jams. Now I work hard from early morning until late at night to feed my family and to make a comfortable home, and I've never felt so good."

If I harbored any doubts about the truth of what she said, I had only to remember the way that Emma and Ivan looked at each other. I must have let out quite a sigh because I woke up Henry.

"Is all this turning out to be difficult for you?" he asked in his most tactful and concerned manner.

"Not at all, darling. Not at all in the way you think," I told him almost truthfully. He knew, of course, all about my past history with Ivan, and I knew he was imagining the worst. "It's wonderful to see Ivan again, but I wouldn't want to be married to him for anything in the world. In fact, I wouldn't want to be married to anyone but you. Actually, I was thinking about Emma—half admiring her and half feeling sorry for her. She carries a very heavy load on her narrow, fine-boned shoulders."

Henry was busy kissing my neck, wanting, I could see, more tangible proof that I wasn't longing to be in Ivan's bed. "Oh, I don't know," he muttered, between little kisses. "I'd say she looked the picture of a happy woman."

I wasn't listening. "She's happy, but can't you see how everything depends on her? Ivan doesn't know what a saint he has in her. He doesn't even begin to appreciate her."

Henry disagreed. "Don't you see, darling, happiness doesn't come in uniform packages. Ivan is a great artist and Emma is a bit of a saint, but they seem to have found their own particular brand of happiness, and that's more than you can say about most people." He had gone past my neck, and the kisses were heading in a southerly direction.

"Except us?"

"Except us." Then, just before I found it impossible to go on talking, I said, "The only thing that worries me is that a lot of saints end up being martyred or crucified."

29

When we got back to New York, I lost no time in finding my way to the new Slade International Gallery. I was curious to see Julian, and damned curious to find out what he was doing about Ivan. Julian very rarely showed Ivan's works in the gallery, and sales were, as far as I could ascertain, nonexistent. Yet he supported them and encouraged Ivan in every way. "Like a kept woman," I said to Henry as I got dressed that morning. But surely Julian had a plan. It seemed unlikely that he would keep on supporting them if he didn't.

Except for the name, nothing had changed in Millicent's town house. It was still as elegant and inviting as it had always been. Once again, I was struck by what the buy-out must have cost Julian. All else aside, the property alone must have been worth close to a million.

There was a new, younger, and prettier version of myself bustling about the main exhibit room. She was tall, thin, Southern, and surely an enthusiastic graduate of Finch College. I wondered if she and Julian were romantically linked, and it occurred to me that of all the things Emma and Ivan had told me about Julian, nothing had been said about his love life.

The room was bare, and I assumed that the gallery was between shows. I was wrong. "Mr. Slade will be down in a moment," the cool beauty said. "In the meantime, would you care to read about our current exhibit and the artist?" I was handed a bio sheet and a rather slick brochure, which featured a pale gray photo of a piece of rope. The show was titled "Optension."

"Sure," I said gamely, peering around the empty room. "I take it there's an exhibit here?"

Her features tightened to show disapproval and she answered with a curt "Of course."

"Oh, good. What fun. No, no, don't show me. I'm just going to stand here until I see it." I started turning slowly in place. The walls were gray. The rug was gray. The light was pale and diffuse. "I'm sure it's here somewhere." I completed my circle. "Okay. It's too clever for me. I give up." I looked over at the girl, but Julian had materialized in her place. He was himself a study in gray—flannel, that is—and exactly as I remembered him. Smart, precise, confident, smiling Julian.

"Maisie," he exclaimed, taking my hands in his and looking quite pleased to see me. "I heard you were in town. And don't you look grand."

"Grand? I look better than grand, buster. I look rich," I said, fluttering my finery at him. I had pulled out the stops getting dressed that morning—the fur coat, the diamonds, the Dior suit—I reeked of wealth and Joy. "I wore all this to impress you. The last time you saw me I was limping out of town on a wing and prayer."

"And, lucky you, your prayers were answered. Emma has kept me fully abreast of your good fortune. I hope you don't spend all your money on baubles. Surely a little art here and there?"

"Well, not if I can't see it! What the hell is going on here, Julian? Is this some kind of joke, because if it is, it's actually rather funny."

Julian smiled. "You should know by now that I never joke about art."

"How true, how true," I agreed. "So? What gives? Is *she* it? Or is *it* she?" I gestured in the direction of young Miss Finch, who looked not at all amused.

Julian led me to the far wall. "He's a very interesting young artist I discovered not long ago. You see, anchored here in the corner is a tension wire. Now let your eyes follow it up and across the full length of the wall to the next corner. See how it's slightly off the mark? You see now how the normal dimensions of the room are refocused? It's quite brilliant, really. He's completely redefined the space we're in. He deliberately mocks our perceptions of space. Throws us off balance. Sets us spinning in the void. Once you get the feel of it, it's very unsettling. Very profound."

"Profound! Bullshit, Julian. God, I *have* been away for a long time. In Paris they're still showing pictures."

"Paris is behind the times. New York is the center of the art world now. And this"—he gestured to the empty space—"is what's happening. This and everything else I show."

"Gosh. Well, then, so much for Paris. Tell me, Julian, how's your gut?"

"My what?"

"I remember a certain little speech you delivered one cold evening at the Cedar about art and what it meant to you, and you said if it didn't grab you in the gut, then it wasn't art. So, I'm asking, does this grab you in the gut?"

Julian laughed. "Maisie, you haven't changed a bit. Still as outspoken as ever. To answer your question, I'll say yes. Everything that's happening these days grabs me and I grab it. Things have changed, Maisie. To stay alive in this business, you move fast and don't ask too many questions. Anybody who wants depth is going to lose fingers and toes."

"My God, you really are serious."

"I take anything that sells seriously. And it does sell. I make it sell. What I show, what I promote, what I endorse, that's what people will buy. At least that's what I'm working for."

"Ah. Now we're getting onto a topic I'd like to talk about. Why doesn't this magic formula work for Ivan? I would have thought you would have made his name and fortune by now. Why isn't he being touted around here instead of this—this glorified clothesline?"

"Maisie," Julian beamed, "you need a drink. Let's go to lunch."

I agreed and the luncheon was quickly arranged by Miss Finch at La Côte Basque. "Coals to Newcastle for you, isn't it, Maisie?" Julian was buoyant as we were led to our seats a short while later. "But I find that if I'm going to eat at all, I must have the best. Otherwise"—he shrugged—"what's the point?"

"Well, it's a long way from cabbage soup on Hudson Street, I'll give it that," I said, taking in the elegant room. You could smell the money, power, and style in this room. Lunching at La Côte Basque was definitely a see-and-be-seen experience, and of course Julian was very much at home, nodding and smiling to any number of people. It wasn't until a remarkably fine bottle of champagne had been delivered to our table and Julian had ordered for both of us that he returned to the topic that was uppermost on my mind.

"So, tell me, how do you find Ivan and Emma? It seems to me that you are not entirely pleased with their circumstances."

"No," I agreed. "Frankly, I find their 'circumstances,' as you put it, appalling."

"Why? They don't want for anything. They would tell me if they did."

"And you would send them more money?"

"Of course, within reason."

"That's what I find appalling. You give them a certain amount of comfort and security and then you warehouse Ivan's work. No one sees it. No one buys it. You're destroying his soul."

"Believe me, I have Ivan's best interests at heart, and though you might not know it, I work as hard for Ivan as I do for my other artists. However, it is not Ivan's time yet. When it is, he'll know it, you'll know it, the whole world will know it. But at this stage of the game, the artist is the least important player of all. I know it sounds self-serving, but what's important is the reputation of the gallery."

I settled back in my chair and lit a cigarette.

"You know, Maisie dear, I am blessed with a remarkable discipline." I found myself staring at Julian's hands. I don't know why I had never noticed them before. They were beautiful and very feminine— smooth, pale, carefully manicured, and disconcertingly clean. "How easy it would have been for me to rush about trying to find buyers for Ivan's work years ago. But how very foolish. I would have been lucky to find even a small handful. Ivan is very much out of the mainstream just now." Julian shrugged. "Oh, I could give him another show. A prestige show. And people would come and praise his work and still we would have to sell for embarrassingly low prices. It would be an insult. And very counterproductive. Every sale at the wrong price is worse than no sale at all."

"But his work is so beautiful . . ."

"Of course it is. But there is no market for it. The public, the art-buying public, wants big, bold, brash images that say something blatant to them. The art market today has no place for anything that Ivan produces. Today's art world is not about artists and their spiritual quests, it's not about beauty, it's not about esoteric questions and academic theories. Art today is about instant gratification. It has to have shock value and it has to be instantly recognizable."

"That sounds disgusting."

"Perhaps. But that's the way it is. You have no idea how much money I've made last year and how much money I intend to make this year. That money is power, and it's going to put me on top. In a few more years I'll have the following and the clout to sell anything to anybody. That's when Ivan will come into his own."

"I don't believe this, Julian. Ivan isn't a trend. He isn't a fad. 'Not this year, guy, but next year. In the meantime, keep 'em coming.' Christ! He's out there working like the devil to produce for you, and you just keep stashing it away somewhere. You ought to know as well as anyone that an artist needs to have his work seen. In a way he was better off in the days when he was starving but showing his stuff at our little co-op gallery."

"That's a thoroughly unrealistic and stupidly romantic notion, Maisie dear. I hate the idea that artists can only be inspired if they're starving to death. *La vie boheme* is colorful only on the stage. Frankly, I don't see that Ivan has anything to complain about. He has enough to live on and to work. He doesn't want more."

I shook my head. "Yeah, and why buy the golden eggs when you can buy the goose that lays them? Frankly, Julian, all this is giving me a headache. Arguing with you about anything has always given me a headache. I still think that what Ivan needs is a sale. A big sale. I don't care what you say—or what he says, for that matter—no one can work in a vacuum. He needs some validation from the outside world. Fortunately, I'm now in a position where I can actually do something about that." I paused to let this fact sink in. For the first time through the entire lunch I had his complete attention. "I want to buy something. But I don't want them to know about it. That's very important. In fact, you needn't even tell him for a few months that a piece has been sold. He might suspect. But now I want to see everything you've got. Will you show me?"

"Music to a dealer's ears," Julian said, grinning. But I thought I detected a note of irritation in his voice.

We went to the warehouse that very afternoon. I could have wept. Hundreds of pieces shrouded in dropcloths, boarded up in crates, wrapped in plastic. But one piece above all others caught my eye. It was the one Ivan had worked on when Emma was pregnant, and was aptly called *Mother with Child*.

"Look at this, Julian. It's so beautiful and earthy and strong."

"Yes, it is." We were silent a moment. As always, there was something about Ivan's work that stunned. "He takes a common subject and transforms it so that we see an eternal truth. I think this is among his finest works. Is this the one you want?"

"Yes. How much?"

"Five thousand."

"Make it ten."

He was quiet a minute, then he said, "All right, Maisie. Sold to the highest bidder." But there was something in his voice I couldn't read. I started to say something, but Julian was all business. In almost no time, checks were signed, papers sealed, and delivery schedules set.

"Now," he said at last, "since our business is completed, I've been thinking—you like theater, don't you? Good. I want you to meet me tonight at a little place I know down on Park Avenue South and Seventeenth Street. Here's the address. I'll be there about ten-ish. All right?"

"That's a little late for a play, isn't it?"

"No. For this one, it's a little early." He winked and gave me a quick peck on the cheek. "Lovely to have you back among us, Maisie dear. But it's time to brush those Parisian cobwebs off."

30

The address Julian gave me led me to a place called Max's Kansas City. To say that this was a restaurant was like calling a Roman orgy a buffet dinner. What I saw as I sat at the bar was a kaleidoscope of simultaneous scenes so bizarre that I wondered about the contents of my drink. A neon sculpture they called *Bucket o' Blood* bathed the room in a pink and green tint. Outside, a crowd halfway around the block was trying to get in. Inside, it was like another planet. The bartenders were gay, the waitresses so beautiful you could cry. Artists mingled with movie stars, fashion designers, photographers, socialites, and uptown Madison Avenue. I saw Andy Warhol drift by, looking haunted and sickly pale. Behind him, Zero Mostel was doing a comedy routine for a table full of black-leather-jacketed hoodlums and their long-legged women, who wore white makeup and skirts cut off at the panty line. I saw lots of big names, such as Henry Ford and Julie Christie and Steve McQueen and Roger Vadim and Bobby Kennedy.

There was no lack of famous faces, but Max's was clearly an artists' hangout. Art hung on the walls and from the walls. Art was the biggest, splashiest, craziest scene in New York, and I was beginning to see what Julian was talking about. We were only five blocks uptown from the old Cedar Bar, but everything had turned upside down. The assumptions were all different, the passions had relocated, and the avant-garde was no longer an isolated few hiding out in the dark scruffy bars of Greenwich Village. It was in the fast track. It was the hot ticket. It was the stuff of business deals, fashion trends, and celebrity. The sixties were in full sizzle at Max's.

I saw a limousine pull up outside. Julian emerged and walked in. I was impressed. He was very visible. He knew everyone. He walked slowly along the length of the bar, looking from side to side, taking it all in, like a spy decoding a cryptic message.

He saw me and waved, and I waved back and I could feel the energy shift to me. So she *is* somebody, after all, it seemed to say. On Julian's arm hung quite the prettiest girl I think I have ever seen, and it took me rather by surprise. As they approached the bar I was even more surprised to see how young she was. Despite the makeup and the slinky dress, she looked like a little girl playing dress-up. Introductions revealed nothing, and as my energy levels were flagging, I thanked Julian for the remarkable show he had led me to and made my excuses to leave. He nodded. "It takes a bit of getting used to." Taking hold of the girl's arm once more, he steered her to a crowded table where he was hailed by one and all.

Right before I left, I heard this conversation at the bar. A Madison Avenue type was describing with great enthusiasm an uptown exhibit he had just seen. The gist of it was that the artist did something called "clean slates," which meant he painted all his canvases a certain uniform shade of blue. "Bullshit," said his companion. "I'm already doing that. I paint apartments for a living." I could have kissed him. In fact, I did.

That summer was a frenzied time—perhaps rightly so, because the times were about to change quite drastically. Henry and I took a wonderful house in East Hampton. It was at the end of a lane off Town Pond, with a backyard that overlooked Hook Pond. In the distance we could see a strip of dune and, beyond that, the ocean. It wasn't a fancy house, but it was pretty and very comfortable. The rooms were big, with lots of light, and there were porches on every side. It was the kind of house one was happy to be in at every season and in every weather—it was cool in the heat of summer and warm and cozy on a blustery winter afternoon. Of course, it had that million-dollar view. The corresponding million-dollar price tag had in no way dampened Henry's enthusiasm. His recent bout with poor health had only made him believe more strongly that we should live every moment to its fullest. To Henry this meant that only the best would do. To me this meant that he was well on his way to recovery, and I was happy to indulge him in every way.

In some ways the scene at Max's seemed to have transported itself to the Hamptons. Everywhere it was crawling with artists, writers, celebrities, and voguish "beautiful people." There were so many that nobody could keep track, and it became the "in" thing not to recognize anyone. Indeed, people would brag about mistaking Warren Beatty for a waiter, or about going to a party and not realizing until the end that they were at the wrong one.

We flung open our doors to any and all, and when the house was full, people actually camped on the lawn. The weekends were long and boozy, filled with rambunctious comings and goings. It was all very gay and silly and exhausting. And as the summer wore on, Henry and I found ourselves escaping more and more often to the St. Peterses farm, where things were quieter but no less hospitable.

Often we drove or walked out to the rocks at Gerard Point or Barnes Landing to pick mussels, or sailed around in Three Mile Harbor, pulling in at deserted beaches to pick up oysters. On early August mornings I'd get Tally and we'd go over to Louse Point and fish for snappers—baby bluefish the size of small trout—which we brought home, cleaned, and cooked for breakfast. In September we went gleaning the potato fields, picking up potatoes the machines had left behind. They were the size of marbles and the most delicious things imaginable. We felt as though we were living in the Garden of Eden.

We spent long idle days on the beach, bringing along lunches and dinners that we cooked over an open fire. Ivan made sand sculptures for Tally, and we spent hours under his tutelage, building elaborate castles or molding gigantic human shapes, only to watch them be erased by an incoming tide.

"Listen to this," I chortled, reading the paper to Henry one morning over coffee. " 'Julian Slade, the art dealer with the nose for the new, is making quite a splash with Southampton's ritziest hostesses. This season you're nowhere without a bona fide artist gracing your lawn, and the Slade stable has got the jet set all agog.' God. I don't know whether to applaud or throw up."

It was true. Julian's splash in Southampton brought him often to the farm. He started showing up with his fashionable entourage, a crew of ladies with names like KayKay and CeeCee and Suzy, women who exclaimed, "How charming. How quaint. How clever," when what they really meant was "How do you stand it?" Julian was all smiles. While the ladies looked at Ivan's work, Julian showered Emma with small, tasteful, and entirely inappropriate presents, which she begged him not to do; and he brought expensive presents for Tally, which delighted the child. For Ivan, Julian doled out more allowance and urged him to "keep up the work." Then he started inviting them to parties, insisting that they come. Ivan and Emma almost never went out. Only rarely did they come even to our house. They were happiest when left alone, so I knew it was difficult for them to haul themselves over to Southampton, where they were treated like curiosities. Emma would come back from these ventures with a quiet, slightly sad expression. Ivan would get on his bicycle and disappear for hours.

He called it "night riding," and one time I persuaded him to let me go with him. It was an experience I will never forget. We rode old, thick-wheeled black bicycles, the kind you see peasant women in France pedaling to market. It was a clear, warm, starry night and there was an absence of automobile traffic that I don't think we'll ever see again. Along pitch-dark roads we pedaled, out into the wide and fragrant night, under the stars, moving slowly, steadily, in unison and in silence. I discovered the wonderful charm of night, night away from houses, night moving by pastures and farms, down marshland roads edged with tall cattails, where the urgent call of the crickets and peepers propelled us on. Night riding was not about cycling but about flying, and I could see why it meant so much to Ivan. In the dark the wheels of the bikes vanished. As we coasted by the still waters of the ponds and bays with the stars reflecting up, the sensation was of leaving the earth, of lifting up into the infinite night sky.

I tried to talk to Ivan about Julian, but he had nothing to say. So the next morning I cornered Emma.

"Why do you let Julian order your life about like this? He's not your guardian. He's Ivan's dealer. And by God he should be doing more for him than making him kowtow to a bunch of sun-baked old biddies."

"Oh, Maisie," Emma sighed. "It's not that. Julian is doing everything possible for Ivan. I know he is. And these contacts are just what Ivan needs. These are the people who buy art. These are the people to endow wings in museums and sit on committees to decide what will be bought for them. You're impatient. I admit, I am too, sometimes. Not for myself, but for Ivan. He needs the outside world. He needs recognition. I look at some of these artists people are talking about, and I get very angry. Especially when I have to watch everyone fainting over some neon and Plexiglas thing that looks like it was thrown together in the dark. I've talked to Julian. He assures me it's only a matter of time . . ."

I started to say something, but Emma kept on talking. "In fact," she said hopefully, "Julian says he's working on a sale for Ivan now. Nothing sure, mind you, but he thinks he's on to something. Wouldn't it be lovely, Maisie?" Her eyes were brimming with enthusiasm. I could have cried. How I wished my secret deal with Julian really would help.

"Lovely indeed," I said briskly. "But I think you've been at Julian's beck and call too much. What do you say we plan a party for him? Let's show him it isn't all caviar and champagne."

We planned a giant clambake. For days we dug a pit, collected stones, gathered seaweed by the ton. We gathered driftwood, huge stacks of it, because the fire had to be kept going for at least six hours. A clambake, lest anyone try to tell you otherwise, is an enterprise that requires the labors of at least a dozen people, and takes about three days to get organized. Even then there are pitfalls.

Julian arrived with a case of champagne just as we were making the final preparations. We had dug a pit and laid in the rocks and boulders. Then we built up a fire and kept it burning for most of a day, until we had a pit full of coals and ashes, which had to be raked away until we could see the heated stones beneath. The hot stones were covered with wet seaweed and then we added our layers of clams, corn, chicken, and finally lobsters. All this was covered with a tarpaulin and sand. "Now," Ivan announced, "this steams for at least four hours. Let's have a drink." Well, we had been so busy with our labors that we hadn't noticed a bit of drama gathering in the western sky, and no sooner had we poured our drinks than the skies opened up and torrential rains came down. We all repaired to our house, where we played records, danced, and waited for our dinner to steam. At one point someone found a collection of old seventy-eights. We adjusted the record player and sank into the sounds of other eras. Benny Goodman, Harry James and his orchestra, Ruth Etting. We danced to swing, rhumba, fox trot, the cha-cha, and even a Charleston. Then someone put on a tango.

The music throbbed, but we had lost all our dancers to exhaustion, all except Emma and Ivan, who danced again to the passionate music that had played such a crucial part in bringing them together. They had perhaps lost some of the wild abandon of that night at Roseland, yet it was no less sensual and exotic as they moved in perfect, stylized unison, each anticipating the other's mood and desire. As the music ended, they froze in place, profile to profile, the color high on Emma's cheek, the arch of her back yielding up her body to Ivan, his silhouette, stiff and erect, poised above her, and such was the breathless passion of that moment that I thought they might disappear in a burst of smoke. I wasn't the only one captivated by the spectacle. Opposite me, standing by the fire, Julian watched, too. His eyes burned with a painful longing. In a flash it was all too clear to me. He loved her still. He loved her more. He would never love anyone else as he loved her. All summer long I had had this feeling that Julian was up to something. He had come into our little group cloaked ostentatiously in the gleaming trappings of success. The car, the presents, the important people—none of it was to impress Ivan. It was all for Emma. Yet here, with naked passion in her eyes, she danced, testifying for all to see that her love for Ivan was stronger than ever.

Within minutes, Julian made his excuses, and over much protestation, he left. It had stopped raining. When we went to check on the clambake, we discovered that the lobsters had crawled away, the heat had dissipated, and all the food was slightly raw and smelled of seaweed. We ordered out pizzas and called it a night.

The golden summer of '64. I wish I could write about those days exactly the way they were, but I can't. I can't because time has gotten in my way, and with it comes the awful burden of knowledge. I look often at the photographs of us from that summer. There is one snapshot in particular of us on the beach. A Moroccan canopy shades baskets of food, fruits, and breads and a giant wheel of cheese, all spread out on rugs on the sand. Everyone holds up a glass of wine in salute to the camera. Dressed in scanty bikinis or flowing beach robes that billow in the wind, we pose and laugh and embrace one another. Nothing mars our perfect day. But in the distance, far enough away that I can't make out whether he's an acquaintance or a stranger, a tall figure stands on the crest of the dunes, looking down on us. Is he waving a greeting or is it a warning? You see, soon after that picture was taken, life—and death—caught up with our innocent, abandoned celebration, and nothing was ever to be the same again.

31

In August we learned that Emma was three months pregnant. We were having dinner at the St. Peters farm when the news was announced. Now here is a strange thing. I have always found it difficult to rejoice at the announcement of an impending birth. Perhaps it is because I have never been pregnant myself, but I am always filled with a vague fear and foreboding. I don't really know whether I fear that something will go wrong or whether I dread the change itself, but to me those announcements are always a little bit like hearing about someone's death. I suppose also that in Emma and Ivan's case, they seemed to be already stretched as thin in terms of money and security as any two people could be. I guess, deep inside, I felt it was a little irresponsible for them to go about bringing more babies into their rickety household. Still, I do know how to observe the social amenities.

"A baby!" I said. "This is wonderful. When will the blessed event take place?"

"Not until February," Emma laughed. "We just found out a few days ago. I'm so happy. Ivan's already puffing about a son. I'm sure he'll be insufferable until the baby is born."

"You know," I said, "I have the perfect gift for you. I think you all should move into the city and stay in our apartment. I'll send Tally to a good school and you can be nice and close to the doctors, the hospital, everything."

Emma and Ivan looked at each other in a conspiratorial way and then explained that they had decided to reject the impersonal, sterile coldness of a hospital delivery room.

"We are going to give birth at home," Ivan announced proudly.

"You mean Emma is going to give birth at home while you pass out or something even less useful," I replied.

"No, no," they both chimed in. "We're going to study and look for a midwife." I looked around skeptically and thought of bringing a tiny baby into this house in the dead of winter. It struck me full force how comfortable my own life had become, and how much of a cushion I had put between myself and want. I had grown used to comfort and the luxury of service, of first-class conditions and the indulgence of my tastes and fancies. I tried to reason with them, but their minds were made up and there was nothing I could say to dissuade them.

Ivan was pouring glasses of champagne, and just before we were about to toast their impending bundle of joy, there was yet another announcement. "We have much to celebrate tonight," Ivan said, beaming from ear to ear. "Julian has sold a major piece of mine and he has sold it for ten thousand dollars!"

"Ten thousand dollars! I say," said Henry, eyeing me suspiciously, "that *is* cause for celebration. Do you know who bought it?"

"No. I know none of details, but let us hope this is the first of many. Is this not the most wonderful news?"

Indeed it was. I was thrilled. "Just think," I said, "of all the things you can do now. You can fix up this house and run some proper heating in here. Maybe even add on a room for the baby. Does Julian know how perfect his timing is?"

"Oh, Ivan," said Emma. "Let's put a floor in the studio before the winter comes." She turned to me. "Ivan freezes on that cold cement."

"To hell with Ivan. He's Russian. He's supposed to freeze. How about a nice fur coat for you, Emma?"

"Don't be silly. What would I do with a fur coat? But we could use a new roof . . ."

Ivan put his glass down carefully on the table and leaned across to take Emma's hand. "No, no, Dyetka," he said gently. "We don't get money from this. None of it comes to us."

"Well, for God's sake, why not?" I demanded.

"Well, piece belonged to Julian," Ivan said simply. "It was not mine. It was part of the gallery inventory."

"Of course, you're right, darling," Emma quickly agreed. "I was silly to get carried away. Still, this is the most wonderful news."

Ivan patted Emma's hand again and then sat back in his chair. "You remember before Tally was born. We haven't seen Julian in long time, and I think we will never see him again, he was in such pain. We could not help it, but you know it was our fault. But suddenly, there is Julian, come to congratulate us, and we are very happy to see him. He likes this sculpture, is called *Mother with Child*, and he is insisting on buying it. He says don't matter what price."

"What was the price?" I asked, fighting down my growing anger.

Ivan frowned as if trying to remember. "I think maybe price was thousand dollars, but was for friend, so I say five hundred dollars. Julian laugh and laugh. He says, 'This is why you need me, Ivan, to represent you. It would be bargain at ten times the price, but you let me have it for next to nothing. Well, I'm going to buy it from you for the five hundred we agreed on, just to teach you a lesson.' He was so pleased with himself. I never see Julian so happy. But I was happy too." Ivan looked around the table thoughtfully. "And you know, he was right. He has found buyer and sold it for ten times more. Now I call that very clever, don't you?"

I was, needless to say, outraged. Emma looked like a limp rag doll. I glared at Ivan, but what could I say? Julian had sold me the one piece that wasn't going to do anyone but himself any good.

"Well," Ivan continued, because no one else could say anything, "we were glad for money then. We don't complain now. We drink, to Julian." He held up his glass and drank it down in one swallow.

I was ready to spit with rage. I knew if I wasn't careful I was going to say something I'd regret, so I tried to be calm. But cold, hard fury was bubbling up inside me. "Well, excuse me for being so stupid." I couldn't keep the sarcasm out of my voice. "But what the hell are we celebrating here? The fact that Julian has managed to get something from you for nothing, and make himself a tidy ten-thousand-dollar profit? You think Julian is your friend? You think he's got your best interests at heart? It's nothing but chicanery. Julian is *using* you. He's *cheating* you." I turned to Henry, feeling hot tears of indignation in my eyes. "Can this be right? Can Julian get away with this?"

Henry considered the question and then answered slowly, "No, it is probably not right, and yes, he can get away with it because he has done nothing illegal."

"Maisie, Maisie, you don't be so upset," Ivan soothed. "You must not be angry with Julian. Always he looks after us. Anyway," said Ivan, "is not so much money that's important. My work is finding its way into the world. That's important."

"Ivan, you're a goddam fool!" I shouted in frustration, pushing myself away from the table. "You are hopelessly naïve about money and business. You're a big, overgrown baby and you think the whole world is here to pamper you and work their fingers to the bone for you. Well, you had better wake up and take a good look around. And the first thing you ought to look at is the circumstances in which your wife and child are living." I burst into tears and ran from the room and out of the house.

Emma got up quietly and followed me. Outside, she found me sobbing and she put her arms around me and patted my shoulder.

"You are our dearest friend. I know you think Ivan and I are living in a dream world, but you mustn't forget that I've known Julian all my life. He is not a bad person, Maisie. He has to do things his way. Ivan and I trust him, and I know he wouldn't do anything to hurt us. But most of all I know that Ivan is completely unable to deal with money and worldly matters. I remember Dance told me once that Ivan could never be completely in this world because he lives so much in his own world, in his imagination." She held me close. "That is the price of being a great artist, and that, after all, is why I love him. Isn't that why you loved him, Maisie?"

"No," I sniffed, trying to regain my composure. "I just thought he had a great body."

Emma laughed. "That's the Maisie I know." She led me back to the porch and we sat for a few minutes looking out at the stars. "Look at how bright that one is over there," she said, pointing. "I tell Tally she's got a star up in heaven that's just for her. If she's good, her star will shine the brightest one of all. Well, that's your star tonight, Maisie. It's the brightest one in the sky."

Shining star or not, I was going to kill Julian.

"Of course you're angry," he said when I stormed the inner sanctum of Slade International. "Your little subterfuge didn't work. That sort of meddling never will. Now listen to me, Maisie. I have everything under control. I always have and I always will. I know better than you, better than anyone, the right way to handle Ivan's career, present and future."

"Like hell you do. You cheated me and you've cheated them."

"Cheated? Hardly. You got what you wanted. Ivan is thrilled with the sale. I daresay it will be an inspiration to him. Sales always are."

"But they didn't get any money."

"No. But if that's all that's worrying you"—Julian opened his drawer and pulled out a large checkbook—"I'll send them money. I'll send it today. Five thousand dollars? Does that sound right to you?"

I nodded. There was still something that wasn't right about it, but I wasn't exactly sure what. Nevertheless, five thousand dollars wasn't going to do them any harm. I left Julian's office that day, and if I'd had time to think about it I might have realized what was bothering me. The money wasn't earned free and clear. It was still a handout from Julian. But I didn't have time to think. Henry's tuberculosis was troubling him again, and so we were forced to fly back to Switzerland.

32

$\mathcal{E}$mma gave birth the following February. In 1965 the notions of natural childbirth and home birthing were new ones, and those involved considered it a romantic and morally superior thing to do. Ivan and Emma prepared with great attention to detail, insisting on the "natural" way. Every bit of the baby's clothes had been hand-knit or sewn by Emma. Ivan had carved the baby's cradle. It was to be born in the bed it was conceived in, and Ivan himself would cut the cord.

Toward the end of Emma's term, Ivan all but stopped his own work. They read books by the dozen—everything from medical journals to translations of obscure Norwegian midwifery manuals. Emma was confident. She remembered almost nothing of Tally's birth, and that distressed her. "We are creating a new life," Emma wrote in one of her letters to me, "and I want to be conscious of every moment. Nothing is born without pain. I've learned that from watching Ivan create. I will make the pain my ally, not my enemy. We will witness the birth of our son together.

"I know I must sound ridiculous to you, but I'm sure it is a son. I can tell by the way he moves inside me, by the strength of his kicks, by the sheer heft of him."

Her labor pains started early in the morning. Tally was sent to school as usual and came home expecting the new baby to be there. But the cradle was still empty.

"Darling, will you fix dinner for Papa and yourself? Can you make some peanut butter sandwiches the way I taught you? You're a big girl now, and will have to help me take care of Papa and the baby," Emma said.

"Why isn't the baby here, Mama?"

Her mother's worn face and perspiring forehead made Tally feel uneasy. They had said the baby would be here when she got home. Why wasn't it? Why did they have to have a baby anyway? Tally wanted her mother to smile and tell her everything was going to be okay, but Emma was not smiling.

"Honey, I can't explain now, but"—Emma took in a sharp breath —"oh, God, Tally, go now. The baby will be here soon, darling. But Mommy can't talk to you now. You go and see about supper, that's my girl."

Tally felt as though she were nailed to the floor. She couldn't move. She couldn't leave her mother. She waited until Emma's breathing was more normal. She waited until Emma opened her eyes again. "Mama, are you going to die?" she asked, her eyes wide with fear, but her voice as steady as she could make it.

Seeing her daughter's distress, Emma gathered all her strength. She took Tally's little hand into her own. "No, darling, I am not going to die. I promise you. But listen to me, Tally. Having a baby is a very, very hard job. Sometimes it hurts, and the rest of the time it takes all my energy and concentration. That's why I need you to help me by taking care of the house, taking care of Papa. Will you do that, darling? Will you go and be a big girl so I can be proud of you?"

Tally went. But not before she had heard her mother sob, a gasping sort of sob that wasn't nice. It wasn't at all nice.

Ivan never came down to supper, and Tally sat alone and desolate at the kitchen table, ignoring the cold cuts and bread and spooning large dollops of ice cream into her mouth. Her father came down to see about her once, and then hurried back upstairs. She tried to go back into her mother's room after a while, but her father sent her to bed.

The hours passed. Ivan sat by Emma's bed, his voice jovial and strong, encouraging her, holding her hand, mopping her brow. And they waited, talking little, counting, breathing as Emma braced for wave after wave of intense contractions.

She tried to muffle her cries into the pillow so as not to wake Tally, but the pain was intense, more than she had anticipated.

Ivan was fretful. "Enough, darling Emma. I will call doctor."

"No, Ivan. No. Hold on to my hand. In just a little while we will have our baby. You and I. You are so strong. Just a little more."

So it went for an hour, then two, then three hours more. But the baby was not coming and Emma was pale with exhaustion, worry, and pain. She tried to hide this from Ivan. There was something wrong, Emma could feel it, and as she braced for another contraction her eyes filled with helpless tears, not so much from the pain but from an eerie premonition that her baby was doomed.

Ivan now paced the room and cursed the howling wind and rain that beat against the windows. He had called the doctor, but the doctor was attending an accident on the highway and his wife could not reach him. She had promised to go for her husband if he hadn't returned within the hour. Each minute seemed an eternity. Ivan could hardly bear the agony on Emma's face. The next contraction brought a heartrending scream from her, and Ivan fell to his knees in frustration and rage and panic. Please, please, God, he prayed, let them be all right. Let them be all right. I'll do anything. He could not grasp what was happening. He only knew everything had gone wrong. So wrong. And his wife and his unborn child were in terrible danger. He was to blame. He knew this. It was all his fault.

"My God, man! What the hell is going on here?" Dr. Daniels stood in the doorway. He was exhausted from the night that had already taxed his skill and his energy. A baby, his wife had said. A baby. Well, there was nothing to bringing a baby into the world. It had sounded routine.

But the scene that confronted him was anything but routine. There was a woman lying in blood-soaked sheets, her breath coming in irregular gasps and her fingers clawing at her face and hair. Her pulse was irregular and her blood pressure was out of sight.

"Get up," the doctor shouted at Ivan. "Go and call an ambulance." The doctor stripped his coat off and rolled up his sleeves. Ivan remained kneeling on the floor, all the strength drained from him, until the doctor turned and yanked him to his feet, slapping his face hard. "Get going, man. Your wife is bleeding to death. We need to get her to the hospital before it's too late." Ivan made the call; the Springs volunteer ambulance would arrive within minutes, but it would be too late for the baby.

In the dim light, Ivan watched as the baby was pulled from Emma's womb, heard its weak and feeble attempts to take in air—one gasp, then another, then nothing. Mercifully, Emma had lost consciousness and did not have to witness the death of her son.

When the ambulance did arrive, Ivan was pushed brusquely aside. An oxygen mask was clamped over Emma's face, and blood was fed to her veins. Then she was strapped to a stretcher and carried down the stairs, her face drained of all color. For all Ivan knew, she had died, too. He stood on the porch watching as the flashing red lights disappeared, then turned back into the room. There in the cradle he saw the lifeless infant—his flesh, his pride, his son—lying naked and forgotten. A man from the rescue squad had stayed behind to wait for the coroner. Now he took a towel and draped it gently over the child. Though the gesture was clearly made out of common decency, Ivan lunged toward this stranger and drove him out into the hall. Then, with a howl of utter, gut-wrenching despair, he collapsed on his knees and buried his face in the pillow where Emma had been.

In the next room, Tally clutched her teddy bear and sobbed for her mother.

33

The ordeal of childbirth had nearly claimed Emma's life as well. Mary Kitchen, a local woman, came in to care for her and look after the household, and it was her I got when I called for news.

"Doctor says she'll be okay, but she'll never have another baby," Mary told me in her flat, unemotional voice. "Other than that, she'll be fine. It's him that's the problem." I gathered that "him" referred to Ivan. "To look at him, you'd think it was the end of the world. He don't eat, he don't talk, he's like a big storm cloud 'bout ready to burst."

I asked her about Tally, but her response was a terse, "Oh well, you know what kids are like."

I didn't know what kids were like, and I worried about her. I'll never know what it's like to lose a baby after carrying it for nine months, and certainly I cried for Emma, thinking of her grief. I knew, too, that, for Ivan, not ever to have a son was a terrible loss. But I worried most about Tally, and I think that my heart was sorest for her as I imagined the pain and confusion she must have felt in the emotional chaos that surrounded her.

I've never accepted the notion that childhood is a happy, carefree time, a kind of vacation en route to the burdens of adult life. Adults, it seems to me, are much happier precisely because they are not helpless and totally dependent on the whims of the people who take care of them. Tally had led a sheltered and idyllic life. I don't know what she thought of getting a new baby sister or brother, but what could she have thought about it? She had no say in it. What she experienced while Emma endured the pain of childbirth I don't even like to think about. And what did she feel in the ensuing weeks, while Emma and Ivan grieved? What did it do to a sensitive young girl to have her safe and secure childhood world turned upside down? Tally lost much more than a baby brother. She lost a whole world, a world in which her parents could protect her from the kind of unhappiness she was now to witness. That winter Tally lost her innocence, and for that she would grieve all her life.

With the coming of spring the world quickened and turned green, and I honestly believe it helped to heal Emma. Chicks were hatching, trees budding, tulips blooming, birds nesting. The garden needed planting; there was no more time for grief. But there was no such help for Ivan. He lived in an abyss of gloom from which there seemed to be no relief. I think he was suffering as much from guilt as from grief. Like a character in a Greek tragedy, he'd been struck down by his own hubris. He lost weight, the color left his cheeks, and a haggard, grim look settled on his face. He tried to seek solace in his work, but there was a desperate emptiness in his gaze. That look told Emma that even the healing power of his work had deserted him. He shut himself in his studio for days at a time and threatened violence to anyone who tried to get him out.

One day, early that summer, Tally set a little table by the side of the road and made a hand-lettered sign advertising lemonade and cookies. A big jug of freshly cut peonies, poppies, and irises decorated her table. Much to her surprise and delight, business was brisk. One man who stopped to buy some cookies bought all her flowers. She didn't have change for his ten-dollar bill, and he told her to keep it. Another woman stopped to ask Tally if she knew where she could buy fresh eggs. Tally asked the woman to wait, and ran back to the chicken coop. The woman bought two dozen eggs. By the end of the day, Tally had made forty-two dollars. That evening Emma and Tally got busy baking more cookies, and decided to take a chance on a couple of pies. In the morning they cut more flowers and divided them into bunches; they gathered eggs and piled them up carefully in a basket; they gathered fresh herbs and tied them together with colorful ribbons. Tally's table was overflowing with good things. By the end of the week they needed a bigger table.

As the summer progressed they added homemade pickles, jams, and jellies. Mother and daughter were busy as they had never been before, and they were flushed with the pleasure of success.

Ivan was another story altogether. His work was virtually at a standstill. For the first time ever he failed to find any comfort or release in it. Everything he did was stale, familiar, and boring. Emma begged him to be patient. Time would heal everything, she told him. But as time passed, Ivan's output only continued to decline. Many days he couldn't work at all, but sat alone in his studio, staring at the wall, staring at nothing.

Just before Christmas, Emma took Tally into the city to do a little shopping and to visit Julian. He took them to lunch at Rockefeller Center. Tally's jaw dropped when she saw the giant Christmas tree and its thousands of multicolored lights. "Oh, Mama. Oh, Mama, look, look," was all she could say, and when Emma and Julian laughed, she hid her face in Emma's skirt, overcome with shyness.

They had the best table overlooking the skating rink, and both mother and daughter glowed with excitement as they watched the skaters circling round and round to the familiar waltz tunes. Julian presented Tally with a pair of figure skates, an early Christmas present, and treated her to a lesson with one of the instructors at the rink. Then he and Emma sat by a window inside, drinking coffee and watching Tally learn to twirl across the ice.

"Look at her, Julian. I haven't seen her so happy in months. I know just how she feels. I remember the Christmas I was eight, and you know how Gram was, so rigid in her traditions. No one under twelve was even allowed downstairs on Christmas Eve. That was the rule. But I couldn't wait. I came sneaking down the stairs and, oh, there it was, the Christmas tree. She had done it all in silver and blue and she was alone in the drawing room, putting the last bit of decoration on it. I had never seen her like that before. She was actually rather disheveled and terribly concentrated. I couldn't help myself, I just ran into the room and hugged her. She hugged me back and she seemed so pleased to see me, I thought for a minute she was going to relent. But then she pulled herself together and said, 'Emma, you go right back upstairs to bed. You are only eight years old.' " Emma's imitation was perfect, and both she and Julian burst out laughing.

"I remember all those Christmases in your house," he said. "They were very jolly compared with my own. I'll bet if I think back for a minute I can even remember the blue-and-silver tree." He was silent then and so was Emma. Then she reached over and laid her hand softly on his. "Thank you for this, Julian. It does my heart good to see Tally enjoying herself. This has been a terribly hard time, and I'm afraid that Tally has had to suffer a heavy burden."

"Emma, my dear, you know I would do anything to make you and Tally happy, to make you more comfortable. You need only to tell me you want something and it will be done. Why not come stay with me more often? In fact, why not abandon your lout of a husband and come live with me?"

"Julian, Julian, don't be ridiculous," Emma laughed, a becoming blush spreading across her cheeks.

"I may be hopeless in my desire for you, Emma. I am most certainly misguided in my attempts to make you see reason, but I am never, never ridiculous. However, if you persist in continuing this inappropriate marriage, there is very little for me to do except supply the occasional civilized lunch." Julian's voice had grown husky with emotion.

"I don't know why you do this to yourself. We've had this conversation a million times. Of course I'm not going to leave Ivan, and I'm as sure as I can be that you wouldn't really want me if I did. But it is Ivan I wanted to talk to you about. You know that he hasn't been working well. He's terribly worried about it, and I'm worried about him. I'm also worried about the money you send us every month. It really doesn't seem right for us to take it when Ivan isn't producing anything. So I think for the time being you had better stop. No, Julian, let me finish. I don't want any pressure on Ivan in any way. Taking the money from you may be adding to the problem."

Julian, to his credit, would hear of no such thing. He was extremely reassuring. He knew, he said, that in the long run Ivan would get back to work and he was not worried about the sums of money he was advancing now. He declared himself much more concerned with Ivan's state of mind and said he had been thinking it over for many weeks and at last had hit on an idea that might solve the problem, at least temporarily. Then he made a suggestion that seemed to Emma at the time to be a very good one. Indeed, the more he outlined his idea, the more her spirits soared. He told her that many artists had experienced the kind of thing Ivan was going through, and by the time she returned home she was full of hope, enthusiasm, and Christmas spirit. Julian's plan would make all the difference to Ivan. She only had to find the right time to tell him about it.

34

Emma was determined that they would celebrate a real Christmas. Almost a year had passed since the baby's death, and it was time, she felt, that they got on with a more normal life. She had bought special presents in New York. Art books for Ivan from Rizzoli. A dollhouse for Tally from F.A.O. Schwartz. And then, from a tiny Austrian import shop on Lexington Avenue, she had bought dozens and dozens of exquisite, hand-blown glass ornaments for the tree, in sparkling silver and midnight blue. These fragile cones and starbursts were each wrapped in tissue, and Emma held them carefully in her lap all the way home on the train.

The next morning the three of them drove around to the nurseries to pick out a perfect tree. Emma and Tally had laid down strict requirements, and Ivan went along, saying very little. After much discussion and debate they decided on a blue spruce that was eight feet tall. It took all afternoon to trim it, but in the end they pronounced it the most beautiful one in all of East Hampton if not the world.

Tally and Emma were very much in the Christmas spirit, and had chattered happily while decorating the tree. They did not seem to notice Ivan's morose mood or the fact that he had been drinking steadily all afternoon. To them the day was very special, and they could hardly contain their excitement. Dinner that evening was special, too—stuffed, baked mushrooms, roast Cornish hens, and wild rice.

"Julian had a wonderful idea for you, darling," Emma said brightly when dinner was finally on the table. "He's very concerned about everything, and he's going to find you a teaching position. He's going to scout around the colleges and universities in the New York area. You know, Julian said that many artists have periods where their work isn't going well. He said that it can actually be a good thing, like a field lying fallow for a season, so that when you get back to work you will be all the more productive." She looked at him, nervously, hopefully. Ivan was looking down at his plate, saying nothing. Emma felt encouraged to go on. "If you think about it, teaching could be the perfect solution for the time being. It wouldn't have to be more than one day a week, so you wouldn't be away from us or anything. Julian said that teaching is a most honorable profession for the working artist. He said that many of the best artists have held teaching jobs. And you know, darling, when you talk about your work, you're so eloquent, so inspiring. I think you would make a wonderful teacher."

Ivan continued to stare at his plate. His food was untouched. He said nothing.

Emma was growing impatient. "I told him I would talk it over with you and let him know soon. Darling, what do you think? Julian said—"

Ivan slammed his fist down full force on the table. The stuffed mushrooms popped like Ping-Pong balls, scattering over the tablecloth and onto the floor. Tally giggled but quickly repressed it.

"I won't have it!" Ivan roared. "I will not have you conspiring, plotting, scheming behind my back. What is it you and Julian wish to do—sell me into slavery? Well, why not! That would be better than this other . . . this travesty."

"Ivan, calm yourself. No one—"

But Ivan had only paused to catch his breath. "You think I would wish to humiliate myself, debase my art to be teaching pimple-faced adolescents how to look at *Mona Lisa*. You, of all people, should know better. But no, I am wrong. Very wrong. You don't know me. And don't care nothing for me. Well, then, leave me. Go away. Go back to Julian. Marry him and live in bourgeois comfort that you obviously desire."

Neither Emma nor Tally was prepared for the flood of anger that was erupting at their usually quiet dinner table. Nor was Ivan able to stop the flow of his paranoid rage.

"If I wanted to be teacher, I would have stayed in Europe. There at least teacher is treated with some respect. American saying is 'Those who can, do. And those who can't, teach!' " he shouted. "You and Julian are so damned sure that I can't *do*. Why you don't say it straight out? Don't give me soft talk and fancy food. You are Judas." His voice shook with rage, and rising from the table, he lifted it up and flung it, complete with dishes, food, and flatware, across the room. Emma, beside herself with anxiety, rushed to his side, trying to calm him, to explain, but he was beyond calming. He was an enraged beast. He turned and grabbed her by the shoulders and shook her. Then he called her one sharp word, "Bitch! *Suka!*" and slapped her hard.

She fell to her knees crying, and Tally rushed to her side. "Mama, Mama!"

Emma held her child and watched in horror as Ivan strode across the room, lifted the decorated tree in one motion, and, hurling it against the wall, shouted to no one in particular, "Enough. I've had enough. Farce is over. Is over. I am rather be dead. I will jump off bridge! I should have done long ago." He slammed the door and was gone.

Emma, still on her knees and holding Tally, surveyed the scene before her: the broken crockery, the scattered silverware; the roasted Cornish hens, ruined and oozing stuffing onto the rug; the overturned furniture; the million bits of broken blue and silver Christmas ornaments; the tree, lying as if asleep on its side; the gravy stains across one wall. Emma looked at it all, she looked down at Tally who regarded her with teary astonishment, and she began to laugh. She shook all over with the force of the laughter, deep and long buried. She laughed as though she'd heard the best joke in the world and had finally got the punch line. She laughed until her stomach hurt and her eyes filled with tears. She laughed until Tally shook her, saying, "Mommy, Mommy! Are you crazy? Why are you laughing? We've got to do something. Papa's going to kill himself. He said he's going to jump off a bridge."

Emma kissed her daughter and soothed her. "Don't cry, darling. Papa's not going to kill himself. He's not going to jump off any bridge. There is no bridge. No bridge at all. There, there. Everything is going to be all right. I know it looks terrible in here, but it will be okay. Papa's going to be all right, too. He had a big hurt inside him and it had to come out. Now that it has, everything will be just fine."

"But, Mommy . . ."

"Hush, darling. Remember what I told you. There is no bridge."

I van was gone for two days, and when he returned he went straight into the studio, locking himself in. Emma put his dinner on a tray and left it outside his studio. He remained in his studio all night, and when Emma knocked on his door the following morning he let her in.

I have a long letter from her describing the scene:

I was shocked. The studio was in a shambles. It looked as if a bomb had hit it. Shattered plaster casts were everywhere, molds were broken, sketches ripped in two, tools flung about and buried in the debris. But worse was Ivan's appearance. His face was haggard and profoundly sad. He looked exhausted. There was no anger, no defiance, only defeat. We held each other for a long time. You know how big Ivan is, Maisie, but just then he seemed to have shrunken, and I felt I was holding a small wounded boy. My heart went out to him but I didn't know what to say so I went on holding him, hoping I could soothe him with warmth and love. After a long while he pulled away and motioned for me to follow him outside. We sat on the little bench Ivan had built into the big oak. The day was crisp and clear, no wind and the sun very bright, making it quite warm for December. It was the kind of day that inspires false confidence about getting through the winter easily. Everything sparkled and glittered and the sun beamed down warmth and benevolence. Look, it seemed to say, winter is no problem at all. Ivan held my hands in his and finally he spoke, "I am failure! I can do no more here," he gestured to the open doors of his studio. "For weeks I've barely slept or eaten and even drink don't give me peace. I am face-to-face with truth, Emma, I see my weakness, my poverty and my nothingness. I no longer have hand to work, not will, either." His gesture was one of sheer hopelessness, empty and devoid of all vitality. I knew better than to try to reason with him then. There are no words of comfort for the despair he felt. I know it can't be true, I know it will get better, but how can I convince him? What do you think, Maisie? Is there hope for him? Is there help? What is to be done? I watched him lock and bolt the studio doors. He handed me the keys and said in a strange and strangled kind of voice, "The muse has left me, my art is dead. I will never work again." His forehead was very warm and I think he was quite feverish. We went back to the house. I made him eat some soup and drink some tea and put him straight to bed. He did everything obediently and seemed childishly grateful. Now he is sleeping and my heart hurts with the burden of his sorrow. But worse than that I feel a kind of gnawing fear. He has always been such a tower of strength to me. I can hardly bear to see him brought so low. And I realize how very much his weakness frightens me. Will I be strong enough for both of us? Oh Maisie, forgive me for writing such a discouraged letter.

The weeks passed and Ivan's spirits did not improve. The weeks turned into months. In the spring, Emma wrote to Julian. She told him not to send any more money. "Ivan is taking a kind of sabbatical," she said. "He needs time and freedom. Until he works again, it would be better for him not to feel obligated in any way. As a separate matter, however, I would like to negotiate a business loan for myself. I am going to expand the farm stand. I want to buy a tractor."

And there followed in Emma's neat hand an itemized list of things she needed. Materials for building a proper roadside structure, down payment on a used garden tractor, money for a larger chicken coop, more hens, a bigger garden, and perhaps a small greenhouse. Included in her proposal was a strict repayment schedule. What Julian thought of all this I can't easily imagine, but he sent Emma enough money for her to proceed with her plans. I felt very removed on my Swiss mountain and could do little more than send encouraging letters and occasional packages of luxuries for Emma and Tally.

Spring arrived early. Ivan behaved like a lamb—he was sweet to Emma, he was sweet to Tally. For a while it seemed as though his decision to stop working at his sculpture had brought him a new peace and tranquility. He worked quite cheerfully around the house, making much needed repairs. He rebuilt the chicken coops and in April he threw himself into the task of building Emma's farm stand.

Today, all these many years later, farm stands dot the landscape of Long Island's East End. New Yorkers' appetite for farm-fresh produce is seemingly boundless, and their pockets, as every local person knows, are very deep. Many former farm stands have become large markets: the Green Thumb in Watermill, Doug's Vegetable Patch in Wainscott, Round Swamp Farm on Three Mile Harbor Road in Springs, and the Farmers Market in Amagansett. The Montauk Highway is dotted with smaller stands and flatbed trucks loaded with produce. But wonderful as many of these are, none of them ever held a candle to Emma's Place. For one thing the little building itself was a gem of imaginative architecture and whimsical decoration. It was the result of a happy collaboration between Tally and Ivan. Emma wanted something practical, big enough to display her goods and sheltered to some extent from wind and rain. Tally wanted something pretty, "something with flowers on the walls," she said. Ivan, his muse still on vacation, applied his skills to produce a charming, portable building that was extremely pleasing to the eye. It was round and gaily reminiscent of a circus tent. Tally insisted on selecting the flowers that were painted onto the gray wooden walls. One side was a trompe l'oeil, a stand of hollyhocks which looked completely real. The other walls were decorated with garlands of red poppies, blue cornflowers, and yellow coreopsis. All around these was a border of small purple pansies, the kind my grandmother called Johnny-jump-ups. These were Ivan's favorite flower, and everywhere in evidence at the St. Peters place. But back to the farm stand. There was no other like it. Not only was it beautiful, but word spread quickly that no other cookies were as good as Tally's Cookies, no other bread as deliciously wholesome as Emma's Wholegrain Bread, and no other eggs as fresh as the brown eggs at Emma's stand. For many weekenders, Emma's stand was the first place they went upon arriving and the last place they visited to stock up on good country produce for the week in New York. The demand for her produce grew so great that Emma soon hired Mary Kitchen to help out and organized a network of home bakers who supplied her with pies and other baked goods.

Everything seemed to be going swimmingly, but with the coming of summer, Ivan changed. He continued to help in the garden and with their flourishing farm stand, but he was like a man who was empty inside, and with the passing of time he seemed to shrivel up and turn even more inward.

From time to time Emma invited Julian out to see Ivan, to talk to him, but whenever Julian came, Ivan was simply not around. He would sneak out the back door and stay away until Julian was gone. Since he had stopped working, Ivan shunned nearly all their acquaintances. For a long time, Emma and Tally were his sole companions. But neither Emma nor Tally had time to serve in attendance as they once had. The farm stand kept them both busy, and often Ivan would find Emma sound asleep in a chair with the ledger books open in her lap. Of course, it was not her exhaustion that was coming between them, it was her exhilaration. Emma was flourishing while Ivan lay fallow. Everything about her had taken on a glow. Her mind and hands were fertile things and in them ideas became realities. She was clever in ways neither he nor she had ever imagined. She knew how to manage people, how to organize her time, how to be frugal and at the same time where to take risks with her steadily increasing profits. He admired Emma. He found he was amazed by her—by her strength and ability and ingenuity, by her heroic efforts to hold their family together. But every victory she seemed to win served only to strengthen the bars of his own cage. He felt trapped.

In time he came to believe that it was she who was suffocating him. Try as he might he found he could not regain his original feeling for her. When he reached for her physically there was a coolness in his touch and where once there had been energy and passion, he now felt a kind of sorrow and hollowness. He knew she could feel it, too. And how very like Emma not to make an issue of it, not to reproach him. After a while he did not touch her at all, he did not even go near her. His drinking increased, and though there were no more displays of temper, I think that Emma would have preferred the angry scenes to the withdrawal of the man himself. Summer came and went. Autumn. Then, once again the winter. Ivan started to disappear for long stretches at a time. First it was for an afternoon. Then it was every afternoon and every evening until there came a time when Ivan was gone for days at a time. Sometimes he was off doing odd jobs—mindless, undemanding work that provided him with a few dollars that didn't have to be meted out by Emma. But more often than not he was taking solace at a local roadside bar called Jungle Pete's. That's where he met Rita Hayes.

36

They called her Miss Rita at Jungle
Pete's. She worked behind the bar, and when she wasn't working, she
hung out. I never met her, and if I had, I suppose loyalty to Emma would
have made me despise her at the time. But now, with distance and
perspective, I see her more as a victim than a seductress, feel the desperate longings in her more than I condemn the sluttish behavior. It was
an ugly and tragic time for everyone, but in the end it was Rita who paid
the greatest price.

She was the town bad girl, the girl whose skirts were too tight and
lips too red, the object of locker-room boasts and idle speculation. She
was a luscious, red-haired, green-eyed beauty, and had she had a few
breaks, her looks might well have opened many doors. As it was, she
ended up used, abused, and finally dead.

Finding someone willing to talk about Rita was easy. "Rita Hayes?
Yeah, I remember her. 'Rita Chiquita' they called her. That gal was wild

for a good time—plain wild, I guess. I remember her back in high school. She was so pretty it drove all us guys crazy. We all said she should go to Hollywood like Lana Turner, ya know, or Jane Russell. She sure had the face for it, everything else, too. Came to a bad end, didn't she, though? Yeah . . . Jesus, haven't thought about Rita Chiquita in a long time."

Finding someone who was willing to be compassionate about her was more difficult, but I did run into a robust, balding fisherman with the unlikely name of Cookie, and he was. We met at a cocktail party for the local baymen not long after I started this project of recollection, and as we drank gin and tonics out of plastic glasses, I had ample opportunity to take his measure. It was hard to see him as a young swain, hot on the heels of the pretty high school girl Rita Hayes had been back in the fifties. Cookie, whose real name was Lester Cooke, looked older than his fifty-odd years, but as I surveyed the crowded room I could see a lot of young men in their twenties who'd one day look very much like my drinking companion. Cookie had lived in Springs all his life, as had his people before him, on back to the first settlers in 1648. Like his ancestors, he has made his living on the bays and shores of the South Fork. His hands were swollen, his fingers sausages of rough, red skin from years of hauling in his traps and nets. His eyes took on that faraway look as he searched back in his mind to recall for me a barmaid at Jungle Pete's, a once-pretty girl who lived too fast and gave too much, too many times.

Jungle Pete's has been bought and sold and renamed at least three times since those days, and in its latest incarnation it's a far cry from the rowdy roadside joint it once was. Inside was a pool table and a huge semicircular bar where "a beer and a bump" was the drink of choice. It was strictly a hangout for local people. Anybody else who went in there was slumming.

"Yeah." Cookie inhaled deeply. "Miss Rita give us all a run for our money. No, no, that's not it." He clarified. "She never took no money. She wouldn't nohow. Nothin' like it. But she sure was a tease. It made a lot of the guys real mad, and 'course the madder they got, the worser they talked. I was as bowled over by her as the rest, I reckon. They all figured I had somethin' going with her, but I didn't. Not like that, anyway. We was friends. I'd be embarrassed to tell you the things she got me to do for her, though. Everything was make-believe to her. Like in a movie. She got me to row her out on Accabonac one night, to go skinny-dipping out there in the moonlight. One night we broke into the old lighthouse out on Cedar Point. Me? I was spooked. But not Rita. She was crazy to play this game. She ran way up to the top in the pitch-dark, shouting some poetry she'd learned in school—'Hark, hark, the lark . . .' You know, that kind of stuff. She knew it all . . . God, I remember that night. We were up in that tower and the moonlight was all over her. It was like something out of an old storybook. 'A damsel and her fair knight' she called us . . ."

Cookie paused, and he was light-years away from the baymen's cocktail do. After a minute he sucked down the rest of his drink, ice and all. "I don't know why she never got out of this place," he said firmly. "She talked about it often enough. Oh, she was goin' to make it big. She was going to Hollywood and get herself discovered. She used to send off for all this junk in the mail, movie star clothes and movie star underwear, and once she showed me these cutouts—you know, like stencils—of famous movie stars' mouths so's you could paint on lips just like Rhonda Fleming or Marilyn Monroe. I told her that was dumb. She had a great mouth all her own. She did, too. But she was always dreaming, always makin' plans. Even after she'd had a couple of kids and had to support them, she'd talk about moving up-island to sing in a night-club or getting a job on a cruise ship. Stuff like that. But to be honest, she didn't look so good after she started living with Karl. That's when she really started boozin'. And the live wire in her kinda turned surly. Couldn't blame her, though. Karl was one mean sonofabitch. Never could understand why she took up with him. Good-look' enough, I guess, the kind of asshole wears gold goddam chains around his neck. Had a big boat, a custom cruiser, and everyone thought he was running in drugs and such. I don't know about that, but I know he used to be a cop upstate somewhere and then he came out here and didn't do much of anything except go out on his boat. I guess Rita sort of gave up hoping for the big time after Karl. She didn't have much going for her at the end. Pretty sad story."

"Did you know she had an affair with Ivan St. Peters?"

"Hell, that ain't news. I remember when it got started. This guy Ivan started comin' by Pete's, and he had a funny way of talking—he was a Russkie or somethin'—and mostly he came in and drank quietly, you know. He wasn't too friendly or anything. We'd heard he was an ottist or somethin' and didn't pay nobody no mind. Rita bought him a drink one night, just to find out who he was. Man, I guess she was some impressed with him and maybe he was some taken, too, 'cause suddenly he got fancy manners, you know, he was kissin' her hand, and drawin' pitchers of her, and before you knew it he was buyin' drinks for the house and slappin' everybody on the back. Oh, he was somethin', all right."

I asked Cookie to tell me more, but he shook his head. "Don't know any more. Me and Rita had a falling-out. I told her this guy had a wife and kid. She told me to, well . . . mind my own business. So I did. I surely did." He shook his head, looking so distressed that I suddenly felt as if I had intruded on some very personal thoughts. I thanked him quickly and started to go, but he caught my arm and said, "You talk to Mary. She'll tell you about Rita. You do that."

Mary Kitchen had been at the top of my list of people to talk to, but she didn't have much to say until I told her what Lester Cooke had said.

"That man was in love with her from the first," Mary snorted. "He never gave up hoping Rita would fall for him. He was a fool for her, always was. Don't think she ever knew how bad he was stuck on her, and if she did, she didn't seem to much care." I was expecting Mary to be all pursed lips and disapproval about Rita, but Mary was a funny one. She had her loyalties and she kept to them fiercely. Other people's opinions meant nothing to her. "Yeah, she was lucky to have Cookie on her side, and she had me, but I guess except for her kids she never really had anyone else." Mary thwacked her dishrag on the sink. "You want a cup of coffee?" she asked, and I knew I was in.

"Rita and me go way back," she said, lowering herself into her chair after fixing us the coffee and pulling a pound cake out of the refrigerator. "She was a funny kid. I can see her now. She came to a birthday party of mine when we were in grade school. All the other girls was dressed up in organdy and Mary Janes—you know, frills and bows—but Rita, she came dressed up like it was costume party. She had on a long lacy kind of dress and a pair of old high heels and a big hat with a feather in it. The kids laughed at her, but I was real impressed. I thought she looked great.

"The summer Marilyn Monroe and her husband, whatsisname, came out to Amagansett, Rita was sixteen. She hung out at the local beauty parlor until she got herself a job cleaning up and so on, just so she could be there when Marilyn came to have her nails done. Pretty soon she was walking like her and making herself up like her, and I think she would have dyed her hair blond if she hadn't been so vain about her own hair. It was beautiful and real fiery red!

"We went all through school together until Rita dropped out. The other kids made fun of her something terrible. Some of it was because she wore funny clothes and acted so high and mighty. But most of it had to do with her taking up with the boys who came in the summer. You know, it's always been a trouble here about the summer people. Let's face it, we depend on them coming. We like their money, but God, we don't much like *them*. Summer is hard. The kids own the town during the winter, but in summer, suddenly the rich kids show up with their expensive cars and preppy clothes and bad manners and they take over. There'd be trouble and some boys would bait those guys and trash their cars or whatever. Girls were just expected to stay clear. But not Rita. She was crazy for those summer boys. She'd get all dolled up and parade up and down Main Street and get herself picked up. I'd see that hair of hers flying around town in their convertibles. She couldn't see how they used her. They called her a whore almost to her face, and she never noticed. She lived in this fantasy world. She would take up with one after another every summer. She pretended like it was a big romance, the real thing, but it wasn't anything of the sort. She was all of seventeen when she got pregnant the first time. She came crying to me. Hell, I didn't know what to do or say. We tried to figure out how she could get the boy to help her, but in the end he got his father to send some lawyer around saying she had no case and no proof. It was awful. She didn't have anyone. Her mom was dead and her dad kicked her out. You ever see those funny little stucco cottages down by the railroad tracks? Well, that was where she lived, and she got a job at the lumberyard, typing in the office. She had the baby and kept it. She had some fool notion that the boy who'd got her that way would come around, but a'course he didn't. I coulda told her. In fact I did, but she just looked at me kinda sadlike and said I didn't have no imagination.

"God, she was a dreamer, though. When her baby was born, she used to dress him up like he was a prince and walk him up and down the street as proud as a peacock and never let on she knew what people were saying about her. She was like that. She was a tramp and she lived like a tramp, but she held her head high. It took that scum beatin' her to death to pull her down."

I was pretty sure Ivan wouldn't talk to me about Rita, but he surprised me. In a way I think he was grateful to get it off his chest, though it was so many years later that we talked that maybe all the sting and pain was out of him.

"I don't know, Maisie," Ivan told me honestly, "I had to have her. I had to have woman like her. It was not natural desire . . . I was man drowning. I was trapped by despair. I wanted woman who would bring me a burning, vibrating thrill. I couldn't go near Emma. I couldn't touch her. Something in me couldn't even be in same room with Emma. I never stop loving Emma, not for a minute, but inside I feel vile, and to touch her repulsed me because it would defile the image I have of her.

I felt like vampire—tired from centuries of living, bored and disgusted. I wanted to hit bottom. I wanted to sink as low as I could. I started going to that bar in the afternoons. That was the worst time of day in the house. Emma, so busy with the farm stand, and Tally rushing in from school and starting her little jobs and I was so lonely then. So afraid of what was happening to me. This Jungle Pete's was perfect place for me. Not just the drink, but it was dark and music was loud and the people keep to themselves. Pretty soon it was the only place where I feel like anything.

"The men in the bar treated her like dirt, they were rough to her and she was rough back. I was fascinated. She would come over and talk to me if the bar was slow. She liked that I am artist and she ask me to draw her. I could see she was once upon a time pretty. Is still, but she was hardened, too much drink and running around. I sketched her face on the back of bar check, but I make her younger, prettier—I know what I am doing. I draw not the woman, but the girl she was once. It was amusing me to see her gratitude. I play the gentleman. I kiss her hand. I speak to her in French. She liked sketch so much, she is begging me to do real portrait. I liked the way she flirt with me and tease me with her body. I went to bar almost every afternoon. It was a game with us. She was good at stirring me up, and I am feeling alive in sexual way after very long time.

"I know I was driving her crazy with desire. But I wanted her to do everything, to take charge of everything. I am wanting the feeling of being seduced.

"At last I agree to do the portrait.

" 'A friend of mine has a summer cabin out on Sammy's Beach. I have the key,' she says. She gave me instructions how to get there and next day I am driving out there. Rita is already waiting."

Here Ivan stopped and he was silent for a long time. I knew he might stop the story here, because he was not a confessional sort of man. He rarely talked at all about himself in this way, but then when he did, it was deliberate, detailed, sometimes harsh, as if he were digging at truths by exposing old wounds.

"She is waiting like a ripe plum, juicy, ready to bursting. I am making busy with my pencils, fixing curtains for light. Outside is raining, but room is too hot from the fire. She is nervous and edgy, chattering away about nonsense. I should have had pity in me, I should have felt sorry for her. I know she was living with man. I know she have two children. But I care nothing about that, God help me. I cared only about my lust.

"I started to sketch and soon she is very quiet. I can see she is watching. Every time I look at her, she is staring at me with wanting. I could hear her breathing.

" 'Come here,' she say. She was sitting on the end of a cot, and she leaned back. 'If you don't come to me, I have to come to you.' Still I didn't move. She laughed and got up. 'Okay, I know what to do. I know what you want.' She came and she took my hand and put it on her breast. 'That feels so good.' She sound lazy now, but she know what I wanted. 'You let Miss Rita do for you.'

"I was her slave. I did only as she commanded me. Sex had transformed her. Her one wish was to have me, to satisfy me. She made it clear I could do anything I pleased with her, and she was expert. She knew everything about physical sensation. I was helpless with her hands on me, her mouth and tongue all over me. She was tireless, and she never stop whispering her desire for me.

"At last everything in me is alive again, and I knew then what I had become. There was no beauty in me, there was no love, there was only animal."

Following that afternoon, Rita lay in wait for Ivan at every turn. She grew bolder every day, and soon enough she wanted more from him than just the infrequent stolen afternoons in the beach cottage. Rita thought she was being so clever, but she hadn't a notion of how closely watched she was by the man she lived with. He was known for his temper and his jealousy. He was rough, and he kept to himself. Rita had a baby when she met Karl, and a teenaged son, too. Maybe she thought Karl would help her out with the kids. Maybe he did on some counts, but one thing was certain—Karl was the kind of man you didn't cheat on.

Rita and the baby, Nicki, lived in a flimsy cottage out near Promised Land. When he wasn't on his boat, Karl lived there, too. It was never proved that Karl was mixed up in drug dealing, but he was a secretive man and spent an inordinate amount of time cruising off Montauk Point. Rita probably thought she was safe, but as her affair heated up, so did her carelessness. More and more she left the baby with a neighbor and grew bold in her obsession.

Before long, rumors of the affair reached Emma. She chose to ignore them. Her manner remained loving and stalwart, intensified even, for she was determined to throw a veil of indifference over the whole matter. Rita was not dumb. She seized on this and grew bolder. She found out about Emma's movements, her hours at the farm stand. And then she would lay in wait for Ivan on his very doorstep.

It was agony for Emma. It was as if Ivan were taunting her, punishing her and himself. It made no sense to her. I think that's why she said nothing and did nothing. She trusted Ivan to come to his senses. But after a while she wasn't sure.

In her diary she writes:

I woke up at midnight and Ivan was no longer in bed. I knew even as I came downstairs to look for him the house would be empty. I can feel it when he's gone. The doors leading to the porch are wide open. The moonlight casts an eerie white light over every object like a spider's thin web, and Ivan is nowhere to be seen or heard. I feel more alone than I have ever felt. I sit here in the rocking chair and I know I should do something, feel something, but I am immobile. I don't know what to do. Ivan is making my life intolerable. The drinking, the inactivity, the infidelity—these things are bad enough, but it isn't any one of these that gives me so much distress. It is his need to live in turbulence. It is his destructive nature. I don't know how long I will be able to tolerate that. I ache for him. Physically, my body aches for him to touch me, to hold me. I remember the first time with us. I remember giving myself to him, how it was, how he filled me up with his hands and his eyes and his body and how everything in me rushed to meet him. We were bound together. It was everything, and I knew there would never be anything ever again like it. I can't believe how he has let our passion die, but I know I am a dead woman without it and without him.

37

The scene that took place in Rita's cottage that night was brutal. Much of it was reported in the local papers. She must have suffered great pain. I can hardly bear to imagine it, and yet I do. That very afternoon she had been with Ivan, wild and abandoned in his arms. That night she was beaten unconscious and left on the floor of her messy kitchen.

Rita opening her eyes, feeling the cold linoleum on her swollen cheek, tasting the blood in her mouth. There was too much pain to move, to turn her head or sit up. Her features were battered beyond recognition. She could hear the baby crying in her crib but she couldn't move. She didn't dare. She had thought he was going to kill her.

He had been sitting in the cottage drinking beer when she got home, and the smell of him was sour and ugly. She had learned to hate him by then. She hated coming home to him after Ivan. She hated having to talk to him, be nice to him, fix his dinner, and, worst of all, let his clumsy hands touch her. Not after Ivan. Ivan, who knew how to kiss her and where and when. Ivan didn't love her the way she loved him, she knew that, but he needed her, and out of his need, she thought, he would perhaps find love. It was only a matter of time. Ivan was everything she had ever dreamed of in her whole life. He was better than the Ivy League college boys of her youth, better than all the men she had ever been with, put together. He was real. She was through with Karl.

Karl would have agreed, had he been inclined to talk about it rationally. As it was, he stuffed her mouth with a dishrag so she couldn't scream, and then he began to beat her. He knew just how to do it. He knocked the wind out of her, then set to work on her face. Her beautiful face. Her nose was broken, her teeth knocked out, her mouth split. And all the while, softly, so the neighbors wouldn't hear him, he'd whispered his venom.

"After I get through with you, no man will ever want you again, you whore! You think you and that artsy-fartsy artist can make a fool of me? You think you can spread your legs for him again? No, not for anyone, but especially not for him."

When he was through with her, she lay still on the floor. She could hear the baby making noises and she was so afraid. She had watched him get his gun. Oh, God in heaven. He was going to kill her and the baby. But he seemed calm now, almost normal. He came over and knelt beside her and she closed her eyes as if she had passed out.

"You don't fool me, Rita," he said. "Just remember that. You don't ever fool me. I know you inside and out, and none of your playacting ever fools me. I know you can hear me. I'm going out now, but I'll be back and I want you to get up and clean yourself up. I'm going out and I'm going to find your boyfriend, you hear me, don't you? I'm going to find him and kill him. I know how to do it so it will look like self-defense. He beat up my woman, isn't that right, Rita? He beat you up and I went after him and he tried to get me. I can make it stick because he's a drunk and a weirdo." He prodded her face with his finger, and she moaned.

She heard his car back down the gravel road and listened as he gunned the motor on the main road. Then she tried to get up, but the effort was too much for her and she lost consciousness again. The baby started crying louder and louder, until old Mrs. Vanderveer from next door knocked gently on the door to ask if she could help. When she got no response and the baby continued wailing, she pushed open the door and found Rita lying gagged in a pool of blood. She picked up the baby and called an ambulance. Then she called Mary Kitchen. Mary and the ambulance and the police all got there at about the same time. Rita regained consciousness. Crying and holding on to Mary, she told them about Karl's threats. The police took off in pursuit of Karl, and the ambulance left for the hospital. "I don't know," said Mary, shaking her head when she told me this part, "I just don't know why it all went so wrong for Rita. She told me what happened. She kept clinging to my arm and the tears wouldn't stop. I was with her all the way to the hospital. I stayed right there in Emergency. Rita fought for her life, and they worked and worked over her. But she just didn't have enough fight left. Right before they took her into surgery, she looked at me and whispered the names of her kids."

38

Emma was writing in her diary when she heard a car coming up the drive. It was going fast, too fast for the narrow dirt road. She debated whether to put the light on for Ivan or let him find his way in the dark, but it wasn't Ivan's car. She knew the sound of his wheezy old motor. Her hand went to her throat. She felt a terrible foreboding as she peered out at the moonlit drive. An unfamiliar car screeched to a halt. Something was very wrong. She was sure they were coming to tell her Ivan was dead. Putting on the porch light, she stepped out into the dark.

An angry, menacing voice pierced the dark stillness of the night. "Where's that shit St. Peters? You get him out here, girlie. Tell him Karl Hoffman wants to see him."

Emma was suddenly all too aware that she and Tally were alone. If she told him Ivan was out, he would know she was alone.

"Can't this wait until tomorrow? Ivan is asleep and I don't want to wake him."

"Don't give me that crap! You tell that chickenshit asshole to get out here."

Emma turned to go inside, but the man was instantly on the porch, grabbing her by the arm. He twisted it hard, hurting her. His face was contorted with rage. He stank of alcohol.

"No sonofabitch gonna fuck with my woman and get away with it," he whispered hoarsely in her ear. "I'm gonna shoot off his fuckin' balls." Suddenly he raised his voice and shouted at the top of his lungs, "Get the fuck out here, you bastard!"

There was a noise inside the house, and he pushed Emma away, whirling around, a pistol in his hand. Emma fell against the side of the house. She could see the man in the full light of the porch now. He had dropped one knee and was pointing his gun straight at Tally's head. Emma screamed, but Tally remained absolutely still, and bravely held her ground. She looked at the man, her little eyes blazing, and said, "You get out of here. Leave my mother alone. Leave us alone. I've called the police." Karl didn't know what to do for a moment, but there was something in the child's manner that disarmed him. His hand dropped. In the distance there was the wailing of a police siren and now he cursed, scrambling down the steps and off across the yard.

When the police arrived minutes later they had him, now hand-cuffed, in tow. "I want that man put away," Emma told the police sergeant. "He tried to kill my child."

"Don't worry, ma'am, they're going to throw the key away on that one. He beat up his girlfriend. She just died. We were on our way to pick him up when the dispatcher got the call from your daughter."

There were by now three police cars, eight policemen, and a dozen or more curious neighbors milling about the St. Peterses' front yard. In the chaos, no one had noticed that Ivan was standing in the doorway. He was in shadow and his head was bent low.

It took Emma a while to get Tally back to bed. Now that the danger was over, the little girl clung to her mother and could not stop crying. "Hush, hush, baby," Emma soothed. "We're all right. We're fine."

"But, Mama, who will take care of us? I don't want him here. I don't want him to scare us. Who will make sure he doesn't come back?" Tally sobbed.

"The police will, baby. They've taken him away."

"I don't mean the man," Tally sobbed. "I—I mean Papa."

She buried her wet face in Emma's neck, and Emma's hand never stopped stroking Tally's head. Finally, when Tally had fallen asleep, Emma went downstairs to find Ivan. He was sitting at the kitchen table, his head in his hands. Emma sat down across from him and studied him for a long moment. When she spoke, it was very softly, but there was a firmness in her voice that he had not heard before.

"Ivan, I want you to listen to me very carefully because what I have to say I will only say once. I'm leaving you. I'm taking Tally and we're going away. We will leave as soon as I can get our things together. I am no longer willing to watch helplessly while you destroy yourself. After tonight, I know for certain I can't do it anymore."

"Emma, please . . ."

"No. Let me finish. I don't care what you have to say. You've degraded me and our marriage, and I'm done with all that."

"But I love you . . ." Ivan wailed.

"If you do, you have a damned funny way of showing it."

"And you love me . . ." He was pleading.

"Maybe I do, Ivan. Maybe even after all this I do. If so, that's my problem and I'll deal with it. But it doesn't change anything."

"Don't do this, Emma." Ivan was crying without restraint now. "I beg you not to do this. I always tried to live my life with honor, with pride. Now I have nothing but shame. If you go, I have nothing at all. Nothing."

"I'm not thinking of you, Ivan. I'm not even thinking about myself. It's Tally. She can't live here after tonight. It's unthinkable. She needs me, and you must let me go so that I can look after her."

"Emma. My Emma. Please . . ." Ivan's voice choked and he reached out his arms for her.

Briefly she allowed him to embrace her, then pushed him away. "I feel sorry for you, Ivan. There is a woman dead tonight because of you. You will live with that fact for the rest of your life, and I know it won't be easy, but I have no more comfort for you. This is as painful for me as it is for you, and I hurt more than you'll ever know. But this is something that has to be." She turned and walked out of the room and up the stairs. When she reached the bedroom, she quietly closed the door, though her hand gripped the knob to stop its violent shaking. "Oh, dear God, give me the strength," she whispered. And then her throat tightened into a hard knot, and the tears fell silently.

39

Thus, Emma and Tally came to live with Julian. In many ways Emma needed Julian more than she needed anyone else at that moment. He was a link to her past. Indirectly he renewed her sense of herself, recalling to her the person she had been before Ivan. I think it gave her the distance she needed to think things through.

Julian, of course, took them in with open arms. He kept an elegant suite of rooms in his penthouse apartment always at the ready to put up important visitors from all over the world. These he now turned over to Emma and Tally. Tally was enchanted. Her fondness for her Uncle Julian intensified. He bought her expensive gifts, took her to her first Broadway show, treated her to afternoon tea at the Plaza Hotel. In her eyes, Uncle Julian led a magical, wonderful life. Suddenly she was a part of it, and she was very happy.

Julian pulled a few strings and had Tally enrolled in an exclusive girls' school. She loved her new school, and blossomed there. She loved her uniform and the kind, firm attention she received from her new teachers. I think, apart from the luxury of her surroundings and the generous attentions of Julian, what Tally loved best of all was the sense of structure and order in her new life.

Emma and Tally had been living with Julian for just over three months when Julian decided to give a party. Quite predictably, it was like no other party Tally had ever been to. She thought everyone there was grand and beautiful beyond belief. She liked the rich clothes and expensive, luxurious furs. She inhaled the heady perfume of the brightly chattering women, watched as they bent their cheeks toward one another with high-pitched amiabilities on their lips. She thought the men all quite charming though a tiny bit ridiculous as they flattered her and flirted with her as if she were a grownup. Still, it was quite nice to listen to them, and one day soon the flirting and flattery would be in earnest. At nine years old, Tally had vowed to herself she would be every bit as sophisticated and elegant as these people gathered in Uncle Julian's wonderful penthouse apartment high atop the City of New York.

For the party Tally wore new velvet trousers that buckled just below the knee, and a loosely flowing pale yellow blouse with a casual "school-boy" tie at the neck. On her feet were velvet slippers; her legs were encased in silk stockings. She looked like a royal page at court.

Julian himself had taken her shopping. Up and down Madison Avenue, in and out of all the smart boutiques. Then he had made an appointment for her at a beauty parlor, although he had explained to her that in New York it was called the hairdresser's. There her thick, unruly hair had been cut in dozens of uneven layers so that after the blow-drying it resembled an upturned mop. She loved it. At lunchtime Julian had ushered her into the fanciest restaurant she had ever seen in her life. A grown-up restaurant where the menu was in French and the desserts came rolling up to your table on a trolley.

The only person who did not seem to be enjoying the party was Emma. Not that she didn't try. She was circulating, talking to people, smiling, even laughing from time to time. And she looked lovely. But there was a deep reserve about her and a profound sadness. Tally didn't know what to do about her mother's sadness, and she found herself feeling angry with her for it, for not trying harder to enjoy her new life. She never allowed herself to think about her father. He had been bad, worse than bad, he had been terrible. He had allowed terrible things to happen to them. And with the pitiless judgment of the very young, she put him out of her mind.

Tally saw her mother beckoning to her from across the room and she went, though grudgingly, because she was afraid her mother was going to make her go to bed.

"No, not tonight, darling," Emma assured her. "Julian's already very put out with me because I want to leave the party. I'm not as used to this sort of thing as I once was. But you can stay as long as you don't get in the way." Emma's hand, cool and soft, trailed across Tally's cheek. "You look mighty pretty, my precious. And very grown up."

"Oh, I hope so, Mother. I want to be grown up. Just as fast as I can. It's . . . it's so much fun, isn't it?" She gazed around the room in rapture.

Emma looked thoughtfully at her daughter. Then she laughed. "Yes it is. Almost as much fun as being nine. Be a good girl and come get in bed with me before you go to sleep."

Tally kissed her mother good night, happy that she would be really and truly on her own for a while. Then she drifted around the large room. Mostly she listened to what people were saying, and because they talked so brightly and with such conviction, she was sure it was very important. They talked of the parties they had been to and the parties they were going to. They gossiped about the latest scandal. They said lots of names of famous people. They seemed to know everybody, and they were in on all the secrets of the adult world. One would have thought there was nothing and no one they didn't know about. Tally listened, enthralled. It all seemed to her wonderfully right. This was the kind of life she dreamed about. Someday, she told herself, the party would be her party, the people would be her friends. And she would greet them like a queen.

She heard one woman remark on the room. "There isn't another like it in New York," was what she said, and Tally beamed proudly. Julian had taken her around this room soon after she and her mother had arrived. He had named things for her and told her why they were beautiful and important. This spacious room with its Aubusson carpet on the floor, its lovely Impressionist paintings on the wall, each one in a gilt frame and lit by a tiny golden light. He had told her the period names of the chairs and occasional tables, such lovely, regal names—Queen Anne, Edwardian, Tudor, Louis V, Venetian . . . Beyond the room was a large terrace, edged by Chinese willows in clay urns. And beyond that was New York City. Spread out like a blanket of tiny diamonds, the apartment afforded a three-sided view that stretched from north to south and west across Central Park. It was breathtaking. That's what her mother had said. "Simply breathtaking." She had heard people say that the apartment and its view cost Julian a fortune, but that didn't seem to matter. He had a fortune. He was the richest man in the world. Oh, how wonderful to have pots and pots of money. And how important!

The thing that struck her most about the new surroundings was not only their beauty and richness but the sharp contrast to the house she had left behind in Springs. It made her feel bad to compare, but still she couldn't help it. The shabby furniture, the mismatched china, the narrow bed in her room, with its worn flannel sheets and musty-smelling quilt. Here her bed was plumped up with feather comforters, goosedown pillows, and satin-edged sheets of the softest linen. She had her own private bath and there was never a shortage of hot water. Indeed, there was never a shortage of anything. Here, life was effortless. Here, life proceeded reasonably—no one made scenes, no one shouted, no one threw furniture about. It made her shudder to remember . . . and then she instantly felt guilty. If only Mama wouldn't be sad, she thought. Then life would be perfect.

40

Years later I asked Ivan to talk to me about the time that Emma left.

"It is very hard for me to recall it, Maisie," he said, "not so much because of pain, but because most of that time I was like sleeping man. I was living *cauchemar,* you know, nightmare. I think the soul went from my body and I was like walking dead person. Do you know that in so-called primitive societies people believe that your soul can leave while you dream. Then, until soul returns, there is no rest, no work, no sleep. That is how it was when Emma left me.

"I was alone, you know, completely. I saw no one. And because I could do nothing else, I would walk. Walk for hours. At first it was aimless—anything to get out of lifeless house, anything to exhaust myself, to keep dark terrors from my mind. I got to know beaches and coves, woods and dunes, everything, all the places around, and I began to see nature like I never saw before. I found comfort being alone, sitting for hours, studying ebb and flow of tides and patterns everywhere.

"One day I was on beach for long time, looking at ocean, watching tide turn to come in. For first time in years I don't feel pain and I began to see glimmer of hope that the sickness that has me might be cured. It was a drizzly day in November and very cold. Suddenly I took off clothes and ran into crashing sea. The shock was stupendous. I screamed and yelled—I think I would frighten anyone who heard, but beach was deserted. I had all over again in that moment all the pain in my life— my parents died again, I was dragged from streets by the Nazis again, my son died again, Emma left me again, Tally left me again. I couldn't swim, nothing, I think maybe I'll die, but huge wave pick me up and throw me like piece of rubbish onto beach. I caught breath and crawled to where clothes are, spitting out water and sand from mouth, I suddenly am thinking this is like I am reborn. Ocean has spit me out second chance—to live and work and love again.

"I turned and looked again at ocean and I think I don't ever see it again as just, you know, pretty view, nice place for summer picnic. Ocean is living force. I understood what primitive peoples know, what ancients knew. Sea and wind and air, everything, beaches and beautiful tall grasses, everything, everything is emotion, is feeling. I don't know if I'm saying right, but was very, mmmm, mystical. It make me whole again."

Of course, the healing process Ivan was talking about took many weeks. He spent his days in the open air, his evenings by the kitchen fire with a spartan supper. He learned to find comfort in silence, his thoughts no longer demons to be avoided. His pleasures, such as they were, were simple, straightforward things, and the very simplicity of them pleased him immeasurably. It wasn't as if he were not lonely. He was. He missed Emma and Tally in a way he never knew possible. But there was something new in his solitude that soothed him.

41

I had lunch with Julian in Zurich in September of 1967, a few months after Emma and Tally had gone to live with him. The recent events had shocked me; the idea that Emma would actually leave Ivan was incredible. Julian, of course, was puffed up and smug, all but crowing—I told you so, I told you so.

It was not unusual for him to be in Europe, and Zurich was an important stopover for him. Slade International now boasted galleries in more than a dozen cities throughout the world, and Julian's manner and appearance reflected his success. In Europe he was considered the preeminent dealer of American avant-garde art, a market that continued its steady and highly lucrative growth.

I saw quite a bit of him on those trips to Europe—I was lonesome for the old days and news of my friends, and Henry's illness would not allow me to travel. So Julian became my only real link to the affairs of Ivan and Emma. Ivan never wrote, and Emma had little to say. Perhaps they didn't want to burden me with their troubles when I had quite enough of my own.

"It's not as if I hadn't foreseen this long ago," Julian said. "Frankly, I am astonished it has taken Emma so long to come to her senses. Ivan may be a great artist, but he is impossible to live with. Emma should never have taken up with him in the first place."

"I hope you haven't said that to her, Julian. It would hurt her terribly."

"Of course I haven't. I've been the very soul of tact and grace. At the moment, Emma doesn't need criticism, she needs taking care of. I've hired a personal maid for her, and she has the run of my house and the services of my staff. I've enrolled Tally in the best private school. The child is positively glowing. She was downright scruffy and wild when she first came, now she's beginning to behave like a proper young lady. I've seen to her clothes, taken her to the theater and ballet, given her riding lessons, introduced her to people who matter. Ivan, the great artist, seems to have neglected his child in every area including the one in which he might have given her the most. She has no culture and very little education. The child can hardly work her way through a French menu, and Ivan, need I remind you, speaks better French than English. I can tell you I have my hands full. But it is a pleasure to teach her, she is so eager and quick to learn. And I think Emma is pleased with my success with Tally."

"I wonder," I said, half to myself. It was easy enough to imagine an impressionable child being bowled over by such largesse, but I couldn't help feeling that Emma was between a rock and a hard place. There was no doubt that she needed to get away from Ivan, at least for a while, I could see that; but I could also see that Julian was hardly a disinterested benefactor. After all these years he still hoped to have Emma back for himself.

"And why shouldn't I?" he demanded to know. "I admit I was wrong about Emma in some ways. There were things, many things, I didn't know about her when we were engaged. But I was right about one thing: she was never cut out to be the drudging wife of a destitute bohemian. She should be surrounded by beauty and luxury, not rotting vegetables and pickup trucks. She should be with people of culture, not temperamental idiots. It was Emma's weakness to want a man like Ivan. She would have found strength with me, even as she does now. As for Ivan, I believe the man has simply run out of luck and talent."

"I hope you don't actually believe that, Julian," I said incredulously, "because if you do, you're riding for another big fall. Emma and Ivan were made for each other. Hard as it may be for you to understand, there are some things that haven't a price tag on them. Whatever difficulties they're going through now will never extinguish the love—yes, Julian, love—they have for each other. And their love has nothing to do with Ivan's talent. You've never been able to sell Ivan's work, so you dismiss him, but personally I don't think Ivan's lost his way at all. I think he's evolving. Dealers like you just suffocate talent. You try to mold everything into something you can sell. That's what it's all about, isn't it? The big sell?"

Julian smiled indulgently and dabbed his lips with his napkin. "Well, Maisie dear, that's a fact of life, whether *you* like it or not. You seem to think that good art naturally finds its own way into the spotlight of public attention and respect. You think it's a natural process, like gravity. Water will find its own level. Truth and beauty will out. Well, let me tell you something. You are very naïve. The history of art is, in fact, the history of rich patrons.

"Where is Michelangelo without the de Medicis, or where is Cellini for that matter? In the modern world, the art dealer has replaced the patron. It's the art dealer who makes great art possible. Where would nineteenth-century art be without the great Duveen? Where would the Abstract Expressionists be without Lloyd and the Marlborough Gallery?"

"Oh for the love of God, Julian. Get off the soapbox, will you?"

"It amazes me, Maisie, that with all your money and the years you've lived among civilized people, you still haven't acquired a particle of sophistication. Heaven knows, you've had every chance."

"I'm afraid I've been a sad disappointment to you, Julian, but to tell you the truth, I'm very satisfied with myself as I am."

Julian and I were used to this kind of verbal dueling, and usually I quite enjoyed our matches, but his influence over Emma genuinely worried me. I could see how smug and self-satisfied he was with this turn of events, and I could imagine the grim realities of the situation. If only Henry hadn't been so ill, I would have flown to America and taken a more active role. Of course, in retrospect, I see that nothing I could have done would have changed the course of subsequent events.

42

It was in January, nearly six months since Emma had left, and Ivan was eating a bowl of cereal next to the open stove one night when he heard a loud crash coming from the studio. He rushed out into the night and found a teenaged boy groaning in the bushes. Clearly he had fallen from the upper story of the studio, and though the bushes had broken the fall, the boy was hurt and bleeding. He was also scared and angry, and he cursed and struggled like a wild thing as Ivan half-dragged, half-carried him into the house.

"Are you gonna call the cops?" the boy demanded as Ivan lowered him onto the sofa.

"Can't," Ivan muttered. "No phone. It's okay, though, you can steal whole place clean if you like."

"I'm not a thief."

"Oh? Please forgive me then. Now let me look at leg." The boy's face was white with pain, but he didn't flinch while Ivan gently manipulated his ankle. "Looks like bad sprain. You need doctor."

"I ain't going to no doctor. I just came to get what's mine." The boy tried to stand, but sank back onto the sofa with a groan of pain.

"Yours? Again I am sorry. I don't know there was something in my studio that was yours. And did you find in middle of the night in the dark what you were looking for?" Ivan laughed gently and laid his hand on the boy's shoulder. "Please lie back. I'm going to wash your cuts and wrap your ankle. But first I'm going to make tea with maybe a little brandy? Eh? You don't look so good, my friend."

The boy did as he was told. The fight had gone out of him and he seemed suddenly exhausted. Still he watched Ivan warily as he moved about the kitchen as unperturbed and genial as if he had been expecting the boy all along. When the hot, steaming mug was brought to him, he again tried to struggle up, but found he was so weak he could hardly move. Ivan put his arm around his shoulder and fed him tiny sips of the bracing drink.

He was thin, but not from lack of nourishment. Tall and wiry, he had the face of a boy and the hands of a working man. There was something almost exotic about him. Rough, straight, jet-black hair, almond-shaped green eyes. He'd be a very handsome boy indeed, if only his face didn't look so pinched, so angry, and so scared. Something in the eyes, Ivan thought, something so familiar.

"Yeah, I found it," the boy said suddenly. "I knew where it was."

"Oh, you have been here before, then, yes?"

"Yeah." He was defiant now, proud of himself. The brandy had loosened his tongue, and he felt warm and boastful. "Lots of times. I was here day before yesterday. I followed you all the way over to Maidstone Jetty. I've seen all your stuff in there. All your tools, everything."

"You like tools?" asked Ivan.

"You don't. You don't take care of yours. They're all rusted from the damp. You ought to oil them, you know."

"So you like to admire my tools. Is that what you come for?"

"No." His eyes flickered to a bulge under his jacket, and then looked quickly away. "I told you I come for what's mine and I don't give a fuck what you say or anybody, it's mine!"

Ivan shrugged. "If you say so. I don't care for what's in studio. Nothing there that means anything to me. You are welcome to anything you want, you know, but I'm curious. What is under coat there? May I see it, please?"

The boy's chin came up and he started to deny it, but then he shrugged. He pulled out a rolled-up canvas that was wrapped around his waist under his coat. Ivan took it and walked under the light. He stood looking at the unrolled canvas for a long while. It was the portrait he had made of Rita Hayes. She looked out at the world through smiling, hopeful eyes, as if her smile held an invitation to join her in a great joke. Ivan looked back at the boy. "You are Rita's boy, yes?" Ivan said. "It's all right, I know you are. I know you. I am very sorry."

And that was how Zack Hayes came into their lives.

The next day Ivan agreed he would not call a doctor or otherwise inform anyone of Zack's accident, if Zack would promise not to leave until his ankle was better. He fixed the boy breakfast and watched him devour a huge amount of food. They didn't speak much, but it wasn't an uncomfortable silence. In the afternoon while Zack slept again, and for the first time in what felt like a lifetime, Ivan went into the studio. The air was still and musty and cobwebs sparkled everywhere in the sunlight that filtered through holes in the roof. Plaster models in various poses stood around looking like ghosts, and on close inspection he found that most of them were covered with a fine film of mildew. A fluttering noise in the rafters informed him that squirrels were nesting up there. It amused him in a strange way to notice that nature cared little enough whether Ivan used his studio or not, whether Ivan was working or not. Life in its myriad shapes and forms went on all the same. Dust, mildew, and decay were as much a part of the process as anything else. Ivan gathered up an armload of his tools and brought them back into the kitchen. All day he scraped, cleaned, and polished away, until not a speck of dirt or rust remained. Zack watched at first but soon was helping, picking up what needed to be done without having to be told. Then after supper Ivan explained the tools, their history, their uses. It was technical talk mainly, and Ivan was surprised to find that Zack knew as much about them as he himself did. He liked the way the boy held the tools, solidly but with respect. They talked late into the night and then Ivan went to bed. In the morning he found that Zack had polished the remaining tools. Everything lay in neat rows, ready for their master's hand to put them to good use. Zack was nowhere to be seen, but Ivan knew he'd come back.

And he did. In the weeks that followed, they found they had much to teach each other. Ivan opened the studio, and he began to talk to Zack about his work—about space, motion, form, and nature. He showed him how the tools were used and how he worked with clay and plaster. He talked about the difficulty of translating ideas into physical objects. He was pleased to discover that Zack had an unerring eye for balance and an easy grasp of technique.

Slowly, in bits and pieces, never all at once, Zack's story began to unfold. Fifteen years old, he'd been on his own for three years already. His childhood might have been invented by Dickens. He'd learned early on to leave his mother's house quickly and silently whenever she was "entertaining." At first he would huddle near the door, willing the time to pass so that he would be allowed back in, but soon the sounds from within drove him to roam farther and farther, and eventually his mother's busy social life became his ticket to freedom.

Ivan said little whenever Zack talked about his boyhood, but the intensity of the boy, his determination, reminded Ivan of himself so long ago, when he, too, was a boy who walked alone, without the protection or security of a family.

Two lost souls had found each other. Out of that small miracle came another: Ivan began to work again. His artistic passion had returned, and with it a deeper, truer expression. Soon he was working from early morning to late at night, sometimes all night. And Zack was there so often that before long Ivan began to take his presence in the studio for granted. Zack, with his meticulous attention to detail, his ability to stay with the most boring but necessary tasks, became an able and invaluable assistant.

I t was spring, and Julian wanted to take Emma to Europe. "It appalls me that you've never been," Julian said as he snuffed out his cigarette and poured another cup of espresso. They had finished lunch and were sitting in the large, oak-paneled library of the triplex apartment. "I'm flying to Paris next week, and then Rome. We could go to London as well, or Switzerland, and you could see Maisie. Would you like that?"

Emma smiled. "You're so good to us, Julian. Really, you're doing too much."

"Nonsense. You hardly let me do a thing for you. I think Tally's done more and seen more in New York in the past ten months than you have. Don't you think it's time you stopped moping about and started enjoying your life? God knows you aren't bound to Ivan now, but you act as if you were. You're like one of those whaler's wives in Nantucket. Remember the summer when my mother took a house there and you came to visit? There was a widow's walk on the roof, and we used to climb up there. That's what you remind me of. A woman waiting for her sailor to come back. You never go out. You never want to do anything."

"Oh, Julian," Emma sighed. "Don't pay any attention to me. I promise I'll try not to be so mopey, but, really, I don't want to go out. I want to think and be quiet."

"But you don't look well. You're pale and you've lost far too much weight. A trip would do you good, and it would be amusing to show you all the places one should see."

"I don't think so, Julian. Not right now. But thank you. Thank you for everything. Most of all I thank you for Tally. She's quite taken with your world."

"My world? It's yours as well. Or should be. I've never forgotten who you are, even if you have. Please Emma," he scolded, "stop acting so fidgety. I want you to look at me and to listen to me. You've become very adept at avoiding me, though you know very well what it is I want to say."

Emma looked down at her hands. "Please, Julian . . ."

"No, I need to say this. I've wanted to say it for so long. You can't be very surprised to know that I love you. I've never stopped loving you. I've never stopped believing that someday I might have you again. I want you to marry me, Emma. I want you to be with me from now on. I want to give you the life you should have had. Now, now, don't interrupt. Let me finish. You were born to a certain way of life and you should have it. I can understand how you might not want a fast-paced social life. Maybe you won't believe this, but I don't like it much myself. I do it for the gallery. Frankly, I spend most of my time with people who either bore me or patronize me. Neither one is very pleasant. I've done well for myself, and I enjoy what I do, but I needn't keep on doing it. Nothing is as important to me as you are. Nothing in business could ever make me so happy as making you happy. Please let me try, Emma. Please let me back in your heart. Let me heal what has hurt you." He got up and came to where she was sitting. He took her hands, which were as cold as two lumps of ice, and pulled her into his arms. She was like a limp rag doll.

"Oh, my darling, darling . . ." His voice was choked with emotion as he pressed her body to his.

She was still for a moment, and then, gently, she reached her hand to his head, stroking the back of his neck. "Julian, Julian, you mustn't say these things . . ." And she started to say something else but suddenly she stiffened and pulled away. Her eyes, which had been gentle and sad, were now bright and alert. Her cheeks were inflamed and her hand went to her throat. Julian stepped back, confused.

"Whatever is the matter with you, Emma?" he said. From downstairs and muffled by the thick doors of the room, he heard Tally's voice squealing with delight.

"Papa! Papa!" Tally flew into Ivan's outstretched arms. "You're here. Why didn't you tell us? Oh, Papa, I've missed you so much." Her kisses rained tiny damp imprints on his cheek. In a single instant she had forgiven him everything.

"Shush, shush now, my Natalia. I miss you, too. Give me big hug. I miss you too. Look. You are grown-up young lady."

"I am. I am very grown up. Julian says he's polishing my rough edges. And you see, he has. See my fingernails? All polished by the manicurist at the hairdresser's."

Ivan laughed. "I kiss my sweet girl's hand. Now tell me about your mama. Is she all right? Is she as happy as you?" He lowered his voice. "You think she will see me?"

Tally stood back and surveyed him solemnly. "I don't know. But you're not to make her cry. She doesn't let me see her cry, but I hear her sometimes at night."

"No, no. I want Mama to be happy. I am here to see that she is happy."

The door behind Tally opened, and Emma was there. They stood still, saying nothing, looking at each other for a long time. So long, in fact, that Tally, whose wisdom often surpassed her years, quietly withdrew. Finally Emma broke the silence.

"Hello, Ivan. How are things with you?"

"With me?" Ivan paused, then burst into a loud, booming laugh. "Emma, my darling Emma. I am fantastic. I must tell what has happened to me. I want to tell you all about my work. I want to talk to you. I must talk to you. Not here . . ." He looked around as if realizing for the first time that he was in strange surroundings. "This place suffocates me. Come walk with me, my Emma. Come walk in beautiful spring air."

Emma did not hesitate. She took the hand that was offered to her, and stepped out into that perfect day in May.

Manhattan sparkled. The temperature was a balmy seventy degrees, with just enough of a breeze to make you welcome the warmth of the sun on your skin. Ivan and Emma walked down Fifth Avenue along the park, then turned east to avoid the midtown crowds. No doubt they drew admiring glances from other strollers—they did still make a very handsome couple—but like lovers the world over, they were oblivious to anything but one another.

"Emma, Emma, I'm working again and everything is changed. When baby died, something died in me, because I was untrue to myself. I was lying to myself."

Emma barely heard what he was saying, she was so overwhelmed by his physical presence, by the strength she felt emanating from him. Never before had she seen him so lit up, so illuminated with energy. Everything about him glowed with strength and confidence. He was a giant among men, this husband of hers, she had always known that. The long three years of his malady dissolved in the light air, and nothing else mattered but that they were together again. Only now, she sensed, it was different, stronger somehow for all the trials and pain they had been through.

"I looked at you with the dreamer's eyes." Ivan stopped walking. He was looking at her closely, intently. "You walked into my life and you were woman in my dreams. I kept you there. You were inspiration to me. But I was not willing to let you be. Emma, I want you back, but not as someone who lives in my dream, who exists in my fantasy to inspire me. I want you back as my wife, to live beside me, and I with you. I love you, Emma, and I want you to be with me now and for the rest of my life."

They had been walking for hours, and they now found themselves in a small park abutting a schoolyard. They sat down on a bench in the playground, in the shade of a maple tree.

"I know it now. Nothing stands alone," Ivan continued. "In new work, every piece remembers connection with others. Like life, Emma, like my life. I cannot look at you without remembering Tally and our baby and Dance and so much more. I wish I could show you sculpture I am making, so you would understand. Wait. Here . . ." He leaped up from the bench, extracted a piece of chalk from his jeans pocket, and walked out to the center of the playground.

"I call it the Circle of Desire." He began to sketch forms onto the black asphalt. He drew quickly and with a sure hand. "Seven pieces. Desire has many faces." One by one, a circle of figures began to appear on the empty playground floor.

"I will create desire in all forms, every mood. Pieces will move like air and wind, and each one will flow from one to next, so together they will form one motion, one space." Ivan paused. The circle was complete. He beckoned for Emma to join him in the center. "This is how piece should be seen. From inside circle. Heart is here." They stood together, hand in hand, encircled by the images he had drawn. He took her in his arms and buried his face in her hair. "Emma," he whispered. "I give you my heart, my life, my work. I beg you, come back to my life again."

Emma put her arms around him, holding him tight. "I was never very far from you, Ivan. I never will be."

Ivan roared a loud, happy laugh. "We will go home, Emma. We go get our daughter and go home." As they walked out of the playground, he had his arm around her waist. But before they turned the corner, he glanced back at the chalked circle he had drawn. He stopped abruptly. Emma, too, looked back and then at Ivan. "What is it, darling? You look as if you've seen a ghost."

His hand gripped hers tightly. "Is nothing," he said, "nothing at all. Let's leave them just like that, I think. Maybe children will invent new game with it. Hopscotch." He laughed his hearty, booming laugh, the laugh she had missed for so long, and hugged his wife again.

44

Emma returned to Springs that very day, though Tally, with only four more weeks of school left, stayed in New York with Julian to finish out her year. I don't know what Julian felt after Emma left, he never confided in me, but he couldn't have been all that happy to have the only woman he had ever wanted slip through his fingers one more time. I do know that he was genuinely happy to have Tally stay on. There was a real bond between those two, and when they put their heads together and had their hearts set on something, they made an irresistible force.

Tally came home on weekends, taking the Long Island Rail Road out on Friday afternoons. I think perhaps she was a little sorry when school came to an end and she went back home for good. She liked having a foot in each world. She liked spending weekdays with Julian, living an ordered life of immaculate luxury, and attending a very good school, where, incidentally, she had done very well indeed. Her teachers liked her, as did her classmates. And she enjoyed spending weekends in the country with her parents, who spoiled her in different ways.

"There is boy living in cabin," Ivan had told her on her first weekend home. His name is Zack Hayes. He is helping me with new work. You will like him." But Tally was not at all pleased with the idea.

"A boy?" she asked. "What boy?"

"Local boy . . ." Ivan started to say, but Tally was not interested.

"But, Papa, why must he live in our cabin? It's really my cabin, you know, you told me it was. You know how much I like to play there. I was planning to use it a lot this summer. Can't he live somewhere else? Why doesn't he live with his parents?"

"No, Natasha. He has nowhere else to live. He is orphan boy. Besides, I need him in studio."

When it became clear to her that Zack was to join them at dinner every night, her hostility increased. Meeting him in person did nothing to change her mind. She could not abide this skinny, ugly boy who hadn't any nice clothes or proper manners. She despised him for having any place in her father's affections, and hated him for daring to pretend to be Ivan's assistant. She resented the fact that *he* was allowed to be in the studio when Ivan was working, while she was not. Her anger honed itself to a fine, bitter edge.

Like most children her age, she was an expert eavesdropper. One evening she heard her father telling Emma the story of how Zack had appeared in his life. She didn't quite understand everything until she heard her mother ask in a quiet voice full of sorrow and pity, "Do you mean Zack is that poor woman's son?"

Tally immediately knew who "that poor woman" was, and she was shocked and angered by this horrible revelation. How could her papa do this to them? How could her mama allow it? Was she so very weak? Didn't she have any pride? Tally crept back to bed and lay in the dark with indignant tears streaming down her cheeks.

From that day she declared total war on this lout who had insinuated himself so perversely into her family. She made it a practice to lie in wait for him and hiss, "Thief, thief," as he passed her by. Fifteen-year-old Zack had no idea what to make of Tally's hostile behavior. She seemed a very spoiled brat, but since Ivan was his mentor and benefactor, Zack was willing to put up with whatever he had to from his spiteful daughter. He adopted the only strategy available to him, and did his best to ignore her.

Julian spent a month in Europe, returning as self-possessed as ever. Neither he nor Emma ever mentioned his proposal again. When he went out to see Ivan's new work, he was impressed. Whatever he might have felt personally, he had always been constant in his appreciation of Ivan's talent. However cynically he may have pursued his fortunes as a dealer, pandering to passing fads and fashions—when he wasn't actually creating them—he knew, he had always known, that Ivan was the real thing. The new work was not only important, it was the breakthrough for which he had been waiting, work that was, just possibly, strong enough to buck the tides of fashion and turn the eye of the art world back to the classical values of beauty, truth, and passion. Never one to waste time, he demanded to know when they would be ready to show.

"Look, it's time you had a one-man show. Can you push a little and have them ready to ship to me next June? That gives you a whole year . . . well, a little under a year. But we could open the fall season with your show." Julian's enthusiasm was unmistakably genuine. Much to his surprise, however, Ivan did not jump at his offer.

"Julian, Julian, my friend, how can I tell you when sculptures will be ready? Many are not yet born. They are tiny embryos in the womb of my imagination. I cannot say how long entire Circle will take, maybe year, maybe rest of my life. But I agree. Is time for Ivan St. Peters to show the world his work. Why not show the work you have in warehouse? None has been seen. I like to see them exhibited. I want to see people around my sculptures. I want this, Julian, and I want you to do this for me. You say you appreciate my work. You say you understand what I am doing. Circle of Desire is direct descendent of all that was before. You cannot know one without the other. Do you remember, Julian, how you promised me you would make people love my work as you do? Do you remember on Hudson Street, when you were starting out in business and I was accepting you as my dealer? I want you to show my early work, Julian, then we will show the Circle when it is complete."

I don't think that Ivan had ever expressed himself so strongly to Julian before, and Julian was impressed. I believe he also saw the strength of Ivan's position and knew that for once the artist was right. The time had come. Despite the late date Julian agreed to have a show that autumn. He promised Ivan the full treatment—publicity, advertising, and a VIP opening. He also promised to talk to dealers in other major cities and arrange a tour for the exhibition.

When it was announced that Julian was staying for an early supper before driving back to the city, Tally ran upstairs and changed into one of her city dresses. She even tried to get Emma to change as well, but Emma looked up from her preparations and said, "Don't be ridiculous, Tally. This is not a dinner party. We're just giving Julian a nice home-cooked family dinner. Would you please shell these peas?"

"Is Zack going to eat with us?"

"Of course he is!"

Tally eyed her mother. "Don't you think that sometimes, like when we have guests, we could have dinner without him? Why can't he go eat with someone else? Why can't he eat by himself? After all, it's not like he's family or anything. He's just the hired help, isn't he?"

"What on earth has gotten into you, Tally? Zack is no more 'hired help' than . . . well, than you or I. We don't have hired help. Zack is living with us because your father invited him to. He's a very gifted boy."

"But didn't Papa say that Zack is his assistant?" Tally went on stubbornly. "Doesn't that mean that he's paid to help out in the studio?"

"Yes."

"Well, then, he's the hired help, and I think he should eat in the servants' quarters."

Emma finished placing a tray of biscuits in the oven. She resisted a temptation to slam the oven door shut. "Tally," she said, "stop what you are doing and listen to me. Look at me and listen very hard. Zack Hayes is not a servant, and I don't seem to remember any servants' quarters around here. He is an apprentice to your father. Being an apprentice to an artist is a very honorable and very old tradition. While he is an apprentice to your father, he is a member of our family, with all the rights, privileges, and responsibilities that come with that. Do you understand me? I don't want to hear any more of your nonsense about this. Now finish shelling those peas and set the table. There's a good girl."

They ate clam chowder, grilled salmon steaks, and peas from Emma's garden, and finished up with strawberry shortcake. Everybody was hungry and ate with enthusiasm. Only Tally, overdressed and uncomfortable, sat primly picking at her food. She shot disapproving glances at Zack, who was noisily downing his chowder. As Julian was telling Emma about his plans for Ivan's show, Tally interrupted: "Excuse me, Julian, could you speak a little louder? I can't hear you very well over the noise Zack is making." Emma let this pass, but she was not pleased with her daughter's behavior. After dinner, Zack cleared the table while Tally did the dishes. Every time Zack came into the kitchen she whispered venomous insults, calling him a thief, a slob, and worse.

With dinner over and last-minute business details attended to, Julian was about to leave for the city. "Well, now, we're all set. Don't make me wait too long for the new work, Ivan. Tally, my dear, if you'd like to come into New York next week, I'll take you to a nice lunch and we'll do a little shopping."

Tally flung herself into Julian's arms. "Oh, Julian, that would be wonderful. What day? Mama, what day can I go?"

"Not next week, Tally," Emma said, softly but firmly. "Thank you, Julian, but Tally will have to stay closer to home for a while. I really can't spare her just now."

"Oh, Mama, why?" Tally howled like a wounded animal. "Why can't I go for just one day? It's not fair . . ."

"That's enough, Tally. I want you to go to your room and wait for me. Go. Now."

Tally ran up the stairs and threw herself across her bed in a paroxysm of preadolescent despair. When she heard Emma's footsteps, she tried out her most heartrending sobs, but Emma was unimpressed. She closed the bedroom door behind her and stood waiting to be heard.

"Tally, sit up, wipe your face, and be quiet."

"You're horrible to me, horrible, and if I can't go to see Julian in New York, I'm simply going to die."

"I doubt that, Tally. But unless we get some things straightened out and understood, you can be sure that it will be a good long time before I allow you to go to New York, or anywhere else for that matter."

"But, Mama—"

"Tally, I heard you saying those ugly things to Zack. Can you explain yourself to me? Can you explain how it is possible that my daughter has turned into a mean little spoiled brat? I have never been so ashamed of anyone in my whole life."

Tally was honestly crying now. Emma had never before spoken so harshly to her. Everything seemed terrible and confusing, most especially the turmoil of her emotions.

"Why do you hate Zack? I've never known you to be unkind before. Talk to me, Tally."

"I hate him because . . . oh, I don't know, I just hate him. He doesn't belong here. He's not one of us. Papa treats him like he's so special, but he's not. He's horrible and stupid. He's . . . he's *common.*" She was all choked up with sobs again. Emma took pity on her. She sat down on the bed and held her until she quieted down.

"You're wrong, you know. Zack is not common. No one is. That's an ugly, snobbish expression and people use it because they are either ignorant or afraid. I want you to think about that. And I want you to think about your feelings. I'm sorry that his being part of the family upsets you so much, but you're going to have to learn to accept the situation. Now promise me that you will never say those things to Zack again."

"I promise, Mama. I won't, really I won't."

"One more thing, Tally. Since when do you call Uncle Julian by his first name?"

"I don't know. I only thought it would sound more grown up."

"Well I don't want to hear you do that again. Understood?" Tally nodded. "Don't be in such a hurry to grow up, my darling. It will happen soon enough all by itself. Try to enjoy being a little girl as long as you can."

That was not, of course, the end of Tally's troubles with Zack. They spoke to each other only when they had to, and for the rest of the summer they were like two old cats who had grown beyond the hissing stage, still bristling when they saw each other.

Tally had discovered that a number of friends she had made at school in New York came out to East Hampton for the summer, and she plunged into a social life that included picnics, beach dates, and slumber parties. Ivan was working like a man possessed, and there was no one to notice that Emma was not quite herself. Her face was often strained and drawn. Her energies flagged, and she simply could not keep up with all the projects that usually surrounded her. It was nothing, she told herself. Probably only an emotional reaction to the strain of the winter and her long separation from Ivan.

As Emma watched her growing daughter, she realized that Tally seemed not to need her the way she had in the past. But this made her happy. Until now Tally had always seemed a lonely girl, who preferred the company of adults to that of children her own age. Often it had reminded Emma of her own isolated childhood, and she was pleased to see Tally with girls her own age.

Two of Tally's girlfriends were playing at her house one day. They had had a long day at the beach, and now were down in the meadow, where they were consuming alarming quantities of cookies and lemonade. They could see Zack's cabin and they watched him come out and walk slowly, absorbed in his thoughts, over to Ivan's studio. Tally was amazed to discover that her girlfriends were intrigued. In fact, the ultimate compliment was bestowed on his lanky form. He was pronounced "Rilly, rilly cute!"

"Who is he?" they wanted to know.

"No one." Tally shrugged. "He's just a boy who works for my father."

"Oh, come on, Tally. Why have you been holding out on us? Are you in love with him? Has he kissed you? I bet he's a great kisser." The girls wouldn't let up, and as their teasing became more intense, Tally desperately tried to think of a way to divert their interest.

"Hey, listen, I've got an idea. There's a rowboat down by the water. Let's take it out and go across." She pointed across Accabonac Harbor to a spit of undeveloped land belonging to The Nature Conservancy. They thought this was a great idea. The boat was a little harder to push out than Tally had imagined, but still with persistence she was able to get them out into the inlet. There was much giggling and shrieking as they made their way across the shallow inlet. Perhaps they were engrossed in their girlish jokes, so they never noticed the leak until the boat capsized and they had to abandon it. The water was no more than waist-deep—there was no real danger except to the boat, which sank ignominiously, but their feet were a little cut up by the gravelly bottom, and they had a longish walk home in their sopping clothes.

Ivan and Emma were furious, of course, but Zack was distraught. It had been his boat, which in the fall months he used to go scalloping. In a good season the scallop harvest could provide almost enough money for him to live for the rest of the year. He was upset about the boat and even more upset at the uproar in the St. Peters household. Tally was made to apologize to Zack while Ivan and Emma looked on. She was going to pay for the boat out of her allowance. There would be no more trips to New York until full restitution had been made.

Tally was contrite in the presence of her parents, but humiliated by having to beg Zack's forgiveness. It was a bitter wound and it festered. One day when they were alone together Zack tried to tell her that he, too, was sorry that there had been so much trouble. "I wish we could be friends, Tally," he said, and held out his hand to her, but she was unwilling to accept his generosity. Before she could think, she was shouting "I hate you, I hate you, I hate you!" She stomped her foot and her lovely young face was contorted with rage. "You could never be my friend."

Zack looked at her and started to walk away. Then he turned and said calmly but with deadly seriousness, "All right. But I'll never ask you again. And someday you'll regret it."

Tally held her head very high and watched him defiantly as he strode down the path, but she was conscious of an odd feeling of regret. She almost wished she had answered Zack Hayes differently.

I flew to New York for the opening of Ivan's show in October. To say it was a huge success would not do it justice. Julian had outdone himself. He had given over the entire gallery to Ivan's work. It was all there—pieces from the early days in the studio on Hudson Street, later works from Springs, sketches of the work that was to come. The critics, the public, everyone who saw the show was enchanted. A critic from the *Times* wrote, "Ivan St. Peters shows us the myriad encounters of the heart captured in bronze . . ." Sales were excellent, and it was clear to everyone that Ivan's genius had finally been recognized.

After the opening, Ivan was much in demand and Julian insisted that he stay on in the city for a week or two so he could be taken around and introduced at various dinner parties. After the years of isolation and hard work, he found suddenly that he enjoyed the attention he was getting, and he especially enjoyed the society of people who were constantly singing his praises. Emma had been at the opening but had begged to be excused from the rest of the social agenda. She was as thin as a rail and had a relentless, racking cough. It was a chronic bronchitis, she said, made worse by the fact that she was allergic to almost every kind of antibiotic. She needed rest and she was going home to get it.

By the holidays Emma was better. But in the aftermath of the success of the New York show, Ivan was called on often to travel. A museum in San Diego had purchased a major piece. The civic center in Cincinnati bought three pieces to place in its park. Seattle had bought several pieces for a municipal sculpture garden. And so on. The installation of every piece had to be personally supervised by Ivan, and he was busy hopping from one end of the country to the other.

Julian, of course, was in his element, wheeling and dealing to beat the band. Among his plans was a show for Ivan at the most prestigious gallery in Washington, D.C., a coup that even he might not have pulled off without the help of the well-known hostess and collector Penny Frankenheimer.

She was Penelope Duvall Frankenheimer, of the Philadelphia Duvalls, widow of Supreme Court Justice Augustus Frankenheimer. She'd been a rich young heiress when she had married, and over the years she had managed her wealth skillfully. She was forty-four years old when Ivan met her, and worth nearly forty million dollars. Her cool head and savvy ways had earned her respect in the business world, but money and business were not things Penny cared about excessively. What Penny did care about was art. She collected it herself, and she helped museums acquire it by donating money and advice. And in her spare time she collected important people. She was the doyenne of Washington hostesses. In a town where the right dinner invitations meant everything, hers were always sought after, and no one ever turned her down.

Ivan went to Washington for a week early in April to supervise the installation of his show. He'd been traveling almost nonstop since Christmas, and his time at home was brief and hectic. In many respects he dreaded yet another trip, but as anyone who lives on eastern Long Island knows, spring comes very late. In April there are no leaves on the trees, and only a few hearty flowers are peeking through the damp soil to remind one that winter is nearly over. Washington, on the other hand, is glorious in April. Spring is voluptuously in full bloom. And so it was when Ivan was there.

One evening he was to be the guest of honor at a dinner party given by Penny Frankenheimer. He knew through Julian that she had already bought several of his pieces and was encouraging the National Gallery to do so as well. Wanting to share his excitement with Emma, he called home, but got Tally, who was in tears.

"Natasha, Natasha. Calm yourself. I cannot understand one word of what you say. Where is your mama? Let me speak with her."

"No, no, I can't, Papa. She's asleep. She isn't feeling well." Ivan could hear the girl blowing her nose, trying to compose herself.

"Is she running a fever? Has she called the doctor?"

"No, Papa. She's says it's nothing. Just a cold coming on."

"Then why do you cry like this, Dushka?"

"Oh, Papa, it's the chickens. They're all dead. Every one of them," Tally sobbed. "Their feathers and bones are scattered all over the yard."

"The chickens! What are you talking about?"

Ivan had to wait for several minutes until she had calmed down enough to speak again. "Some dogs got into the hen house. They went crazy, Papa. They ripped all the chickens to pieces. Even Jack. They killed Jack the rooster!"

Tally was sobbing. At last he was made to understand the extent of the disaster that had befallen them. There had been at least thirty chickens in the hen house. Tally and Emma were much too sentimental about their hens; even the older birds, who could no longer lay eggs, they kept on in contented retirement. He knew that for Tally every bird had a name and a history, and his heart ached as he heard his daughter crying for her dead chickens.

"My poor little girl. I'm sorry. There, there. It must have been terrible for you. What does your mama say?"

"She doesn't know. I didn't want to upset her, and she's been asleep. Zack cleaned up the mess and—oh, Papa, please come home. I want you to come home right now."

At last Ivan was able to soothe his daughter. He promised they would get all new chicks that spring and he would build her a strong, impenetrable hen house. A fortress of a hen house, he said. He would be home in a few days and all would be well.

Ivan enjoyed Penny's dinner party. He enjoyed making Penny Frankenheimer's acquaintance as well, and the chicken disaster was soon far from his mind. Penny had a warmth and directness about her that put everyone instantly at ease. Ivan found himself flattered at every turn, and when Penny led her guests out to the garden of her Georgetown house, he was pleased to find two of his early sculptures. He was eager to know more about his hostess. They talked all through dinner, and Ivan stayed long after the other guests had gone. He and Penny drank brandy and talked late into the night. He discovered in Penny a woman with an astounding knowledge of art and a great deal of sympathy for, and understanding of, the problems confronting the working artist. He found himself telling her things he had never really voiced before— about his fears and expectations of success, about his mistrust of a certain breed of collectors who were only in it for the money, about his wish to control the destiny of his art. Penny listened, understood, and sympathized in a way that Ivan hadn't experienced from a woman in a long time. It was strange, this feeling he had around her. It wasn't overtly sexual, and yet it had all the elements of attraction. They were drawn to one another. There was no hint of impropriety, but no denying the attraction. When Ivan finally said good night to Penny Frankenheimer, it was with the sure knowledge that she was a woman he would be seeing again.

46

Despite Ivan's well-intentioned promise, there would be no more chickens at the St. Peters farm in Springs. When Ivan returned he found Emma pale, weak, and in bed. She insisted on calling it a lingering flu, but there was something in her eyes that told him a more bitter truth. He went to see her doctor as soon as he could, and his worst fears were confirmed. The doctor's words fell like heavy blows. It was cancer. By the time she had come in, it was everywhere. There was nothing to be done but to keep her as comfortable as possible. Emma was dying.

Ivan felt as if the very air around him had been sucked away, as if he had been cast into the blackest void. The doctor reached for him and touched his shoulder, murmuring a soft condolence. Ivan stood. He tried to speak but he could not. He strangled on the words he was about to say. Unable to speak, unable even to breathe, he strode from the room. Outside, it was an unusually warm April day, the temperature having reached into the low eighties. The balmy weather was particularly welcome after a long and frigid winter. But the heat of the sun could do nothing to dispel the chill in Ivan's heart. He started walking, leaving the car in the doctor's parking lot. He hurled himself through the town of East Hampton and noticed nothing, saw nothing, felt nothing but the need to keep walking. It took him less than an hour to walk the four miles to his home. He never broke his stride, but entered the house and went straight to Emma. She was sitting on the porch, looking out across the harbor. Emma looked at him and smiled. Ivan knelt and laid his head in her lap and started to cry.

"Poor darling," Emma whispered. "I couldn't tell you myself. I couldn't do that one thing for you."

"You're going to be all right," he said. "Please, please, dear God, you're going to be all right."

She stroked his head. "I'm going to die, Ivan."

They said nothing for a very long time and then she said softly, "I hate it. I'm not afraid of it, but I hate it all the same. You see, I've had time to sort it out and think it all through. But you won't have that. And that's what I hate so much. You must try very hard, my darling, to understand as I do. Our spirits are eternal, Ivan. Our love will take away any fear. There is no death for us. We will always be together. You told me that yourself when I first came to you that Christmas Eve. Do you remember? You must try to recall that sureness of feeling and hold on to it now. It will make it easier for you. You've suffered enough, my darling. Now you must let me go and then go on with your life and your work."

"That is impossible. You are my life. You are my work. You are everything I am or will be."

"Then I will always be with you." She reached up and removed the magician's coin that she had worn on a gold chain everyday of her life since their marriage, and pressed it into Ivan's hand. She closed his fingers around it and held his hand in both of hers. "Remember what you told me . . . our journey together will never end. You and I, Ivan, we will live always together. For us, there is no death." She began stroking his head until his shoulders relaxed and the tension of his body began to fade. They held each other for a long time, Emma soothing Ivan until at last he could look at her. In her eyes he saw only peace and tranquility.

They made a pact not to speak of death anymore. They would live each day as it came, they would savor it, enjoy it, and let it go. To his credit, Ivan pulled it off heroically. He split himself in two. When he was with Emma he was cheerful, patient, and loving. It wasn't even that hard. Their love for each other was as luminous and palpable as ever. Now it sustained them in the pleasure they could still find in each other's company. But alone in his studio, Ivan cursed God and the universe. He railed against the fate that was to steal his beloved Emma from him. He cursed his own petty ambitions and lusts. He cursed all the meaningless temptations of life. The thought of life without Emma was unbearable to him. And the knowledge that he was losing her ate away at his heart like a maggot. He knew as certainly as he knew anything that he would never find peace again.

In the weeks that followed, time belonged to no one. It was no longer measured in minutes or hours, but became at once a precious and cruel presence in the life of the house. Emma's discomfort grew, as the doctor had said it would, and a nurse was hired to take care of her. Soon she no longer came downstairs. Tally was told that her mother was very ill, but no one mentioned death. Ivan worked in his studio while Emma slept in a haze of painkilling drugs, and when she awoke he sat by her bed, playing the guitar and singing to her the Russian songs of his childhood. Tally sang, too, and often accompanied him on her recorder. They worked up quite an act together and joked about going on the stage.

These were the happiest times. The room where Emma lay became a world unto itself, a tightly bound cocoon in which the three of them were together as they never would be again.

When I flew in from Switzerland to visit them, Ivan picked me up at the airport. The minute he saw me, his composure fled. We stood in the crowded airport and I held him sobbing in my arms. He said my name over and over again as he held me, and then he stepped back and said, "The doctor says it won't be long now." I nodded and took him back into my arms.

"She is dying before my eyes, Maisie. I see the ashes under the skin of her beautiful face. I put my arms around her and I can feel her receding into death and I am willing to enter death to follow her, to be with her. She is so much a part of me. I feel her inside of me. I feel her gestures in my gestures and her voice in my voice. Her expressions are my expressions, and her sadness and happiness mingle with mine. She is everything I am."

There was nothing for me to say, so I said nothing. We went and had a drink at one of those dark, smoky airport bars where it is the middle of the night twenty-four hours a day. Then we drove to Springs.

By the time I got there, Emma had reached the stage where she was more in the next world than in this one. I spent many hours sitting by her bed, talking a little, resting while she drifted off to sleep, picking up our conversation when she woke. She was very weak but she was at peace, and often while she slept a smile hovered on her face. I remember a particular afternoon. Sunlight flooded the airy bedroom. I was working on some needlepoint when I heard Emma say, "Maisie? I'm so happy you're here. I was having the most wonderful dream. It was my birthday and I had on a dress—my pale yellow organdy. I wonder where it is. I haven't seen it in years. I was in a meadow, a glorious, sunlit meadow filled with wildflowers in so many colors. The air was perfumed with their scent. And I was running through the meadow looking for someone. Oh, Maisie, it seemed so important, and I can't remember the rest." She sighed and closed her eyes. Then she opened them once more and reached for my hand. She said, "Don't go away, Maisie. I'm just going back there for a minute. I want to find what I was looking for. I won't be long." I watched as she fell into an easy sleep and her face relaxed. The clock on the mantel ticked loudly, and I could hear the strokes of the standing clock downstairs in the hall. I wonder if it's just in the houses of the dying that one becomes so acutely aware of the presence of clocks. As she slept, Emma looked so young. I could tell she was dreaming by the little twitches of her expression. I knew her dream was much more vivid now than what had become of her waking life. Suddenly her eyes flew open and she sat up and reached out her arms and called, "Ivan, Ivan, I'm here. Don't lose me. I'm just here." Her voice was the voice of a young girl—happy, vibrant, and so very much in love. The words were the last she ever uttered.

She died a few days later. We were all there, Ivan, Tally, and I. She never regained consciousness while we kept vigil over her. I think we hoped that if we watched her very carefully we might yet prevent the inevitable. Ivan's eyes never left her; he studied her face as if he were chiseling it on his brain. He listened to her breath. Emma's delicate features blurred in his vision. Then he took her hand, stroking the soft skin. Across from him, Tally held her mother's other hand. But in the end she eluded us. Her life slipped away as lightly and easily as a sigh escapes the lips.

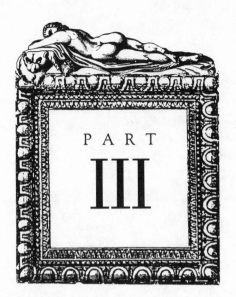

PART

III

47

As I get older, I find I enjoy thinking about myself, where I've come from, the people I've met, what I may or may not have learned from the various turns in the road. The mistakes I've made don't seem quite so colossal now, or the triumphs so important. All in all, things are beginning to even themselves out. I find my fifth decade a very comfortable stage of life. And though I experience an occasional longing to feel once more the mad passions of youth, I am content, by and large, to sit back, observe, and thank my lucky stars that I am saner, wiser, and more grounded now. Today's generation of young people seems different to me. Where my generation was driven by its passions and desires, at the expense of all comfort, security, and prosperity, today's young people seem to be pursuing the very bourgeois values we despised. When we were young, when we were the new bohemians turning the world on its ear, the misunderstood genius, starving and creating in an unheated, uncomfortable garret, was the role model for every artist. Kids from all over the country couldn't wait to come to Greenwich Village, to be poor, to be hip, to be creative. Poverty was raised to the status of a positive virtue. Today the misunderstood genius is despised and avoided. Today he is just a failure. Donald Trump is the man today—aggressive, vain, bombastic, vulgar, culturally illiterate, but successful, always and infinitely successful. Today's young people are dedicated to the worship of success. I don't claim to understand it any more than my parents understood me, but circumstances thrust me into the very heart of this success-oriented artistic milieu.

But back to my story. Ten years have passed. Henry died in 1970, not more than a year after Emma. It had been coming for a long time, and we both knew it. His illness had gone on for an eternity and had weakened him so much that he truly welcomed the end. He left me a good deal of money, but his greatest gift was that he provided me with a new direction for my life. The last years of his illness had kept him bedridden, and I became his only source of contact with the outside world. I used to go out of my way to poke around places, talk to people, find out little stories, anything and everything to amuse him. He would tape-record my stories, saying he wanted to play them back when I was away. In fact, what he did was hire a secretary to transcribe the tapes. These he sent off to a friend in the newspaper business, with the result that I was asked to write a weekly column for a small chain of newspapers in the Midwest. It was called "Notes from Abroad." It became incredibly popular with readers, so that within a year my column was syndicated in over 250 newspapers, and thus I arrived at a career at a time of life when most people are beginning to look forward to retiring.

"Notes from Abroad" kept me very busy. I traveled all over the world. I met many people. I had a wonderful time. There were lovers but I was never tempted to marry, and remained happily independent. I could easily appreciate Jane Austen's very sensible observation that "a single woman of good fortune is always respectable." Every few months I made a point of being in New York, and I would check in on Tally and Ivan. Now, you ask, with Henry gone and Emma, too, did I entertain thoughts about Ivan and me together again? The answer, strangely, is no, I did not. Dance had all along been right about me. It takes stamina and selfless dedication to live with a genius. Nurturing Ivan was never going to be my calling. I was too busy nurturing myself.

Ivan and I would always have a very special kind of friendship— very trusting, very loyal—but it was Tally who became my love. Tally is an adult now, and any minute she will come through the double doors of the apartment I keep in Paris. I can almost set my watch by her, because she is the most punctual person I have ever known—pretty good luck for a chaperone, which is what I am, for lack of a better title. Now isn't life funny?

Paris is my home when I'm not traveling, and for the last three years it has been Tally's, too. But before I allow my beautiful and complicated young Tally to come through that door, let me bring you up to date on her.

I guess Julian and I more or less took charge of Tally after Emma died, Ivan being worse than useless. Emma's death had left a space between Ivan and Tally that was filled with sadness. The sadness went away in time, but left an emptiness. Ivan turned to his work. By then he was already famous, and his fame just increased. His work was praised from every quarter. The critics loved him; the public loved him. And Julian's energy never flagged. Ivan's works were exhibited, sold, and honored throughout the world.

I don't doubt that Ivan loved Tally, but he was never well equipped to see to the needs and sensitivities of a girl growing into womanhood. In truth, he wanted Emma back. Failing that, he wanted a daughter as much like Emma as possible. And in Tally there is much that was Emma's. She has Emma's height and her natural grace and that porcelain skin, and, though darker, that luxuriant hair, but look into Tally's eyes and you will see not Emma but Ivan. Look into her heart . . . well, but who am I to say what was in Tally's heart? The heart of a beautiful, bright, headstrong young woman is something about which I am no longer expert. Thank God!

Ivan's trouble was that he failed to look at Tally at all. I suppose he couldn't help it and it would hurt him to hear me say so, but the fact is that he was a terrible father. I don't know if he would have been a better father to a son, but in many ways he failed Tally completely. It has taken me all these years to realize it, but Ivan's ideas about women are outlandishly medieval and destructively romantic. I think his worst failure as a parent was in never being able to think of Tally as a person separate from himself. He expected her to love, comfort, obey, and care for him. Worse still, he expected her to leave him alone and not bother him with the irritating demands of a teenaged girl.

When Tally finally elected to go away to boarding school in Connecticut, Ivan never obliged her in the small ritual ways that would have meant the world to her. He would never show up for Parents' Day, or moving-up day, or even graduation, yet he would appear unannounced on a weeknight or during exam week, demanding to see her, to take her out, to hug her and be off again. He treated her like a delightful toy to be taken out and played with on a whim. In vain she waited for him to praise her excellent grades. Instead he teased her and called her a grind. She learned French and spoke knowingly about art and literature, but Ivan dismissed her notions and corrected her pronunciation.

Then there was the matter of Penny Frankenheimer. In Tally's senior year, Penny moved into the house in Springs. The romance had been brewing for a long time, and to be sure, Penny still maintained her houses in Washington and Palm Beach, her apartment in New York, and assorted pieds-à-terre in Europe. But in the Hamptons she lived with Ivan. Tally was furious. Furious? More like Vesuvius erupting. Her anger was monumental. I know; I was the one who had been dispatched to tell her. For all his ego and bravado, Ivan was more than a little timid of Tally.

She would not have it, she said. She would never again set foot in Springs as long as that woman was in her mother's house. She would not speak to her father. She would barely speak to me or Julian until we had sworn undying loyalty to Emma's memory and denounced Penny Frankenheimer in no uncertain terms. Julian rather overdid it, I thought, but he probably did wish that Ivan would simply go on working for the rest of his life, without any females around to distract him. I guess I felt sorry for her more than anything else, but my primary loyalty was to Tally, who needed all the support she could get. She was consumed by the most awful feelings in the world—feelings I recognized from the long-ago past and hoped never to experience again. Jealousy, betrayal, and fear wreaked havoc with the poor girl's reason, and no amount of arguing or coaxing could allay her anger. A week later I got a telephone call from her. With a steely voice she told me that she had written to Vassar and withdrawn her acceptance. She would not be going to college. She would not even stay in America. She was coming to Paris to live with me. Nothing mattered to Tally but that she put as much distance between herself and Ivan as possible.

I was delighted. Ivan was relieved. Julian was hurt. It was, I think, the first time in recent years Tally had ever made up her mind about anything important without consulting him first. The day after graduating at the head of her class (Julian went; Ivan wasn't invited, although I know she had hoped he would storm the barricades and surprise her), Tally sailed out of New York harbor on the QE2.

For the next three years Tally was a whirlwind of determined energy as she meticulously orchestrated her own education. The St. Peters name opened many doors, and Tally was far from shy about using it. She carried a full course load at the Sorbonne, and arranged for tutorials with some of the leading art experts in France besides. She traveled extensively, not for fun but for edification. She took up photography and discovered she was quite good at it. Inside of a year she had studied with three of Europe's top photographers and had built an impressive portfolio.

She also took a job working as an assistant to a popular fashion photographer, an attractive older man known as a playboy. She had an affair with him—not her first, she informed me. "I decided to lose my virginity on the Atlantic crossing. He was a very nice Princeton boy and he was very fond of me. I think a shipboard romance is a good way to lose one's virginity, don't you? It's so removed from everyday life and then, quite conveniently, you arrive at Le Havre and it's over. But of course it left me still very inexperienced sexually, so I decided the older man should come next."

"But, honey," I exclaimed, "you sound as if it were all a matter of test-driving a car. Don't you want to feel something in your heart?"

'She thought about it for a minute. "Well, of course I do, Maisie. But I certainly wouldn't want to lose my head over the whole thing. I'm not looking to be an emotional basket case, I just want to know what it's all about."

"Okay. I'll accept that for now. But you tell me this again someday after you've fallen head over heels in love with someone."

She grinned good-naturedly. "I will. But, you know, Maisie, I think sex was a much bigger deal for your generation." That shut me up for a bit.

Of course, what was really going on was something completely different. Tally was confused and, underneath that, afraid. She had had some pretty unhappy experiences, and I'm afraid in her heart she took the blame for them on herself. I knew that with the right man her feelings would change, but I was not the one to convince her of that. I let it go.

If I have given the impression that Tally was a prig, I have done her an injustice. She had humor and keen perceptions about people (well, most people), and to be with her was always to be entertained. Despite the rigors she put herself through, there was a freshness and vivacity about her that came not only from her youth, but from her enthusiasm for life. There was enormous generosity in her, and she never left a kindness unpaid. Indeed, the only person who suffered at her hand was Tally herself. The admirable if impossible goal she set for herself was nothing less than the attainment of perfection. Still, there were times when I wanted to shake her, muss up her hair, and goad her into some sort of abandoned silliness, and then she would give me a big hug and tell me that I had gone a little daft in my "old age."

We were completely at ease with one another, without any of that forced jocularity that often comes when friends are of different generations. I found it more agreeable to talk with Tally than almost anyone of my own age. We joked and laughed and chaffed one another, told each other secrets, argued over our differences, and wept at exactly the same moments in sentimental movies. I fancied that in Tally I could see Emma and Ivan and even farther back, to Louise Blackstone and Ivan's ballerina mother, all playing themselves out in the fluid and vivacious features of my lovely young companion. Strong will and passion were her legacy, and I hoped she would learn to manage both before either one could overwhelm her. Three years in Paris did in fact soften Tally's attitude toward her father. It was Penny she couldn't, or wouldn't, come to terms with. Still, we were happy and content until one spring afternoon when a thick letter arrived addressed in Penny Frankenheimer's flowing hand.

I sighed. As I waited for Tally to come in, I had a feeling things were about to take a dramatic turn in our lives. I was right.

Tally came bounding in. She was unusually aglow and flushed with excitement. "Wonderful news," she said, waving a manila envelope under my nose. "Do you remember the photographs I took in Italy this winter? Well, I've sold them! Of course, it's not much money, but that doesn't matter for now. They want to see more of my work . . ." She chattered away and I nodded and smiled.

As always, I felt a tug at my heart that Emma was not here to see Tally grown into such a beautiful young woman. The high color on her cheeks and the sparkle in her eyes reminded me in an instant of the time one winter day, so long ago, that Emma had rushed up the four flights of stairs in the old warehouse on Hudson Street and burst in the door with the news that she had taken a job. "A job?" Ivan had growled. "What kind of job?" "Well," said Emma, pausing for effect, "Macy's has hired me as a spy!" Silence. And then we three, Dance, Ivan, and I, collapsed laughing. But Emma was unruffled. Yes. It was so. She was to be a floorwalker. Oh, how we teased her. We improvised shoplifting scenes and made wagers that she would not last out the week. But she did.

Of course, the job took its toll. She was exhausted from standing on her feet all day, and after two weeks she had still seen nothing suspicious. Her boss called her on the carpet and told her to sharpen up. Ivan demanded that she quit. But Emma was determined. And then one day she came home sobbing as if her heart would break. It was in the afternoon, and Emma had been watching the clock like a hawk. Only one more hour. Please, God, let me get through one more hour, she'd prayed.

She was on the second floor, in budget ready-to-wear, when she saw a woman in an old brown woolen coat, standing in front of a table stacked with cheap Ban-lon sweaters. The woman was short and dumpy, with an unhealthy gray complexion. Emma could see that her hands were swollen with chilblains. But what particularly caught Emma's attention was the expression on the woman's face. It was as if she had discovered the pot of gold at the end of the rainbow. Her dull eyes were filled with wonder and awe. She stood staring at the bright colors and the headless mannequin with the very pointed breasts in the middle of the table, sporting one of the sweaters. She was transfixed and, watching her, Emma, too, was transfixed. She saw the woman reach out and select first the yellow—no, the blue—ah yes, finally, it was the red one. A bright, garish red Ban-lon sweater on special for Five-ninety-five. Then to her horror Emma saw her carefully stuff it under her coat before she turned and headed for the escalators.

Emma was paralyzed. What was she to do? Sound the alarm? Arrest this woman for . . . for what? For stealing a cheap sweater that would probably fall apart after two washings? Was this poor, miserable woman with her five-ninety-five theft going to affect the corporate health of R. H. Macy, Incorporated, owners of the largest department store in the world? Emma felt the tears streaming down her face. Never, never, if she lived to be a hundred years old, would she forget the look on that woman's face. A look of such longing and desire. Oh, why hadn't she wanted a fur coat or a gold necklace or suede gloves? How pitiful. How pathetic. The red, V-necked Ban-lon sweater, and now she, Emma St. Peters, who had always had the best of everything, was supposed to report her and have her arrested. She couldn't bring herself to do it, but the unhappiness and misery would not leave her.

Emma wept. She wept all the way home She cried all night in Ivan's arms, and the next day, alarmed, he took her to the doctor. The diagnosis was extreme fatigue owing to overwork and pregnancy.

And now here was that baby all grown up, and Emma was no more. Perhaps none of us had come to terms with Emma's death even after so many years. It still seemed to me a very harsh and cruel twist of fate.

Tally's eyes fell on the letter, and her bubble deflated in an instant. "What does *she* want?" she asked, eyeing it suspiciously.

"Darling, I don't know of a better way to find out than to open it."

Tally opened the letter and I watched her face as she read it. She was impassive. When she'd finished it, she handed it to me without a word.

The gist of the letter, written in Penny's straightforward manner, was that in the fall, the Guggenheim Museum would mount a major retrospective of Ivan's works. It would be the most important show of his career, and in Penny's opinion, it was time for Tally to bury the hatchet and come home. "He needs you, darling," she wrote. "He misses you terribly and he needs his daughter to be with him this summer and by his side for the retrospective. Perhaps after so long a time we can all meet each other with a new perspective and make a new beginning. Won't you come? Your father's birthday is in two weeks. Shall I tell him the best of all possible gifts is coming home?"

I thought Penny put it very well, but I could see without asking that Tally was waging a fearsome battle inside herself.

Perhaps because I had been thinking of Emma, perhaps because without knowing it, I, too, had been wondering just how long she was going to stay in exile, I went to Tally and made her look at me. "Penny's right. Your father misses you terribly. You know, honey, you've turned yourself into an accomplished young woman, worthy of your father's attention and pride. It's time you went home. If I've learned anything, it's that we're given so few choices in life. Almost everything that happens has nothing to do with whether we would have it so. Make the right choice now."

Her shoulders stiffened. For a minute I thought I had said the wrong thing, but then she took a deep breath. "Of course I'll go. I'm only sorry Julian didn't tell me this news about the Guggenheim. Surely he's known about it all along. Yes. I'll go. I will go and do what I can to help." Her voice was thin and her body tense.

This attitude was not exactly what I'd had in mind. A postscript from Penny included me in the invitation. I decided I'd better go along, too.

I knew things were going to be tough for Tally when she got home, and I told her so, but Tally was like her father in that you really couldn't tell her anything. She had made up her mind how things were going to be, and that was that. She wrote Ivan immediately, congratulating him on the coming retrospective, and, anxious to impress upon him that she had much to offer, she volunteered to make a photographic record of Ivan's sculptures as they were being readied for the exhibition. She wrote a gracious but formal note to Penny, thanking her for her suggestions and saying she was coming home. And she called Julian to chide him for not keeping her fully abreast of the big news about her father's career. Inside of a week, we were off in fine style; we had tickets on the Concorde, as a conciliatory gesture from Julian.

Tally had been away from home for over three years. At her age this seemed like a lifetime. She was filled with fantasies of what her homecoming would be like, and so from the beginning she was bound to be disappointed. I could tell by her barely suppressed excitement as the plane was coming in for landing that Tally expected to be in her father's arms momentarily. But, most unfortunately, Ivan was nowhere to be seen and I could only watch as she stiffened her upper lip and tried to put a good face on things. No one met us at the airport, no one, that is, but the limo driver sent by the always tactful Penny.

Perhaps it would have been better if we had taken a slower form of transportation, taken more time to anticipate what was waiting for us on the other side of the Atlantic, but, in truth, nothing could have prepared Tally for the changes that we found at the end of the long, twisty, unpaved driveway in Springs.

We were met by Penny, looking cool and elegant in white linen. Her welcome was genuinely warm as she kissed us, handed us tall glasses of lemonade, and generally made a fuss about our comfort and convenience. She was every inch the gracious hostess—the generous, warmhearted mistress of the house. Tally was bearing up pretty well, but I could tell that she was impatient to see her father. And where the hell was he, I wondered, starting to get a little hot under the collar myself.

Penny explained. "I know you're longing to see Ivan," she said to Tally. "He made me promise to tell you he loves you. He'll join us around seven, and in honor of your arrival, he won't work tonight." Penny delivered her speech bravely, but she was uncomfortable and even she could see that Tally was crushed.

"Darling," she said sympathetically, "I know it sounds awful of him. But do try to understand. He can think of nothing but this retrospective, and apparently he's got this one piece, his masterpiece, and he's got to get it finished before the end of the month so it can go up to the foundry, and, well, I don't have to tell you what living with an artist is like . . ."

"No," said Tally quietly. "You don't. I guess nothing ever really changes, does it, Maisie?"

"Oh, I don't know about that," I said looking around and desperate to change the subject. "The house looks pretty different. Is this a new room or a new old room?"

Penny took us on a tour. There was little left of the ramshackle old farmhouse that had been Tally's home ever since she could remember. Walls had been torn down, floors relaid, windows enlarged. Half of the whole second floor had been ripped out, so Tally's old bedroom was only a memory, hanging disembodied and invisible in the open space above the new dining room. Emma's cozy, messy kitchen was remodeled beyond recognition. Gone was the old-fashioned stove, with its peeling enamel, tricky pilot lights, and roomy warming ovens. Gone was the old stone sink with the hallowed-out space to hold the bar of kitchen soap that Emma always insisted worked better than any modern detergent. Gone was the big oak table where we had spent so many hours eating, drinking, talking, arguing, laughing, and being happy together. The new kitchen was all shiny, cool surfaces, mostly stainless steel and marble, and it housed every modern appliance and improvement. "I don't think Mama would have known what to do with most of those machines," Tally confided in me when the house tour was finished. I had few words of comfort to offer. Emma was gone, and the present went on irrevocably displacing the past.

A new wing had been built, a great, barnlike structure with soaring ceilings and one wall of glass facing onto a series of grassy terraces reaching down to the harbor. Here one could visually experience the intense productivity and vigor of Ivan's work. The studio and lawn had filled up with sculptures over the decade, and now they spilled out onto the land. At first Ivan had placed his sculptures outdoors in the fields for lack of indoor space, but later it was to study them in an unconfined and uncluttered area. He had graded the land and built stone pedestals on which pieces were placed. Thus, the house in Springs, and the studio that housed the hundreds of drawings he had done in the solitude of night, became an extraordinary, one-man museum. In the open his sculptures took on a oneness with the natural surroundings and a brilliance of unity that was lost in a gallery or museum.

We settled into our rooms and Penny tactfully left us alone. I didn't want to give Tally any time to brood, so I burst in on her with an idea.

"What do you say we go over to Louse Point for a swim? I always feel disgusting after traveling from one continent to another." Tally looked up at me with her gorgeous blue eyes, her father's eyes, and, fighting back her tears, gave me a look of gratitude and affection. I sat down on the bed beside her and hugged her.

"I think it's a great idea, Maisie. Let's get the hell out of here. Let's go for a swim."

Louse Point in those days was unknown to the fancy crowds that swarmed all over nearly every other beach in the Hamptons. The unlikely name had come from the old days when Connecticut people had come across the Peconic Bay to fish and almost starved to death. "Not enough there to feed a louse," someone had said, and the name stuck. A few baymen kept their boats there. A handful of local people went there to fish for snappers or to jump into the channel for a swim. The view from Louse was exquisitely beautiful, but it wasn't much of a beach, and the sun worshipers had many more attractive locations to invade. Louse was for locals who didn't want to mix with the New Yorkers. Bill de Kooning could come here and fish, and the only conversations he would have would be with some other fisherman about bait or tides or the weather. Saul Steinberg could go there and sketch and no one would pay him any mind. The people who came there to swim and relax for a couple of hours in the sun all mostly knew each other. There was an unwritten but very specific beach etiquette. Everyone knew that certain spots belonged to certain people. The patch of sand just below the rosa rugosa was Yetta Feinbloom's. Yetta was a poet and a painter and everyone knew that she liked to work just there, just as everyone knew not to bother her unless it was after five o'clock. Then, as likely as not, she would pull out a thermos of martinis and bag of potato chips and invite you to sit for a cocktail and a bit of gossip. Farther in on the spit of land there was another patch that belonged just as surely to a group of elderly ladies who played cards every afternoon. If you got on their good side you could rely on them to supply you with a spritz of insect repellent to protect you from the vicious green flies that arrived in August.

Tally and I took the Jeep and drove the four miles around to Louse Point. We parked at the very tip and ran down to the water and dove in. There was no wind, the sun was hot, and the water was cold but not frigid. It was the perfect temperature to make you catch your breath and force you to swim, to use muscles that ached to be moved, to let the water wash away the tensions that afflicted body and soul. Swimming in that crystal-clear blue water was the nearest thing to total bliss that I have found on this earth. The water soothed, revived, and put things in perspective. Nothing could be all that bad when one could come to Louse and swim. When we finally came out of the water, we flopped onto our towels and stretched out on the hot sand. Now the sun felt good as it dried the moisture on the skin, leaving a salty afterglow. We were laughing, talking, finally feeling a sense of well-being at having returned to this wonderful place, and I must have dozed off for a few minutes. I woke because a shadow blocked the sun and made me feel a chill. The sun was in my eyes and I couldn't make out who it was looming over us. Then I heard Tally shriek, "Papa, Papa!" and she flew up like a bird and was in his arms.

It was a heartwarming scene. Father and daughter embracing, talking, laughing, crying all at once. Ivan looked great. Neither the past ten years nor the fame they had brought him had altered him at all except for turning his hair a shocking, brilliant snowy white. He was still a robust giant of a man, with a big voice and extravagant gestures, and as he swung his daughter around and prepared to fling her into the water, I looked around and thought of the stories that would be told over drinks tonight in houses around the Hamptons. I watched them swimming and listened to their talk as it carried, crystal clear, across the water to the ears of all who sat entranced on the beach.

"How did you get down here, Papa?"

"I try to work, but only I can think of you. Penny tells me you are here, so I grab old bicycle and so I am here, too. Ah, Natasha, Natasha, my lovely daughter. You look like mermaid from fairy tales of my grandmother. How many men will be destroyed by their desire for you? Poor hopeful fools. I pity them. I do."

"Stop it, Papa. You're embarrassing me. Look, people are listening to every word you say."

Ivan looked around, then grabbed Tally and lifted her high up in the air, shouting, "Look! Look! Everyone! My daughter, Natalia St. Peters, is come home!" And would you believe it, people up and down the beach of Louse Point stood up and applauded. Ivan St. Peters had his audience in the palm of his hand. And he put on a good show.

You wily old fox, I thought to myself. How the hell do you get away with it? Doesn't bother to meet his daughter who has been away for three years, quits work a whole hour early, and is now a hero. Tally has forgiven him again. Women always forgive Ivan. Women. Ivan's women. What a pliant and forgiving lot we are.

It turned into a wonderful evening. At six o'clock the sun was still warm but the beach was now almost completely ours alone. Soon Penny joined us, arriving with beach chairs, blankets, sweatshirts, and a picnic hamper filled with cold champagne, fried chicken, a spicy black bean salad, and crisp baguettes still warm from the oven. We spread out on the sand, ate and drank, and didn't go home until we had watched the sun set in hues from fiery pink to delicate mauve.

I marveled at Penny's intelligence and ingenuity. She had managed to orchestrate a homecoming that was free of tension and resentment. A good time was had by all, and by the time we returned home we had only energy enough for a bath before getting into bed. I went to sleep with high hopes that this day would set the tone for all the days to come.

In fact, for several days things between Ivan and Tally did stay friendly and loving, but after that I'm afraid they reverted to form. As I watched I realized that, if anything, Ivan had become even more grandiose in manner, more self-centered, and more arrogant. Soon enough, Tally realized that she had been foolish to think she would take charge of Ivan's house. Penny wisely stayed as far in the background as possible, but once you met Penny, even briefly, there was no question about who was in charge. Penny ruled the roost. She did it graciously, kindly, considerately. But Penny was a queen bee and that was that.

I must say I rather liked her, though we were not destined to be close friends. She had tall, reedy good looks and a way of dressing that was both elegant and comfortable. She was organized and efficient; at the same time she was quite warmhearted and helpful, shedding a kind of bubbling intelligence and sophistication over everything. She had a marvelous laugh, and her devotion to Ivan was sincere. She was Ivan's confidante. She advised him about his business affairs and his shows, orchestrated his social life, and generally protected him from the irritants of the outside world. She did for Ivan what no one else could do, but Tally, alas, couldn't or wouldn't see it that way. To her, Penny was an interloper. She had trespassed on private property and, worse, did not seem to know it. I don't really know whether things would have been any better if Penny had been a meeker sort of woman, but the situation remained much as I've described it. In the ensuing days and weeks, everyone behaved nicely enough, but I never stopped having the feeling that we were living on top of a volcano that could erupt at any moment.

But all that lay ahead. That first night back in Springs, Tally slept the happy, exhausted sleep of the prodigal daughter who has returned to the bosom of her father.

A few days later we were gathered to celebrate Ivan's birthday. To Ivan this day was the most important holiday of the year, and he was never embarrassed to say he wanted it celebrated with as much fanfare as possible. This year, with Penny in charge, it was a black-tie dinner for twenty. The highly acclaimed chef from the American Hotel in Sag Harbor had been in the kitchen all day, preparing a feast. The house was suitably festooned with flowers, and outside all the trees from the terrace down to the water were strung with thousands of tiny white lights. I must say, despite my partiality for the comfortable days of Emma's kitchen and mismatched china, it was an impressive and beautiful display and it did set a celebratory mood. Tally looked fabulous in a flowing white Norma Kamali gown. Her high cheekbones were flushed with a hint of sunburn, and heavy silk ropes circled her head so that her luxurious dark hair tumbled like a waterfall onto her shoulders. She looked like a classical Greek goddess, yet very modern at the same time, and I was a very proud godmother.

It was a warm evening and we were on the terrace for drinks. The sun was setting in a very showy manner, and the sky was bathed in a glorious golden light. On the surface we were all very jolly and ready for a good time, but there was a hint of drama in the air, and beneath the façade of smiles and kisses, tempers were smoldering. I was watching Penny now as she greeted Julian.

"Julian. You're looking very well."

Julian did indeed look well. His rather bland, handsome features had acquired a distinct cragginess and a hint of decadence, too, which made him much more interesting-looking in his middle years than he had been in his youth. But I suppose to most people the most fascinating thing about Julian was the glow of success and prosperity that emanated from him like a golden light. He looked polished, expensive, and very well kept. His hands were manicured and soft, his clothes were tailored on Savile Row, and his Italian shoes were made from the skins of snakes.

"And you, Penny, are looking very brown. The summer seems to have found you already." They bent toward each other and kissed ever so lightly. The look was all warmth, but even from across the room I felt the frostiness between them. Ivan had of late become increasingly picky about which sculptures he would sell and to whom, and he had been producing his new works in groupings that he insisted must be sold ensemble. Julian, of course, felt that the gallery should have a free hand in all matters that related to sales, and he suspected—rightly—that it was Penny who was encouraging Ivan to take such stands. I think he was happy to have Tally back on the scene because he knew that Tally disliked Penny even more than he did.

Indeed, Tally was making Julian laugh by mimicking Penny behind her back. "Oh, do have a drink, Julian, darling." There was something about the way Penny smiled, quick, on-and-off smiles, that was easy for Tally to imitate and exaggerate, and she did this now as she told the bartender how to fix Julian's very particular martini.

"Let me decide for you. Let me pour it for you. I'll even drink it for you because that's what I do best. Everything!" Her laugh tinkled through the air.

"Stop it, Tally. She'll hear you. What a little actress you are."

"Yes. But not nearly so good as you, Julian. You actually looked delighted to see the mistress of our happy home."

"And why not? Penny and I are the best of friends."

"Julian, you are every inch the gentleman and I love you for it. Now come and help me arrange the placements. Penny allows me a few of the odd jobs around here, and I think I shall put the two of you together since you're such *good* friends."

"Darling, I see Penny just about as much as I care to, as it is. Put me next to you. I have something I want to talk to you about."

More people arrived: a young South American artist who had just taken New York by storm; a psychiatrist who had written extensively about the creative process and was also a big collector; an English playwright whose hit play had just been made into a film with an East Hampton location; an English actress who had starred in the playwright's movie and who was rumored to be the playwright's mistress though otherwise happily married; the two charming owners of the bookstore in East Hampton; an investment banker who was famous for his collection of postwar sculpture; a neighbor and writer whose book on Jackson Pollock had just been published and his wife, a painter whom Ivan much admired. The guests seemed to be a perfect cross-section of the cultural community and the affluent who supported it. There was much chatter, much gossip. But the party had not yet begun. And it wouldn't until Ivan arrived.

Penny looked elegant and relaxed in a black Halston sheath. She was greeting a very tall young man who, I must say, cut an elegant figure in a tuxedo. They kissed affectionately and appeared to be on quite intimate terms. In a moment Penny had him by the arm and was leading him in my direction. Imagine my surprise to discover that this sophisticated young gentleman was none other than the ragamuffin of old, Zack Hayes.

"Maisie," he exclaimed, "how wonderful you look! How wonderful to see you."

"Well, thank you. But truly it is you who look wonderful. I seem to remember a rather scruffy, very shy teenager. How are you, Zack? What have you been up to?"

"Oh, this and that. Finishing up school. As a matter of fact, I quite literally finished yesterday. You see before you a fully accredited but very unemployed architect." He gave a modest bow, but I could see that he was pleased with his new status.

"Zack, that's wonderful. Congratulations. Yes. Now I remember. You went to Yale?"

"Yup. Me and Yale have seen a grueling seven years together. Who'd a-thunk it, Maisie? Local boy makes good. Well, I wouldn't have done any of it without Ivan. But you know that." He smiled the most charming and warm smile, and I felt my forty-five-year-old bones melting in those big hazel eyes. "Where's Tally, by the way? I guess I haven't seen her since . . . well, let's see . . . since before she went to Paris. Ivan is so pleased to have her back. He told me she'd be here tonight."

"Not just tonight. She's here for the summer. And I am, too, so we'll see a lot of each other, I hope. Oh, and I think Tally's inside." I couldn't help wondering what Tally would think of the new Zack Hayes.

"Great! Then, if you'll excuse me, ladies"—he gave a lazy sort of half-bow and grinned—"I'm going to get myself a drink and find out what three years of Paris have wrought."

I turned to Penny as Zack departed. "Wow!" I said, like a starstruck teenager. "I always thought he was a nice-looking kid, but, my God, he's gorgeous."

Penny smiled tolerantly. Obviously she didn't dwell on the physical attributes of younger men. "He's a charming, wonderful boy," she agreed. "And so loyal. Ivan quite dotes on him, you know. He could never have been as productive as he has been if it hadn't been for Zack. Ivan says that Zack is technically more proficient than he is himself, and he relies on Zack to supervise all the foundry work. That's quite a responsibility for such a young man."

"I'll say. How he managed to work for Ivan and get a degree in architecture at the same time is a miracle in itself."

"I know. I don't know how he did it. Ivan got him into Yale and hired him over the holidays and summers, but Zack got through mostly on scholarships and night jobs. And even with that workload, every time Ivan needed him, which was often, Zack would jump on a plane and fly here."

"Well, good for them," I said. "Good for both of them. It's a miracle they found each other. I know it's trite to say so, but I always think that Zack came into Ivan's life to replace that poor little dead baby boy, to be the son he never had."

"Yes," Penny agreed softly. "You know, I'll never forget something I saw, quite by accident, when I first came to stay here. It was a summer night, very warm. The moon was full, so it was quite light out. Ivan was working late and I was very much by myself, but quite happy about it, because I was by myself, but not alone. Do you know that feeling?"

I nodded.

"I decided to walk down to the water, and as I passed the barn I heard music. It was an old-fashioned Viennese waltz. The barn doors were open and I walked over and peeked in, attracted by the music and thinking I would catch sight of the artist at work. Well, there was Ivan with his arm around Zack, leading him through the steps of the waltz, singing, 'One, two, three; one, two, three; one, two, three.' It was charming and very touching. You see, he was teaching the boy to dance. I began to understand their relationship then. Zack would be Ivan's heir. I don't mean to his fortune or anything material. But Ivan was passing on to Zack everything he knew about being a man. He's given that boy the gift of his heart. What a lucky boy, I thought, to be the beneficiary of such an inheritance. But Zack deserves it. He has worn the mantle well and is worthy in every way of Ivan's gifts."

It was at that moment that Ivan chose to make his appearance. All the guests had arrived, wine and conversation were flowing, and only the host himself was missing. Penny spotted him and was by his side in an instant. They made an impressive couple. Ivan looked truly regal, the white dinner jacket and shocking white hair accentuating his tanned face and piercing blue eyes. After all these years I was still awed by his size and presence. I knew he was a big man, but still, I felt he was bigger than life. Ivan Rex, I muttered to myself, and Penny beside him, very much his queen. Together they walked around and greeted their guests and shortly afterward we went in to dinner.

We were very splendid at table. The settings were magnificent—fine china, heavy silver, sparkling crystal. The windows were all open to the night, and a sweet, heavy scent of roses permeated the air. We ate caviar and oysters, cold salmon and lobster mousse, asparagus mimosa and baby lettuces in champagne vinaigrette. As I ate and drank and enjoyed myself thoroughly, something jogged my memory back to another birthday so long ago it seemed like centuries.

I had met Ivan only a few weeks before, and I was wildly in love with him. Dance told me Ivan's birthday was coming, and we spent two days cooking a crayfish gumbo. It was Dance's only culinary talent, and as he presided over the cast-iron pot, muttering dark incantations and coaxing the roux to a perfect deep chocolate brown, he told ghost stories of the Savannah low country—haunting, macabre tales of dueling oaks and ravaged brides who walked at midnight while the moon shone through webs of Spanish moss. To my joy, I found three very old etched-crystal champagne flutes in a stall down on Canal Street, and they seemed just the thing that ladies and gentlemen of the Old South might have drunk from on the veranda. Though they cost me most of a week in tips, I had to have them. And so the birthday came. We toasted Ivan with those glasses filled with French champagne, and then, on impulse, we all threw our glasses against the brick wall of the loft. It was such an extravagant gesture. It was such an extravagant night. We ate like trenchermen, stuffing ourselves as only the very young can do, and then we went to the Five Spot to hear some jazz.

Much later we ended up at the Café Rienzi where Dance had organized a surprise. The Café Rienzi always had the reputation of having the prettiest waitresses, and Dance had organized six girls to bring out a cake and, in a chorus line, sing "Happy Birthday" to Ivan. Ivan roared his approval, and after the performance the girls surrounded him to administer birthday kisses. He looked so beautiful and so happy that I remember thinking it was almost a shame the girls had to get back to waiting tables. Almost. Later that night I was only too happy to have him alone and all to myself.

I looked at Tally and tried to understand how it was possible that all those years had flown by since that birthday party at the Café Rienzi, how it was possible that I was once as young as she was tonight, and I wondered where that girl had gone. I brought myself back to the present and tried to see the party through Tally's eyes. I could tell that her face fairly ached with being pleasant. Oh God, she was pleasant, though I could see in an instant that the young and handsome South American on her right was not to her liking. It was in the eyes. Carlos had what writers often refer to as "laughing eyes." They were big and brown and edged with long black lashes. He liked his eyes. He wrinkled and twinkled them like castanets. I watched Tally sigh with boredom. Up and down the long pine table the guests were eating and laughing and drinking quantities of wine. Tally's glass was almost untouched, though the wine was excellent. Tedium always made her want to drink less, not more.

I could see her watching her father at the far end of the table. He was regaling several rapt listeners with what appeared to be a very funny story, because Penny was laughing her "delighted" laugh, and everyone seated around Ivan had followed suit. There was nothing Ivan loved more than an appreciative audience, and he had one now. We could all tell he was in a good mood. It was a certain way his whole body seemed to relax. And this very relaxation radiated from his body like a warm current that was, as ever, infectious to anyone who came near him.

I watched Tally looking at Zack, and wondered if she was as taken with his dark good looks as I was. Frankly, I didn't see how any girl could resist him. Billie Wingdale, who was sitting on his right, was certainly making no effort to resist him at all. Billie, though no longer young, was still very attractive. Now in her middle forties, she was slim, vibrant, blond, and beautiful. She was the kind of female other women loved to hate, and in my mother's day she would have been called a man-eater.

Herself a painter of mediocre landscapes, she had been on the fringes of the art scene for as long as I could remember. She lived off a small trust fund and the generosity of her richer men friends. Many years ago she had taught high school briefly, but her career had ended in disgrace when it was discovered that she was sleeping with one of her sixteen-year-old students. Her men were always either very rich or very young. Quite obviously she had set her sights on Zack that evening.

We had reached the end of the meal. It was dark now, and the candles cast a warm glow over the assembled guests. At an invisible signal from Penny, Annie, the beautiful black pastry chef, appeared bearing a cake sparkling with birthday candles. Ivan beamed like a happy child. He rose from his chair. "Dear friends," he bellowed, "today is great occasion. It is the anniversary of my birth, so I would like to propose a toast." He raised his champagne glass, looked around the table, and pronounced gleefully, "Happy birthday to me!" Everyone stood and sang the traditional chorus. Ivan joined in:

> Happy birthday to me.
> Happy birthday to me.
> Happy birthday to me-ee.
> Happy birthday to me!

When the applause had died down, the candles had been blown out, and the cake cut and distributed, Ivan spoke again. "My good friends. Bring your wine and come with me." He had risen suddenly from the table and was urging everyone else up. "I have something I want to show you. Something very beautiful. Come. Come. We go to the studio."

I was surprised, to say the least. Ivan hardly ever let anyone in the studio. He claimed it invaded his senses and confused his thoughts. Indeed, the studio was always a cool and silent place. The old barn had long since been torn down, and in its place stood a clean circular structure of white pine and glass. Zack had designed and built it with Ivan and the help of just a few carpenters.

We all trooped down the path with our glasses of wine, the ladies tottering a bit in their high heels and Ivan in the lead like the Pied Piper. Inside, the studio was dim, but in the center of the room on a platform was a sculpture about twelve feet high. It was held in place by a series of ropes and pulleys that reached up to the very top of the building. When they had all come into the space, Ivan walked quickly to a master switch, and at a flick of his wrist the network of bronze was bathed in light. Tally sucked in her breath.

No one said a word. Not for a long time. And then Ivan started walking slowly around the sculpture and he spoke in a low voice, almost as if he were talking to himself. "There are seven pieces in the circle I call Desire. Each one has many faces. Desire calls to us and seduces us in hundred subtle ways. *Love, Power, Knowledge, Glory, Passion, Joy,* and *Fortune.* All these I have known, and I have searched in mind and heart and all senses for the forms that make up these human enchanters. Today, at last, Circle of Desire is complete." He stopped and stood at the base of the ramp. But it seemed as if he were not standing but floating. There was something strange about his relationship to the piece, almost as if he were an integral part of it.

"Only in center of circle, in center where the self lives, are we free from the gravity of desire. Here is peace and tranquility. Here is beginning and end. This is *Heartsease.*" There was a moment's silence, then Ivan went on. "Julian," he said, "today is birthday, so you must humor me at all costs. There will be only one *Heartsease,* and it will remain here in Springs. I will place the Circle of Desire in fields that I have loved, on land that has nurtured me and cared for me. It will be my testament to the power of nature and the power of love. That is my wish."

It was clear that *Heartsease* would be hailed as one of Ivan's most powerful works. There was an energy and life emanating from the graceful sculpture that was breathtaking. Indeed, part of its visual pleasure lay in the fact that although the piece weighed thousands of pounds, it was so delicately balanced that it seemed the slightest push would topple it to the ground.

Everyone started walking around the platform, and Ivan moved with them, explaining how the bronze had been slowly and painstakingly polished to a mirrorlike finish. Only Tally remained where she was, and opposite her stood Julian. She could see that he, too, was moved, but what she saw on his face confused her. It was unabashed admiration, and yet there was also a strange emotion that was hard to define—almost a look of envy, envy mixed with rage. She looked quickly away, then Ivan caught her hand.

"You come with me, Natasha. I want to show you myself, because is yours as much as mine. I wanted you to see this first with people around it. Our *Heartsease* always will look best when there are people. You see how she embraces them and holds them near." He led Tally around for a closer inspection, and then stopped and put his arm around her. It was a rare moment of intimacy between father and daughter. Ivan cleared his throat and tried to speak, to tell Tally something, and it was obviously very difficult for him to say, but his eyes welled up with tears and the words would not come. He hugged his daughter roughly to his chest.

The moment was soon over, and without further explanation Ivan was leading his guests back to the house. As Tally started to follow, Zack caught her hand and gestured for her to remain behind. When the rest of us had left, he hopped up on the platform and helped her up to stand with him. It was the first time all evening they had had a chance to talk or be together.

"It's beautiful, isn't it?" Tally said, feeling strangely shy.

He nodded. They stood looking for many minutes. Then he spoke. "I think I know what your father was trying to show you." His voice was low and soft.

"Show me?" Tally asked.

"Come," he said, gently taking her arm. He led her closer to the suspended sculpture. He pointed to a place that was almost hidden from sight. There, placed in a crevice beneath a wing that jutted out into space was the gold magician's coin. Tally bent her head and looked closely. She could barely decipher the words carved around the coin, but when she did, her lips moved slightly as she read them: "To Emma, who keeps my heart for all eternity. ISP."

A large lump came into her throat and she looked away. And then at Zack. Then she looked at the floor. She didn't want him to see her cry.

He didn't say anything for a minute, and then he said, "There never was another woman like her." His voice was low. "In a way, you know, for a few lucky months, she was my mother, too."

Tally nodded. "Everyone loved her."

"You must have missed her badly."

"I still do. Oh, not in the way I did after she died. I was just a child. I needed my mother the way children do. But now I think I miss her more. It's like something was taken away, some sort of link—a solution to the puzzle. I don't know. I told myself that I was coming home for Ivan, but I think I really came home this summer to try to find my mother. Does that sound crazy to you?"

"No."

"And in a funny way, I think she's here. Something of her, anyway."

"Well, she's anywhere your father is. She's everywhere in his work."

Tally frowned to fight back more tears. She couldn't understand why she felt so constantly on the brink of crying. Ever since she had come home, she had felt as if she were on an emotional roller coaster. It must be jet lag, she told herself firmly. She turned once again to look at the giant bronze sculpture. "I wish I had my camera right now. Things look so different in the night, don't they? I mean the spotlights and the shadows on the wall. I love shadows, I mean I like to photograph them." She was beginning to chatter, and she couldn't stop. "I was planning to photograph all of Papa's sculptures for the show, but maybe I should just concentrate on *Heartsease*. What do you think, Zack?"

He grinned. "Hey, I'm not paid to think, lady. I'm just the muscle around here."

Tally laughed. She began to relax again. "Do you mind if we stay here for a while longer? I don't feel like partying anymore. Or do you think that will upset Billie?" she asked coyly.

"I don't think anything could upset that woman. I don't know how she managed to eat her dinner when her hands were all over me. Save me from her, Tally, I beg of you."

The loud buzz of the intercom interrupted them. Suddenly Penny's disembodied voice filled the studio.

"Tally, darling, the musicians are here. Your father won't let anyone start dancing until he has the first dance with you."

"Well," Tally sighed, "I guess there's no escaping the party. Her majesty commands our return." She let Zack lift her down from the platform, and marveled at his easy strength. For a second it was like floating. He continued to hold her arm as they made their way back to the house up the path lit by Chinese lanterns.

It was a small Gypsy band, two violins, a concertina, and a tambourine. The music was wild and wailing, and tugged at your heartstrings with longings for something romantic and unattainable. Ivan danced with his daughter, and they whirled and swirled to the stirring waltz. Everyone stood and watched until Julian marched up to the dancing couple, touched Ivan on the shoulder, and cut into the dance. Then the floor was open to the rest of us. But before the dance was over, Zack, taking his cue from Julian himself, cut in and waltzed off with the lovely Tally. They made a breathtaking couple—both tall, dark-haired, and lithe.

"Aren't they the very picture of young lovers?" I said to Julian, who stood beside me.

"Maisie, dear"—his voice was dry and sardonic—"you are ever the hopeless romantic. A towering confection of sentimental hogwash. I'm sure Tally has far too much intelligence to get herself involved with an unsuitable and penniless artist's apprentice."

I found his smug tone particularly irritating. "But, darling Julian, in my experience, and I believe in yours as well," I said with sweet bitchiness, "it seems that intelligence has very little to do with it."

" 'It'? What 'it'?"

I patted his arm. "Love, Julian. Love."

50

Well," Tally announced wickedly late that night, perched on the end of my bed, "I hear you're trying to make a match between Zack Hayes and me."

"Christ." I threw up my hands. "Julian has a big mouth. Of course I'm trying to make a match. He's so sexy."

Tally laughed. "Maisie, you're worse than a bunch of horny school-girls, but I love you for it. Yes, Julian told me all about it, and he doesn't approve. Nor do I. I'm not here to run around after sexy young men, so I'll leave all the ogling of Zack to you and Billie Wingdale. I, for one, have better things on my mind. Just wait till I tell you my news! Julian thinks he can get me a spot in the Guggenheim to show my photographs of Ivan. I mean, it's just in the talking stage and he's very cautious, but if I know Julian, he can swing it. Julian can do anything, and he thinks my work is good. He said so."

"But, darling, you haven't got any photographs of Ivan," I pointed out.

"Well, I soon will have. I'm ready to go. Julian is going to kit out a darkroom for me in the basement. I've got the best cameras money can buy, and I've got an inside track on my subject."

"Does Ivan know about this?"

"He knows I'm going to photograph his work. I'm going to get really familiar with it, all the different stages, and then when I've got something to show, I know he'll let me do him."

"I don't know, honey," I said dubiously. Ivan was well known for his abhorrence of publicity. For all of his extravagant personal gestures, he hated celebrity. It was, he said, one of the few aspects of American life that appalled him. Over and over again he had watched good artists first bow and then finally grovel before the god of celebrity. "It destroys," Ivan said. "The artist is no longer free but a slave to his image. Soon he believes himself to be the work of art." Ivan wanted attention focused only on the work and not on him, and to that end he was almost manic. No interviewers were allowed on the grounds, no photographs of Ivan appeared in the press. As a result, there wasn't a reporter or photographer around who wouldn't give his right hand for an exclusive on Ivan St. Peters. I wondered why Julian was encouraging Tally with such a plum as the Guggenheim. But she looked so bright and eager that I couldn't help but encourage her, too. Maybe for her Ivan would relent. I hoped so.

"And tomorrow I'm going over to the foundry," Tally bubbled on. "Zack tells me they're casting a piece. It's a lost-wax casting, and that's a very delicate procedure. Isn't it exciting?"

Yes, it was, I said, and then kissed her good night and sent her packing to her own room, glad I was not young and ambitious and that I had reached an age when the best thing about going to bed was reading a few more pages of Proust.

The next morning I watched as she went off driving the cute little Volkswagen convertible that Penny had arranged for her to use over the summer. Tally had wrinkled her nose when she first saw it, deriding Penny's sense of what was appropriate for "young people," but I thought she looked darling as she drove off in the bright summer morning.

The foundry was on the North Fork, about forty-five minutes from Springs. It was a large, plain, brick building, once a blacksmith shop, that had no adornment to suggest anything beyond honest sweat and toil. By the time Tally had arrived and unpacked her equipment, the workday was well started. If, in the back of her mind, she had been expecting some small fuss to be made over the arrival of the artist's daughter, she was no doubt disappointed. Zack and the workmen had been at it since dawn, and she was all but totally ignored. If she expected

Zack to be the courtly gentleman he had been the night before, she was a bit disappointed about that, too. He greeted her hurriedly, and un-ceremoniously handed her a bundle containing a pair of dirty, baggy work pants, an overshirt, safety glasses, and ear plugs. Then he led her to the top of a narrow catwalk, where, with much gesturing and shouting over the ferocious din, he pointed to various welders, polishers, and mixers, all working at once. Tally nodded curtly and set up her camera equipment. When she looked for him again, he was gone.

Minutes stretched into hours. Down below, Zack and the foundry workmen moved about purposefully, seemingly unaware of the inferno that surrounded them. Tally found that she could not keep her eyes off Zack. It was irritating. It was exciting. She adjusted her lens and tried to focus on something of the chaos down below, but Zack loomed more and more in the viewfinder. His jeans were tight over his long legs and low on his hips. He was lean and handsome. His face reminded her of portraits she had seen of American Indians, his skin a tawny brown, his face all angles and high cheekbones, his straight black hair pulled sharply behind his ears. She refocused on a plump man who was perspiring heavily. Then Zack took off his shirt and she felt her throat tighten. Christ! She looked quickly away, then back. He moved with the assurance of a man fully in charge, and what she noticed most was that he took no notice of her. What the hell were they doing down there? she wondered. The noise and heat of the foundry were almost unbearable, but she worked, resolutely setting up shots, trying to make some sense of the process by which molten met-als were transformed into the shapes that would eventually be the gleaming sculptures her father had imagined.

Suddenly something seemed to be happening. A new form had been wheeled out on a dolly. The workmen stood back, and Zack stepped up to it with a hammer and a chisel. His body was very tense, and she saw him stop once, then twice, undecided, and then everything about him seemed to relax, and with the precision and grace of a conductor with a baton, he tapped the giant form here and there, and the plaster began to fall away in sheets. From within, a curving, graceful, soaring thing emerged. Her heart pounded and she felt close to tears. Black with slag and rough at all the edges, to be sure, but it was . . . well, Tally thought, her camera forgotten in the moment, almost like witness-ing a birth. Zack ran his hands over the sculpture, stepped back and walked around it, got on his knees and peered under it. Then he held his thumbs up, grinning with delight. There was much handshaking and back-slapping and then Zack turned to where she was and signaled for her to wait there. A few more gestures, a few more words with the foreman, and then he came bounding up the steel stairs to her. He leaned close to her and said something, but she couldn't hear. Then he started to help her with the equipment. It was over. The day at the foundry was done. Tally was both relieved and supremely disappointed. She wished she had been more a part of it, that she had been in the middle of it and not a mere bystander. She got her things together and started down the stairs after Zack. Near the bottom, he turned and offered her his hand.

In the next three weeks, Tally learned much more. She had been to the foundry three times. She knew all the details and steps of the lost-wax process. She knew it was anxious and difficult work. Zack and the foreman had explained it to her the next day after work. They had all repaired to a nearby bar, and Tally had liked sitting in the cool, dim place, surrounded by men still gritty from their work. Zack showed none of his Yale polish. Here, as on the work just cast, he let his rough edges show. Having made a plaster model of the figure to be cast, he explained, Ivan copied it in wax, which was spread in a thin coating over an inner core of clay. Then Zack covered the finished wax model with a thick layer of plaster to form the mold, and when this was heated, the wax melted and ran out through little holes. Then the molten metal was poured into the mold, filling all the space where the wax had been, and the bronze was left to cool and set. At last the mold could be broken away, and if the casting had gone well, the hardened metal appeared in the exact shape of the wax model, needing only to be smoothed, polished, and finished with the patina of Ivan's choosing.

Zack was an exacting craftsman. While he talked of his work, his face was deadly solemn, and Tally found she wanted nothing more than to poke him out of his seriousness and see him smile and laugh. He had a wonderful smile, and then there was that certain something that made her catch her breath and flush.

"Of course," Zack continued, "not all of Ivan's work is cast in the lost-wax process."

"Oh?" she said attentively.

"Some pieces—*Heartsease*, for instance—are made from a permanent cast or mold. Ivan always decides at the outset how many pieces will be made, and then he destroys the mold."

"But why?" Tally was aghast. "Why destroy it?"

"Because everything has its life," Zack answered easily. "Ivan likes editions of three and seven and nine. After that, the mold becomes meaningless to him. After all, he's an artist, not a manufacturer." Zack said this lightly, but Tally was offended. "Of course he isn't," she answered, at once irritated and feeling vaguely like someone who had made a great social gaffe. She did not like the feeling. How was it that Zack knew so much more about her father than she did?

The darkroom equipment arrived as Julian had promised, and Tally spent hours developing and printing her photographs. The dim red glow of the safelight was relieved only by a solitary shaft of white light from the enlarger. Tally studied the negative image on the easel. A large truck stood in the yard, next to the open barn doors of the studio. Sculptures were everywhere, waiting to be loaded onto the truck. She raised the head of the enlarger all the way to the top, and when she refocused, all the clutter had been eliminated from the scene. Now there loomed the solitary figure of a man. He was standing, legs spread wide apart, hands on hips. Even this negative image of him, with its unearthly glowing eyes, caused a quick tightening in Tally's belly. When she had the figure framed, she switched off the enlarger and, reaching into the paper safe, extracted a sheet of eleven-by-fourteen photographic paper, placed it on the easel, and made the exposure.

As she slid the exposed paper into the developing tray, the dark-room light lent an eerie quality to the scene, making her look almost witchlike as she stood gazing at the shimmering liquid.

She watched the paper in the tray intently now. The image of Zack began to appear—faintly at first, like a shy spirit at a séance, but finally with crystal clarity and fine, sharp lines. Finally there was nothing ghostlike about him. He was real.

Now she lifted the photograph from the developing tray. After she had fixed and washed the print, she tacked it up on the wall, impulsively running her hand across the surface to remove a few drops of moisture, she thought, but her touch lingered on his bare chest. What if she did that to him really? What if she had done it this very morning, when she had first noticed the drops of perspiration glistening in the silky hairs on his chest? What if she had buried her face in the warm wetness? Would it have tasted like tears?

But the eyes in the photograph seemed to be watching her, teasing her, and the tiny hint of a smile on his lips seemed to say that he knew what she was thinking, and suddenly, in a blind fury, she ripped the picture off the wall and tore it into tiny shreds. Then, not bothering to clean up, she ran upstairs.

51

The next day was a bust. Tally woke to the sounds of an argument coming from below. When Ivan was angry, his accent was worse than usual. Penny's voice, too, carried up the stairway. Tally gripped the pillow around her head and then, angry herself, threw it across the room and got up for a shower. On the way down to the kitchen, she met me coming up the stairs.

"I wouldn't go down there if I were you," I said, "unless you have a white flag. They're all having at each other in the study."

"Who?"

"Julian, Penny, and your father. Who else? Julian and Penny are at loggerheads over Ivan's decision to break the mold for *Heartsease*. Penny, of course, is all for it. Julian says Ivan is being too hasty, that he should wait until after the exhibition and that he will see that the mold is kept under lock and key in the warehouse. Penny says she'd like to unlock a few doors in the warehouse herself. I don't think those two trust each other. Did you know, Tally, that there has never been an inventory of the works Julian has?"

"No. As a matter of fact, I didn't. But I can't see what the problem is. Penny just likes making a fuss over everything. What business is it of hers anyway?"

"She loves your father and she's a smart woman. She's only trying to protect him."

"From Julian? My God, that's ridiculous and you know it. Julian's done everything for Papa, and he's certainly been around longer than she has. Julian is the best friend this family has!"

"Penny certainly doesn't believe that. When Julian said he wanted to hire security guards for the summer to watch the studio, Penny said, 'Whatever for, Julian? No one's going to steal anything. You're the only art dealer around.' Julian didn't like that at all."

"Nor do I," Tally sniffed. "What does Zack say about all of this?"

"Oh, Zack has been sent to New York to check out the lighting plan at the museum."

Tally's heart fell. So there went the day. Ivan would be in a terrible mood, because he always was when he had to talk about business. Zack was gone. She went back to her room and decided to take her camera and wander down to the harbor to take pictures of the house and studio from that perspective. Zack's cabin was down by the water, the cabin she had so resented his moving into when she was little.

Tally put on her oldest jeans and a faded sweatshirt. Loading her camera and putting an assortment of lenses in her canvas bag, she ran from the house, glad to escape the black cloud that was brewing in the study. It took her almost half an hour to get to the cabin because she decided to go around by the road instead of through the tall grass, and when she got there she was quite out of breath. Now here was something that had not changed at all! She was delighted. It was exactly as she had remembered it. Even the old rowboat, was there, tied to the dock. It would be fun to go out in it, to paddle about in the harbor, maybe shoot pictures from the water. Tally had one foot on the deck when she heard something from inside the cabin and it startled her so, she instinctively moved back into the tall grass.

The door opened and a girl stepped out. Tally couldn't see her face, but she could see the most extraordinary tangle of red hair cascading down the girl's back. She could also see that the girl was wearing shorts and no top. The girl stopped for a moment and stretched her arms luxuriously to the sun; then, as if she had forgotten something, she turned and stepped quickly back into the cabin.

Tally felt her heart pounding and she stayed very quiet and very still until she calmed down. Then she crept away.

Goddam him, she muttered walking angrily back up the road. And she instantly hated herself. Why was she so angry? Why shouldn't he have a girl? Goddam, goddam, goddam, she muttered with each pounding step on the dirt road. Admit it, she told herself. Admit you've imagined all sorts of things about Zack. Admit you imagined him kissing you. Admit you've reached out for his naked flesh. She shook her head in anger. She had imagined just about as far as she could, and all the while he had some bimbo girlfriend waiting for him in his hideaway shack! She was furious. Worse, she was jealous. Zack Hayes would be quite the catch for some *local* girl.

The whole thing was ridiculous. She had merely been lonely and bored and so she had momentarily fancied herself attracted to someone like Zack. Well, Julian was right. She and Zack Hayes were worlds apart. She gave herself a stern talking-to. She would go into New York this afternoon with Julian. She needed a good dose of city life. That was where she belonged. And Julian always made sure she had the best of everything.

But the house was empty when she got back. Julian's car and bags were gone; he had already left. Once again she cursed Zack as if it were his fault that she had missed an invitation from Julian to go to town.

Well, to hell with it. Zack Hayes was not why she had come home this summer. Forget Zack. She had come home to be with her father. She had talent and good instincts, and out of that she would fashion a photo essay about Ivan and how he worked.

In the darkroom she selected the fifteen best prints she had so far. They were good. She couldn't help admiring them yet again.

Ivan was sitting alone in the studio when she went in.

"Papa?" she said. "Are you busy?"

Ivan looked up and then waved her to come in. "I was thinking about you, my Natasha. I was sitting here in the quiet and I—well, I don't really know why it comes to me, but I was remembering the time you were a little girl, no more than a baby. We had just come to East Hampton, before we got the house here. We were living in town over the store, and I remember your mama and I put you in a pushcart and walked you up and down, up and down the main street. That was really all there was for us to do. We didn't have money for anything. Well, there was this old man who lived in the town, and every time he would see us with you, he would come out and bend down to the cart and he would say, 'Your papa loves you and your mama loves you and God loves you. But I love you most of all.' You thought that was so funny. You laughed and laughed. And the old man laughed and . . . oh, I don't know. It means nothing. All these things . . ." He smiled a faraway smile.

"I don't remember."

"No? Of course not. It is not important." Ivan shrugged.

Tally felt as if she had missed something, but she didn't know what. She thrust the portfolio in front of her father. "Will you look at these, Papa? Julian says I can show them at the Guggenheim exhibit, if you approve. I have more, but these are the best."

She watched his hands as he leafed through the stack, not daring to watch his face. Finally he came to the end. Carefully he stacked the photographs together, tying the string at the top in a neat bow.

"I'm sorry, darling girl," he said finally. "These are not for exhibition."

Tally felt a hard ball tighten in her stomach. "What do you mean?"

"Just what I say. These pictures are work of beginner. There is no shame in that. You are beginner. Everybody must be beginner at first. Someday maybe you will be genius photographer, but not yet. Natasha, listen to me . . . you don't start at the top because you are my daughter. Work hard. Someday, when you earn it, you get show at gallery or museum, but not now. There is nothing here."

He turned back to his worktable and, after a moment's deliberation, picked up a sharpened pencil and fitted it into a drafting tool. He was already lost in his work when Tally left.

And so the day ended. Tally was in a foul temper and stayed in her room until she heard Ivan leave to go out with Penny. Then she went downstairs and wandered aimlessly around the house, which was still as unfamiliar to her as a hotel. Ivan frustrated, annoyed, and irritated her. She didn't see why she had to take his criticism. She didn't see why she had to stay here all summer. He didn't need her. He didn't want her. It never occurred to her that she needed and wanted him.

52

She was reading a book when Zack came up on the screened-in porch. She was surprised to see him, but she concentrated on her reading and didn't look up.

"Hi," he said. "I was wondering if you'd have dinner with me. I was just going out to get a hamburger."

She glanced up. "Hmmm. I don't think so, Zack. I'm not really very hungry." She looked back at her book.

"Oh. Well, maybe some other time." He waited. Tally kept on reading. "I saw the model of the installation today. It looks good. Maybe you'd like to see it with me the next time I go in."

"I'll see it sooner than that," she said. "I'm having lunch with Julian in a few days, and he'll take me around to the museum." She kept her voice deliberately flat.

"Good." His voice showed irritation, which pleased her. "Sorry to have disturbed your reading." He turned to go, but then he turned back.

"I almost forgot. Ivan said it was okay, but I wanted to ask you, too. My sister stays with me sometimes, and I don't have hot water down at the cabin. If it's not too much trouble, could she use the spare-room shower?"

"Your sister?"

"Yes."

"Oh well, yes, of course. Anytime she likes, and . . . I didn't know you had a sister."

"Well, I do. She's really my half-sister, and she's a lot younger than me. She's fourteen."

"Is your sister here now?"

He nodded. "Would you like to meet her? Because she'd love to meet you. She's a little weird, even for a kid. But I think you'll like her."

A half hour later, Zack and Tally and Nicki Hayes were bouncing along in Zack's pickup truck on their way to eat at Bobby Van's in Bridgehampton. Zack had been right about his sister. Nicki was about the weirdest fourteen-year-old Tally had ever come across. She was slim and tall and precociously beautiful. She was dressed in old clothes, scraps really, out-of-date bits of things, old oddments, moth-eaten things, tattered castoffs. Everything was too big on her, she was too thin, and yet somehow, taken all together, she looked marvelous. Her hair was a mess but so extraordinary that all she had to do was flop it this way or that and it looked fabulous. She was sweet, innocent, vague, charming, and silly all at the same time. Tally couldn't take her eyes off the girl.

"People must tell you how beautiful you are," Tally finally said.

"Oh sure," Nicki giggled. "All the time. I was walking down Main Street the other day and this man got out of a sports car and came over to me and stood there for the longest time. Finally he said, 'You have the face of an angel.' "

"What did you do?"

"Nothing. I didn't have to, because right after he said it he sort of groaned like he had a stomachache and then ran back to his car." And then Nicki groaned and fell over laughing.

"Jesus, Zack," Tally said. "He ought to be arrested. What kind of thing is that to happen in broad daylight in East Hampton?"

"I know, I know. I worry about her all the time. But Nicki knows how to take care of herself, don't you, honey?"

"Zack thinks I'm a dope." She stuck her tongue out at her brother.

"I don't think it, I know it. She never goes to school, she's flunking out, and all she does all day long is wander around town wearing these crazy clothes!"

"I don't know. I sort of like the look, Zack." Tally appraised Nicki's costume. "Do you like dressing up?"

"Yeah. I like all the old stuff. I practically live in the Thrift Shop, and they save things for me. I go to the dump, too. You wouldn't believe what people actually throw away. I'd rather play dress-up than anything."

Tally nodded vaguely, but her mind was churning. Nicki Hayes was a natural model, what they call in the fashion business a "money bones." Tally thought any photographer in New York would simply die for her.

"Listen, Nicki," she said on impulse. "I have a great idea. Would you let me take your picture? And will you let me fix you up? I mean like the models. I worked on a fashion magazine in Paris, and believe me, you've got the look."

"She's too young," Zack cut in.

"Are you kidding?" Tally winked at Nicki. "The top models these days are even younger, some of them."

Nicki giggled. "Oh, don't mind stuffy old Zack. He doesn't approve of anything I do. Gosh, Tally, would you really? Take real pictures? Zack said you were a professional photographer, and I was gonna ask you, if I ever met you, if you might do me. I've practiced and practiced in front of the mirror, but it's not the real thing. I bet I could be a model. I mean, I know what my best side is and I know just how to suck in my cheeks . . . see, like this . . ." Only Nicki both sucked in her cheeks and crossed her eyes, which made them all collapse into a fit of giggles. Zack, too. Then Zack turned up the radio and the sounds of "My Sharona" blasted into the night and they all took up the song. Tally felt as if she had been drawn into an enchanted spell.

Tally set up her equipment down at the cottage the next morning. Zack left them, promising to be back for lunch.

"Make that *with* lunch," Tally shouted after him, and Zack nodded and waved.

That afternoon she developed the first rolls of film. They were good enough, but Tally decided what she needed was a real studio, with proper lighting, professional makeup. When she found out that the local photography store had just such a setup, she instantly rented it for the following week. She spent most of the intervening time gathering costumes and props.

On the day of the shoot, she picked up Nicki with makeup, hair gels, and three suitcases of dresses and accessories.

"Can't I look now, Tally? Please?" Nicki begged. She had been sitting for what seemed like hours while Tally wove ribbons in her hair and then slowly, painstakingly made her up. Last had come the dress, an old net formal from the fifties, strapless, with pink checked gingham trim. This Tally had ripped and torn into wispy shreds so that the effect was at once fragile, campy, and funny. At last Tally sat back on her heels and, with a final critical once-over, pronounced Nicki ready for the shoot. She led Nicki to the corner, where there was a full-length mirror.

Nicki stood peering at herself, transfixed. "Oh gosh, Tally. Oh wow," she breathed. "Look at me."

"I have been looking at you, you nit, for the past two hours. You like the effect?"

Nicki just nodded. Tally had transformed her from a rather messy child into a fantastic version of the kind of things she saw in the top fashion magazines. She was very chic, punk, very now. And she was gorgeous.

They worked for the next five hours. Pausing only to change costumes, rearrange hair, touch up makeup. Tally took dozens of rolls of film. She knew the results were going to be fabulous. And they were.

Tally and Julian were lunching at Mortimer's. "Look, Julian. Look at this girl. She is a natural. Isn't she fantastic?" Tally could hardly contain herself as she placed one blow-up after another in front of Julian. She had called Julian and insisted he drop everything to see her. "She's a photographer's dream—completely uninhibited, her face is stunning from every angle, she's long and lanky and perfect for every imaginable type of clothing." Tally knew the photographs were good. Better than anything she had ever done. "God, I could sell these right now. I know I could."

Julian set the portfolio aside and signaled the waiter to bring them another round of drinks. "Sell them? To whom? Listen to me, Tally, your little friend is quite attractive and these are amusing, but all this is just child's play. It's not serious. It's not art. Frankly, I am a little disappointed. I thought you had finally captured the great artist on film. Perhaps Ivan didn't like your initial presentation, but don't give up on that idea. You're good enough to photograph him as you set out to. Don't let yourself get waylaid by . . . this."

"You don't like them?" Tally was incredulous. "These are good pictures, Julian. Much better than anything I showed my father. I hate to admit it, but he was right about those pictures. They weren't very good. But I'm excited about Nicki, Julian, I really am. To tell you the truth, I feel much more comfortable and inspired doing her than Ivan."

Julian smiled and patted her hand. "Of course, you're nervous. Anything worth doing has that effect. Don't take the easy way out. These photographs are good, I'm not saying they aren't, but use them to build your confidence. You have what it takes, Tally. I know you do. I've watched you grow up, and if I have only one talent, it's that I recognize talent. You can photograph Ivan St. Peters. It's never been done. It's special. It's unique. It's the kind of thing that will get noticed. But send these photographs to an agency in New York, and what do you think will happen? Will *Vogue* come rushing to your door, demanding your services? I doubt it. The girl will simply be snapped up by some agent or another and some editor or another. Another pretty face in the Seventh Avenue rat race. You and your work won't figure in it at all. You don't want that, do you?"

"Well, no, I guess not," Tally admitted. "But I don't want to let Nicki down. I more or less told her I could do something for her."

"And so you can. Send her to me. I know a great many fashion editors. I'll see that she gets around. You send her to me, and in the meantime, Tally, you listen to me. I'm far wiser than anyone gives me credit for. Ivan can't see beyond the nose on his face. He's under a lot of pressure and he sees you as his little girl and all that. No wonder he rejected your work. But I tell you it is good enough for the exhibit. I can *make* it good enough. You need to work, of course, work hard. And you need a critic, someone who can take what you have and shape it, but the essential quality is there. The feeling is there. Believe me, I know. I have a sixth sense about you, and I always have. You're not Ivan's daughter for nothing. You've got what it takes."

Tally beamed. Coming from Julian Slade, this was high praise indeed. And it was just the sort of thing she needed to hear. Julian was right, as always.

53

Tally returned to Springs with renewed vigor. She was everywhere that Ivan was, her cameras slung around her neck, her face intent, her purpose clear. It was exhausting to watch her, and I think we were all beginning to feel the tension that was building between Tally and Ivan. If it hadn't been for Zack, I think the cork would have popped far sooner than it did. He was a master of diversionary tactics. But then, he was a man in love.

One day Zack took Tally sailing.

"I want a big career and a big life," Tally said as the sails on Zack's boat unfurled and caught the southerly wind. "You have to think big —that's the only way to get it—I won't stand for being anonymous." The boat slipped smartly out of the marina. "I don't want to be just the daughter of someone. I want to be that someone."

Tally held on to the starboard rail. She was suspicious of sailboats; it always seemed to her that the damn things were going to tip over.

Zack steered his way through the dozen or so anchored boats in the harbor.

"This exhibit is just a start, of course. Julian thinks my work is good enough, even if Ivan doesn't. If I work at it, really work for the rest of the summer, he says I can still do the exhibit at the museum. So what do you think, Zack?"

"I think it's great. If that's really want you want to do."

"Of course it is. What else would I want?"

He shrugged and smiled at her. "Maybe a beer? They're in the cooler."

"I hate beer," she said, reaching in for one for him. "Say, now. You've got champagne in there, too. Are you celebrating something?"

"Only the fact that I've got you in this boat. By the end of the day I expect to turn you into a real sailor."

She made a face. "That's what they all say. But I warn you, if we tip over I'll scream and then I'll drown and then I'll never forgive you." They both laughed, but Tally grew serious again. "Zack, you've been really nice about helping me with my work, but I'm not completely stupid, I can tell you aren't enthusiastic. Will you tell me why?"

"It's not that, Tally. It's just that I—well, Ivan hates stuff like this. He never talks to interviewers. I don't think he's even seen a photograph of himself in twenty years. He doesn't understand what you're trying to do. I mean, 'photo essay'? He doesn't know what that means, or indeed why it should mean anything." Zack held up his hands in a what-are-you-going-to-do gesture. "I think maybe Julian is out of line about this. He knows how Ivan feels, but he's still trying to push this idea along, and I've got to wonder why."

Tally felt her defenses rising. "Why not? It's not going to hurt Ivan. It's not going to do anything but be an interesting footnote to the exhibit. Look. I'm not kidding myself into thinking I'm going to make a name for myself on this. But I think I have something unique to offer. You're right about there being no photographs of Ivan for the last twenty years. That's shocking. And really a shame. Posterity will be curious about him, how he worked, how he looked while he worked. Don't you agree with that?"

"I don't know, Tally. It all seems like something else is going on here. Julian's not happy about Ivan's decision on the molds for *Hearts-ease*, and frankly, I think he's using you."

"You don't like Julian, do you?"

"Hey, we're supposed to be having a good time, not a third degree. Now hang on, sailor. I'm coming about." Tally ducked her head and hung on as the boom reversed itself and then, with a snapping of sails, the boat swung out toward the bay.

"But maybe Julian is right about not breaking the molds," she continued. "Papa's an artist; he doesn't know about the business end of things, the way Julian does. Maybe Julian's right and Ivan's wrong about this."

"It's not a matter of right or wrong, Tally. It's what Ivan wants. We're not talking about business, we're talking about art. He's put everything he is into *Heartsease*. It's the culmination of everything he's tried to express. It's not a commodity, it's an extension of his life. I don't think Ivan intends to ever sell *Heartsease*. And he certainly doesn't intend to make recastings of it."

Tally started to say something, but the day was too perfect for argument. The wind was steady and warm. They sailed out of Three Mile Harbor into Gardiners Bay, and the cool spray from the sea relaxed her. For a long time they didn't talk at all. That was one of the very nicest things about being with Zack. They could go for hours hardly saying a word to each other, and yet there was never an awkward silence between them. She was comfortable with Zack, and had she stopped to think about it, which she didn't, she would have realized how rare that sort of comfort was.

"Hey," he called to her, "have you ever been on Gardiners Island?"

She shook her head. "I've seen pictures of it, but I didn't think anyone could go there." Gardiners Island was a five-mile strip of land, just a few miles from Springs, that was privately owned by the Gardiner family and had been ever since King George II had granted it to them in 1743.

"I used to go over there all the time when I was growing up. I know a wonderful place. We could have our picnic there. Do you want to?"

"Sure. If we won't get attacked by guard dogs or something." Tally was excited. She had lived in Springs most of her life and had stared across the bay for nearly as long, wondering what it must be like to live on your own private island. Though the family maintained a few houses and windmills on the island, the forest, one had read, stood as it had since prehistoric times, the beaches were pristine, the flora and fauna all but untouched by civilization.

Zack sailed his boat to one end of the island. The main house, he explained, was at the other end. They anchored a little offshore and waded in. The beach, deserted and pristine, was like no beach she had ever been on before.

"I feel like I'm a million miles from civilization," she said in a hushed voice. "Like we're on another planet, even. Why is that, Zack?"

"I think it has to do with the fact that no one can come here. It feels like that, don't you think? It feels big and empty and fresh. But come with me. We'll take our picnic on the high ground."

The island was long and narrow, and they walked for a while in the dunes, but soon they were climbing a steep slope. Tally was quite out of breath when Zack turned and pulled her the final few feet to the top. They stood at the edge of a meadow. She had never seen such a meadow before. It was a big, round basket of tall grasses, filled with hundreds of brilliant wildflowers. Reds and blues and the brightest of yellows dipped and blew in the breeze so that the field seemed animated, a wild, abandoned dance of color. On the far side there was a forest of large, dark trees, a virgin, primeval forest.

"My God, Zack," she whispered, "the Garden of Eden must have looked like this."

He didn't say anything, but took her hand. He led her straight into the blowing grasses until they came almost to the far side. Here the ground was covered with soft moss, and Zack laid the blanket down and the basket of food on top of it.

"We can explore for a while, if you want to."

"No. Not yet. I just want to sit here for a while and let this sink in."

"I know how you feel. I remember the first time I came here. It's hard to know how incredibly perfect the natural world is, because it really doesn't exist anymore for most of us. There are highways next to parks, and marinas on the water. We put up signs about deer crossing, and plant flower gardens and build houses for birds, and pretty soon all that seems like nature. But it isn't. The natural world has all but disappeared. Oh sure, you can find it if you're willing to travel long distances and backpack hundreds of miles, but most people aren't ever going to do that. And here we are, only a few miles from the modern world, in an untouched wilderness."

They were silent for a long time, and then Tally turned to Zack. "Why was it I hated you so much when we were little?"

Zack smiled. "Did you really hate me?"

"Oh yes. At least I thought I did. And I did! Don't you remember?"

"Well, sure. I remember a lot of stamping of feet and shaking of curls. I didn't have much experience with girls then. I guess I figured it came with the territory."

She wondered what his experience with girls was now. "I was pretty awful. I felt like you had taken something from me. Stolen it. Now I'm not even sure what it was I thought you'd taken. I guess I was jealous of you and the relationship you had with my father, but that wasn't it exactly. It was something else. It was as if you had taken something even more precious from me, and I wanted it back."

"Well"—Zack paused, staring off in the distance—"there was the issue of my mother. Maybe that was it. It was a pretty upsetting time, and maybe it seemed to you like I was a part of it." He was silent for a minute. "It must have been hard on you. So many things are hard to understand when you're young."

"Why can't people just *behave* themselves?" Tally added. "I mean, it seems to me there should come a point when you stop indulging yourself and get on with your life."

"Yeah. Well, I don't think most people can. Emotions have a way of taking over. Passion almost always triumphs over reason. But it hits kids the worst because they can't do anything but stand by and watch. You always look at the older generation and think, 'Well, God, they had it all figured out.' You look at old photographs, and there they are, looking so confident and grand and grown up. I have a feeling that's why Nicki dresses up in those old clothes all the time. She thinks that gives her some sort of wisdom."

"You worry about her, don't you?"

"Yes. She's so different from me, but I feel close to her. She looks a lot like my mother but sweeter, and . . . more trusting than anyone I've ever known. I didn't see much of her when she was growing up. I was thirteen when she was born, and pretty much on my own. As soon as I can get settled, I'll be able to take care of her myself."

Tally remembered when she was thirteen. That dark, silent year after her mother had died. She remembered how she had tried to do things the way her mother had taught her, and how hard she had tried to make things nice in the house, but somehow nothing she had done had made anything nice. Her father had withdrawn more and more into his work and the studio. And she remembered Zack. He had been seventeen that year. Zack and Ivan in the studio for hours, sometimes all night, while she sat alone in the house. Until Julian had stepped in and stopped all that. Julian had made all the arrangements for her to go away to school, and paid for it, too. Dear Julian. Thank God for Julian.

She shook away the gloom of that year and inhaled the sun-filled air and the damp scent of the earth underneath her. "I suppose the worst part of growing up is finding out that the older generation didn't know much at all. Certainly not as much as we thought."

Zack nodded. "My mother . . . well, my mother was a woman who never did have her two feet squarely on the ground. She was a big dreamer."

"Tell me about her, would you, Zack? I'd like to know something about her, because I never—well, no one ever really talked about her around me."

Zack's face was impassive as he reached into the picnic basket and got out a bottle of wine and opened it. He rummaged around in the basket, then said, "Hey, we forgot glasses."

"We don't use glasses in Eden." Tally reached for the bottle, tilted her head back, and took a long swig. "We can pretend it's a goatskin." She handed the bottle back and felt the rush of warmth from the smoky red liquid flood her veins. Then she flopped back on the ground and waited and watched Zack. He drank, and she noticed his neck and throat for the first time, and how the muscles ran in two thick cords, spreading down into his chest.

"Are you sure you want the whole story?"

"The whole nine yards, nothing left out."

"Well, I guess I would have to say my mother was sort of like one of those ladies in the fairy tales to me. It was like some wicked spell had been cast on her and sometimes she was wonderful and other times she was under the spell. She had this thing about men. One day, one of them would turn into a white knight and rescue her. She used to talk about it. 'Our ship will come in one day,' she would tell me, but our ship was always in the form of another man." Tally felt herself being drawn into another world as Zack talked. She felt something else, too. It was deep in her heart and it was something she had never felt before.

Life with mother had had its ups and downs, Zack remembered on that sunny day on the edge of a field of wildflowers, but no matter, he had loved her. He had thought she was the most beautiful woman in the world, and she had always told him he was her best beau. He'd learned to accept the steady string of "uncles" in his life, but he had never liked any of them. He wouldn't let himself like them because he was so afraid she might really fall for one of them, and then he wouldn't be her best beau anymore. Zack was going to grow up and rescue his mother. Someday he would be her hero. A real hero who would treat her like a lady and buy her nice things. On the increasingly rare nights they were together, they would sit up eating popcorn and drinking Cokes, talking about what they would do when their ship came in. Rita was never at a loss for ideas.

"When Mother talked about her plans for the future, she made them sound as if they really could happen. There was a time when I believed our lives could have changed for the better. It was right around the time Nicki was born. My mother loved babies. She was so happy being pregnant, and just cuddled and cooed over Nicki like she was the greatest thing. Yeah," his voice was far away, "that was the best time. But then Karl Hoffman came on the scene and everything changed." Zack's face clouded over, and Tally was afraid he would stop, but he continued. After a few months, Karl's brutality forced Zack to run away. He was taken in by an old, retired fisherman who owned a shack and a gas pump out on one of the piers in Three Mile Harbor. Zack earned his way by helping dispense fuel and fishing gear to the baymen, but the work was seasonal. The rest of the time Zack spent either in school or by himself. He learned everything he could about the sea and air and land. He loved the outdoors. And then his mother met Ivan. And Zack knew she was doomed.

"She went kind of crazy, I guess. She knew it was her last chance, and she probably knew it wouldn't work out. I think of them like two stars out of orbit, each one careening off track . . . but who knows, really? It seems like a long time ago. I don't know what I felt when she died. Someone lent me a baggy suit and I stood at the grave and I think all I really felt was a kind of relief."

Tally lay down on the blanket, shielding her eyes with her arm. It gave her intense pleasure to watch Zack talk. To watch his lips, which were soft and gently rounded. To watch his eyes squint in the sun. To watch his moods and the way his cheek muscle jumped when he was being serious.

He turned, suddenly smiling down on her. "Hey, you're not going to sleep, are you?"

She shook her head and started to push herself up. But he reached for her and held her down. "No, don't move."

And she didn't. Not a bit. She lay still, but her heart had started to beat harder and she felt her breath shallow in her throat. He was still looking at her, and she found she could not unlock her eyes from his. There were no sounds except the wind playing in the tall grasses and, in the distance, the call of birds. The sun was warm and she felt it deep in her bones. She felt everything. The blood beating in her veins, the nerve endings tingling on her mouth and in her belly and at the very tips of her nipples. Her legs trembled and she could feel a heat, an energy deep inside her, gathering irreversible force. She had to have him. It was as strong and powerful an urge as she had ever felt.

"Oh God, Zack," she moaned. "Let me kiss you." His arms went around her in an instant and she reached for him, pulling his mouth to hers. For just a split second, he held back and she saw in his face a look of triumph, but it didn't matter. Nothing mattered but his mouth on hers, the feel of his hard, lean body against hers, the urgency in him matching her own. He was as overwhelmingly and terrifyingly, hungrily in need of her as she was of him. And when, a minute later, he pulled away, she gripped his shoulders as if she were fighting for her very life.

"No, wait, baby," he whispered gently. "Don't let's go too fast. Let me see you. Let me look at you."

She lay back in the soft grass and let him hold her and kiss her. He kissed her mouth and then her eyelids. He kissed her neck, and his hand gently stroked the very tips of her breasts under the thin cotton T-shirt. She felt herself grow hard, her nipples aching. His fingers were sure and strong as they tugged and twisted and stroked the burning nerve ends of her breasts, and she thought he must have done this to many women before her, but she was glad because she wanted him to be sure and strong. He unzipped her jeans and his hand slipped down beneath the elastic of her panties and he started taking off her clothes. She sighed as they came off. She felt free. Free of any constraint. She was naked and she watched him as he looked at her and she knew she was beautiful. Her body was a thing of perfection. She saw it in his eyes and she felt the knowledge grow in her, making her languid and sultry like a cat. Now he was standing over her, taking his own clothes off. Watching him sent deep currents of desire sweeping over her body, so that without his even touching her, she could feel her body moving and rocking with the ecstasy inside. He was like a statue, hard, his legs muscular and tight, the dark tangle of hair in a straight line on his belly reaching down to the full erection with a single drop of moisture at the swollen tip, glistening in the sun.

He knelt down beside her, watching her face as he spread her legs, feeling the wetness there, so soft, the flesh like velvet—slippery wet under his finger, her hips lifting each time he stroked her until she moaned and reached out for him, her voice one she had never heard as it begged him to come to her.

Then he melted so deep and gradually into her that she could hardly tell where his body left off and hers began. He moved slowly and deliberately inside her until there was nothing left in her to resist him. She would never know this again, or she would know it forever and ever. She couldn't hold back anymore and cried out to him, "Now, please now," but he wanted her too much to let her give in. "No, not now. Not yet." His hands and his tongue were gentle as they slowed her down, rocking her gently back down to earth until her eyes opened and looked into his and then her teeth bit gently at the edges of his mouth and her tongue sank deeper and deeper into him until she could feel his belly harden and his arms tense and then he lifted himself above her and brought her legs up around him and now, now, there was nothing on earth but this moment and this thing that was happening to them. They couldn't get close enough, and each felt such a longing for the other, for love and need, for release of a long-felt passion, that there was now no holding back. Everything seemed so right, so good, so unbelievably good, and they reached higher and higher into each other until they were there at the very top together, bursting, suspended in the sun while a sea of wildflowers swayed in the wind.

Afterward they lay in each other's arms, still shiny with sweat, and hugged each other close. They kissed. Over and over until it seemed they should just let their lips lie against the other's, not kissing, not daring to pull apart. Finally, Tally burrowed her face into Zack's neck and whispered, "God, Zack. How can anyone feel like this? How can this happen?"

He pulled her close and kissed her forehead. "I don't know, Tally. But it's happened to us. I've never even come close to this with anyone else. I love you. I think I've loved you for a long time. Maybe more than you'll ever know."

54

In love, in love. Is there any other sensation in the world like being in love? On a summer night, say, with his arm around you, his lips to yours. Dear God. Could there be anything finer than that? Is anything else in life so worthwhile?

I often think of the weeks that followed as a kind of lull in the storm. Zack and Tally were like every young couple I have ever known who have just discovered love. They were sure no one else on earth had ever felt such momentous emotions, and they were very secretive and private, as if we jaded ones could only mar the perfection of their feelings. For the first time I can recall, Tally did not keep me in her confidence and avoided my company. Inwardly, I cheered. Not just because two very lovely and deserving people had found each other, but for the suddenly relaxed and very pleasant time this gave Ivan and Penny. In fact, with everyone in the St. Peters compound suddenly all lovey-dovey, I elected to take a short trip. Okay, I'll admit maybe I was feeling a little out of it, surrounded by all the billing and cooing. I decided to hie myself off to the fat farm for a dose of clean living and pampering. I arrived back two weeks later, having lost ten pounds, and I felt as marvelous as I thought I looked. Zack had been dispatched to pick me up at the airport.

Naturally, I asked Zack how went the course of true love. He was not really the confiding sort, but he liked me and we felt at ease. "You know her better than anyone, Maisie. I don't get it, I guess. For a while everything seemed perfect and then she changed. I don't know what happened, exactly. I mean we feel so strongly one minute and then she backs off, like it's all a big joke or something. I love her. I love her more than anyone I've ever known. More than Ivan, even. But she won't let me get close to her."

"You mean she's, ah . . . cold?" I said incredulously.

"Oh no. Not that way." He grinned. "God, Maisie, she's"—he hesitated and glanced at me—"well, hell, she's the most passionate woman I've ever been with. That's not the problem."

"Well," I said, relieved, "then what is?"

"That's just it. I don't know what the problem is. For one thing, she wants to keep this whole thing a secret. We have to act like we're just friends—not even that—acquaintances. I'm not even allowed to wave to her if I'm driving by in my truck. She actually sneaks out at night to see me. She's terrified of people finding out. I don't get it."

"Well," I said, "she's in the midst of her first real love affair, I know that for sure. And she wants some privacy. I can understand that. The competition with Penny, the difficulties with Ivan, yes, I can definitely understand it. But it bothers you, doesn't it?"

"Yeah. It does. Maybe it shouldn't. Maybe I'm going too fast. Listen, I never thought I'd be the one who was rushing things. I thought the last thing I wanted was to fall in love, but I have and I don't want to screw things up. Maybe I should just back off."

"Don't do that." I was serious. "Go with what you feel. Playing games doesn't help anyone. And trust Tally. This is not an easy time for her. In the fall, after the retrospective, things should even out."

Zack nodded, but I could see he was still perplexed. I can't say that I understood it either.

Ivan, too, was irritated with his daughter. He tried not to show it. He had tried not to show it ever since she had come home, but the truth was she got on his nerves. He knew what she was trying to do with her photography and he didn't want it. She could do anything she liked, go anywhere, take up any interest she cared to, but he didn't want her there in the studio, taking pictures of him. It seemed the more he didn't want her there, the more she was.

There were times he could see his beautiful Emma in Tally. He knew it was unfair, but he so wanted Tally to be like her. And sometimes, if he walked into a room, coming on her unexpectedly, or if he caught her laughing, or lately, when he saw her talking to Zack, why, she was almost a spitting image of Emma. It was in the softness of her cheek, in the way she held her head, sometimes in the graceful flutter of her hands as they gestured when she spoke, and then, oh, he would catch his breath trying to hold on to that moment. But alas, they were fleeting and all too rare.

Why did Tally have to set her mouth so, he thought, watching her as she busied about him with her camera, and why did she worry herself about such trivial things? A career? What was a career? He didn't know. You did in life what you had to do. There was no label for it; you didn't run your life by what someone else wanted you to do. What nonsense her talk was, and her plans. To take pictures of him and show them? It seemed a foolish thing, and it annoyed him to no end.

"Enough. Enough. Enough," he bellowed, and then instantly softened his voice. "My girl, it is enough for me today. I cannot think with all that noise."

"Noise? What noise? Do you mean the camera shutter?"

"Yes. Yes. The camera makes a noise and I don't like it. It makes me jump inside. Besides, is too hot today to be cooped up here with me. Go to ocean. Why don't you ask Penny to go? You never do anything with her."

"You're just trying to get rid of me. I'll go, but please don't try to push Penny on me. We have nothing in common and she gets on *my* nerves."

"Ach." He was impatient. "You be nicer to Penny. She has done nothing to make you so rude. You make me ashamed."

Tally flared. "Oh, do I? I can't think why you should be ashamed of me. I'm not the one who's meddling and interfering and trying to run everyone's life around here. If you ask me, it's Penny who ought to be ashamed. She's done nothing but make Julian's life a misery, and mine, too, for that matter."

"But I don't ask you. No. We don't talk about Penny this way. You know nothing. She has been great friend to me."

Tally sniffed. She snapped her camera case closed. Just then, Zack drove by on his way down to the cabin. He beeped the horn as he always did if he saw her in the yard or at the window. Two quick taps on the horn, that was all it was, but to Tally, who was trying to keep her romance under wraps, it was like the town crier passing through.

She knew her cheeks were flushed, so she ducked her head down as if there was something tricky to getting the camera back in its case. When she straightened up, she saw her father grinning at her. *"Nu! Da!* So. You think I don't notice, but I do. Mainly, I wonder why the work is behind schedule and why my assistant is gone all the time. Then I see why. I see you and I see Zack and I know everything." He tapped his temple and beamed at her.

"What do you know?" Her voice was measured and cool.

"Oh, Natasha, my daughter, don't be so secretive. You don't need to hide this from me. Nothing makes me so happy as you and Zack together."

"And then she left, slamming the door as if I had said something wrong." Ivan paused and held his hands up in that way men do when they think they've confronted a woman being irrational. "I don't know . . . I don't know." He shook his head.

Penny, Ivan, and I were on our way to the opening of a friend's show at the Parrish Museum in Southampton. Penny was driving us, as she always did, in her very smart forest-green custom Mercedes. Ivan sat in the backseat like a sultan, with his eyes closed. Penny, I could see, was waiting for an opportunity to plunge in with her usual forthright manner.

"But, darling, you're being totally unfair. If Tally wants to keep her affair with Zack a secret, you shouldn't tease her. Teasing does nothing but cause tension, and we've enough of that as it is. As for her career, you're living in another century. Every woman today wants a career. They're very serious about them, and they should be. For once I almost agree with Julian. Tally has the makings of a very good photographer. If she's a bit naïve and immature, well . . . it makes it all the more charming. It's not, after all, as if her exhibit were going to be prominently displayed, and I'm sure that we will be able to select some quite presentable work. You just don't like having your picture taken, and that's silly of you."

"Ah, Penny, Penny. You always stand up for Tally, and she is wrong to be so rude to you." Ivan's sigh was deep and tragic.

"She isn't rude, darling, she's upset because she thinks I've taken her place. We've talked about this, Ivan. As you told me, one of the last things Emma said to Tally was that she was to take care of you. Well, she comes home to do just that, and finds me in residence. She's young and passionate and she's your daughter. I would say she's been remarkably civil, all things considered."

Penny was on to another topic now, and as I looked out the window at the passing scene, I marveled at how agile and efficient she was. Having reassured Ivan about Tally, she moved smartly on to the protocol of the Southampton social scene.

Penny was almost too perfect, and I understood why she irritated Tally. Penny did, too, in general. But of course she had no idea how very off-putting a perfect person can be. As for me, I like perfect people. I'm so far from being perfect myself that I find it comforting that there are some people in the world who are capable and qualified and keep everything running smoothly. I find it soothing. In fact, I often go a bit sleepy-eyed when I'm with Penny. She looks at me oddly sometimes. Perhaps she thinks I drink. It was true that after long stretches of time with Penny you got the feeling that she was the only one on the tennis court playing the game. Her energy was unflagging, her form and follow-up admirable. She played by the rules, and her rules were fair and honest. But in the end she always won. No wonder Tally had problems. Tally wanted to win, too.

They both wanted to be the perfect woman, but in the contest for Ivan's attention, Penny was the clear front-runner. He needed her. At this stage of his life, he was almost totally removed from practical matters. As Emma had done before her, Penny did everything for him. She organized his social life, orchestrated the running of his house and his business affairs, kept on top of his obligations, organized his trips, and in general ran every aspect of his life outside the studio. She was good at it and she loved it. Her only cross to bear was Julian, whom she disliked and mistrusted. On this one issue, Ivan did not give way to her better judgment. But, as I said, she was unflagging in her pursuits. Given time, I think she would have had her way about Julian.

Yes, Penny was perfect—even to the extent of her respect for the memory of Emma. Though she had never met Emma, she spoke about her in terms of affection, and accepted her preeminence in Ivan's life agreeably. Penny knew full well that she would never be the major love of Ivan's life, but she also knew that if she had to have a rival for Ivan's affections, she could do no better than to have a dead one.

Perversely, I did on occasion wonder about what went on in their bedroom. Time had not diminished my memory of Ivan St. Peters in the sack. At fifty-two he appeared as virile and sexual as a man of thirty. Still, it was hard to imagine Penny in the throes of passion. But I was wrong. Years later she told me how she had felt about him.

"I was forty-four when my husband died. He was much older than I, and his illness lasted quite a few years. Later, when I met Ivan, I thought I had put all that behind me. We met briefly once before Emma's death, at a dinner party at my house, and something between us sparked. It was intoxicating. It was so unexpected. I remember walking around for days afterward feeling rather giddy. After Emma died, Ivan became quite reclusive, as you know. Frankly, it never even occurred to me to try to see him again, but I was so drawn to his work and so eager to see it that I quite naturally went to the Slade Gallery when the new show opened. And there he was, just as I had remembered him. I knew from the minute I walked into the room that the spark was still there for me. I never looked back. I wanted him. I went after him like one of those female types you see in the movies. I was very bold, but he was bolder than I. He made it clear from the beginning that I was his." Penny paused and went quite pink. "He had such a way about him, didn't he, Maisie? It didn't seem to matter that I was a woman of fifty. Ivan simply loved women. He knew so much about the inner heart. And he found in me what had been there all along but was almost forgotten." Her eyes went a little misty. "The finest thing about it was that he showed me how very much more passion existed in me as a woman then there ever did when I was a girl. It was an incredible gift."

55

Alone in her bedroom, Tally stared at herself in the full-length mirror. She was composed. Her hair was neatly combed, her face scrubbed and glowing from her shower. Only an hour before, it had not been so. Only an hour before, she and Zack had been swimming off Louse Point, naked, the water dark and silky soft on their skin as they floated on their backs, the millions of stars overhead reflected in the inky waters so that she had felt as if she were at the center of a starry universe.

Slowly now she undid the sash of her robe and let it slip to the floor. She studied her body. It was the same body, it looked the same, but she had only to close her eyes and remember Zack's hands, his tongue and his smell and his breath, and it was no longer her body, but something separate and alive of its own accord. It was bliss. Her hand trailed down her stomach to the tangle of hair, and she pressed her hand against the mound, marveling at the renewed lust she felt, wishing she could have him again—and again.

Sex with Zack was nothing short of fantastic. She had only to see him walking across the yard to the studio or waving to her as he drove by in his truck to go all weak-kneed and mushy inside. And then nothing, no amount of concentration on her work, no brisk diversions to the ocean, could keep her mind on anything but him. And with him, "it," the great, indefinable "it," was always fantastic. In his cabin, on the beach, in his truck, anywhere, everywhere—over and over again it was fantastic.

The way they fit together. The way they knew without words, without any sort of preamble, what the other wanted. Sometimes it was funny and they played like naughty children. At other times, it got so far beyond them, so deep, that there was no way they could get enough of each other.

"So what's the problem?" I asked, when she had finally confided this to me.

"No problem," she answered. "It's the perfect summer romance. Sweet, short, and then over."

"Come on," I said. "Who are you kidding? What are you saying? That this is just a fling? It must mean more to you than that. Why, you are the picture of a woman in love. What is this 'summer romance' bit?"

"But that's just it," she answered brightly. "We are a summer romance. This whole thing will be over with when the summer is done, I'm sure of that."

"You're very sure of yourself, indeed."

Tally nodded. "Yes. I am."

Later I would realize that Tally was actually terrified by what she felt for Zack. What she wanted was control, or a sense of it, anyway, and what she had with Zack felt very much out of control. Every generation, I guess, reacts against the one before, and somewhere along the line Tally had decided she didn't want the kind of wild, disjointed, abandoned life she thought her parents had had. She wanted well-marked boundaries, respectability, and, most important of all, financial security. Love and passion and freedom, all those things my generation craved, spelled chaos to Tally. She aspired to a completely different kind of life, filled with material goods and strict social patterns. Love, it seemed to her, was a dangerous, unpredictable thing that needed to be kept at bay.

"Look," I said, "I like my creature comforts, too, but not at the expense of love. You talk as if your feelings didn't matter."

"Oh, they matter," she said patiently, "but I can't allow them to run away with my life. You see, Maisie, passion is not love, or at least it's not the kind of love you should base your life on."

I was silent for a moment. "Then what do you think love is?"

"I think the purest kind of love is friendship. Most people think friendship is less important, but when you think about it, it's the best of love. It's not all tied up with feelings of jealousy and possessiveness and uncontrolled passion. You're not confused by it. It's easy and natural, it's a commonality of tastes and interests and affections and kind feelings. And there's desire in it, too. The desire to make the other person happy and content. It's completely unselfish, whereas all this heart-throbbing sort of thing is totally selfish."

"Selfish? I wouldn't call it selfish but honest. Passion has everything to do with love, honey. It's the very essence of it."

"Oh, Maisie, you sound like Papa."

"Thank God. He's never lost it. And it's a wonder that you've never found it." Tally looked hurt, and I didn't want that. "Look, honey. Maybe I just don't understand. I'm a hopeless romantic. I admit it. There's nothing worse than a mother hen trying to force a match where there isn't one. Maybe I've wanted something that just isn't there from you and Zack—"

"You haven't talked to Zack about this, have you?" She was instantly on the defensive.

"Oh, honey. Of course not," I lied. "I'm not quite so meddlesome as that. You and Zack have your own lives to work out. I'm only an interested bystander who loves you very much and wants the best for you." I reached over and took her hand, a remarkably soft hand for one so hardened in her opinions and resolves. "When I was your age, I was just as sure of myself as you are. Things become less clear as you grow older. Look, you may be half right about what you say. Then again, I may be half right, too. The only difference is I've reached the age where I can listen and you haven't."

Late that night or early that morning, Tally was awakened out of a deep sleep.

"Tally? Are you awake?" Nicki's voice was soft, but Tally woke in an instant.

"Yes. Nicki! What are you doing here? God, I was dreaming. What time is it?"

"Gee, I don't know. I guess it's late." Nicki stood in the doorway of Tally's bedroom. "Everyone's asleep."

"Of course they are, it's three in the morning." Tally squinted at her clock. "Jesus, Nicki . . ."

"Oh, Tally, don't be mad. I had to come and see you."

"How did you get in?"

"Easy. You never lock the doors. I used to come in the house all the time. Mostly at night, but lots of times when Ivan was in the studio and no one was here. I love this house."

Tally was wide awake now. "Hey. Come here and get in bed with me. You're freezing, Nicki. Your feet and hands are like ice. How can that be? It's August, for God's sake."

Nicki didn't say anything, but she curled her body against Tally's. Instinctively, Tally put her arms around her and was shocked at how thin she was. She rubbed Nicki's hands in her own, and felt the girl sigh and snuggle closer.

Inwardly, Tally sighed. Nicki was getting more and more difficult for her to take. She was a ward of the state and would be until she was sixteen. Zack was her only family, but he didn't qualify as her guardian. He had no permanent home and no money, and until recently he had been too young. Nicki adored her big brother, but it was Tally she loved.

She knew Nicki loved her, was devoted to her, and she wanted to do the right thing by her. But she really didn't know what that was. She was like a lost puppy. God, she was cute, but what was one supposed to do about it? One of the things Tally tried not to think about was Nicki's life. Nicki didn't like to talk about things like school and her foster parents and such. And Tally was afraid of digging too far into Nicki's life. Her foster parents didn't seem to be much good, and were probably keeping her for the monthly check it brought them. After a while Tally gave up asking. She never knew what was true anyway, and often wondered if Nicki did.

So she was surprised one day when Nicki suddenly and quite out of the blue recounted to her the violent end of Karl Hoffman. Karl had been tried and sent to prison after Rita Hayes died. But the manslaughter charge sentenced him to a mere ten years, with time off for good behavior. Unfortunately for Karl, he got himself killed in prison. "But that was lucky for me," Nicki said in her breathless way, "because he always said he was my real father. That's why they put me in a foster home, 'cause they were gonna give me back to him when he got out. But I know he wasn't my real father. I just know it. And Zack says he doesn't think he was either. But anyway, after he died I was too old to get adopted, so I went to some other foster people and I have to stay with them until I'm sixteen, then Zack and me are gonna go off somewhere together and live. Zack promised. I wanna go to California but he doesn't, so I guess we won't, but it sure would be fun, huh, Tally, to live near all the movie stars and Disneyland."

All summer, Nicki had been glued to her. It was flattering to a point, and then it was . . . well, if not a nuisance, problematic. She tagged along everywhere. She begged for attention, constantly asked advice, and chattered incessantly, mostly about plots of movies and her whimsical daydreams. Zack was no help because he didn't know what to do about her either. He said that all Nicki needed was someone like Tally. Someone she could count on and turn to. It seemed to her that he expected her to take care of Nicki. At first she had gone along with this unrealistic notion, but Nicki's problems had turned out to be far beyond Tally's realm of experience. She was a dreamer. God, that child lived in the land of make-believe.

"Nicki, honey, don't go to sleep. Tell me why you came here."

"Oh . . . you know. I can't sleep where I am."

"But, sweetie, they'll be worried about you at home."

Nicki let out a big sigh. "That's not my home. Not to me. I wish this were my home. I guess you'd be pretty mad at me if I told you all the times I used to come here. I started coming over to the house to find Zack when I was little, and then I just started coming on my own. I used to hide in the bushes and come in when the coast was clear. I saw you a lot before you went away to Europe. Then, when you did go off, I used to come up to your room. I didn't do anything or take anything, but I liked to sit on your bed and pretend you were my big sister and that you had told me to take care of all your things while you were away."

Tally hugged her closer. "Did you?"

"And you know what, Tally? Maybe you are my sister. I mean my half sister, just like Zack is my half brother. 'Cause I know all about what happened back then. I know that my mother and Ivan were in love with each other . . ."

"No, Nicki. They weren't in love . . ."

"Yes, they were. I bet they were. And then she had me. I was her 'love child.' I saw a movie one time about a love child. Only the father was a musician, but he was just like Ivan only he died, and the mother—"

"Nicki, Nicki! Honey, I can tell you this is all a fantasy. It's not like the movie. It's all pretend. Oh, sweetie, I'm not your sister or your half sister, but I am your friend. And I'll always be your friend. Okay? But you mustn't make up these stories. They're not real. Now look, you go to sleep and tomorrow we'll go shopping and out to lunch and . . . oh, I don't know. We'll have a whole day together."

Nicki nodded sleepily and then turned over, pressing her back against Tally's warmth. "When you and Zack get married, we'll all live together, won't we, Tally? Won't it be fun?"

Tally lost no time in getting Zack alone the next day. "Married! You haven't told her we're getting married?"

"No. I think I might have mentioned it to you first." He grinned. "Don't get so riled up, Tally. She's just a child. All children play make-believe."

"She's not a child. She's fourteen years old. When I was that age I certainly didn't play make-believe."

"Well, maybe you should have."

"What's that supposed to mean?"

"Nothing. Look, I'm sorry she upset you. As far as I can see, the only bad thing she's done is sneak into your house uninvited, and I'll speak to her about that."

"That's the least of it, Zack. I mean, the next thing you know she'll be telling everyone about us. Saying we're getting married. I can't have that. I won't stand for it."

"Hey, hey, slow down. Let's back this up to the beginning. Now that you mention it, what's so bad about that?" He stopped what he was doing, which was patching the sails for his boat. They were out on the small dock next to his cabin.

"Oh, come on, Zack. Be serious."

"I am being serious."

"You want our sex life blabbed around to everyone?"

"No. I want to marry you."

Tally, who had been pacing up and down the boards, stopped dead in her tracks. Her look could not have been more incredulous.

"Marry me! My God, you're as balmy as she is. Please don't joke."

"Do you see me laughing? I couldn't be more serious. After the show opens, I'm going out to Colorado to spend some time with an architect there who's got a grant to come up with housing solutions in Third World countries. He's going to Africa first, and says there's a place for me if I want it. It's exciting. And it's a pretty good offer. It's the kind of job where I can do—or anyhow *start* doing—some of the things I think ought to be done. I want you to come with me."

"And what am I supposed to do while you're out building the better mud hut? Chew juju leaves and put rings in my nose like the other female chattels?"

He laughed. "That's not exactly what I had in mind. Though you wouldn't look half bad with a ring in your nose."

"Zack, don't tease me."

"No? Okay, so let me put a ring on your finger."

"That's not what I meant."

"I know it. I've thought about it, the two of us. There are so many places we could go, so many things we could do together. I love you, and I even like your rather acid tongue and temper." He laughed. "Except that it always seems to be coming my way."

"This whole conversation is ridiculous. You're asking me to share your life, and you don't even know what your life is going to be. It's totally unrealistic. It's absurd. Besides, I don't want to live life on a pittance from some government grant. There's no reason why I should."

"You can live on very little in Africa, and in Europe, too, for that matter."

"You're so impractical, Zack. You never think things through. I've lived in Europe. Do you think I could go back there traveling on second-class tickets, putting up at third-rate hotels, without a bathroom, and eating at cheap restaurants? I want to have fun. I want to do all the things that people do. And I want to do them with ease and style. I want the best of everything. I want to be at the center of things, not stranded in some Third World village. I want an interesting, important life, filled with interesting, important people."

He smiled. "So do I. See? We're perfect for each other."

"Zack, be serious. We don't mean the same thing at all."

"Look, Tally, I guess I'm jumping in a little fast, but I've never wanted anything more than I've wanted you. I don't know how I got to be so lucky. I don't even want to think about it. But you're the one for me. I can't make promises about what our life together would be like. We'll just have to go out there and see. I don't want to lose you. I don't even want you out of my sight. I love you, Tally."

She looked down at her hands. "Whatever that means," she said uncomfortably. She did not like the drift of this conversation. Not at all.

"It means I love you." He was by her side now, and he pulled her to him. "Sometimes I even like you. And sometimes . . ." But he didn't finish the sentence because he was kissing her, and though she meant to resist him, she could feel a wave of pure lust undulating from just above her belly clear down to her knees. The sun was hot on her back. She liked that. He held her head with his fingers twined in her hair and kept on kissing her until she gave in and allowed every last ounce of resistance in her to disappear. When he could feel it, too, he lifted her out of the hot sun and carried her into the dark coolness of the cabin.

"No, Zack, please don't. I can't marry you. I want to talk to you. You have to listen to me. I don't want to do this."

He paid no attention to her. She wanted to stop him from undressing her, but she couldn't. She wanted him so much, her whole body was limp. And, frightened by her need, she couldn't stop talking. "This isn't what I want . . . it isn't right. You can't solve every problem with sex. Please let me go . . ." But she didn't mean it. He knew it and she knew it. He pushed her back gently until she was leaning on her elbows. She tried to say something more, but she couldn't. And now her passion was so heavy in her that she could only watch as he knelt between her legs.

Her breath came in short gasps. Oh God, he was good. So good to her. He knew everything about her. Every secret place, every tiny little change of mood and desire. She felt she was jumping off from a high place and was falling, down, down, and just when she knew she could stand no more, that surely she was going to die with the pleasure of it, her body shuddered in ecstasy and she cried out with an unrestrained sob of pure pleasure.

She lay back on the bed, her arm flung across her eyes. She couldn't speak, and for a long while she couldn't think. From the way Zack looked, she could tell he thought she had accepted him. That she was going to marry him! How could he think that? This was not at all what she had been prepared for. Zack was a summer affair. It was the kind of thing that didn't last, and Tally knew it *shouldn't* last. She didn't trust what she was feeling for Zack. She didn't trust it and she didn't want it to get in her way. And it was for damned sure she wasn't going to throw herself on the mercy of so unreliable a thing as sex. All of a sudden she felt angry. Why was he ruining everything? Slowly she got off the bed and dressed. She didn't dare look at him. When she was dressed and composed, she turned to him.

"I meant what I said, Zack. I won't marry you. If you'd stop for a minute and think about it, you'd know I was right. We don't want the same things in life. We'd be miserable in a matter of months. You think all this breathless tumbling around in bed should lead to marriage? You don't stop to think about the other ninety percent of the time. Can't you see that life can't be organized around passion? Sexual love doesn't last. And I think it's a terrible mistake to think that passion is love. What you and I feel for one another is wonderful. I don't deny that. I will never forget this summer. But it never even occurred to me that it was anything more than a brief, wonderful affair. We can't let it take hold of us to the exclusion of other things, things that are more important in the long run. Passion is like a drug, it makes you think things you wouldn't normally think. It distorts your vision."

"Distorts? I think it clarifies it. It expands it. I don't believe you, Tally. I don't believe what you're saying. Passion is the only really honest thing two people can give each other. Passion is what we are. Passion gives you freedom."

"I don't want freedom. I don't want to be unsettled. I can't see the point of it. I want a completely different kind of life from the one you want. When I marry, I want it to be to a man who believes exactly as I do. Who wants the same things. I don't apologize for what I want. I want beautiful things and a well-ordered life. And you don't. You live in a world I can't fathom. It's idealistic in the extreme, and that may be fine for you, but it's all wrong for me."

"Wrong? In what way?" He spoke in a slow, infinitely calm way, but she could see that she had gotten to him and he was angry. "No, no, don't answer that. Let's talk about you and me. The two of us, without all the crap about beautiful things and ordered-up lives."

"Oh, Zack," she sighed. "We've had an affair. We've felt good about each other. Let's not get all muddled up. Can't you see it for what it is, can't we enjoy it and then let it go when the time comes for it to be over? We're lucky to live in a time when two people can have an affair and get it out of their systems and get on with their lives. That's what I intend to do, and you should, too. I don't want to change you, and you shouldn't want to change me. Can't you listen to reason?"

Zack shook his head. "But I don't think it is reason. All summer you've talked about success and money and the things it buys, and comforts and having fun and being noticed. I wish you could see how little that all means. You have no conception of how exciting life can be if you live it in your gut. It's intoxicating. It's liberating. You're not at the mercy of petty things like invitations to parties and one-upping the next guy. You don't have to own things to know a happy life. I should think it's a burden, if anything. Your trouble is that you don't trust your feelings, Tally, and if you don't trust them, you've got very little else to go on."

"No, I don't trust feelings. Not the kind of feelings you're talking about. I want my future mapped out, I want clear boundaries. You don't get that by being ruled by your emotions. I want what's real, Zack. I won't allow romantic fantasy to control my future. All my life I've listened to stories about how wonderful love is. But I've also watched and seen where all this love gets you. My mother gave up everything for love, and what did she get? A lot of hard work, cancer, and an early grave. I know her family disapproved of her marriage to Papa. I'm not so sure they weren't right. In any case, that is not what I am going to do with my life. I am not going to give everything up for something as tenuous as love . . . whatever that is, anyway."

He said nothing and neither did she. Then she moved toward the door. "I'd better be going."

He stood aside. "I won't stop you."

"You couldn't, Zack, even if you tried. You've never had that power over me." She left quickly, but not before she saw the look on his face. She had hurt him terribly. It was visible in his eyes, and despite her resolve, it went straight to her heart.

56

Tally was miserable, and Zack no less so, but with things getting more and more hectic as the day of the opening neared, no one paid much notice. Tally, I think, was looking for an opportunity to talk to her father, but I must say he didn't make it easy for her. The summer was coming to an end, and she was no closer to getting through to him. It seemed to her that she was thwarted at every turn. Ivan was all but inaccessible while he was working. For the few hours in the day when he wasn't in his studio, Penny was invariably by his side. Penny organized, soothed, fetched, carried, amused, and entertained, and she was always there. When he was in the studio, Zack was there, doing for Ivan in his work what Penny did in his private life.

Tally felt alone and confused. There seemed no place for her in her own home. She avoided Penny as much as possible. All of Penny's kindnesses and thoughtful gestures did nothing but irritate Tally further. And now she was avoiding Zack as well. Her feelings about him were ever more complicated, and she blamed him for spoiling their wonderful time together by suddenly turning serious and marriage-minded. It seemed to Tally that everyone around her was being contrary and was somehow against her. But Ivan was the worst of all. She had expected her father to pay attention to her, to support her ambitions to be a photographer; at the very least, she had expected his cooperation. In both of these things he had disappointed her.

"I'm his daughter, Maisie. But he takes no interest. I have talent, I know I do, but he won't even talk to me." She was angry, and in many ways I didn't blame her. It must have hurt to see the attention and interest Ivan had lavished on Zack over the years, while she, his own flesh and blood, had been held at arm's length. "Darling, talk to him. Here you are, fussing and fuming to me, when it's he you need to speak with. But let me remind you that honey catches more flies than vinegar."

"And what is that supposed to mean?"

"Honestly! You girls today have thrown out the baby with the bathwater. Men like Ivan—or, to put it in a less inflammatory way, *people* like Ivan, because I'm sure there are women in this category as well—need to be sweet-talked and cajoled. If you want him to pay attention to you and do something for you, don't start by arguing about every stupid little thing to show off how smart you are. Set your mind on your goal and then butter him up until you get it."

Tally was looking glum and unimpressed. "Oh, Maisie. I'm not a child begging for a new toy. I'm serious about what I want, and I don't see why I have to play silly games."

"You know what your problem is?" I asked.

"What?"

"You are too much like him yourself. You're both stubborn and proud and willful. But he's got thirty years of experience on you. If you lock horns, he's going to be the winner."

Tally didn't say much in response, but I knew she would think about it.

That night, a stifling hot one, Penny was in New York, making party arrangements for the opening, and Zack was at the foundry. Tally made a pitcher of fresh lemonade, changed into a skirt and blouse, and headed for the studio. Ivan seemed glad to see her.

"So, Natasha." He motioned to her to join him on a long bench. They straddled it, facing each other across the tray of lemonade and glasses. "Talk with me. Tell me how young love progresses."

"Now, Papa, don't start. That is not why I came to see you. Besides, you're all wrong, you know . . ."

"*Nu, nu* . . . I have eyes. I see everything. Zack is walking with a black face, like a storm cloud. My daughter has sadness in her eyes. You have had lovers' quarrel. But I know these quarrels . . . it will pass. It is nothing. A small misunderstanding?"

"Small enough," said Tally wickedly. "Zack seems to think that I should marry him and follow him around the world while he decides how poor people should live."

"I see," Ivan said seriously. "Well, that is something. And what did you say?"

"I said no, of course. The whole thing is ridiculous."

"What is this? Ridiculous? What does this mean? Surely a man does not propose marriage to be ridiculous. I think maybe he did not ask you in proper way. But you must forgive, Natasha. He is man with much on his mind. When he works he can think of nothing else. In that way, he is much like me."

"He is rather like you, isn't he?" She didn't bother to conceal the bitterness in her voice.

"Yes. I think so. We understand same things, he and I. We look at things same way. I see myself in Zack when I first meet him. And Zack helped me to see again what I had lost in myself. He is very important to me, to my work. Yes, I would say we are very much alike."

"But listen to me, Papa. I don't want to get married. And I certainly don't want to marry Zack. I want to do my own work and live in my own way. He's all wrong for me. Can't you see that for yourself?"

"Natasha. You talk with your mind and not your heart. Of course, you don't marry if you don't want to, but everyone sees you are in love. What is problem? I don't understand. Zack has great talent, great abilities. He will go far, but he needs you, darling daughter, to care for him. To love him as woman should."

"What are you saying to me? Zack has nothing to do with this. Love is not the issue. We're talking about my life. Doesn't anybody care what I want to do? I have my own dreams."

"Natasha, Natasha. Love has everything to do with it. You are woman, Natasha, young, beautiful, impetuous woman. You must listen to your heart. Think of your mother, Natasha. What Emma would do. That way you can never go wrong. Be more like your mother, Natasha, and you will be happy as she was."

Tally was suddenly and quite uncontrollably livid with rage. "My God, but you are an insufferable egotist." She willed her voice to be steady, but it trembled in the back of her throat. "You and your precious protégé Zack! What sort of men are you? Women aren't servants put on earth to take care of men. We aren't blithering idiots who have to be 'seen to' and 'managed' and brought around. You think you're so clever and noble and wise—and good! You talk about love, but what do you really know about it? You say you loved my mother, but what did you even care about her beyond your own comforts and needs? What did you ever do for her besides work her to death and demand that she love it because it served you? Even when you came to Julian's apartment to get her back, you cared only about yourself. I've often wondered what would have happened if Mama had turned you down. She should have, you know. She should have taken charge of her life right then and there, and maybe she would have had a chance to really live. But you didn't care about Mama. You've never cared for anyone but yourself."

Ivan was momentarily speechless. Then he said, "Be very careful what you say about Emma, young lady."

"Oh yes, Ivan. I'll be very careful. Because it wouldn't do to upset you, would it? Because the great Ivan St. Peters must never, never be upset or worried or inconvenienced. No, that wouldn't do at all. It wouldn't do to make you really see what you lost and how you lost it. My mother died because you were so busy massaging your ego. You made her give everything she had to you, including her life. You thought the only reason she had for living was to stroke your goddam genius. And she believed that crap. Well, so much the worse for her, but don't expect me to be that dumb."

"Quiet!" Ivan roared. "How dare you speak of mother like this! You know nothing. You understand nothing. You dishonor your mother's memory. There is nothing in you of her."

"How would you know what's in me? You've never even bothered to look. I'm a flesh-and-blood person, not a ghost. I don't act like her or look like her because I'm not her. But that's all you've wanted from me, from the very day she died. And now you're trying to palm me off on Zack, whom you approve of because he is so much like you! It's you who dishonor me."

"You are more stupid than I thought," Ivan said, throwing up his hands. "What do you think in that thick skull of yours? You are blessed with greatest good fortune in that young man. But what do you know of that? What do you know of honor? What do you know of love? You want everyone to love you, but you offer nothing in return except insults. You want me to tell you you are talented and beautiful and gifted and . . . what else? You want me to see these things in you, but I don't see. You make it impossible to see anything but bitterness and unhappiness. You know nothing of love. Your mother knew. She never measured her love. She loved because that was what she was. Every breath in her was love."

"If I am bitter and unhappy, you made me that way. You're nothing but a hypocrite. You've dedicated *Heartsease* to Mama, but look at you! Have you found your peace? Or are you still using her so you can thump your chest and crow to the world what a great artist you are?"

"Natasha. Natasha." His voice was filled with sadness. "You don't know what you are saying. I cannot explain these things to you. They must be felt."

"You think I don't feel? But I do. And what I feel for you is disgust. I think you are a fool! And I'm a bigger fool for having tried to talk to you about anything that really mattered."

Tally turned on her heel and left, slamming the door with all her might. Outside, the air was suffocatingly hot and sticky. She ran blindly across the lawn, stopping when she came to the drive and leaning against the big willow to catch her breath. The night air was thick with tiny insects; they buzzed in her ear. Her breath was caught in her throat, but she was determined not to cry. Not here. Now now. Not ever for him anymore. She would get out of here as soon as she could. God, for once she was going to do exactly as she pleased. To hell with Ivan. To hell with Zack. To hell with the whole bloody mess of them. She would go back to Europe. Why hadn't she thought of that before? There she was treated exactly as she wanted to be. With respect. With admiration. She had some money. She would leave tomorrow. Tomorrow night she could be back in Paris, in Maisie's comfortable house, where she should have stayed all along. She had been wrong to come back here. She would do anything, anything it took to find her own life. She didn't need Zack and she certainly didn't need her father. In the distance she heard Ivan call her name. Loud and clear, it echoed in the still night air. She put her hands to her ears. Well, she wasn't going back in there. She wasn't going to apologize. She wasn't ever going to pander to him again! She took her hands away and listened. There was silence.

She stood against the tree, fighting down the choking grip her emotions had on her throat. A small sob escaped from her lips. In the silence it sounded harsh and unreal. But the sound had not come from her. There it was again. What was it? She turned back toward the studio. Then she started to run. He was calling to her.

It seemed such a long way, but in reality it was just a few hundred feet. She ran up the drive and past the house. In the moonlight the studio seemed like a great white animal. The blood in her chest pumped furiously as she tried to run faster, but as she came near the door, she slowed. There was dread here . . . she was afraid.

"Papa, Papa?" she gasped at the door. And then everything became like a dream. The awful sight she saw couldn't be real. She tried to scream, but she had no voice. She tried to move but she could not.

The giant sculpture had slipped from its ropes and, like a juggernaut, had begun slowly, inevitably to roll forward. Ivan's legs were trapped, and his massive arms strained helplessly against the immense weight. There was nothing Tally could do but watch in horror. For an agonizing moment he strained against his fate, and then, with what might have been a shrug, he collapsed and the three tons of metal eased on top of him in what appeared as slow motion. And then she saw, she saw it clearly, his head rolled back and out of his mouth the spirit and soul, breath and life of him left his body in one long, agonizing, silent scream. Tally stood and watched as her father was crushed to death.

Zack found her there minutes later, out of breath from wailing and nearly insensible.

57

It seemed impossible that Ivan was dead. Even today, all these years later, I cannot describe the loss we felt. There was, suddenly, a big black hole in our lives. Ivan had been so big, had taken up so much of our emotional and psychic space, that the world seemed suddenly a smaller and drearier place. For the first time I felt old. Death was making me old. One by one, the people who had meant everything to me were gone. Where were they? Where were those days, those minutes and hours, we had spent together? Those moments soon to be forgotten altogether? What did those moments mean? Was there any meaning to them at all? They were all dead now: the beautiful boy that was Dance; sweet, sweet Emma; my Henry, so sick and in pain; and now Ivan, invincible Ivan. I struggled hard to retain fragments of our talk, to see images of the life we had loved. I struggled hard to remember. But the very act of trying to remember discouraged me. What was the point, if there were only memories left? I mourned Ivan's death more deeply, I think, than I had mourned the others. I wept for Tally. I wept for Penny and Zack. But most of all I wept for Ivan. He was the very thing that life was about. Vibrant and strong. Curious and childish and filled with the capacity to feel. I wept inside myself because I didn't know what else to do. It was a horrible night, filled with sirens and police and coroners and wave upon wave of people. People who had loved him, neighbors, the local newspaper, doctors, and women bearing cakes and soups.

Within hours, Julian arrived from New York and took charge. He immediately hired a full-time nurse for Tally. She had suffered a terrible shock and was in a frenzy of grief, rage, loss, and guilt. It was wisest, they felt, to keep her sedated.

Around midnight, Julian issued a message to the press:

> IVAN ST. PETERS IS DEAD AT FIFTY-TWO, THE VICTIM OF AN ACCIDENT. HE WAS SUDDENLY AND TRAGICALLY REMOVED FROM THE WORLD, BUT HE WILL NEVER BE REMOVED FROM THE WORLD OF ART. HE WILL BE BURIED NEXT TO HIS WIFE IN A PRIVATE CEREMONY. THOSE WHO KNEW HIM WILL GRIEVE HIS PASSING, BUT HIS HAUNTING SCULPTURES WILL NEVER DIE. AND THE RICH PANORAMA OF HIS ACHIEVEMENT WILL FOREVER GIVE VOICE TO THE HARSHNESS AND SERENITY, VIOLENCE AND TRANQUILITY, JOY AND DESPAIR OF THE INNER HEART.

Penny took charge of the funeral arrangements. To tell you the truth, of all the people who were left behind to mourn for Ivan, my heart went out to her the most. Tally, devastated as she was, was young and blessed with Ivan's own brand of self-centered vitality. Her loss was great, but she would recover. Zack, who had adored and worshiped Ivan, was also young and in a hurry to get on with creating his own life and world. But in a way Penny had lost the most—a lover and companion. She had been given the rare gift of passion and joy late in life, and now these were truly irreplaceable. But she bore her loss with great dignity and arranged the funeral and the reception with her usual skill and gift for organization.

Most of us grieved and tried to console each other. Julian took a more businesslike approach. The following afternoon, vans from Slade International arrived and began removing every remaining sculpture from Ivan's studio.

Zack was distraught. It seemed to him that things were moving much too fast, and he tried in vain to see Tally, but the nurse insisted that she not be disturbed. Finally he pushed his way into her room. I was there, too, and I shook my head at Zack, but he was paying no one any mind. He came to her bed and reached for her, holding her as close as he could and whispering something into her ear. He told her over and over again that he loved her and wanted her to depend on him, but Tally was unable to think or cope. She was like a limp rag doll, and when Zack tried to tell her about Julian's rush to remove the sculptures, she closed her eyes and I saw tears there on her lashes. She waved Zack away and insisted that Julian was in charge. She begged Zack to leave her alone and to trust Julian as she did. Julian, she said, would do exactly as she would do. Zack was hurt, I could see. In the corridor outside Tally's room, he begged me for help, but I had no solutions to offer. Tally was Ivan's closest relative. Without her consent, it seemed to me, we could do nothing. Zack was not so sure. He was determined to confront Julian. And so he did.

"Yes?" Julian hardly glanced up from his lists of inventory.

"I'd like to talk with you."

Julian leaned back in his chair. "I've been expecting you, Zack. Please, sit down." He indicated a chair and Zack sat in it. "I understand you've been to see Tally. I think that for the moment the less she is involved, the better it will be for her. She's had a terrible shock."

"Haven't we all? But I hardly think keeping her constantly sedated is going to help."

"Doctor's orders, Zack. Frankly, I don't know what's best for Tally, but it seems to me she should be spared all she can be right now. My concern is getting her over this terribly difficult time as best we can. Now what can I do for you?"

Zack marveled at Julian's cool efficiency. "Well, aside from wanting to do something for Tally, I would like to know why everything is being removed from the property. Aren't you moving a bit hastily here?"

"Yes, I certainly am. And I'll tell you why. The retrospective must go on as planned. I trust you think that wise?" Zack nodded. "If you want me to put it on the line, Zack, I will. The sad truth of it is that an artist of Ivan's stature is worth a great deal more dead than alive. Yesterday Ivan St. Peters died, and today every single piece of his work has skyrocketed in value. Overnight this has turned into a multimillion-dollar estate, bigger than you could imagine. You see me sitting here doing business as usual, and you think I don't feel as you do. Well, you're wrong. I feel the loss as deeply as anyone, but I have a responsibility to get Ivan's estate in order and protected. That responsibility, to Ivan and to Tally, outweighs my feelings right now. Do you understand?"

"I understand what you're saying, but I can't say I feel better about it. You can hire guards if you're worried about theft. I think you should wait until Tally can deal with this. I think you're out of line to presume to take anything away right now."

"Presume? What kind of talk is that? Of course I presume. Ivan gave me responsibility for his works years ago. I'd say that you are the one who is out of line, young man. I understand how you feel, but I'm afraid you don't know what you're talking about. I respect the relationship you had with Ivan, but not enough to let you sit here and tell me what I should and shouldn't be doing. I think you should leave now."

Zack remained sitting. "The mold for *Heartsease* is still at the foundry. Do you want me to get it and see that it's broken? That's what Ivan wanted, you know."

Julian appraised Zack coolly. His answer was quick and to the point. "Understand one thing, and get it straight. The affairs of Ivan St. Peters are in my hands now. Nothing you have to say has any bearing on what will or won't happen. As far as I am concerned, you are no longer wanted or needed. Now leave this studio."

Zack got up slowly. "Tally won't let you get away with this, Julian. That I promise you." He walked out. Julian merely shook his head.

Services, mercifully brief, were held at the studio, attended by friends and family, neighbors, admirers, reporters, and the merely curious. Tally arrived flanked by Julian and a nurse, but when Zack tried to comfort her, she collapsed in tears, and was led away by Julian. Afterward, everyone was invited to stay on for refreshments at the house. Only Zack and Penny and I made the short, sad ride to Green River Cemetery, and only we heard the hollow sound of the earth as it was shoveled onto Ivan St. Peters's grave.

58

I'm afraid that in the days following Ivan's funeral, there was little of the pulling together that often occurs in a family when death strikes. Zack was embittered and disappointed to find Tally so inaccessible. I tried to console him, but he felt none of my optimism about how things would work out for him and Tally. Penny had decided to leave. She was not a legal entity. Death had rendered her completely irrelevant in matters concerning Ivan. She had her dignity and she certainly didn't want to compromise it. Tally didn't want her around, and Julian made it plain that he felt she was an intruder in the St. Peters household. As for me, I was the old faithful dog who hangs out no matter what. It was a sad and depressing week, but before too much else could happen, there was one very important bit of business to attend to: the reading of Ivan's will.

We gathered together one last time in the large living room. As the lawyer read the will, I saw that Tally was staring out the window, out onto the graceful terraces of grass where stood dozens of the fruits of

Ivan's genius. Her look was so intent, it was almost as if she were trying to will him to appear, to conjure him in the flesh out of the stone and metal images he had left behind. I think I realized just then that Ivan, who in the flesh would never again laugh with us or embrace us or cause us happiness or pain, would do all that and more, still and forever, through his work.

The lawyer, a local fellow who at first seemed rather nervous, nevertheless read the articles of the will slowly and deliberately. Ivan had been generous with all those who had loved him. He left me a beautifully bound portfolio of his early drawings, many of them sketched in the loft on Hudson Street. And he entrusted to my care Emma's diaries. They were mine to read and to pass on to Tally whenever I judged she was ready to have them. I was moved to tears and knew I would cherish Ivan's trust and bequest for as long as I lived.

Penny was left a series of statues that would complete a study he had done soon after he had met her. Zack was given a sum of money and the entire collection of Ivan's tools, and with it a statement that read, "There is nothing to the end that is not there a hundredfold at the beginning. I give you the beginnings and thank you, my friend, for all that you have shown me."

But a bombshell dropped when the lawyer announced that it was Tally, not Julian, who had been named executor of the estate. Julian at first blanched, then the color came back to his face with a vengeance, and he angrily challenged the validity of the will, claiming that as little as a year earlier, Ivan had assured him that he was named executor. It was a hideously awkward moment. In one stroke, Ivan had rendered Julian and Slade International virtually powerless over the future disposition of his work. The tension in the air could have been cut with a knife.

The lawyer assured Julian that the will was quite in order, having been drawn up at the beginning of the summer. Julian shot a venomous glance at Penny, then quickly recovered himself.

"Managing the works of an artist of Ivan's stature," he said, "is not something one can do or even learn to do without years of experience in the art market. Ivan trusted me with his work from the minute we met, and I stuck by him through all the lean times. I never stopped believing in him. You may think me self-serving, you may think I am flattering myself, but I honestly believe there is no one living who knows better what to do with Ivan's estate than I do. Be that as it may, I bow, of course, to Ivan's last wishes. Tally knows, I am sure, that I will always be available to advise her to the best of my abilities."

It was a very effective little speech. I doubt whether Tally had heard a word of it.

That very afternoon, Julian suggested that Tally and I move into his apartment in the city. It made good sense. There was no point in staying on at the compound. It would only keep Tally in a state of depression. A change of scene would do everyone some good. It was settled. But once ensconced in the grandeur of Julian's Fifth Avenue digs, I was not so sure we had made the right decision. Everything seemed blown out of all proportion. The market value of Ivan's work had, as Julian had predicted, shot straight into the stratosphere. Collectors, museums, and investment groups were busy trying to put their hands on any and every St. Peters before the retrospective, which was expected to drive prices even higher. Also, Ivan's death had bestowed a kind of instant celebrity on Tally. I don't think anyone had quite realized how much Ivan's work meant to people outside the art world. People who otherwise cared nothing for art were mad for his sculptures. They stood before them and were often moved to tears. There was a quality about Ivan's work that was utterly generous. It stood for all things human, and encompassed everything from highest joy to deepest despair. It was natural enough that Tally would receive some of the attention that had formerly been her father's, but none of us expected the storm of media attention that enveloped her. Television, newspapers, magazines—all wanted to interview her. Invitations flooded the mails. But Tally kept herself in seclusion. She had nothing to say to the world. She was still trying to come to terms with the events that had overtaken her in such a grievous fashion. She looked to Julian for everything, and Julian continued to pamper, coddle, and protect her as he had always done.

Little more than a month later, Tally and I were sitting out on the terrace of Julian's apartment on a late afternoon, when he came bounding in with a most anxious look on his face.

"Darling? I've been looking everywhere for you. And here you are, shivering on the terrace. Maisie, what ever has come over you? She'll catch her death. Come inside, both of you. We'll have a fire. Who would have thought it would get so cold?" Julian led Tally into the living room of his apartment, rubbing her hands and wrapping a soft cashmere throw around her shoulders before ringing for hot drinks.

"You spoil me, Julian."

"Of course I spoil you. I've always spoiled you."

Tally grinned. "I remember when Mama and I first stayed here. This was the grandest, most beautiful room I'd ever been in, and I was so impressed. I still am."

"Good. I like for you to be impressed with me. I like for you to rely on me. And"—he paused while a maid bustled in with cups of steaming hot water and honey, mixed with a very potent amount of brandy—"I very much like it that you are here with me. Are you glad you moved into town?"

"Yes. I couldn't have stood being in the house alone. But I'll be glad when Papa's show is over. It seems like it's been a long time coming."

"Only six weeks, but I know what you mean. It is rather like having a command performance hanging over your head, but it's so important that you be there." The steaming glasses were passed around, each held in a quilted linen cloth. How like Julian to have a special set of glasses and their "cozies" just for hot toddies, I thought. "Have you thought about what you want to do afterward? Not that I want you to do anything." He went on. "I'd be honored if you'd stay on with me indefinitely. You have no idea how much I enjoy the company of a beautiful young woman. You do know how very fond I am of you, don't you?"

"Oh, Julian. I hate it when you act all formal and fuddy-duddy."

Tally made a face at him, but her heart wasn't in the teasing. "Are you sure there's nothing I should be doing for the opening? I feel so useless."

"No, darling. I want you strong for the press preview. You will have to face them, you know, and I want the world to see what a beautiful and brave young woman you are. Don't worry about anything else. I have it all under control . . ." Julian paused and sighed.

"What is it, Julian? There is something troubling you, isn't there?"

"Well, as a matter of fact there is." Julian's face registered concern. "I hadn't planned to bring this up—in fact, I had hoped to be able to completely spare you—but some disturbing facts have come to light."

"Oh?" Tally's entire body tensed. I had a feeling she wasn't going to like what was coming. Julian's voice had taken a grim and businesslike turn. He was watching her closely and choosing his words with care.

"The day after Ivan died, I called the foundry and had them lock the molds for *Heartsease* in a storeroom. They assured me they would be safe, and with everything else that had to be attended to, I relied on that assurance. However, when we went to pick them up, they had disappeared. It didn't take very long to trace the culprit. Zack Hayes had removed them the day of the funeral."

At the mention of Zack's name, Tally began to look ill.

"As you know, there was a good deal of controversy over whether Ivan should break the molds or not. Had Ivan lived, who knows what he would have done in the end. But he is gone now, and he will be remembered as one of the most important artists of the twentieth century. To destroy anything he left behind would be a crime."

She cleared her throat. "What does Zack say?"

"He is a most arrogant young man. I don't know what his game is, but he's quite adamant about what he wants. He readily admitted taking the molds, but he refuses to hand them over to me. He insists on seeing you. I've held him off for weeks now, hoping to come up with a solution, but so far there is none. Now, I'm afraid, it's up to you to talk some sense into him. You must demand the return of what's rightfully yours."

"I don't want to see him, Julian. Can't you send your lawyer or someone? You have the power of attorney. Take care of it for me. Please, Julian."

This was news to me. I had no idea Tally had given Julian power of attorney.

"I could have him arrested today," Julian went on, "but I don't think we want to create such unpleasant publicity just before the exhibit. I know it's hard for you, darling, and I wouldn't for the world want to upset you, but I don't know what else to do at this point."

Tally looked miserable and kept shaking her head, but I saw a chance for a reconciliation. I leaped in feet first and encouraged her to go. If she saw him, if she got back onto familiar ground . . . "Honey, I think Julian is right. Zack has meant too much to you. You should go. I'll go with you. I have some business in East Hampton anyway."

The drive to Springs was agony for Tally. Why couldn't they leave her alone, she asked over and over. Julian had been wonderful. She was grateful for the attention and care he gave her, but nothing could diminish the cruel images that flooded her memory. She braced herself as the car turned up the dirt drive, but, oddly, there was no emotion in her when she saw the house and the studio. She asked the driver to stop and she got out. It was so quiet. A cool, clear autumn day, the sun dappling through the trees that were bright yellows and reds. Zack, she had learned from the caretaker, was still in the cabin and she decided to walk. It would calm her, she thought. She had never dreaded anything quite so much.

But again she was surprised. Zack was standing on the dock. He had been watching her approach, and now he waved once and smiled. Despite herself, she waved and smiled back. His truck was in the drive, and she saw that it was packed with all of his gear.

"Are you leaving?" she asked.

"Yes. Tomorrow. I'm glad you came, Tally. I was afraid you wouldn't."

"I didn't want to come, but now I'm glad I did, too. It's so beautiful today, isn't it? After the city . . ." she didn't finish the sentence. They were quiet for a minute. "I know we've got some business to discuss, but maybe we don't have to talk about that right now."

He was relieved. "Good. Let's just sit here in the sun. Here, let me get you a cushion . . ." he started for the cabin.

"No that's all right . . ." She tried to step aside, but blocked his way instead, and they bumped into one another. Then they both burst out laughing. In an instant she was in his arms and he was kissing her and she was holding him close.

"My beautiful, beautiful Tally," he said, stroking her cheek with his finger, and she felt herself sighing with contentment. "God, I've missed you. My poor baby. I didn't know what to do."

It felt so good, his arms enveloping her, her head buried in his shoulder. The smell of him—like the dune grasses and a clean flannel shirt, and his skin, she knew just the taste of it, a little salty and warm, so warm.

"Zack?"

"Yes?"

"Nothing. I just wanted to say your name. It's such a nice name to say."

"Is it?" He was kissing her again. She could feel his teeth and they were hard, but his tongue and his lips were gentle. She kissed him back and felt such a longing for him. She knew he felt it, too. But she had to stop. Stop him and stop herself.

"No," she said. "Don't."

He looked surprised. "Why?"

"Because I don't want you to." He didn't believe that. She looked quickly away. "Maybe we should talk about why I'm here after all."

He watched her for a moment. "Okay. But I said it all in my letter."

"I never got a letter."

"Yeah. Well, that figures. I sent it to Julian's. I understand he keeps you under lock and key."

"That's ridiculous. Julian has been wonderful. Which is more than I can say about you. I never got a letter, but I know from him what's happened. You had no right to take the molds, Zack. They don't belong to you."

"I know that. They belong to you."

"Well, then, fine. Give them back."

"It's not that simple, Tally. Nothing is. I don't think you've ever really understood about *Heartsease*. Ivan worked for ten years on it. He sketched it hundreds of times. Nothing else in his life obsessed him like this one thing. He made models of the sketches. He made them in plaster and clay and plastic and stone. None of them were right. And he destroyed them. He destroyed the drawings. There was to be no other *Heartsease* except the finished piece. Not a drawing, not a model. Nothing but the one and only *Heartsease*, dedicated to his one and only Emma. He was adamant. Somehow I've got to make you understand that, Tally. I owe him at least that much."

"If he felt that way, why didn't he break the molds when *Heartsease* came from the foundry?"

"Because Julian begged him to wait. Julian knew damned well that Ivan intended to destroy the molds, but he was playing for time. Wait, he said, wait until the piece reaches the museum safely. Accidents can happen. Well, Ivan agreed to wait. *But he never agreed not to destroy the molds.* I know, Tally. I was in the studio when they argued about it."

Tally frowned.

"You remember what Ivan said that night in the studio? He wanted *Heartsease* to come home to Springs. He didn't want it sold or copied.

He didn't want second and third strikes sitting in Houston and Hong Kong and God knows where. He wanted it here. Give him what he wanted, Tally. You can do it. Tell Julian to fuck off. He's the only person who stands to lose by honoring this wish. But he's not the executor; you are, Tally. What you say goes."

Tally felt a twinge of discomfort. All those papers she'd signed . . . she couldn't bring herself to tell Zack how easily she'd given up on her responsibilities. "You're wrong about Julian, Zack. I know you are. Julian is not trying to win or lose anything. He only wants what's best."

"You're a fool to think that, Tally."

"Don't you tell me what to think." She could feel her anger rising. "I want those molds returned to me. As you say, I'm in charge of the estate. I decide what to do."

"Yes, you decide. Not Julian. Don't let him sidetrack you from doing what's right. Don't listen to his arguments about posterity. Ivan knew how he wanted to be remembered. And you should know it, too. Why do you think your father made you executor? Because he was afraid of what would happen to his work if anything happened to him. He was counting on his own flesh and blood to honor his wishes."

"Are you telling me he mistrusted Julian? That's Penny talking. She never liked Julian and she tried to turn my father against him. Ivan owes everything to Julian, and I'm not going to degrade that friendship because of her jealousy and your paranoia. Don't you see, Zack?" she pleaded. "The retrospective will cement my father's place in history as one of the great twentieth-century artists. Julian is the only person who knows how to handle that. Selling his works, placing them in the right museums, getting the right price, all that is Julian's job. I can't turn on him now and tell him I don't believe in his judgment. My father would have changed dealers if he hadn't trusted Julian. Or he would have said something to me, but he didn't. Now you want me to fly in the face of everything they built together over the years. Of course, *Heartsease* is going to be returned to Springs. I particularly asked Julian about that. But it will tour the world first. It should be seen by the whole world, Zack, it's the most impressive thing Ivan ever did. What if it's damaged? What if it's stolen? Things like that happen all the time. If we broke the molds now, we could lose it forever."

Zack was pacing up and down the dock now. He stopped and put his hands on either side of Tally's head. "God. I wish I could shake some sense into you. Ivan always said you were as stubborn as he was, and now I see what he meant. I only wish you had a little of his sensitivity. Ivan didn't want *Heartsease* to travel. He wanted the world to come here to see it. He wanted people to see it, experience it in the environment that helped to form it. Jesus! Don't you realize what Julian Slade is? What he stands for? He's a parasite. A leech. He's gotten rich sucking the life-blood from your father. If he gets his hands on the molds, he can do anything he likes. He can recast *Heartsease* any number of times, and to hell with what Ivan wanted. You're standing by and letting that man make a mockery of everything your father stood for. Letting him? Good Christ! You're helping him."

Shaken by Zack's words, Tally rose, her face drained of its color. "Are you going to give me the molds?"

"I always intended to. I only wanted to see you, to talk to you away from Julian's influence. I loved your father, Tally. But, more important, I love you. I want to help you. I don't want to see you make a mess of things."

"I have all the help and good advice I need." Her voice was as cold and hard as steel. "*Heartsease* is my responsibility, not yours. I want no further business with you after this. It's over, Zack. I only wish it had never begun. Do you understand?"

His eyes squinted, appraising her, and it was as if he were seeing her for the first time. He waited a long, measured time before he spoke, and when he did, his voice matched hers. "The molds will be delivered to you tomorrow. As for you and me, for the first time you've finally said something I agree with."

A week later, Tally entered the enormous spiral lobby of the Guggenheim on Julian's arm, to the applause of hundreds of invited guests, come to pay homage to Ivan St. Peters and the extraordinary legacy of his genius. The exhibit was splendid, and Tally felt her heart swell with pride. Her elation quickly faded, however, when Penny Frankenheimer walked up to her, greeted her coolly, and got straight to the point.

"Is it true that the *Heartsease* molds have not been destroyed?"

Tally nodded curtly.

"I was afraid it was true," Penny said. "Whatever are you waiting for?"

Tally took a deep breath. "None of this is your business, Penny. From now on, please remember that." She then turned rudely and walked away.

□

Still, the show was a smashing success, and Tally found that in the weeks to follow, she was one, too. Julian conducted her through a whirlwind of social events. The New York art world was quite taken with the beautiful daughter of the great sculptor. Through it all, she depended on Julian for everything, and he was not slow to provide. Then, playing boldly on her trust and affection for him, not a month after the exhibition, Julian proposed marriage to Tally.

She was moved to tears, she confided, by his proposal, which had been humble, almost apologetic. He told her he hardly dared to speak to her about marriage, but the thought that she might leave him had made him bold. He said that in the past few weeks, though one part of him had been in mourning, the other had been blissful and buoyant, and all because of her. He knew that if he didn't speak now, the moment would pass forever and someone else would capture her heart. He had no right to it—indeed, he didn't expect her to love him the way he loved her—but if she would consent, he would spend the rest of his life trying to make her happy.

Tally reasoned it out. Julian was kind, considerate, and capable. As his wife, she would lead an extraordinary life, and she wondered if this all hadn't been predestined for her. It didn't take her long to make up her mind. She would marry Julian Slade, and someday she would come to love him as deeply as he seemed to love her.

I was astonished. She was chic, mannered, and cool—very much in control of the situation. "Of course you're surprised, Maisie," she said, completely understating my horror. "I was, too. And Julian as well." She laughed. "Maybe he was the most surprised of all that I agreed to marry him. It was simply a matter of the two of us looking at each other a little differently from the way we had before, and suddenly it all seemed very right. Julian wanted to wait to let everyone get used to the idea, but I didn't. And so we've set the date. This time next week I will be Mrs. Julian Slade III."

"Next week!" I was speechless. I looked out the window of Julian's sleek car—his own personal limousine and chauffeur, which I knew cost him upward of fifty thousand dollars a year to maintain. I felt weak. I'd gone to California for one week and all hell had broken loose. I felt as if all the life had suddenly been drained from me. How in God's name could I stop this? I took a deep breath. "Now, Tally, listen to me. This whole thing has gotten out of hand. Surely you must have doubts. If you don't, then I do. Quite serious ones. You've been under a terrible strain. Julian has been a prince, I'll give him that, but, my God, you can't marry the man out of gratitude."

"But what's wrong with that, Maisie? I love Julian's life. I always have. I've always dreamed of having exactly what he's offering."

"My God, you're thirty years younger than he is."

Tally smiled indulgently and shook her head. "How much younger were you than Henry? And you were both wonderfully happy. I know there's a big age difference, but it doesn't really matter to me," she said. "Julian is what he is, and I feel much more comfortable with him than I do with almost anyone. He's lived a grand life. He has marvelous experiences to share. He's by far the most cultured and captivating man I've ever known. And I've never encountered anyone sweeter or more considerate. He's everything a woman could want."

"But what about Zack?" I was flustered. This whole thing had caught me so off guard that I felt I was making no sense.

Tally blushed ever so slightly, but, Lord, what control that girl had! "Zack was a mistake—a silly mistake, and one that I don't want to dwell on now. I'm counting on you, Maisie, to stick by me. If you can't, well, I'll be sorry, truly sorry, but it won't make any difference. I've made up my mind. You've got to see this from my point of view. I'm a person who needs a clear view of what's ahead of me. I've never wanted the bohemian life the way you did, or the way Zack seems to want. Julian is the only person who has ever understood me. He's never wanted me to change. He makes me feel exactly right. I think that's what I love about him the most. This feeling of being wanted. When I go to a party or walk into a roomful of people with Julian, everyone looks at me differently. They treat me differently. It's a lovely feeling."

She had me half believing it. No wonder she believed it herself.

The car came to a halt in front of the canopied entrance to Julian's apartment. The liveried doorman stepped smartly up and held the door. There was nothing to do but get out.

"You go on up, honey," I said. "I'm going to stretch my legs and take a walk in the park."

She nodded and then grabbed my arm before I could leave. "Please be happy for me, Maisie."

I must have walked for hours. When I came back, it was almost dark. Julian and Tally were together in the library. They both came and gave me a hug. "Well, Julian," I said, holding fast to Tally's hand, "you're the luckiest man alive."

He beamed. "I know it."

That night we feasted on pheasant and champagne in Julian's dining room. The table glowed with silver and candlelight and crystal and polished mahogany. Tally sat at one end, her skin a pale porcelain against the black velvet gown she wore. Julian, at the other end, was beaming as he chattered on about the plans he had made for their wedding trip. I sat in the middle, getting a little drunk and marveling at the ease with which Tally had seemed to step into her role as mistress of the household.

The topic turned to an upcoming sale at Sotheby's in London, in which two of Ivan's sculptures would go on the block. Accordingly, London would be the first stop on the honeymoon. Tally listened eagerly, her eyes aglow. Julian talked at length about market strength and testing the waters and . . . oh, I don't know. I guess I'd long since tired of hearing about the business side of art. In truth, it bored the hell out of me.

We drank more champagne to celebrate their upcoming nuptials, and soon they left for a late party from which I had begged off, saying my trip had tired me. They asked me one last time to reconsider, as the butler brought in their wraps—identical midnight blue cashmere capes. If I hadn't wanted to cry, I would have died laughing. I finished the bottle of champagne by myself that night and stared out over the city, lost in melancholy thought.

A week later we gathered in the drawing room—just a handful of well-wishers. The ceremony was small and private. It was witnessed by me and two members of Julian's staff, and then the new bride and groom promptly left for London on the Concorde.

61

I went back to Paris for the better part of a year. I might have stayed there indefinitely writing my column, seeing friends, traveling, and otherwise leading a very pleasant existence, but for a chance meeting that sent me packing back to New York. I'd been sitting one evening in a noisy café near my house, watching the passing scene, as was my custom. The night was warm, and the feeling in the air was exhilarating. I guess I was lost in my thoughts when suddenly a man walking past me stopped and, with a grin, strode up to my table.

"Good God!" I said. "Zack Hayes. Sit down and have a drink. What are you doing in Paris?"

"Just passing through, I'm afraid," he said with obvious disappointment. "How frustrating, especially now that I've stumbled on you. I was changing planes at Orly, but I couldn't resist one night in Paris, so I switched my ticket for tomorrow's flight."

I made a face. "That's no way to see Paris. You need at least a month. But what has been happening in your life? The last I heard, you were on your way to Africa."

"Well, you heard right. I've been there all year. I'd be there now, but I have reason to be in the States." He paused as if he might tell me that reason, but then evidently thought better of it. Instead he treated me to a lengthy description of life in the bush.

He looked older. Perhaps it was his deeply tanned face, but somehow he seemed more rugged. Whatever it was, he had lost the cheerful, boyish look I had come to know, and appeared a much more serious and solemn fellow. He told me of his travels in Africa, of the professional possibilities he saw there. We chatted amiably enough, but we both knew we were just passing time. It occurred to me he might not know about Tally's marriage, and I didn't much like the thought of telling him, but the subject had to be broached, so I asked him outright. His face went a little funny, and he cleared his throat.

"Yes. I left New York the day they announced it in the papers. It disgusted me. She disgusts me."

"Yes, well," I said, rather alarmed by the anger in his voice, "it was pretty much of a shock to me, too, but if I've learned anything, it's that you can't control someone else's life." I paused, but he said nothing. "She's not unhappy, Zack," I said softly. "I mean, she seems to have found a niche for herself, and for the moment I think it's got to be a relief from all the pain and grief of Ivan's death."

His expression revealed nothing. His eyes were cold. "Relief? I doubt it, Maisie. If she had any feelings at all, she would have grieved and felt the pain honestly. Instead, she's chosen to live without feeling. It was a masterful thing she did, marrying Julian. She's protected, insulated, untouchable. At least she thinks she is. You know, she's quite like Julian in many ways. I think they deserve one another."

"Well," I said, refusing to be disloyal to Tally, "I can understand how you feel. But I think it's splendid that she's getting involved in the gallery. Her taste is impeccable and her judgment good. She might be Julian's equal in that way."

Zack smiled coldly. "Face it, Maisie, her judgment stinks. But that doesn't surprise me. Frankly, what surprises me most is you." I wasn't sure I knew what he meant, but the conversation, in any case, was clearly over. Zack had risen from the table. Our little reunion was over. I invited him to dinner, but he excused himself, saying he had another engagement, and off he went.

I went home and called Tally's number in New York, but a maid informed me that Mrs. Slade was resting and did not wish to be disturbed. I hung up feeling rather empty and dejected, and it seemed to me that I had been feeling that way for a long time. Just seeing Zack had made me admit, at least to myself, that what I had known all along was true. Tally's marriage was wrong. Terribly wrong. Things were not as they should be. I felt it. I had to return to New York. I owed it to Ivan and Emma. Most of all, I owed it to Tally.

I took an apartment in the Carlyle Hotel and informed my editors I was changing the focus of my column to reflect the change in my address. "Notes from Abroad" would become "New York Notebook."

A few days after I had settled in, Tally and Julian threw a dinner party in my honor. Though there had been many telephone calls, we hadn't actually seen each other since I had been back, and the vision that greeted me on the grand staircase of Julian's apartment was a shock. Tally was stunning. She wore a stylishly cut black silk suit. It was rather severe for one so young, but she wore it with the careless confidence of a woman to whom it is second nature to wear expensive clothes. She was chic from the fashionable cut of her hair down to the tips of her rose-painted nails.

It was hard to reconcile the sight of this stylish, perfectly gotten together woman with the disheveled and visibly lovestruck young girl who, just a year ago in Springs, had strolled onto the terrace with Zack, trying, quite unsuccessfully, to act as if they had not just been making love. Tally hugged me, and when I exclaimed over her chic beauty, she only laughed and said, "Tell Julian. Goodness knows, he's worked hard enough at turning me out." Tally was the very essence of a smiling, gracious, and attentive hostess. I began to wonder if I hadn't been rather hasty in my intuition that something was wrong with her life. She seemed so fully in control. I longed for a quiet moment with her, but until that time I decided to relax and see what would happen next.

At dinner I sat next to a talkative man who turned out to be the art critic for *The New York Times*. He was younger than me, but intelligent and, for a critic, charming enough.

"Well," he said finally, "you'll be surprised at the bohemia of today. It's a far cry from the Greenwich Village days. In fact, the new artists stay as far away from the Village as they can. The new scene is all Hell's Kitchen, TriBeCa, and of course Avenue C, that's where most of it is all happening. The artists today embrace materialism and glamour. They long for fame and they long for money. They're not in it for the spiritual quest. They're in it to get discovered. Remember how artists in the fifties were tortured by the idea of making money? Of selling out? Well, young artists today are tortured by the idea of not making money. Twenty-one-year-old artists, and all they talk about is tax shelters and American Express gold cards. They make frivolous art, and they will do anything to get attention. Bohemia used to be a place to hide, but now it's a place to hustle."

I grimaced. "I'm beginning to think I'm going to have to do a lot of legwork to discover New York in the eighties. I'm as ignorant as my readers out in Iowa. Probably more so."

"Well, that's not a bad angle. The blinding leading the blind, so to speak. The art world now is pretty tricky. It changes like quicksilver. The best galleries in town seem to be the nightclubs."

"I hear that's what's in store for us after dinner. Tally said we were all going to an opening of a new club."

"Yes. It's called Club Paradise. It's quite something. I've had a preview at a press party two nights ago."

"Well, I hope it's worth all the fuss they're making of it. What does it look like?"

"Oh, you'll see. I don't want to lessen the impact. But prepare yourself for a shock. Leo Thorn's clubs are known for shock value, and I think this one outdoes all the others."

"Who is he?" I said. "Or should I know?"

"My dear Maisie, you are talking about Mister Downtown himself. If you don't know who Leo Thorn is, you don't know anything."

"Listen," I said, "I got left behind when Pop Art came along, and I've never caught up. So tell me."

He nodded agreeably. "Leo Thorn is what you might call a very successful con artist. I mean, he has the last word on everything that happens downtown, and downtown is a force to be reckoned with. He started out in public relations and he's turned it into kind of an art form. He made a fortune opening discos in the sixties and seventies and promoting the hell out of them. Then he turned art collector and made a big name for himself as a discoverer of new talent. He and Julian have become very thick. Leo's collection got so big he hit on the idea of turning his clubs into galleries. Julian's invested heavily in this new club. They've commissioned some of the top young artists to design the interior. The results are sort of neo-punk, post-modernist fairyland, if that says anything to you."

My head was swimming. "You sound very knowledgeable on the subject."

"Oh yes," he laughed. "I've got a lead story in the Sunday *Times*.

I've been immersed in this so-called new bohemia for months now. At first I was appalled. It seemed all mockery and confusion, but now I've come around to it. A lot of it, anyway. In any event, it's what's happening now. New York is a very old city and the artists are very young, and if I've learned anything in my life, it's that everything has to change."

After dinner I followed Tally up to her room to powder my nose. I was chatting away about how much fun I was having and how exciting her life seemed. When I turned away from the mirror, I saw Tally sitting on the edge of her bed, her eyes vacant, her whole body rather wilted, with her hands folded neatly in her lap like those of a schoolgirl.

"But, darling, whatever is the matter?" I was astonished. It was as if a bright light had gone off.

"Nothing," she said trying to force some gaiety back in her voice. "I'm tired, I guess." She got up quickly and bustled about, avoiding my eye.

"Well, if you're tired, let's not go out."

"Oh no," she said quickly. "We have to go. Julian expects it. He's made all sorts of plans for tonight. He's got a whole slew of people coming from various dinner parties all over town. It's a big night for him."

"Fine, then let him go alone. Maybe you're getting the flu."

Tally smiled. "No, mother hen. I'm not getting the flu. I'm not sick. I'm tired. Weary of the scene, I guess. We do this almost every night. We go to parties and openings and clubs and galas. Look, I want to show you something." She crossed the room and flung open a double door. Inside were enough clothes, shoes, accessories, coats, and hats to stock a fair-sized boutique. "Everything is arranged according to event. Ball gowns, luncheon suits, dinner dresses, daytime casual, daytime chic, nighttime elegant, late-night trendy. Lots of things I wear are sent around by designers, but of course I have to send those back. A nice girl named Trudy comes every so often to accessorize things, to throw out the old and make room for the new. If I tell her what I need for an occasion, she'll go out and shop for it."

"I don't believe this. It's rather fantastic."

"Isn't it? I remember all those years dreaming of the day when I'd have all the clothes I wanted, and now I do. With a vengeance." She closed the doors smartly. "It's the old childhood fantasy of being let loose in a candy store. Let me tell you something—it gets to be nauseating pretty quickly."

A voice in my head kept saying, I knew it, I knew this marriage wasn't working, but I was biding my time. "So who is this new partner of Julian's? I never thought he would be interested in nightclubs!"

Tally shrugged. "You'll meet him at the club tonight. His name is Leo Thorn, and God, is he ever the thorn in my side."

"Yes, I've heard about this Mr. Thorn. I can't wait to meet him. I hear he and Julian are very thick."

"Like glue." Tally wrinkled her nose. "I don't know, Maisie. Sometimes I can't figure anything out. I thought Julian had the perfect life. He's at the top of the heap. He has everything. He is surrounded by beautiful objects and important people, but it's never enough. Now, all of a sudden, it seems our whole life revolves around this Leo Thorn. Julian is smitten with him, and he's constantly around. He's crude, he's sleazy, he's offensive. But he has some sort of control over Julian. For a while I was helping Julian to scout for new artists for the gallery. I think I saw every half-baked show and gallery in New York. I really worked my ass off, and you know what Julian did?"

"What?"

Tally shrugged. "He called in Leo. He said Leo would show me the ropes, introduce me to the artists that mattered. It was as if nothing I had done meant anything to him at all."

"Oh, Tally . . ." before I could get any further, the door opened and there was Julian.

"There you are. Both of you. We've been waiting for you. Darling, the cars are here and everyone is ready to leave. I think we should go, don't you?"

"Yes, of course, Julian. I'm sorry. It's just that Maisie and I got to talking and—"

"Time enough for that tomorrow." Julian winked at me. "Isn't she lovely, Maisie? Isn't she beautiful?" Tally picked up her fur wrap and walked to the door. Julian took her arm.

The Paradise Club was in Alphabet City on the Lower East Side. The limousine whisked us to a neighborhood distinguished primarily by its shabbiness, its filth, and its derelict population. As we pulled up in front of a quite ordinary-looking building, the crowds and lights from the television cameras blocked out much of the ugliness, but I still had the feeling I was kicking my way through Needle Park as I made my way to the entrance. Two very large men stood guard outside the club, choosing those who might enter from among the hundreds of anonymous hopefuls. Many would stand outside all night.

Inside there was a long blacklit corridor, the floor of which was covered in a rainbow of shag carpet and the walls were swaddled in Day-Glo fake fur. The ceiling was made of bubbles of liquid foam, and everywhere were plastic toys, inflatable animals, and blowups of sitcom characters. Along the corridor that wound down to an enormous room for dancing were show windows, and inside these were artworks from various artists. There was everything in those windows—images from television, suburbia, pornography, cartoons, Hollywood, the grocery store, church, science fiction, even literally the kitchen sink. I stopped to watch one of the artists who was fussing over his exhibit. He was a nice-looking fellow, and I asked him if he minded talking to me about his work.

"Oh sure," he said, looking pleased. "What would you like to talk about?"

"Well . . ." I looked in on a sea of crushed beer cans surrounding a replica of the Statue of Liberty crown. "How did you come to make this?"

"My feelings are these," he said soberly. "Plunder, plagiarize, steal —do anything you have to, but have fun doing it. I like to have fun. I think having fun is being happy. I mean, you definitely cannot have too much fun. So I want to have fun when I'm working and I want people to have fun looking at my work. When I think about what I should do next, I think, 'newer, better, nower, funner.' Don't you think this is the fun-est place you've ever been to?"

I nodded. "Fun-er? Fun-est? Oh brother!" I proceeded to our table, feeling a little bemused but still intrigued. Julian had pulled together a glittering crowd, and it was almost impossible not to get caught up in the music and the energy. The dance floor vibrated with a thousand young limbs. I had forgotten how beautiful young men in their twenties are, and how sassy the girls, all blissed out on the sweet drug of limitless expectation, and probably some other drugs as well.

Tally seemed to have revived and was busily seeing after her large table of people. Champagne flowed. I felt pleasantly lost in the moment, swept away by the noise and movement of the crowd. I hadn't felt this way in a long, long time—a time when I was as young as the girls I saw here, a time when a party materialized almost every night. There had been thousands of parties. The word would spread through the Cedar Bar like wildfire that someone, somewhere was expecting some important gallery people, or maybe just happened to have some extra booze around, and suddenly the astonished host would find himself confronting a battery of crashers. We never came empty-handed, but we did come in hordes. I loved those people. I loved the parties. I loved that scruffy place in time where artists toiled in a friendly swamp of collective obscurity.

Out of the corner of my eye I saw Tally rising to her feet and looking very surprised as two people approached her table. The man appeared to be in his forties. He was dressed entirely in white and looked utterly dissolute. With him was a very young, very beautiful girl in a slim-fitting lace evening gown, a corsage on her shoulder, pearls at her throat. She was more than just beautiful, she was almost unearthly, with her pale face and cascading red hair. She looked oddly familiar. I looked at Tally. I looked back at the girl. Then I remembered. It was little Nicki Hayes, from Springs.

They could hardly hear each other over the din. Tally shouted in Nicki's ear, and Nicki wrote down something on the back of a napkin. The two embraced and then Nicki was led away by the man who turned out to be none other than Mister Downtown himself, the infamous Leo Thorn.

62

The evening seemed to be over soon enough, though I was shocked to discover when I got home that it was four in the morning. I slept most of the next day. The day after that, Tally came for lunch and related the following account of her reunion with Nicki Hayes.

"I was so shocked to see her, Maisie. So surprised. I didn't even know she was in New York. I feel terrible, but I guess I put Nicki and everything else about last summer out of my mind when Papa died. You see I sent her to Julian, who said he could help her with her modeling. But then Papa died and I never really followed up on Nicki. I mean, everything was so crazy then, and I just assumed she was still in East Hampton. But she isn't. She's living with Leo. I can't believe it!"

"How in the world did she get to him?" I asked.

"Well, I gather Julian sent her to Leo. She says Julian assured her she would have a big career in modeling, and that Mr. Thorn was the man to see. She's been in New York as long as I have, but she didn't call because Leo told her not to. Said to wait until her career took off, but of course it hasn't, poor thing. But you wouldn't believe how they live, Maisie. I've never seen anything like it. The loft is the size of half a city block. There are no carpets, no rugs, only a vast stretch of varnished oak floor. There are a few plants—more like trees, actually —and one sofa and an enormous stone sarcophagus that serves as a table. It's really kind of macabre. Otherwise there was no furniture. No beds, even. They sleep on futons, which are rolled up in the morning. Everything is stripped down and hidden away in invisible compartments.

"At one point I asked for a glass of water, and she said she didn't think there were any glasses. 'Of course there are, Nicki,' I said. 'Everyone has glasses.' I mean, she's been living there for months and she doesn't know where the glasses are. But I couldn't find them either. The kitchen had this one austere metal utility island, you know, and everything else was hidden from view. I mean, there were cabinets, but they had no knobs; you had to press buttons under hidden ledges to open them. We settled for drinking beer out of a can. Or rather I did. Nicki didn't have anything. She says Leo says she has to stay thin, but God, she's a rail as it is."

After seeing Julian, Nicki had gone back to East Hampton, unsure about seeing Leo as Julian had suggested, and wanting Tally's advice. But of course Ivan had died and Tally had not been available to anyone. So she'd taken everything she owned (actually, she wore it all), and with fifty dollars she'd saved up, she headed for Greenwich Village. Two days on the streets had convinced her that looking up Leo Thorn wasn't such a bad idea after all. He took her on as a "secretary"—just until her career got going, of course—but one thing had led to another and, "Well, here I am," she told Tally, "having fun, fun fun."

"Are you?" Tally asked. "I mean, is he good to you?"

"Good! He's the best. I mean it. He buys me clothes and takes me around with him and introduces me to all sorts of people who are going to help my career."

"Oh? Is this the modeling we're talking about, or something else?"

"Well, modeling, of course. And maybe I'll be in a movie. Leo says the sky's the limit. He says I'm a natural."

"Look, Nicki," Tally said, exasperated, "I don't want to throw ice water on all this, but you're just a baby. Leo Thorn is a high roller. I mean, has he introduced you to any real agents? Has he seen about having professional pictures taken? Have you been on any 'go sees'? If not, then he's using you."

"Using me! But how could *he* be using *me*? He's the one with all the money."

"Oh, honey, come on! I mean for sex. You're living with him, for Christ's sake. He's old enough to be your father. You're just fifteen."

"So? Julian Slade is old enough to be *your* father."

"But that's different . . ."

"It's not different at all." Nicki was indignant. "I know why you left Zack. You wanted security. You wanted to be taken care of. You didn't want to take any chances. Well, I wanted the same thing. I learned from you, Tally. I modeled myself after you as much as I could. Whenever I was unsure about something, I'd ask myself, 'Well, what would Tally do?' "

"Nicki! This is terrible. How could you think that living with someone like Leo is like my marrying Julian? I've known Julian all my life. My parents knew him and trusted him. What do you really know about Leo Thorn?"

Nicki was up and pacing back and forth. Clearly she was upset. "God, Tally, you don't know. You really don't know anything. I'm happy here. So what if I have to sleep with him? I don't mind. It's not kinky, and even if it was, a little, what's so wrong with that? I mean, men aren't like us. They're different."

Tally was upset now herself. "Nicki, I want you to listen to me. You are a child. You should be at home, going to school, not dressing up every night and going to clubs on the arm of some fifty-year-old sleaze-bag. I know him. He's bad news. You don't belong with him."

Nicki looked desperate. "What are you asking me to do? Go home? I don't have a home. You and Zack were the only home I ever had, and you left me behind. You didn't even say good-bye to me. And Zack tells me he's going to send for me when he's settled somewhere. But when? He doesn't know. He doesn't even tell me where he's going or for how long or anything. I just hated it when you two split up. I figured there was nothing much left to believe in."

"But, Nicki, Zack and I weren't right for each other. It wasn't our fault. It wasn't anybody's fault. Just because we decided to end things doesn't mean you should run away. I'm sorry, but this"—she gestured to the large living space—"is not where you should be. You should go home and go back to school."

"Will you please stop saying that!" Nicki stamped her foot. "Listen, you want to know about my 'home'? I'll tell you. A foster home isn't a home. Foster parents, at least mine, aren't kindly old folks who love orphaned children. They're in it for the money. For the check that comes once a month. Do you think they care whether I'm happy or doing well in school or having a good time? They don't. They care if *they're* having a good time, though. My foster father started coming in my bedroom when I was nine. He would make me take off all my clothes and then he would jerk off all over me. When I was eleven, he started making me have sex with him. He said I was a slut, just like my mother. He said I was a liar and that no one would believe me if I told. Shit. Who was I supposed to tell? My foster mother? She hated me."

"Oh, Nicki, Nicki, honey, why didn't you tell Zack?"

"Yeah, sure. Tell Zack. Zack would have killed the sonofabitch and spent the rest of his life in jail."

Tally felt angry and sickened. She wanted to grab Nicki and take her home, but what home? Home to Julian? Julian had sent her here in the first place.

"Don't be sad, Tally. I'm really happy here. Leo leaves me alone most of the time 'cause he's so busy. He's nice to me. He gives me an allowance and takes me around like he's really glad to have me with him. It's not gonna last forever, I know that. But then nothing does. And, you know, I believe him about making me a star. Why not? Why not me?"

Tally was fishing about in her bag for a hanky. "Yes. Why indeed not." She blew her nose. "Now listen to me, Nicki. I'm going to write down my private telephone number. You're to call me, anytime, day or night, if you need me. And I don't mean if it's a big crisis. Call me for anything. If you're lonely or bored or want to talk over something. Promise?"

"Sure. I promise."

"In the meantime, we'll see each just like we used to. Okay?"

"Yeah. I'd like that. So do you have to go now?" She clung on to Tally's arm.

"Honey, I do. Julian and I are . . . God, I don't know what we're doing, but it's for damn sure we're doing something. Now look. I'll call you in the next few days." They hugged and kissed at the elevator, then Tally stepped inside and pushed the ground-floor button.

63

Tally confronted Julian demanding to know why he had sent Nicki to Leo. But Julian only shrugged. "I thought you wanted me to do something for her, so I did. What happened after that is hardly my business or yours."

Tally didn't know what to think. She became more and more edgy and temperamental. She found her only relief was walking. Quite literally, she took to the streets. On the street she could relax; the crowds of people wanted nothing from her. On a single city block she could be witness to a thousand small dramas. It liberated her mind, she told me, and set her imagination free. One day her wanderings took her to Greenwich Village, and on impulse she walked to Hudson Street to see if she could find the building where her parents had lived. Hudson and 12th. Well, if this was it, Tally thought, standing across the street, it was quite elegant. Huge windows graced the large old warehouse, and a doorman stood under a crisp royal blue awning with the name THE

ATRIUM embossed on it in white. The doorman was only too happy to tell her that indeed it was the original building but gutted and redesigned into sixty living units, each opening onto a large, glass-domed rotunda of trees. Would she like to see? he asked. Tally shook her head. "No. This isn't the place I was looking for," she said, and thanked him all the same. And she walked on.

She went to bed early, but awoke at midnight with her heart pounding from a dream unlike any she had ever had before. It was all pure and vivid sensation. She was back on the beaches of East Hampton. Zack was with her and they were running in the warm sand, playing in the surf. The intensity of her feelings grew. She could feel his body close to hers. She felt happy. When he took her in his arms, she could hardly contain the joy she felt, and as they came together in the dunes and began to make love, Tally cried out with her need and long-pent-up passion. It was a wail from deep inside, a gigantic, unbearable realization of what had been lost. Zack possessed the power to help her, but even as they reached for one another, even as his body loomed over her open, waiting, yearning form, she knew she could not have him. She awoke calling his name, the tears streaming down her face. The dream was not a dream, but a longing so real, so powerful that it left her devastated.

She paced back and forth in her bedroom. She was alone. Julian was in Europe. Something big, he said. The full extent of her loneliness, and her great need for Zack, drenched her in fear and rage and despair. She cursed herself. She had thought love was complicated, but in reality it was so simple. It was so sweet. Oh, if only she could find it again. If only there were some way to go back, to retrace the steps that had gone wrong and put them right.

Tally was standing in for Julian at the opening of a show. She had looked forward to it, but instead she felt suffocated. The room was jammed with people and she found it difficult to move. She smiled and nodded and kissed people and shook hands and got kissed. She felt nothing. She felt numb. She wanted to hide or to run away, but she didn't know where.

"Well, well . . . the beautiful Mrs. Slade. Are you pleased with the show?" Tally felt herself shiver in disgust as Leo Thorn put his hand on her arm, but she forced a smile, hoping he would realize it was forced.

"The show is marvelous, Leo," she gushed. "I didn't see you come in. Where's Nicki?"

He was grinning at her in that particular way she found so offensive, a familiar, seductive sort of grin, as if he knew something embarrassing about her.

"I think you'll be pleased with what the critics will have to say about the show," Leo was saying. He grinned again.

Tally shifted uncomfortably, wishing she could move away from him, but the crush around her was impassable. "Yes . . . I'm sure I will. I haven't seen Nicki yet. Where is she?" She asked again.

Leo looked bored. "Oh, you know these kids. At the last minute she changed her mind and didn't want to come." He acknowledged an entourage of young people coming in the door. One girl caught Tally's eye. She was a startlingly pretty blonde, dressed from head to toe in black. Black Capri pants, a black leather jacket, a porkpie hat, and huge eyes rimmed in heavy black liner. Her eye caught Leo's and she flushed with pleasure. "Well, tell her to call me tomorrow, will you?" Tally said, but Leo had already moved away.

Tears sprang to her eyes for no apparent reason, and she had to get out into the air where she could breathe. She edged her way to the door and suddenly, out of the corner of her eye, she glimpsed the tall, dark-haired figure of Zack. Her dream of the night before rushed back to her and left her breathless and unable to move. She saw Zack talking angrily to Leo, then watched as he turned away. It wasn't until then that he caught sight of Tally.

She felt her heart jump into her throat. His eyes locked on hers. He hesitated and then walked over to where she was standing.

"Hello, Zack," she said, feeling faint. "This is a surprise. I didn't know you were in town."

"I hadn't planned to be. I didn't know I'd see you here tonight, Tally. In fact, I only came here to get Nicki. I got a message from her. You don't know where she is, do you?"

Tally shook her head, and then she held her hands to her ears. "This is bedlam. I can't talk to you here. In fact, I was about to make a rather premature escape."

"Escape? Where?"

"Well, I hadn't really thought beyond fresh air. Why not come back to the apartment with me for a drink? It's around the corner and . . ." She saw him frown. "Oh, Julian's not in town, if that's what you're thinking."

Finally he nodded and she led him to the rear of the gallery so that they could slip out unseen through the service entrance. She felt reckless and more alive then she had in months. She could barely look at Zack without all the old feelings rushing over her. Her memory of him was clear—sunshine and wildflowers and sensations that had for so long lain dormant. It had been over a year since she last saw him, and he looked older, more assured, more worldly. She felt tongue-tied and a little breathless, like a schoolgirl alone for the first time with a teacher she has a crush on.

Inside the spacious apartment, she led him up the circular stairway to the drawing room and then quickly dialed the maid on the house telephone to say that she was in but would not need anything. Behind a carved wooden mahogany panel was the bar, and she pushed the doors aside and busied herself with the glasses and ice, well aware of Zack's appreciation of the richness of the room.

"What would you like, Zack? We have just about everything."

"Yes, I would say you do. Van Gogh. Matisse. Constable. Even a Botticelli. I had no idea there were any left in private hands. This is quite a collection."

"Yes, it is. Most people are rather surprised when they see it for the first time. They expect Julian to have nothing but contemporary art on the walls. Julian is very proud of it. In fact, he turns into a rather fussy old maid when it comes to security. His alarm system is so sensitive it once went off when a rose petal fell from a vase of flowers onto the table."

"Well, then, I won't try to steal anything."

"Oh, Zack, that's not what I meant . . ." She was flustered. She didn't quite know what to say. "You haven't told me what you'd like. A brandy? Scotch?"

"Brandy. Thanks."

She handed him the large snifter and started to say something, but whatever it was, it died on her lips. He was staring at her so intently.

"Why did you do it, Tally?" His voice was low.

"Do what?" Her heart was pounding so.

"Marry him."

She was silent. What could she say?

"Was it for all of this? The best of everything? I remember your saying that once."

"Yes, I remember, too. I've said a lot of things I wonder about now. There was a time when I thought I knew what I wanted."

"And now you don't?"

Tally looked at Zack and then walked to the terrace doors. The night air was fresh and she took it in hungrily. He followed her outside and they stood in silence for a moment, looking out over the glittering lights of the city. "I thought Julian had all the answers," she said quietly. "Now I can't seem to remember what the questions were."

"Can't remember? I can. Seems to me it had to do with money."

"Oh, Zack, you never understood."

"Understood what?"

"You could never understand that I didn't want to live like my parents. I didn't want a messy, disordered life. I didn't want to catch as catch can, never to know where the next penny was coming from, to live without beautiful things and a structured life."

"And you think I did? That's where you were so mistaken, Tally. An architect's life is all about order and structure. You know, if we sat down with a paper and pencil and listed the straight facts of how we would both like to live, I think those lists would be remarkably similar. I grew up in chaos. I know how destructive it can be. I don't want a messy life any more than you do. That wasn't the problem."

Tally spoke very softly. "What was the problem, Zack?"

They were very close. She could feel the warmth of him, and knew that if she tilted her face, their lips would be within inches. She had only to whisper low for him to hear her. "What if I said I'd changed? If I said that I was never able to forget about you? That I've never felt for any man what I felt for you? I was wrong about a lot of things I said, Zack. I was wrong to marry Julian." There, she'd said it. She was glad. "I feel as if I'm suffocating. The boundaries, the expectations are deadening. I don't want to be dead. I want to feel something again." Now she did lift her eyes and look into his. "Kiss me, Zack. Please kiss me." He pulled her roughly to him and their bodies came together tightly and she could feel him stiffening, and a heat like slow-moving honey began to spread through her veins. His mouth came down hard on hers and she responded, a hungry, greedy child The kiss was hot and dry and almost hurt, but she was frantic to press herself closer to him for more. His mouth broke from hers and she felt herself moan with desire. "I love you, God, I love you." And she tried to pull him to her once more. But instead he gripped her arms tightly and held her away from him. She gasped in frustration.

"I'm an idiot." It sputtered from him almost as a groan. "I'd give anything not to have done that. I'd give anything to get you out of my mind. I'm the world's biggest fool, but I'm not going to let you fuck me over again. You're everywhere in my life. You've followed me across Europe and into Africa. I've seen you in crowds, I've seen you in vast empty places, and I've grown to hate you, Tally. I loved you once. God help me, how I loved you. But not anymore. Never again."

"Zack!" Tally struggled to free herself. Had he hit her, she couldn't have felt more pain. "My God, Zack. Let me go." And he did, but not without giving her a shake that trembled through his own body. Astonished, she could only stand stock-still, staring at him.

"What sort of fool are you playing me for now? Your ego astounds me. You think you can heave a big, sorrowful sigh about your mistakes, and there I'll be, waiting and willing to have you back. But I'm not willing at all. It's too late for things to be that simple. You've too much explaining to do. You want me back, but I don't hear a word about all the pain you've caused. You don't mention Nicki. You say nothing about *Heartsease*."

"What are you talking about? I haven't done anything."

"Exactly. You've done nothing. You sat by and watched like some high-class whore while that pimp Julian betrayed your father and everything he stood for. You've allowed Julian to do any damn thing he pleased with your father's work. Your irresponsibility is unforgivable. And while we're on that subject, you filled a young, impressionable girl with a lot of garbage about the 'big time.' You set yourself up as her idol. You pumped her up with all those stories about glamour and wealth. You sent her to New York and she came because she loved you, and came to find you. And what did she get instead? Julian Slade. I should have had him arrested for molesting a minor."

"What are you talking about?" Tally's voice rose.

"Your husband, Tally. I'm talking about a very sick man who plays out his frustrations on very young girls. Nicki came to Julian because you said he could help her. He helped her, all right. And when he was done, he passed her on to Leo. I saw Nicki a week ago. I wasn't very nice to her. I browbeat her until she told me what had happened with Julian. I didn't have the guts to ask her about Thorn. He's the lowest. Lower than Julian. She never could have made it as a model, you should have known that. She was easy prey for people like Thorn and Julian. You should have known that, too. And you call all this the best of everything. I call it rape and plunder and degradation. Nicki wanted to be just like you, Tally. She called you her big sister. You should have taken better care of Nicki. You should have taken better care of yourself."

"I'm not going to stand here and have you insult me. Nicki's your sister, not mine."

"Did you know that she's been gone for days?"

"Well, I'm sorry about that. I'm sorry for her. But she's not my charge, and don't blame me for what is your responsibility, not mine."

"You don't know the first thing about responsibility. Your father—"

"Stop going on about my father! Don't you mention him again to me, do you hear?" Tally heard the shriek in her voice, but she didn't care. Her whole body was shaking. "I hate you, Zack Hayes. You wanted to own me. You wanted to control me. It would have been your final triumph as the protégé of the great Ivan St. Peters. Oh, how you insinuated and ingratiated yourself into his life. The poor, pathetic, adoring boy, now the big proud man. But you'll never be the man Ivan was, Zack."

"You have no idea what a man is, Tally. And you know less about being a woman. A real woman like your mother. You're nothing but a spoiled little girl who could never make room in her life or her heart for anyone but herself. When you married Julian, I almost went crazy. I wanted to rescue you from what I thought was certain death. But I didn't. I couldn't. I still believed enough in you to doubt my own self. Thank God. You and Julian deserve one another. The two of you make a great team."

"Zack, please. Stop all this. Stop accusing me. I don't know what you're talking about."

"I'm talking about *Heartsease.* I'm talking about the fact that there are now three of them. Maybe more. I've seen one. It's a good job. Oh, not perfect. Not exactly the way Ivan would have done it. The patina is a hair off. I would have done one or maybe two more polishings. But then, I have a critical eye. Penny called me. A buyer in Paris wanted her opinion on its value. But it's no big secret. Julian's not trying to hide anything. The fact that you don't seem to know about it proves how very unimportant your opinion is."

"I don't believe this. Why . . . ?"

"Because Julian will cheapen anything that's better than he is. He only understands power and greed, and to those ends he must destroy anything that is truth or beauty. Ivan finally came to understand this, and that's why he named you as the keeper of his work. What a pity." He stood looking at her for a minute and then he strode past her, across the terrace, and through the magnificence that was Julian's room—past Gauguin and Matisse and Van Gogh, past the Rembrandt sketchbook and Rodin's reclining nude, past crystal and gilt and intricately woven tapestry threads. It was a room filled with priceless treasure, but when Zack was gone it seemed as empty as all space.

Tally's head ached and suddenly she was so tired. So tired that she had to sit down. She made her way inside and lowered herself slowly, almost painfully, into the corner of the sofa. She sat in the dark. She tried to think. She tried to distance herself from what Zack had said. But she couldn't. Instead she remembered a day when she was fourteen.

Julian had come out to Springs. Perhaps he had driven her out from school—she couldn't quite remember—but it had been a hot day, and when they got to the house no one was there. So they put on their bathing suits and went to the beach. In the ocean the waves rushed over them, tumbling them against one another in the rough surf, and she was knocked down. She came up gasping, not noticing her suit had fallen to her waist, and then Julian was holding her, fondling her, his hands cupping her small bare breasts, and over the pounding surf she could hear his moans. There had been other times before, when she'd been younger still . . . soft caresses, little touches that went on too long . . . Then, swiftly, the way the mind leaps across years, she was lying on a bed in a hotel in France. It was her honeymoon. Next to her the bed was empty and she was staring at the trompe l'oeil ceiling painted to seem like the top of a gazebo in summer in the elegant Old World hotel. Julian was no longer with her. He had come to her, held her, kissed her, ventured his hands to touch her breasts, her stomach, between her legs. She had sighed, kissing him back, waiting for the feelings that would transport her, but she had felt the coolness of his touch. "What is it?" she had whispered in the dark. "What's wrong?" But Julian had said nothing, only sighed with disappointment as if she had failed him somehow. Then, without further ceremony, he had quickly consummated their marriage. There had been other times, too, but it was never pleasant and it was always without passion. Then, many months later, she had confronted him, begging to know what it was that restrained him so. "Oh," he said lightly, "I wouldn't worry about it. Marriage doesn't necessarily mean compatible sex. Marriage is entirely something else. I think we make a great team, even if some people say I'm too old for you. But you see, darling, what they don't understand and what you don't understand is that it's not I who am too old for you, it's you who are too old for me." He had paused, waiting for his words to sink in, and then he had patted her on the arm as if they were old pals. "I think it best if we don't speak of this again, don't you? I shall be discreet in my actions, and should you care to . . . I expect you to be discreet as well. No questions asked." After that night they had never even slept in the same bedroom again.

Outside, a million lights twinkled on and off in the city as the evening hours stretched into night and night into early dawn. Tally never left her corner of the sofa. She never slept that night. She only stared and stared into the abyss of her life.

64

By the end of the week, Tally knew everything. She had gone to Julian's office and opened every pertinent file. One good thing about Julian, she discovered, was that he was precise in his accounts, meticulous in his preservation of papers. She was aware that his assistant was making hurried telephone calls to Europe to alert him of her activities, but she didn't care. She would never care for him again. She now knew that Julian had manipulated her father and his estate, that Julian claimed as his own property every major piece of sculpture Ivan had ever made. There was a file accounting for the trust fund willed to her from her great-grandmother. She knew that he had taken the funds to launch himself in the gallery business. And she knew the worst, that all the generosity she had believed to be his, he had doled out from her very own money and accepted her gratitude—and Emma's and Ivan's, too!

Shocked and disillusioned, Tally couldn't bear to return to the opulence of Julian's apartment. Suddenly she craved, however changed, the friendly coziness of her old home. Tally left for Springs immediately, and when she got there her eyes confirmed what perhaps in her heart she had dared to hope wouldn't be true. *Heartsease,* she knew, was on exhibit in Vienna, but none of the dozens of pieces her father had saved over the years to be preserved on the property were anywhere to be seen. He had placed them so carefully all around the property, in the field, by the water, in the small woodsy area—every single piece was gone. Only empty pedestals dotted the landscape, unhappy reminders of Julian's perfidy. Tally's heart sank. All she could think about were the papers she had foolishly signed, the waivers she had granted—indeed, the complete lack of interest she had shown in her father's estate. Foolishly, she had followed in her father's footsteps, never caring about the business side of art, trustingly leaving it all to Julian. But now she was beginning to see Julian quite clearly for what he was—a man burning with jealousy, a parasite who had fed on Ivan and the wonderful, vital creative spirit he embodied. And she had helped him. Blindly, she had relegated the efforts of her father's life and the genius of his spirit to Julian's ruthless manipulation and greed. The thought sickened her.

The house had been closed for almost a year, and Tally rushed about, opening windows. The exercise did her good. She was hot and sweaty afterward, and she took a long, cold shower upstairs in her room. Her things were all here, just as she had left them, and now she was surprised to see just what she had left behind. Had she taken any of her possessions ᴛo Julian's? Come to think of it, she hadn't. An old pair of jeans came in handy, as did her cowboy boots. Her sweaters and shirts were folded neatly in drawers. Her hand lingered on one shirt, but she didn't dare to put it on. There was nothing really special about it, just a man's flannel shirt. What was special was the night Zack had given it to her. Nicki and Tally and Zack had all flopped on her bed, eating popcorn and watching "Saturday Night Live." Nicki and Tally had been convulsed with laughter over some silly sketch that Zack hadn't gotten. The more he hadn't gotten it, the more they had laughed, until finally he had dumped the entire bowl of popcorn on their heads. That had started it. A free-for-all of food, drink, and anything else handy, until they were covered in the mess, their clothes sticky and wet. So, in the middle of the night, they had all trooped downstairs to do the laundry. Nicki had fallen asleep, her head in Tally's lap, and Tally and Zack had talked almost until dawn about the meaning of life until they both agreed it was the stupidest conversation they had ever had. When she had pulled the clothes out of the dryer, his shirt was warm and soft and she held it to her cheek. "Maybe that's the meaning of it all, Tally," he had said. "Something warm and soft to make you feel better."

She went downstairs to the kitchen. The caretaker had cleared out both pantry and refrigerator, so she went out to the shed and got one of Ivan's old black bicycles down from its pegs. What was it her parents had loved about these? She could barely remember, but now it came back to her. Something about riding at night. Night riding. That's what they had called it.

The country store was open, but old Mr. Miller had retired and now it was his granddaughter and her husband who ran it. They had smartened things up considerably. Homemade pasta, Perrier water, and pâtés stood in place of Wonder Bread and Dinty Moore stew. The granddaughter recognized her. She and Tally had been in the fourth grade together, and Tally practically fell on her with delight. "Yes, yes, of course, I remember you. I do."

That evening she sat on the veranda, wrapped in an old shawl, and stared out over Accabonac Harbor. An occasional car came down Fireplace Road, but for the most part it was quiet and peaceful. Birds flew in low to their nests, the setting sun cast its amber glow, and the wind in the trees made soft, feathering sounds that soothed her. Some things never change, she thought.

Early the next morning she biked to the store to get a paper and a cup of coffee. Mist was rising off the fields and water. Stands of low evergreens looked as if they'd been sprayed with frost. Pusey's Pond had low clouds hanging just over the water, and there was a single white heron standing in the middle of the pond. The entire scene reminded her of a Chinese brush painting. Back at the house she wandered from room to room and finally ended up in the attic. It was dusty, but she managed to open the dormer window for fresh air. Boxes and boxes of things were piled high, and she decided to go through them. There were things her parents had brought from New York. Menus Ivan had sketched on, old photographs, theater programs, posters announcing poetry readings, a leather purse with nine subway tokens in it, and other odd mementos that seemed insignificant, detached as they were from memory.

But here was a box that was filled with memories. It was a faded chintz hatbox, and carefully folded inside were the clothes for her favorite doll. The doll was long gone but she remembered the nights sitting at the kitchen table talking to her mother while Emma sewed. What had they talked about? She had loved listening to her mother's voice because it had a sort of breathlessness to it that very often turned into a laugh. And she liked to tell stories about things she had seen or heard that day and the things she remembered from her own childhood. Now Tally looked closely at the work. It was beautiful. Tiny embroidered flowers circled the neck of a pink satin dancing dress. There was a plaid Highland kilt, a sailor suit, a nightgown with insets of lace, a fairy costume with tiny silver stars sewn over filmy white net. She could touch the clothes, but where was her mother? Where was her soft, breathy voice? Tally folded everything as before and went on to the next box.

It was a jumble of her report cards and the crafts she had brought home from school. She held up a rather dazed-looking clay fish, painted all the colors of the rainbow. Well, you would never take this artist for the daughter of a famous sculptor, Tally grinned. She had been proud of that fish, and hadn't her mother exclaimed over it! For years it had sat on the kitchen windowsill along with the jars of beans and avocado plants, seashells and rocks, a tin box with rubber bands in it, and so many other scavenged things that had made up the clutter of the household.

Inside another box were things from an earlier time: dance cards from cotillions in Boston, photographs of a strange-looking crippled girl, an Episcopalian prayer book inscribed to Emma from the Bishop of Boston. There, too, was her father's wool cap that he had worn all during the war. There were old storybooks, postcards and letters from friends, Christmas messages, reviews, ledger books from the farm stand . . .

Tally got to dreaming, and her mind was flooded with long-forgotten memories. She was five and running across the yard to greet her big, strong papa, who lifted her up and up and up until she thought she was flying. She was seven and helping Emma set the table with all its mismatched china and flatware, and yet Emma had taught her how to set the table properly, each fork set next to the folded napkin, each knife and spoon lined up just so. She was nine, with a case of the measles so bad they had to bandage her hands at night to keep her from rubbing her eyes, and when they held a mirror up for her to see the spots, she cried, "Oh, Papa, make them go away. They're ugly."

And all the days in between. Forgotten days, stories her father had told her by the fire, the time she had sat on a hornets' nest and Emma had plunged her into the washtub filled with starched water to stop the sting, the clambakes, the long, meandering walks on the beach to gather the beach plums for jam. On her tenth birthday they had gone to New York City and met Maisie for lunch at the Russian Tea Room. The restaurant looked as if it had been decked out for Christmas, and Tally loved the costumes worn by the waiters. Halfway through the lunch, Ivan had spotted a ballet dancer who had recently defected from the Soviet Union. He invited the young man and his manager to join them for their meal. Vodka was called for. Much caviar was ordered. Toasts were made and a hilarious, high-spirited lunch ensued, most of which took place in Russian, with many translations for Emma, Maisie, and Tally. At the end of the meal, the cossack-shirted waiter presented Ivan with a bill and very deferentially asked him, "Excuse me, sir, what language were you speaking?" Ivan roared with laughter. He asked the waiter what nationality he was. "Brazilian," was the answer. Ivan laughed again, filling the room with his beautiful male roar. "Wonderful. Wonderful. This is America. We were speaking Russian. At Russian Tea Room. Ha! Ha! Ha! And our waiter is from Brazil. And the cook must be Chinese. Splendid." Ivan doubled the man's tip.

If she closed her eyes, she could hear again Ivan's laugh. Feel again her mother's arms. Sitting in the dusty attic with all the relics of her family and her life spread in a circle around her, Tally wept silently into her hands. She wanted to bury her head in Emma's lap and cry there as she had done so many times. "Mother, Mother, what shall I do?"

Julian returned to New York and formally, as if they were already sworn enemies, arranged to meet Tally at the house in Springs. He arrived precisely at two, so there would be no thought of lunch. Tally greeted him coolly in her father's study, then got right to the point. She accused him of everything. To her surprise, he denied nothing.

"I will not defend my actions. They don't need defending, least of all to you. If anything, I am delighted with what I've done and how I've managed things in the face of a great deal of trouble caused by your father and now by you. You know, Tally, I have been around a great deal longer than you have, and I know much more than you do about the way the world works. It's fine to indulge artistic whims whenever possible, but business is not run on indulgence. Ivan was a great artist. And he will be for all time. But do you know what makes a great artist? People. A great artist is accessible to people. I told Ivan once I would make the whole world love his work as I did. And I have. And I will continue to do so, but only as I see fit."

"And in the meantime you will also see fit to bring millions of dollars of profit your way?"

"Why not? Ivan had a tedious and rather childish notion about *Heartsease*, which I don't happen to share. And what is wrong with profit? You never seemed to think of it as evil before. When I profit, so do you, let's not forget that. I thought by now you had matured enough to be as practical as I am about these things."

"Practical be damned! You're vile, Julian. You are despicable beyond words, beyond anything I ever dreamt possible. You've stolen everything, from my mother, from my father, and from me. You stole my birthright, a legacy that was entrusted to you by a frail old woman. And then you passed yourself off as a benefactor. How can you live with yourself?"

"Your birthright, is it now?" Julian was cool, his voice mocking. "Please don't put on airs, my dear. You had no birthright. You had no business being born. At least not with that Russian for a father. Emma was mine. She had always been mine. Then she made a mistake. And we all paid for it. I never stole anything from anyone. I only took what was mine all along."

"Oh, get off it, Julian. Emma didn't make a mistake. I've heard all the stories about how you proposed to her when she was eleven years old. That didn't make her yours. It just made you a pervert, or something a little less dignified than that. There was nothing wrong with Emma. She just grew up, Julian, and when she met a man, a real man, she fell in love with him . . ."

"And what, pray tell, did it get her? When she left me for *him*, she was an exquisite, beautiful young woman. And I watched her deteriorate over the years until she was nothing but a drudge, a fishwife, with red hands and coarse skin. She chose that over life with me." Julian's voice was as bitter as though this had happened yesterday.

"She chose life, Julian. But I'm not sure that's something you'll ever understand. Emma loved her life—she loved her house, her garden, her chickens. She cared for each little chick as if it were her baby. And she was never happier than when she was knee-deep in muck, shoveling compost onto her vegetable patch. Julian, Emma was happy scrubbing the floor. She loved life! And at least with Ivan she got to live it. If she had stayed with you, you would have locked her away with all your other precious objects and taken her out once in a while just to drool a bit over her. She needed a man, Julian, not a slimy, cold-blooded snake whose idea of sex is polishing the family jewels."

Julian had turned as pale as a ghost. He got up slowly and walked to the door. "You realize that you own nothing except this house. Everything Ivan ever made belongs to me. You can have a divorce if that's what you want, but you will get nothing. My lawyers have seen to that."

"Yes, Julian, I'm sure they have." Tally sounded exhausted. "But you know what, Julian? I've learned a lot in the last week while I was looking for the truth. And I guess the most important truth I learned was that those are only things. They're not going to keep you warm at night, they're not going make you soup when you're sick, and they're not going to give a shit when you die, Julian. No one is, Julian. Keep the sculptures, keep everything. I don't want them and I don't want you. I'm just like Emma, Julian, I want a real man, and you don't qualify."

The door slammed and he was gone.

65

Tally wanted desperately to call Zack, but a combination of shame and pride wouldn't let her. Instead she called me. Of course, I went immediately to Springs, where over the next few days she told me all that I have related here. I was determined to cheer her up, but the more I learned, the more cheerless the situation seemed. It was painfully obvious that Tally had absolutely nothing of her father's to call her own—not even one of Ivan's sculptures had been left in the house. Everything had been taken by Julian. It was an empty house, stripped of everything that had given it beauty and vitality.

It was Tally's idea to call Penny. After Ivan's death, Penny had returned to Washington, and Tally reached her there. They had a very long talk, and from the sound of it I knew Penny was being as reassuring as she always was. She graciously agreed to come to Springs to see what she could do to make sense of the mess Tally was in. She felt positive that all was not lost; Julian played a good game, but she thought there were a few tricks he might not yet be on to. If anyone was a match for Julian, it would be Penny Frankenheimer, and it seemed as if she was more than game for a battle. The fight was just beginning, she told Tally, and she vowed to put all of her legal and financial resources at Tally's disposal. Her confidence boosted, Tally's spirits rallied.

We were sitting in the kitchen a few nights later, and Tally was whacking away at an enormous bowl of risen dough. She had decided to fill the house with the smell of home-baked bread. We had a fire in the woodstove and there seemed such a warm, womblike air about it that it could almost have been Emma's kitchen. We had talked ourselves blue in the face over the past few days, but only in terms of Julian and the disposition of Ivan's estate.

And so I asked, "What about Ivan, Tally? What about your father? Have you found a way to forgive him? To come to terms with all that came between you?"

"Yes," she said slowly. "I think I have. But it's not so much coming to terms as . . . well, maybe it's just growing up a little. I got all confused when Mama died. I wanted to be like her but I wasn't. I thought it was my fault that she died. And I wanted Papa to love me the best and he didn't. He loved her. And when she died I wanted to become her, but of course I couldn't. I think what I wanted most of all was for everything always to be like that one perfect day."

"What day was that, honey?"

"I don't know. It just seemed that once there was a perfect day. But there really was no perfect day, just a lot of perfect moments that I've strung all together. I guess that's the curse of childhood. Your parents don't exist as people; they're supposed to be perfect, like Christmas. Their names are Mama and Papa, not Emma and Ivan. They don't have sex and they don't quarrel. If everything goes along as it's supposed to, you gradually grow up and you gradually accept the fact that they're people. I loved my parents, but I hated Mama for dying and then I hated Papa for being so sad. But what I really hated was the fact that they meant so much to each other."

"But you were the most special part of their life, Tally. You must know that."

She smiled. "I wonder. Everything about them was special and I guess they felt that made me special, too, but I think they were off in some sphere by themselves most of the time. They really weren't of this world. Honestly, Maisie, back then I never wanted an artist for a father. I wanted a father who wore a suit and went to the office every day and came home and didn't throw tantrums or shout and carry on. But now

I know how lucky I was. I had a father who reached for the stars. I had a father who shouted and screamed and carried on until the whole world stopped to listen and see. And I had a mother who knew what that was all about."

Tally gave the dough a punch for emphasis, and then pressed it in a pan and put it in the oven. We were drinking spiced tea and pretty soon the room was enveloped in the smell of baking bread and I guess we were both feeling comfortably reflective.

"Tell me about the Greenwich Village days, Maisie. Tell me about Mama and Papa and you in New York."

"Oh, honey, you've heard those stories a million times."

"I know. I like to hear them. Family stories become part of you after a while, don't you think? You inherit them, like the shape of your eyes and the color of your hair. They're the only link you have to the past. I wish I could have known my parents as those people, the ones who lived in the stories. I wish I knew the difference between what was real about them and what I think I've made up. I don't know what's true anymore."

"Well, the truth of anything is hard to get at, isn't it?"

"I don't know, Maisie. Death is true."

"True, yes. But is it a beginning or an end? Should we celebrate a life or mourn a death? I think where most people get confused is that they expect the truth to be obvious when, really, it's no more obvious than all those magic tricks Ivan used to do. Did I ever tell you about the play Dance wrote about all of us?"

"A play? Really? What was it called?"

"He called it *The Day Girl and the Night Boy*. Oh, Tally," I sighed. "Do you know, I haven't thought about that play in a long, long time, and yet it was . . . well, it was one of the most special nights of my life. The play was in rhyming couplets and it was about a girl who had never seen the night and a boy who was shut away from the day. It was written like a fairy tale, and there were all sorts of omens and witches and dark forebodings, but finally the boy and girl met and fell in love. From that moment on they were inexorably bound. I remember Emma in her golden costume, her hair hanging free, with threads of silver woven through it. In the stage light it gave the illusion of a sparkling morning sun. And Ivan was done up in a black velvet cape and a highwayman's hat. They were breathtaking together. You have no idea how beautiful they were. They were perfect."

"Were you in it, too?"

"Oh God, yes. I was the comic relief. I played Magic and my

costume was entirely in pink crepe paper, and Dance played the Sorcerer. He was in white, with a long silk scarf like the ones that pilots used to wear in the First World War."

"What fun."

"Yes. Fun. We thought so. We also thought it was make-believe. Here we were in our costumes with greasepaint on, and fake props and artificial lights, and yet it was real because it was about us. It *was* us. It was everything we were."

"What happens in the end?"

"Ah, that was the true brilliance of it." My thoughts drifted. For just a moment they were all here with me, Ivan and Emma and Dance, and the four of us were gathered again together for one brief moment before it all vanished. I looked at Tally, whose expression was rapt. "Dance was an exquisite poet, Tally. Someday I'll give you the play to read. What happened was the Sorcerer vanished, Magic grew old, and Day and Night were destined to follow each other in circles for all eternity."

Tally sighed. "I wish I had lived in the fifties. It seems like it was a lot more fun."

"Maybe we did have more fun. And maybe when you have children they will say the same thing to you. I don't really know anymore. Memory is quite tricky that way, and one forgets all the dull days and the depressions and the petty, nitpicking rivalries and jealousies that went on. But sometimes I remember it like a never-ending party—sort of an exhilarating frenzy. There was never enough time to do it all. There never is enough time. I guess that's the one fact of life that can't be avoided. Time passes and swallows up those days and you can never have them back. It's important to understand this. Time never stops. It never waits. You must never waste it. But you can never tell young people about time. They haven't yet the capacity to understand. Understanding is the end of youth." I stopped because Tally was not really listening to me anymore. They do stop listening after a while. I could have told her many things that night. I could have told her a million truths, but she didn't have the ears yet to listen. She needed her own memories and her own interpretations. There is so little that one generation can really tell another. "Well," I said, "I suppose it's always seemed as though the previous generation had the best of it. I'll bet one day you'll be boring some starry-eyed girl with tall tales of the eighties."

Tally laughed and started to say something, but suddenly she stopped and looked at me. "Oh, Maisie," she said, and she shivered as if a cold wind had hit her, "I have the oddest feeling."

"Good God, Tally. Don't scare me. You look as white as a ghost." And she did, too. Tally had gotten up from the table, her hand at her throat. A minute later the telephone started to ring. It was very eerie. We both jumped to get it, but Tally took the call. Her face went from surprise and pleasure to crushing disbelief. I knew something terrible had happened.

"Zack. Oh, Zack. Where are you? Oh my God, no . . ." When she finally hung up, Tally came to the kitchen table and put her head down and cried. I waited till she had pulled herself together, and then I, too, learned the truth.

Nicki Hayes was dead. Her body had been found in the back row of a movie theater. She had gone to see a revival of *Wuthering Heights*. Tally instantly remembered telling her how she thought it was the most romantic movie ever made. Nicki had never even heard of it. The thought of Nicki still acting on Tally's advice reduced Tally to a fresh flood of tears. Leo Thorn had been questioned and cleared. Officially, the death certificate stated that it was a case of heart failure owing to a combination of starvation and diet pills. But we knew, all of us, that Nicki Hayes had died because nobody cared. She had died of neglect.

Tally begged Zack to let her arrange the funeral. A few days later we stood, a small and somber group, by a freshly dug grave in the tiny Green River Cemetery of Springs. Nearby, Ivan's stone and, next to it, Emma's seemed to stand as silent guardians, as Nicki's small, white coffin was lowered into the ground. Penny and I, as well as a few local people, left soon after the minister had read the burial rites, but Tally and Zack remained behind.

I don't know what they said. Perhaps nothing, for talk can be clumsy in the face of all the emotions they must have felt. I know they stayed there for a long time. Perhaps they simply clung to each other in silence and forgave each other the mistakes of the past. Then, in the gathering twilight, hand in hand, they came home.

Epilogue

This is the end of my story. These have been my recollections. I suppose I could have written a much more comprehensive study of Ivan St. Peters, of his times and his work, but I had no wish to do that. I only wanted to write about what I knew and experienced, and about my own knowledge of some quite remarkable people. But of course there are no true endings, and you are naturally curious about what has happened since that very sad evening at the graveyard.

Zack and Tally are married. They have three darling girls—Lily, Elizabeth, and Meg. One of them was born before they were married, because even with the best lawyers, it took two years for Tally to get a divorce and win back a sizable settlement from the trust of Louise Blackstone. Zack never did go back to Africa. Family life changes a man's plans. But I can say in all honesty that I have never seen a happier husband and father than Zack Hayes. They live in Santa Fe, New

Mexico, where Zack is a partner in an architectural firm, and Tally has become quite an accomplished nature photographer, but they come to me and the ocean every summer. The girls call me Grandma, and since there's no one else to fill those shoes, I figure, what the hell.

The rest of the story is not so pretty. Even Penny's battery of skillful lawyers have had trouble getting back any part of Ivan's large body of work. To say that Julian turned out to be a master of fraud and deceit is an understatement. Penny spent well over a million dollars in legal fees to defeat him in court, but it was, in the main, a hopeless case. Many of Ivan's sculptures seemed simply to have disappeared from the face of the earth, or at least from the jurisdiction of American courts. Documents were destroyed, bills of sale altered. Publicly it was a scandal, though some dealers no doubt privately admired and envied what Julian had gotten away with. Unscrupulous dealers have no doubt been bilking the public and screwing artists since the Italian Renaissance, at least. And in all the centuries since, there has never been any law or board or commission to keep a watchful eye on the buying and selling, advertising and promoting of art. If you ask me, the art business is a travesty. I'd love for art to be free—given away to anybody who wants it. But no one's asked me lately.

In the end, Penny decided to drop the suit and expend her energies on the financing of a museum to house those works of Ivan's she was able to buy on the open market. A surprising number of pieces have been donated by collectors, too. The museum is in Springs, and there anyone can come to see the Circle of Desire and, at its center, the beautiful *Heartsease.* The original! Few people know to look for the coin but it's there. The studio stands as a library, and Penny has gathered a sizable collection of art books, reviews, critiques, and photographs (including all the ones Tally took that last summer) pertaining to Ivan and his work. Tally willingly turned the house and studio and grounds over to the nonprofit foundation that manages the collection, but she and Zack kept the cabin down by the harbor for themselves. It amuses me, when they come to stay with me in East Hampton, how within a very few hours of happy chatter and gossip, Tally and Zack start giving each other those sidelong, intimate glances, and as the flush in Tally's cheeks grows a tiny bit warmer, I know they are about to remember a very important errand they must attend to. And so off they go to their ramshackle hideaway on the edges of the beautiful estuary of Accabonac Harbor, with its cattails and marshlands and the great ospreys circling their nests and the intense blues and golds cast on the water by the setting sun. I tell them not to hurry back—and they don't. Not for many hours, not until the girls and I have devoured the pizza I've ordered in, and played an exhausting game of hide-and-seek, and gone out into the dark night to find our stars in the sky. I am a contented woman then. I know that passion and love will never die, and that the best part of desire is in the eyes of eager children looking up into a starry night sky.

But what of Julian? In the world of art dealers and crooks, Julian Slade was one of the biggest. For a time, because of the many lawsuits, he was in disgrace of a kind. Slade International closed. But Julian lives in Rome now, and deals privately all over the world.

I suppose, of all the people in my narrative, I've thought of Julian the most now that the story is put to rest. Where indeed would we all be without him? Where would we all be right now, had not that dapper fellow appeared one rainy afternoon in a walk-up tenement gallery in Greenwich Village? It's unthinkable, isn't it? No Emma? No Tally? And who would Ivan St. Peters have been? What would his work have looked like? You see, it would be so easy to turn Julian into a convenient villain and let it go at that, but strangely enough, I'm inclined to forgive him, though his faults were grievous. He was not a good man in the end. But what of the beginning? Who and what was Julian Slade when he walked into Ivan's loft on Hudson Street and fell in love with the beauty he found there? Let's face it, he did do what he said he would. He did make the world love Ivan's work as much as he loved it himself. He never said he was going to be a gentleman about it. He never said he wouldn't be greedy, jealous, or manipulating. No. He delivered on his promise. And someday, just for old times' sake, I shall probably look Julian up in Rome.

In the end, of course, it's not the Julian Slades that matter. It's not the money that matters. I wonder if even the flesh and blood matter, once one's days on earth are over. What matters are the dreams and imaginings of the human heart and mind. For what more is art than that —the imagination wandering through unfamiliar territory until it comes home to rest in the creation of form?